BOOK TWO

IN THE NECROMANCER'S SONG

TRINITY OF BONES

C A I T L I N   S E A L

Charlesbridge
TEEN

For my mom and dad, who have always
encouraged my love of stories

At the time of publication, all URLs printed in this book were
accurate and active. Charlesbridge and the author are not responsible
for the content or accessibility of any website.

Published by Charlesbridge
85 Main Street, Watertown, MA 02472
(617) 926-0329 • www.charlesbridgeteen.com

Library of Congress Cataloging-in-Publication Data
Names: Seal, Caitlin, author.
Title: Trinity of bones / by Caitlin Seal.
Description: Watertown, MA: Charlesbridge Teen, [2019] | Series: Necromancer's song; 2 |
Summary: Naya Garth is returning to her homeland of Talmir to testify
against Valn, the man who had her murdered and resurrected as a spy; but secretly
she is looking for the necromancy journals which may help her to save her love, Corten,
who is trapped between resurrection and true death—but Talmir is dangerous for
one of the undead, and meanwhile Corten has discovered that someone is seeking
immortality with a ritual that will unleash chaos in the world.
Identifiers: LCCN 2018058503 (print) | LCCN 2019005102 (ebook) |
ISBN 9781632896629 (ebook) | ISBN 9781580898089 (reinforced for library use)
Subjects: LCSH: Magic—Juvenile fiction. | Immortality—Juvenile fiction. |
Death—Juvenile fiction. | Conspiracies—Juvenile fiction. | Adventure stories. |
CYAC: Magic—Fiction. | Immortality—Fiction. | Death—Fiction. |
Conspiracies—Fiction. | Adventure and adventurers—Fiction. | Fantasy. |
LCGFT: Action and adventure fiction.
Classification: LCC PZ7.I.S33688 (ebook) | LCC PZ7.I.S33688 Tr 2019 (print) |
DDC 813.6 [Fic]—dc23
LC record available at https://lccn.loc.gov/2018058503

Printed in United States of America
(hc) 10 9 8 7 6 5 4 3 2 1

Display type set in Java Heritages by Heybing Supply Co.
Text type set in Centaur by Monotype
Printed by Berryville Graphics in Berryville, Virginia, USA
Production supervision by Brian G. Walker
Designed by Susan Mallory Sherman and Sarah Richards Taylor
Jacket design by Shayne Leighton

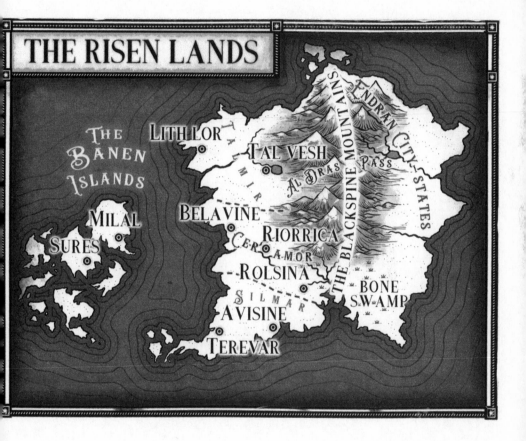

THE RISEN LANDS

THE BANEN ISLANDS

LITH LOR

TAL VESH

AL DRAS

TALMIR

ENDRAN CITY-STATES

SNIS

THE BLACKSPINE MOUNTAINS

PASS

MILAL

SURES

BELAVINE

RIORRICA

CER AMOR

ROLSINA

SILMAR

AVISINE

TEREVAR

BONE SWAMP

THE SNARL

DOCKSIDE

LITH LOR

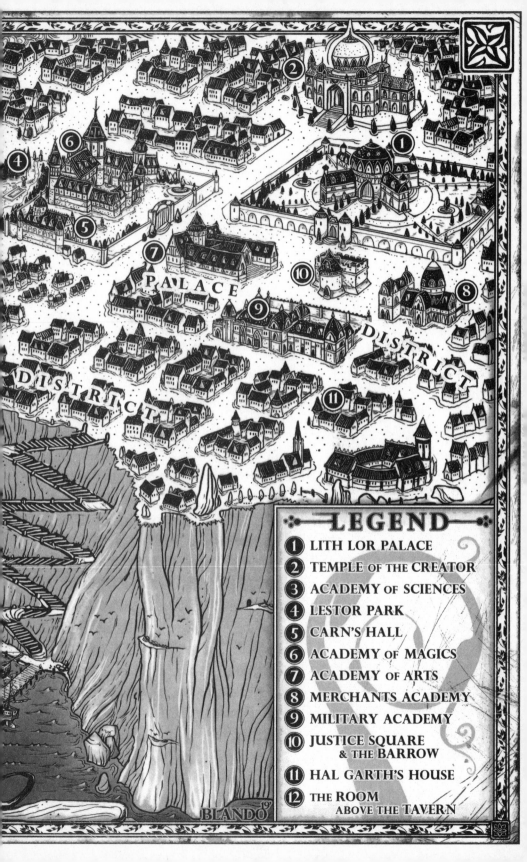

PALACE DISTRICT

BLANDO'19

Chapter 1

CORTEN

Wind howled through the dark and twisting landscape of death. It pressed against Corten's chest as he struggled forward. One step. Another. Up ahead light glimmered through a crack in the darkness. It was a portal, a tiny gap in the barrier between the world of the living and that of the dead. His old mentor Lucia's voice resonated from the other side. The notes of her song were deep and rich, and achingly familiar, as she called him back toward life.

As Corten struggled on, blades of shadowy grass sprang up to wrap around his ankles, and the wind pressed like a thousand hands trying to push him back. Rocky, uncertain ground shifted beneath his every step. The first time he'd died, the pull of this strange landscape had been gentle and insistent. Voices on the wind had whispered of rest and safety. He'd refused them, and now it seemed death was determined not to let him escape a second time.

Corten set his teeth in a snarl and pushed on. Second resurrections were tricky, but theoretically not impossible. He just had to reach the portal.

The ground crumbled under his foot as though in response to his determination. Corten cried out and stumbled to his hands and knees. Struggling to stand, he heard a sound more terrifying than the howling wind. Lucia's voice was faltering.

"No!" Corten forced himself up, fighting the wind and his own exhaustion. He was so close. The song broke off as Lucia coughed. Then she gasped in breath and managed another half-strangled refrain.

"Corten!" a second voice called, higher than Lucia's and sharp with desperation.

"Naya?" Corten reached for the portal. For just a moment, he saw her on the other side, her eyes wide as she reached back for him.

But it was too late. Lucia's voice failed. The light wavered. Then with a crack like thunder, the portal closed, leaving Corten standing with one hand outstretched toward the infinite darkness.

"No," Corten whispered. His hand fell limply to his side. Grass rustled against his legs as the wind's strength lessened. He collapsed to the ground, and the grass blurred and re-formed around the scorched pants he'd been wearing when he died. He shuddered at their touch, more like the brush of heavy mist than anything real. *Probably because they aren't real,* Corten thought. This place was shaped by thoughts and fears. It was an echo of the living world, and nothing here was quite what it seemed.

Naya had told him that when she'd died, she'd felt the shadows like a tide. Others felt invisible hands pulling them away. For him, death had always been this endless grassy field, all winds and uncertain footing. He'd wondered if the landscape would change after a second death, if whatever killed him would shape the scenery into something new. Apparently not.

Corten stood, holding one hand against his chest. Hot pain still lingered where the sword had snapped his rib and sent his soul screaming back to this dark place. How long had it been since he'd followed Naya into the tunnels beneath the burning

Talmiran Embassy? Time was impossible to judge on this side of death, but Lucia wouldn't have waited more than a day or two before she attempted to sing him back.

Images from those last hours before his death flashed through Corten's memory. The fire they'd run through had seemed almost alive as it furiously consumed the building—nothing like the controlled heat of the furnaces he'd worked with as an apprentice glassblower. What they'd found in the tunnels below the embassy had been worse. Yet Naya had faced it all without flinching. Even when her father, Captain Hal Garth, had stood before her and snarled his hate, still she hadn't run away. In that moment she'd seemed a different person from the quiet, uncertain girl she'd been when they first met.

And from what he'd seen in that single glimpse through the portal, it looked as though she'd gotten away safely.

Corten smiled to himself. Of course she'd gotten away. She was trained to fight, unlike him. Creator, he'd probably looked the fool when he'd swung that iron poker at her father. At least he'd managed to break the foul man's arm.

Corten's smile turned to a grimace. Such a mighty legacy he left behind. Corten Ballera: failed necromancer, breaker of arms, and crafter of ugly glass trinkets. Oh, yes, the bards would surely sing his praises. And Naya . . . Well, if she were lucky, she'd forget him and go on to lead a long and happy life. Maybe she would even meet someone new.

The image of her in someone else's arms made his stomach twist. He squeezed his eyes shut, remembering the heat of her lips against his after they'd fled the execution. He must have been mad to kiss her like that. But in that moment, he'd felt so intoxicatingly alive that all his thoughts and doubts had been incinerated. He'd imagined sweeping her off her feet and carrying her far away to find a place where they could both be more than their regrets and the mistakes they'd made.

The wind blew harder. Insistent.

Corten glared at the swirling dark expanse of this dead world that had claimed his soul. "So that's it?" he asked. "That's all I get?"

The wind swallowed his words and carried them away. Corten stood. "This isn't fair!" he shouted. "I still have things to do!" He had a life back in Belavine, friends. Was death at the hands of some hateful merchant really the end of his fate?

The wind mocked him with its constant force. It made him feel like a little kid stomping and screaming at some slight. As that image formed in his mind, the world twisted, perspective warping and light flooding the dark. He *was* a little kid, five years old and fuming over the injustice of his parents' going out for a picnic without him. His father scowled from behind his mustache while his mother rolled her eyes.

As abruptly as it had come, the vision vanished, leaving Corten kneeling as he struggled to make sense of his surroundings.

Well. That hadn't happened last time he'd died. Then again, last time he hadn't missed his chance at the portal. Corten stood on shaky legs. He closed his eyes and searched his memory for every scrap of lore he'd ever learned about death. The longest recorded gap between a death and a resurrection was four days and six hours. No one had ever successfully been resurrected after a second failure, but so far as he knew, no one had tried since the end of the war. And if anyone was going to try, it would be Lucia.

Voices whispered through the darkness, barely distinguishable from the endless rustling of the grass. The back of Corten's neck prickled with the sense of someone watching.

Stop fighting.

Come.

Rest.

When Corten opened his eyes, a figure stood before him.

It was almost human, but its edges were indistinct and its face hidden in shadows. Corten stepped backward, nearly tripping over his own feet.

"Stop fighting," the figure said. The voice was masculine, and the rasp of it made Corten think of old books and mildew.

Corten shook his head. He tried to back up farther but felt the ground shift ominously beneath his heels. His stomach lurched like he was already falling, and he had to fight down a gasp of fear. He reminded himself of all the times he'd gone up on city rooftops, even jumped off some of them just to prove to himself that such falls no longer held any power over him. But rooftops had always felt so stable compared to the loose rocks of the cliff's edge, and there was something very different about falling when you were the one in control of the jump. "I don't want to die," Corten said, managing to make the words come out in something slightly manlier than a terrified squeak.

"What you want matters not. Your life is spent. Now it is time for you to rest."

Something about the figure's words tugged at Corten. Necromancy was as much about purpose and will as it was about carving runes. A necromancer could use their circle to create and contain a portal, and they could use the song to find and guide a soul back. But they couldn't force anyone back into life. What if it worked the same going the other way? "What happens if I refuse?" Corten asked.

"All souls go to their rest."

Corten crossed his arms. "Why? And what are you anyway?"

The shadow man didn't answer. The darkness at the edges of Corten's vision writhed, and the feeling of being watched intensified.

"Will you drag me away if I refuse to go?" He wouldn't let his fear get the better of him. If he stalled long enough, maybe Lucia would figure out a way to open another portal.

"You will go willingly."

"I won't."

"You will. If you don't, the scavengers will consume you."

A chill crawled up Corten's spine. "What's that supposed to mea—" Before he could finish the thought, the ground beneath his feet vanished. His words became a scream as he plummeted into darkness.

CHAPTER 2

NAYA

Naya strode through the hallways of the Ceramoran palace and prayed her nerves didn't show on her face. Servants and low-ranking officials bustled past her as they tended to the daily business of the court. A few glanced her way and whispered behind their hands when she walked by, but no one tried to stop her.

Naya's former mentor, Celia, had once told her that understanding the expectations of others was one of a spy's most valuable skills. Most of the people Naya passed knew who she was. They knew that only weeks ago she'd been spying for their enemies in Talmir. She was Talmiran after all.

However, the people here also knew she'd betrayed her former masters and countrymen. She'd saved the life of the Ceramoran king's chief adviser, Salno Delence. Now she was taking lessons from a tutor in the palace and preparing to join the Ceramoran delegation to the Congress of Powers. She was sure the palace gossips would gladly whisper about her motives or her ties to the Necromantic Council. But when they saw her walking the palace halls, they would expect she was there on official business.

Naya walked quickly, as if she had somewhere important to be, but not so quickly that she would look like she was trying to flee. She kept her head up and her expression neutral. She willed the palace denizens to see her, then dismiss her as just another part of the everyday scenery. Because if any of Delence's allies realized what she was really up to, they would do everything in their power to stop her.

Memories stirred in the back of her mind as she entered a wing of the palace she hadn't visited in weeks. They made her chest ache and her throat tighten with fear. Once, she'd been a master of locking away such things. But locking pain away had been her father's strategy. Captain Hal Garth had taught her to be cold and calculating. He'd seen the people around him as either tools or threats. Including her.

Naya turned a corner and saw a familiar guard standing in front of a heavy wooden door banded with iron. A servant polished the gilt frame of a painting farther down the hall, but otherwise there was no one in sight. The guard, Lieutenant Lila Selmore, flashed Naya a nervous smile as she approached. She was a small woman with lean features, close-cropped hair, and an air of cheerful confidence. Today the aether swirling around her was spiky with unease. "You're sure you want to go through with this?" she asked without preamble.

Naya hesitated, feeling the press of Lila's emotions against her own. As a wraith Naya could detect emotions through the aether—energy that drifted off all living things. It was a skill that had proved useful more than once, but sometimes it felt as much like a curse as a gift. It was all too easy to lose herself under the flood of outside sensations.

"I can do this," Naya said, trying to banish both her own fear and Lila's. "But if you think this will bring too much trouble down on you—"

Lila shook her head. "Let me worry about that part. The Necromantic Council owes you a debt for the help you gave us during the coup." She smirked. "And besides, the Council wants to know what that lying bastard has to say as badly as you do."

Some of the tension in Naya's chest unwound. "Then let's get going."

Lila glanced down the hallway. She waited until the servant finished her polishing and moved out of sight around the corner. As soon as they were alone, Lila pulled an iron key from her pocket and unlocked the door. Naya sensed the wards deactivating as the lock's heavy tumblers shifted. Lila opened the door and led Naya down a long flight of stone steps.

Unease thrummed through Naya as her bare toes touched the first step. Not so long ago, she'd been dragged into this same dungeon to face what she'd thought was certain death. She heard the shouts again, felt the icy cold of salma wood cuffs binding her. She saw Valn looming over her. He'd demanded her help even as he condemned her to die as a pawn in his plans for war.

These dungeons, and the man who waited in the cells below, were reminders of her failures. And no matter how hard she tried, she couldn't lock away the fear and loathing she felt every time she thought of what those failures had cost. Naya pressed one hand flat against the wall of the narrow stairway. She closed her eyes and tried to focus on the physical world, blocking out everything else.

"Are you all right?" Lila asked.

Naya opened her mouth to answer, but her throat was too tight to speak. Her eyes burned with unshed tears, and suddenly the task before her felt too vast, too impossible for words. But she also knew that if she didn't summon the courage to face Valn now, she would spend the rest of her life in uncertainty and fear.

Naya clenched her jaw, trying to convince her stupid feet to keep walking down the stairs. After a moment she felt Lila's hand on her shoulder. Lila's aether flooded through her, a warm mix of sympathy and concern. She'd been with Naya on the night Valn had captured her and thrown her into the dungeons.

Though Lila couldn't sense the aether, she obviously guessed some of what Naya was feeling.

Naya gripped Lila's hand and drew in her comforting energy. The warmth reminded her that there were good people here in Ceramor, people she could trust. She was afraid, yes. But at least she didn't have to do this alone.

Naya opened her eyes and gave Lila a weak smile, trying to offer a little reassurance in return. "Thank you," she said. "I'll be okay. I just want to get this over with."

Another door waited at the bottom of the stairs. Lila unlocked it and led Naya into a square stone chamber with a table and chairs in the middle. Two guards sat at the table with a deck of cards spread between them.

They nodded and let Naya and Lila pass. Lila had called in a few favors to ensure that those on watch this shift would be allies of the Council.

The younger of the guards watched Naya intently. She could tell from his aether that, ally or not, he wasn't happy with his part in this. Well, she wasn't happy about it either. She'd been asking Delence for permission to interrogate Valn practically every day since learning he had survived their last encounter. Delence had refused her every time. So, with time running out before the delegation left for Talmir, Naya had been forced to find a way around his orders.

When Naya had gone to the Necromantic Council for help, Lila had told her about the warnings Delence had issued. Apparently, he was afraid Naya would try to kill Valn. As if she'd be satisfied with giving him a quick death. No, Naya wanted to see Valn stand trial for all he'd done. For years he'd passed out bribes and commanded spies, kidnappers, and murderers as he sought to steal the freedom of Ceramor's people. He would pay. But before that happened, there was something Naya had to know.

"He's at the end," Lila said, speaking softly as they stepped into the long hallway of cells beyond the guardroom.

Naya's attention focused on the cell at the end of the hall. It stood just next to the salma wood chamber where she'd been locked the last time she was here. Despite the despair-drenched atmosphere, Naya felt a burst of vicious glee at the thought of Valn rotting in the same darkness where he'd confined her.

"Are you ready?" Lila asked as she placed one hand on the heavy iron bar set across the door.

Naya didn't feel ready, but she nodded all the same.

Lila opened the lock holding the bar in place, then slid the bar back. The metal groaned. The door swung open, and Naya stepped into Valn's cell.

She heard a soft thud as Lila closed the door behind her. A small, irrational part of her panicked at the thought of being trapped. She tried to ignore it, reminding herself that the door was unlocked. Even if it hadn't been, this cell wasn't designed to hold a wraith.

The dim light of a single rune lantern revealed a narrow chamber with a straw pallet on one side and a waste bucket on the other. Valn had been lying on the pallet, but as Naya entered he heaved himself upright with the help of a wooden crutch.

Naya stared at him in silence. He bore little resemblance to the man she remembered. His suit was gone, replaced with the simple brown pants and shirt of a prisoner. His normally impeccably combed black hair was dirty and tangled, and bruises and scrapes shadowed the skin around his wrists and across one cheekbone. His right leg was wrapped in a thick cast up to the knee, and from the careful way he moved, Naya guessed at least one of his ribs was broken.

Only his eyes hadn't changed. Even here, locked in a dirty cell, he still stared at her with that same gleam of confident superiority he'd had when he'd scheduled her execution. He met her gaze, then dipped his head in the imitation of a bow. "Miss Garth, welcome. I had wondered if we'd see each other again. Does this mean Lord Delence has changed his mind about letting me live to face trial before the noble Congress of Powers?"

Valn's tone was light, almost jovial. Naya's fingers curled into fists. "No," she said. "You'll go to trial. I just have some questions for you first."

"Ah," Valn said. "In that case I hope you won't mind if I sit down. Lord Delence was kind enough to offer the services of an excellent healer, but as you can see, I'm still recovering from the wounds you gave me." He moved carefully, using the support of the wall and the crutch to ease himself back onto his pallet.

"Well, what did you want to know?" Valn asked once he was seated. "I can assure you I've already told Lord Delence and his interrogators everything."

"You told him the runes for my bond came from Talmir," Naya said. As she spoke, she drew in aether, trying to sift Valn's emotions from the aura of fear, pain, and despair that seemed to permeate the very walls of the dungeon. Growing up in Talmir, she'd believed her people would never stoop to using the necromantic magic they so hated. But not only had Valn organized her resurrection as a wraith, he'd done it with powerful runes, which should have been destroyed after the last war between Talmir and Ceramor.

Recognition flickered in Valn's eyes and Naya tasted something sharp and bright in his aether. Was that fear or anticipation? "Did I?" Valn asked. "It's hard to remember all we talked about. Those first few days after our last encounter were . . . difficult."

"Who gave you that journal?" Naya asked, taking a step forward. "Why would a Talmiran have access to illegal runes?"

Valn tilted his head back and laughed. It might have been

a convincing display if she couldn't taste the bitterness in his aether. "Why do you care?" he asked, a harsh edge bleeding into his voice.

Naya didn't answer, and slowly the corner of Valn's mouth curled into a sneer. "You know, back when you pulled that stunt to escape your execution, I assumed you were just trying to preserve your own pointless life," he said. "I never would have guessed your loyalties were so flexible that you'd be willing to switch sides and work for Delence. Perhaps your father was right about what necromancy does to a soul."

Anger, hot and red and sharp, surged through Naya. That heat concentrated in the rune-carved bones of her hand. She drew in more aether and imagined transforming the despair-laden energy into true heat and burning that condescending look right off Valn's face. How dare he speak to her of loyalty! Twice he'd ordered her death. He'd used her and betrayed her. He'd manipulated everyone around him as though their lives were nothing. Valn might not have swung the blade himself, but Corten's death was on his hands, along with those of everyone else killed during his failed coup.

Valn must have seen something in her eyes, because he shifted as though he were trying to press himself back through the stone wall.

Naya clenched her teeth. The aether sang in her bones, demanding action. But she couldn't, wouldn't, burn him. She wouldn't become the monster her father had seen, or the killer Delence apparently expected her to be. She held her hand out to one side and concentrated, releasing the energy in a burst of light that seemed blinding in the dim cell. Valn didn't cry out, but she heard his sharp intake of breath and the rustle of straw as he jerked in surprise.

"Who I'm loyal to doesn't matter to you," Naya said, proud of the cold note in her tone. "All that matters is that you answer my questions. So tell me, where did you get the runes for my bond?"

Valn shook his head. "I already told the interrogators. I had no allies in Talmir. I acted entirely of my own volition. And whether or not you believe me, I acted for the good of everyone in both Talmir and Ceramor." He said the words in a monotone, like a schoolboy repeating a lesson learned by rote.

"You're lying!" Naya snarled. "Nothing good would come from another war!"

"I never wanted war," Valn said, leaning forward. "I sought a transfer of power, a joining of Talmir and Ceramor that would have saved lives."

Naya shook her head and took a step back. "Just tell me, did you get the runes in Talmir or didn't you? Is it true that more works like that still exist?"

A series of sharp knocks sounded against the door, two fast and one slow. Naya cursed silently. That was Lila's signal that someone was coming. Valn glanced at the door, then back at her. "If I said yes, what would you do with that knowledge?"

"Just answer the question," Naya said.

"Perhaps I will, if you tell me why it matters so much to you."

Naya couldn't tell him the truth—that she and Lucia hoped to find an ancient ritual that would allow Naya to step into death and hunt for Corten's soul in order to bring him back. But she had to do something to convince Valn to talk. "I don't trust Delence with those runes any more than I trust the Talmiran government," Naya said slowly. "If they exist, then I want to find them before he does."

Heavy footsteps and shouts sounded in the hallway outside. Naya could feel the seconds ticking away. She kept her eyes locked on Valn's. His expression was intent, and the aether around him shimmered with uncertainty. "Well, it's true that

Talmir's policy on necromancy is more complicated than people like your father have been led to believe," Valn said. His eyes seemed to shine in the dim light.

Excitement and frustration thrummed through Naya's chest. "Stop giving me half-answers. Who are you even trying to protect? Your plans failed. Do you really think anyone in Talmir will argue for you at the Congress? They named you a traitor. It's over."

Valn laughed at that. "Over?" He met her eyes. "For me, maybe. But for you, my little spy, I suspect the war has only just begun."

CHAPTER 3

NAYA

"What war?" Naya asked Valn. Then the door to the cell burst open, silencing any answer he might have given. Delence strode in, followed by four very nervous palace guards. He eyed Valn as though checking to ensure his prized prisoner still had all his limbs.

When he seemed satisfied, he turned to Naya. "Out," he said coldly.

Naya stared at Valn, but his face was now set in a carefully blank mask.

"Now, Miss Garth," Delence said.

"I'm going." Naya stalked reluctantly out of the cell. Delence and the guards followed, locking the door behind them. When they were all back in the hall, Delence turned his glare on Lila.

"Sir—" she began.

"Return to your barracks, Lieutenant. We'll discuss your role in this mess later."

"It wasn't her idea," Naya said.

Delence's already-stern expression hardened. "Of that I am very much aware. Come with me, Miss Garth."

The guards formed a loose perimeter around her, making it clear that Delence's words weren't a request. Heat rose in Naya's cheeks, but she flipped her brown curls back over one shoulder and forced her expression to remain calm as the guards escorted her up to Delence's office.

The office was small, despite Delence's status as one of the king's most trusted advisers. Naya remained silent as Delence settled behind a desk covered in papers. "You know," he said, "several important people think I am making a mistake by bringing you to the Congress of Powers. I'm beginning to wonder if they might be right."

"I only wanted to talk to him," Naya said.

"I don't care what you wanted. I made it clear you weren't to go near Dalith Valn."

"Why?" Naya asked. "I'm the one who stopped him. If not for me, Ceramor would probably be under his control. I think that gives me the right to interrogate him."

"No, it doesn't," Delence snapped. "Clearly I was right to send an extra pair of eyes to watch the dungeon's entrance. Do you have any idea how delicate your situation is? I have spent a great deal of time and effort convincing the world that you were nothing more than an innocent victim in Valn's schemes. I don't need you complicating my efforts by assaulting prisoners."

"I didn't touch him," Naya growled. The bones in her hand prickled with heat and power at Delence's insult. She held the power in, barely, as the rest of what he'd said sank in. What had he meant by an extra pair of eyes?

After a moment she remembered the servant who'd been polishing the picture frame. Of course. Naya had been so wrapped in her own unease that she'd barely given the woman a second glance. The servant must have gone to Delence as soon as she saw Naya and Lila talking by the prison door. It certainly explained how Delence had learned where she was so quickly.

"You still disobeyed me." Delence leaned back in his chair. "Perhaps it would be better for everyone if I leave you behind when we sail for Talmir tomorrow."

"You can't! You need me." Naya stared at Delence. Surely he wasn't serious.

"I don't need anyone who can't follow orders. You're valuable, Miss Garth, but you are not irreplaceable."

Naya froze. She could taste the anger still swirling around Delence. Sharp fear grew in her chest and the prickling sensation in her hand turned cold. Had she pushed him too far this time? Her conversation with Valn had left her almost certain that the necromantic secrets she sought were in Talmir. She needed to get back into the country to find them. After a moment her anger surged back, strong and hot. Delence wouldn't care about resurrecting Corten. He only cared about Naya because he wanted something from her. In the end he was barely any better than Valn. Just like Valn he was ready to throw away anyone the second they stopped being useful.

Perhaps she should let him dismiss her. There had to be other ways to slip past the Talmiran border. After all, she'd grown up in Talmir. She knew the language and the culture. And since she'd died, she'd spent nearly all her time training as a spy. She could reshape her features—and even fight if she had to.

Yes, the prospect of throwing all Delence's offers away and setting out on her own was very, very tempting. But seizing that freedom would come at a price, and Naya wasn't sure it was one she could afford to pay. On her own she would have to find a way across the border that didn't involve sailing in the *Gallant*, the ship she'd inherited from her father. Anyone who recognized the ship might realize who she was—the daughter of a traitor, and a wraith besides. Being exposed as either could be deadly in Talmir without the sort of protections the Ceramoran delegation offered. She'd have to go by land, which would take more time and money than she had.

Naya clenched her jaw and spoke in what she hoped sounded like a calm and reasonable tone. "Who would you replace me with? You need me to testify against Valn. Last I heard, you haven't had much luck catching Celia, or anyone else who could say for sure that Valn organized the spy network and the coup against your King Allence. Not to mention that most of the documents that could have proved his guilt burned with the Talmiran Embassy." Naya was satisfied to feel a brush of rough frustration through Delence's aether. His people had been working to hunt down the dregs of Valn's spy network for weeks.

"And," Naya added, "if you don't bring me, the other delegates will wonder why you left someone with so much valuable information about Valn's crimes behind in Ceramor. They'll wonder if you're hiding something." Which, of course, he was. Delence was one of a very small number of people who knew Naya had been resurrected with a reaper binding, one of the powerful and illegal bindings created during the Mad King's War.

He'd claimed he wanted to help keep the secret of what she was in order to protect her. If the Talmirans discovered the truth, they would demand her execution. But Naya wasn't fool enough to think his reasons were purely sentimental. According to Lucia, Delence had taken all her notes on the reaper binding. With those notes a talented necromancer could make more of the reaper soldiers who had so terrified Talmir's armies during the war.

In keeping Lucia's notes and hiding Naya, Delence was taking a risk. But if something did cause the alliance to fall apart, Ceramor's lack of a standing army would leave it at a severe disadvantage. Resurrecting their dead as reapers could give them the edge they needed to keep from being overrun by Talmiran troops.

Delence watched her in silence for several seconds, then nodded. "It's true that your testimony is valuable," he said slowly. "But your actions today make me wonder if you understand the seriousness of this situation. This Congress is about more than just punishing one man for his crimes. The Ceramoran delegation has a chance to prove we are valuable and trustworthy allies. If we succeed, we can leave Lith Lor with better trade agreements and a more stable alliance. If we fail, we may end up facing another war."

"I know," Naya said.

"Then you should understand why I can't bring anyone I don't trust."

Naya crossed her arms. Obviously Delence hadn't trusted her to begin with, otherwise he would have let her speak to Valn. But if the prickly impatience in Delence's aether was anything to go by, then saying so wouldn't get her anywhere good. "I understand," she said.

Delence nodded. "I hope we can put this matter behind us. Can I trust you to follow orders in the future?"

"Yes," Naya said through clenched teeth. She could break that promise later if she had to.

"Good. Then I suggest you go finish preparing for the journey. We sail with the tide tomorrow." Delence looked down at the papers on his desk, clearly meaning the words as a dismissal.

Naya hesitated. "What are you going to do to Lila—I mean Lieutenant Selmore?"

"I haven't decided yet," Delence said. "I could demote her, or reassign her to a posting in one of the outer villages where she'll be less tempted to cause trouble."

Naya's fingers closed into fists. "She deserves better than that. She risked her life for Ceramor during the coup."

"And I will take that into account." The edge in Delence's voice made it clear he considered the matter closed. "Is there anything else?"

Naya shook her head, then stalked out of Delence's office. As she walked through the castle halls, she thought back over her brief conversation with Valn. The anger in her chest coiled and hissed. After everything, he still had the nerve to claim his intentions were noble. She tried to force her anger aside and analyze his words with the cool, logical calm that had once come so easily.

Talmir's policy on necromancy is more complicated than people like your father have been led to believe.

She wasn't sure what to make of everything Valn had said, but that hint was enough to convince her that she was moving in the right direction. Naya continued to mull over Valn's words and Delence's warning as she left the palace and took a tram up the hill toward the Bitter Dregs Café. Even this early in the afternoon, many of the tables were full. Wraiths, undead, and a handful of living members of the Necromantic Council sat talking and relaxing over drinks and plates of food.

Naya wove through the small crowd to a table near the back, where Lucia waited. The necromancer looked up and offered Naya a thin smile as she approached. "How did it go?"

Naya groaned as she sat down and accepted the cup of dark tea Lucia pushed across the table with her good arm. The other arm was still wrapped in plaster from when she'd broken it during the night of the coup.

"Salno Delence is a terrible human being," Naya said. "I managed to get to Valn, but apparently Delence had left a servant to spy on the dungeon entrance. I only got a few minutes with Valn before Delence barged in."

Lucia winced. "Ah. Well, you're still here. Should I take that as a good sign?"

Naya shrugged. "If you mean how Delence hasn't locked me away or tried to execute me, then yes. But it's going to be hard to get anything done with him keeping such a close watch on me." She felt suddenly exhausted by the day's events. She wished Corten were here. He would have known what to say to make this business with the Congress feel less huge and terrifying. If he were here, then maybe she wouldn't even have to go to the Congress. The two of them could sneak away somewhere and just . . . live. She imagined a little house on the Ceramoran coast, and Corten's body warm beside hers as they lay on the roof and watched the stars.

The impossibility of it made her chest ache. There would be no more rooftop nights or warm afternoons spent watching Corten's fingers shape molten glass into cups and bowls and smiling ducks. Corten was gone and it was her fault. She had to fix that no matter the cost. Naya raised the teacup to her lips, letting the liquid touch her skin until the strong, smoky flavor of it washed through her senses. It wasn't as comforting as actually being able to drink the tea, but it was better than nothing.

"Miss Garth, Lucia, there you are." A tall, thin man with neatly trimmed brown hair sat down in the table's last unoccupied chair and offered them both polite nods.

"Earon," Lucia said, returning the other necromancer's nod.

Earon Jalance smoothed the front of his suit. The aether around him was bright with nervous excitement as he leaned forward to rest his elbows on the table. "So, were you able to speak to our, ah, friend?" he asked Naya.

"We got in," Naya said. "But I didn't learn much before Delence showed up. He wasn't exactly happy to find me there, or to find Lieutenant Selmore helping me."

Jalance frowned. "You would think the man would show more appreciation after all the Council did to help him." He sighed. "Well, Lieutenant Selmore knew the risks."

Naya didn't like the dismissive tone in his voice. "There has to be something you can do to help her."

"Hmm. I doubt Delence will be interested in meting out punishment himself, what with the whole delegation leaving tomorrow," Jalance said after a pause. "Don't worry, I'll find a way to ensure that whatever discipline she's assigned is light." He tapped the table with two fingers in an impatient gesture. "Now, please tell me you learned something worthwhile."

Naya wrapped her hands tighter around her teacup, enjoying the familiar feel of smooth porcelain. Like Delence, Jalance knew what she was. He'd been the one to carve her a new bone after Valn captured Lucia. He knew the runes for her binding had come from one of three journals Lucia wrote more than thirty years ago. Back then Lucia had been an apprentice helping resurrect undead soldiers for the Mad King's army. She'd experimented with magics far stranger and more complex than anything allowed by the current Ceramoran king.

Now Jalance was very, very interested in learning if more of Lucia's work had survived the purges after the war's end. "I think our suspicions were right," Naya said. "I think someone from Talmir is hiding a cache of necromantic works."

"Did he say who?" Jalance asked.

"No. But there are only so many people who could have gotten access to the lab Lucia worked at. We'll find a way to track them." Naya tried to infuse the words with more confidence than she felt. She hadn't wanted to involve anyone else in her search. And she still wasn't sure how she felt about possibly handing Lucia's other journals over to the Council. But when it became clear that she'd need help getting to Valn, Jalance had been her best option. The man kept a secret library of histories and forbidden literature related to the Mad King's War. As she'd suspected, he'd been more than eager to aid her when she'd made her proposal.

Jalance looked between Naya and Lucia. "The Council won't be able to offer you any more help once you leave Ceramor. But there are several people here who would be happy to pay you for whatever you find."

Assuming she could track down the missing journals, and that no one in Talmir decided to kill her for the crime of being undead. Naya nodded to Jalance. She didn't care about the money, or the risk. She just needed to get Corten back.

CHAPTER 4

CORTEN

Corten fell for what felt like eternity. Wind rushed and colors flashed through the darkness, vanishing before his mind could make any sense of them. He squeezed his eyes shut and waited for the impact.

But it never came. The wind died abruptly. Instead of the shock of crashing into the ground, he felt his feet settle gently onto a hardwood floor. When he opened his eyes, he found himself standing in his room above the glass shop. Naya lay on his bed, her features twisted in pain and her skin fading in and out in patches. Her dark curls were spread across the pillow to frame a pretty oval face with delicate lips and wide, intelligent eyes. Corten's chest tightened.

"You don't understand. I'm not who you think I am," Naya said, her voice raw.

Corten took a step back. "What's going on?" The edges of the room wavered. This had to be a memory, like when he'd seen the image of his parents. Even as that thought crossed his mind, anger filled him, as fresh and sharp as the day he had first learned her secrets.

"Ever since I died, I've been working as a spy for the Talmiran Embassy," Naya said. "I helped kidnap Delence. When the guards came for Lucia, they were looking for me."

Corten tried to take another step back, but his feet seemed

locked in place. That day she'd confessed, Corten had told himself that Naya—or Blue, as he'd known her then—was confused. She had to be. There was no way the person he'd come to love had been toying with him this whole time.

"But she did toy with you," a voice whispered from the dark. "She lied and she used you and—"

"No. That isn't what happened," Corten said. He clenched his fists so tight his nails dug into his palms. Naya had lied to him, yes. But she hadn't done it to hurt him. She'd made mistakes, and she'd had the courage to face those mistakes. She'd risked everything to undo the damage she'd caused. Seeing that courage had made him love her all the more. That was why he'd followed her into the burning embassy. He'd wanted to help her stop Valn. Valn, who was a poison, the sort of person who twisted everyone around him toward his own ends. Corten had imagined that if they could only get rid of Valn, then he and Naya could start fresh, together.

The shadowy figure appeared again, materializing from around the corner of a faded and flickering bookshelf. "Is she why you struggle? How could you ever trust someone like that again?"

Corten shook his head. "Why are you doing this?" he asked.

"So you will see," the shadow answered. "You cannot stay here. You cannot return to life. Even if you could, you would only find more strife and suffering. It is better to travel on and accept your death."

Corten frowned. "What are you?"

The shadow didn't answer.

"Why can't I stay here?"

The room flickered, and whispers hissed at the edge of Corten's hearing.

"The fringe isn't safe. You must go," the shadow said.

"Go where?"

As if in answer, Corten felt the wind rise, pushing at his back. The walls of the room faded and shadowy grass pushed up through the floorboards, shattering the illusion of memory.

"Go!" This time the shadow's voice was like a trumpet in the hollow darkness. "They have found you!"

Something black and twisting tore through the far wall. Shining claws. Writhing, impossible limbs. Mouths everywhere that went beyond black into something empty that Corten's mind refused to process. Thought left him. He turned, and letting the wind guide him, he ran.

The thing behind him howled, and the darkness seemed to pulse and writhe in response to its anger. Corten's lungs burned as he tried to get away, away, awa—

The world twisted again. Color flooded into the black and gray, and suddenly the grass beneath him was the faded gold of early autumn. The sky was blue, streaked with wisps of cloud. Up ahead his younger brother, Bernel, ran toward the cliff's edge, clutching a small wooden box in one hand.

"Damn you, give it back, Bernel!" Corten shouted, his breath coming in gasps.

Bernel spun, taking a few steps back and holding the box up. "What, this?" he asked. His tone held a laugh, but there was something hard and angry in his eyes. "Careful, Corten, my palm's awfully sweaty. Wouldn't want it to slip." Bernel shook the box for emphasis, making its contents rattle as he dangled it over the cliff.

Corten slowed, stopping several paces from his brother. The grass was still damp from the previous night's rain. The air was clear and bright, and the leaves were just starting to turn. It was the morning of the town harvest festival and he did not have time for this. "All right, fine," Corten said. "You've had your joke. What do you want?" They stood on a sloping grassy field that dropped off abruptly to offer a dramatic view of the farmlands below. Their family's lands stretched out behind Corten, the house hidden beyond a copse of trees.

Bernel tilted his head to the side, narrowing his eyes. "What do I want? I want to know why everything good always happens to you."

"What are you talking about?"

Bernel shook the box again. "This! You were going to give it to Sasia, weren't you?"

"So what if I was?" Corten glared back at his brother, clenching his fists. Honestly. At fourteen, Bernel was only a year younger than him, but sometimes he acted like such a kid.

"I told you I liked her!"

"So? That doesn't mean she belongs to you. You can't just claim people like they're the last slice of cake, Bernel. When has Sasia ever even said three words to you?"

"That's not the point! You always get everything! If she thinks you like her, then she won't even look at me." Bernel turned toward the cliff. "Well, if you're going to take her, you'll have to do it without this."

Corten cursed, imagining the rosewood box sailing over the cliff, shattering on the rocks below and spilling the little moonstone pendant out to who-knew-where. He'd spent a half year's pocket money on that thing. His parents wouldn't mind if they knew it was a gift for Sasia. His mother had been hoping to make a match of them. And while Sasia and Corten had never had much in common, Sasia was sweet and pretty. Most importantly for Corten's mother, Sasia came from a family whose wealth and bloodlines dated back even further than Corten's own. If she showed him favor, then maybe Corten's mother would stop pestering him constantly about the family lineage and he could go back to focusing on his apprenticeship with Lucia.

Of course, if he lost the pendant with nothing to show for it, he'd only earn himself more grief. And it wouldn't matter if it was Bernel's fault. Bernel would gaze at their parents with those wide, innocent-looking eyes and all would be forgiven.

Corten sprinted toward Bernel, grabbing his brother's arm just before he could throw the little box. They grappled, all Corten's attention focused on the box even as terror rose up deep in his mind.

No. Not this. Not again.

"Let go!" Corten shouted.

The world slowed as Bernel's grip on the box finally loosened. Corten took a step back, triumphant. Then he heard the rattle of pebbles falling down the slope, felt his foot slipping as wet dirt and loose rock crumbled under his heel. He tilted back, and back. Bernel's eyes widened. His hand was still outstretched where it'd been when Corten tore the box free. Corten tried to reach for his brother, but his fingers caught only air.

Then he was falling, the sky blue above him.

The scream tore from his throat. He flailed, trying to grab hold of something, anything. His back hit the rocky slope, sending pain like lightning jolting through him. His body twisted and the world became a spinning chaos of pain.

Then blackness.

Corten found himself on his hands and knees, gasping for breath as the shadowy grass rustled all around. The pain was gone, but his arms and legs still trembled with the shock of it. He pushed himself to his feet. His thoughts were fuzzy, his limbs weak, as though something vital were trickling away from him. Shame and horror rose thick in his throat. Of all the stupid ways to die. Stumbling off a cliff in a fight over a trinket for a girl he didn't even care for. He should have stood up to his mother. He should have let Bernel throw that stupid necklace over the cliff.

If he had, maybe he wouldn't be dead. He turned in a slow circle, trying to get his bearings. Lucia would sing him back, of course. Bernel would run and tell someone what had happened and then . . .

Corten blinked as reality cut through his foggy thoughts.

Wait. The cliff had been years ago. He spun, looking for the monster that had chased him, but there was no sign of it now. No sign of the shadow man either. Even the wind was dying, steeping the colorless world in a silence that was somehow almost as frightening as the beast's howls had been.

What was going on? He'd been trying to escape, to find his way back to the place where Lucia's portal had opened. But now with the wind gone, he wasn't even sure which direction was back.

It is better to travel on and accept your death.

Corten shuddered. "Not yet," he said, the words sounding odd in the hollow quiet. "I'm not done yet." He turned and started walking in what he hoped was the right direction. The barriers between life and death weren't absolute. Nobody knew that better than the necromancers. The monster had been chasing him away from the portal. The shadow man had tried to warn him away, and the wind had dragged him deeper into death. Something wanted to keep him here. Why bother doing all that if there was no hope of him slipping back through to the other side?

CHAPTER 5

NAYA

The next morning Naya and Lucia took a carriage down to the docks to meet the rest of the delegation. Lucia sat stiffly, clutching her plaster-wrapped arm to her stomach. Tears still shimmered in her eyes from saying her good-byes to Alejandra. Lucia's lover had been far from pleased to have her traveling to a country where necromancy was punishable by death. She was even less happy knowing what Naya and Lucia planned to do. But in the end she'd given her blessing, along with the command that Lucia come home safe.

"Well," Lucia said, wiping her eyes after a moment's silence. "I suppose we're really doing this."

Naya nodded. Despite everything, she felt somehow lighter as the carriage rattled toward the docks. After three weeks of preparations and uncertainty, they were finally on their way. "Did you make any more progress on the diagrams last night?" Naya asked.

"No." Lucia pressed her lips together, and the energy around her prickled with frustration. "I went back over those books we borrowed from Earon's collection, but I couldn't find anything new. It's maddening. Every time I close my eyes, I swear I can almost remember the right runes."

Naya shifted uneasily. Lucia had spent weeks attempting to

reassemble the rune diagrams for a ritual she called a shadow walk. If they could finish the diagram, Lucia could sing open a stronger portal that would let Naya step physically into death. Lucia had sketched out a complicated set of modifications that would allow her to add two new bones to Naya's bond as well. If her plan worked, the bones would act as a compass, one pointing Naya toward Corten's soul, the other guiding her back toward life. Of course, it would only work if they could find the diagrams for the portal.

"And you're still sure you can't try sending me through an ordinary portal?" Naya asked.

Lucia shook her head. "That answer will be the same no matter how many times you ask. I'm not certain what would happen if you tried, but even if you did get through unharmed, you wouldn't be able to take your bones with you. You'd have no way to find Corten, and I'd have no good way to call you back to life."

"But—"

"No. We're already taking enough risks." The carriage hit a bump and Lucia winced, touching her broken arm. "I miss him too. But I won't help throw you into death with no protection. If we can find my journals, we'll try the shadow walk. Other-wise . . ."

"Otherwise we'll find another way," Naya said quickly.

Lucia gave her a small, sad smile. "Of course."

Silence settled between them. Naya watched the city's brightly painted houses flash past. Some foolish part of her couldn't stop looking for Corten's face among the people on the streets, or for a glimpse of him running across the rooftops above. She would catch sight of someone from the corner of her eye, black curls or the familiar curve of a smile. Hope would flare in her chest, only to sputter when she turned and saw it was some stranger who bore little resemblance to the boy she loved.

It wasn't fair for Corten to have torn such a hole in her life. They'd barely known each other a few months. Yet somehow those months had seemed brighter and more real than all the rest of her years put together. What had grown between them felt sharper than the fleeting crushes she'd had during her school-days back in Talmir. She didn't know if it was the sort of love that could last a lifetime. All she knew was that the prospect of going on without him left her aching like her chest was full of jagged thorns. Maybe things would be better in Talmir. Maybe there she could stop hoping to spot him around every corner and instead focus on finding what she needed to bring him back.

The noise outside swelled, drawing Naya out of her thoughts. The carriage slowed and she heard the driver shouting for people to step aside. It seemed a crowd had gathered at the docks to see the delegates off. The aether around them was bright with an almost festive air. Everyone hoped this meeting of the Congress of Powers would bring an end to the restrictions the Treaty of Lith Lor had imposed on Ceramor after the last war. But beneath the sweet citrus smell of that hope, Naya could sense fear and anger smoldering like hot coals. Ceramor had suffered for thirty years, and while Delence had long argued for patience and a peaceful solution, that patience was running thin.

They reached the docks after several minutes of jostling. Two ships stood proud against a late-summer sky that shimmered with heat. The first was a large, square-rigged galleon, her hull painted in bright patterns of green and blue. That would be the *Lady*, the flagship of the tiny Ceramoran fleet and one of the few new vessels they'd managed to build since the war. Beside her, small, sleek, and unassuming, was the *Gallant*. Naya's chest tightened when she saw the familiar lines of the ship's bow. Once she'd dreamed of the day when she'd have her own ship and the freedom to sail where she would. Now all her old dreams were tainted by the memory of her father's betrayal.

Naya's feet barely hit the dock before Delence strode over to greet her. "Miss Garth, Madame Laroke, I'm glad you're here." He motioned to one of the sailors, and the man hurried over. "Please show Madame Laroke to her cabin aboard the *Lady*."

Naya frowned. "Isn't Lucia sailing with me?"

"No need to crowd the *Gallant* when the *Lady* is designed to carry passengers in comfort, especially given Madame Laroke's injuries." From Delence's brisk tone and friendly expression, Naya could almost imagine their confrontation the day before had never happened.

The aether swirled thick around them, the mingled emotions making it hard for Naya to guess if there was anything lurking behind Delence's smile. Between working with her tutors, helping Lucia, and planning her meeting with Valn, she'd had little time to think about the *Gallant*. When she'd asked about preparations for their departure, Delence had dismissed her questions with the assurance that everything would be taken care of.

"If the *Lady*'s better equipped, then why bring the *Gallant* at all?" she asked.

"I had thought you would rather travel on your own ship instead of leaving it here to accumulate docking fees."

"You're charging me docking fees?" Naya asked.

"As a member of the delegation, you will have your expenses covered by the Crown. King Allence agreed with me that having a second ship in Talmir could prove useful, and the *Gallant* seemed a natural candidate. But I'm afraid we can only pay for her upkeep so long as she is in the service of the Crown."

Naya felt foolish for not thinking of that little detail before. Creator, she'd spent years training to become a merchant. She should have started planning for this the moment Delence signed the *Gallant*'s deed over to her. She should have ignored his reassurances and insisted he let her help with the voyage preparations. More than once she'd decided to go down to the docks and look the *Gallant* over. But every time she'd found some excuse to put it off—a new book to examine, or a trip to Matius's home to say good-bye. Looking at the ship now, she felt her stomach sink.

The journey to Lith Lor wasn't long this time of year, a week or two at most, depending on the weather, but the price to pay the crew and equip the ship would still be substantial. And once spent, the money would be lost. She had no cargo to sell when she got to Lith Lor. Naya frowned. Accepting ownership of the *Gallant* had seemed the natural thing to do when Delence had offered. But looking at the slim smile on his face now, it felt more like a shackle than a gift.

Lucia glanced uncertainly between Naya and Delence. "I do appreciate the offer of comfortable lodgings, but should anything happen to Naya's bond, wouldn't it be better if I was near at hand?"

Delence waved the question away. "If anything goes wrong, the *Gallant*'s crew can throw up a signal and we'll row you over to deal with it." He turned to the sailor who'd been waiting by his elbow. "Madame Laroke has a chest on the back of the carriage, I believe. Bring it to the *Lady*, please."

"Yes, sir." The sailor started off.

Lucia glanced once more at Naya, then followed the man. "Please be careful with it," she called out. "Some of my tools are quite fragile."

"Which ship will carry Dalith Valn?" Naya asked.

"The *Lady*, of course."

Of course. Even before she'd gotten caught yesterday, Naya supposed it would have been too much to hope that Delence would put his precious prisoner on her ship.

Delence's smile hardened like bread left out for too long. "I hope you haven't forgotten our last conversation."

"I haven't," Naya said.

"Good. Then come with me, we have a schedule to keep. I'll introduce you to the *Gallant*'s standing captain and her other passengers and we can be on our way."

Naya glanced around but couldn't spot Lucia among the crowd. She'd have to figure out how to get a message to the necromancer. Perhaps Lucia could find a way to talk to Valn during the journey.

The man Delence had hired to captain the *Gallant* on this voyage was lean, with a scraggly beard and dark eyes set in a perpetual squint. "Captain Elseran Cervacaro. At your service, Miss Garth," he said with a low bow. "I'll be taking care of the day-to-day business so you can relax along the voyage." Naya returned the bow with a curtsy and took an immediate dislike to the man. There was something condescending in his manner, and she didn't like the roughness of his appearance.

Delence led her down the pier to a spot by the *Gallant*'s gangplank where a young woman in a simple dress stood next to a young man in a suit. They both looked to be in their late teens. The young woman dipped a curtsy, but Naya barely saw it as her eyes fixed on the young man and dread made her stomach plummet. He was taller than Naya, with black hair swept back in the latest fashion and almost delicate features. Necromantic tattoos encircled his neck and wrists, binding his soul to his formerly dead body.

"This is my son, Francisco," Delence said, clapping the young man on the shoulder. "You two will be working together at the Congress, so I thought it would be good if you had some time to get to know each other on the trip over."

Francisco offered Naya a shallow bow. "Miss Garth." His tone was cool, but when his eyes met Naya's, she saw fury lurking there. No wonder. She might not have pulled the trigger on the rune pistol that killed him, but hers was the last face he would have seen before his life faded away.

CHAPTER 6

NAYA

A few minutes after meeting with Delence and Francisco, Naya stood at the top of the *Gallant*'s gangplank, her bare toes inches from the deck. She clutched the rail as a sudden wave of vertigo hit her. The scene before her was achingly familiar. Sailors rushed about, readying the ship for departure while the captain bellowed orders. Sunlight gleamed off the round windows of the deckhouse, and her nose filled with the smells of tar and salt and the pungent, fishy odor of the docks. It should have felt like coming home.

But the sailors were all strangers, and when Naya looked up, she saw the Ceramoran flag flying off the mainmast.

My father really is dead, Naya thought with a shiver.

"Miss Garth, is everything all right?"

Naya blinked, then glanced back at the young woman standing behind her. She was about Naya's height, with a sturdy build, cheerful features, and dark-brown hair pulled up in a practical bun. Her name was Felicia, and apparently Delence had assigned her to be Naya's lady's maid. She was regarding Naya with a worried look, one hand clasped tight to the gangplank's railing.

"It's fine," Naya said quickly. She drew in a deep breath of aether, then boarded her ship.

Captain Cervacaro glanced at her before gesturing for one

of the crew. As the sailor jogged over, Naya saw he was perhaps two or three years her senior. He was tall and lean, with a crooked nose and the coarse, sandy-brown hair and green eyes of a Silmaran native.

The young sailor led her below deck, where Naya discovered her things already stowed in the captain's cabin. She stepped hesitantly inside. The cabin was bigger than her room above Lucia's shop, but it felt somehow far more cramped. Light streamed in through the square-paneled windows along the stern wall, illuminating the surface of a small desk. Between her and the desk was a scuffed table where she and her father had sometimes sat together for dinner. Someone had secured a pair of sea chests against the port wall, next to the room's single bunk, and strung a hammock on the starboard side.

It was surreal seeing the cabin without her father in it. Part of her expected him to step from the hallway behind her and sit at the long table to review whatever work he'd set for her to do that day. She'd been fourteen when her father had finally decided to let her travel with him. Her first night aboard the ship, they'd eaten dinner together at that same table. The food had been simple, but to her it had tasted better than any king's feast. She'd basked in her father's attention as he'd shown her charts marking their route and told stories of his past adventures.

Naya forced herself to look away, blinking as a swirl of conflicting emotions made her eyes burn. This room held some of her happiest memories of her father. But remembering those days only made her anger burn hotter. All those times he'd smiled and praised her, he'd been keeping a terrible secret. He hadn't trusted her enough to tell her about his work as a spy. He'd sent her into danger with barely any warning. He'd killed Corten simply for defending her. She shouldn't feel sad or guilty over what she'd done to him in the end. The kindness he'd once shown her didn't forgive the monster he'd become.

No. He was always a monster. You just didn't want to see it before.
For years her father had been consumed by his hatred of the
necromancers and the undead of Ceramor. He'd been willing
to do anything or hurt anyone if it meant a chance to kill them.

"Well, this is . . . cozy," Felicia said, drawing Naya away
from her increasingly dark thoughts. Naya turned to see Felicia
eyeing the hammock warily.

"You can have the bed," Naya said quickly.

"Oh, I couldn't—" Felicia began.

"I don't sleep. Besides, I like hammocks." And she intended
to spend as little time as possible in this room. There were too
many memories here that she'd rather not examine.

Felicia seemed to consider for a long moment. "You're sure?"
she asked.

"Completely."

"All right. Is there anything you want me to unpack, Miss
Garth?"

"No!" Naya said, more sharply than she'd intended. She
tried to soften the words with a smile. "I can do that later. And
please, just call me Naya."

Felicia raised her eyebrows. "I'm not sure Lord Delence
would think that appropriate."

Naya fought to hold on to the smile. She'd never had a lady's
maid before and she didn't particularly want one now. But
Delence had insisted, and at the time it hadn't seemed worth
pressing the issue. Now she would just have to make the best of
it. "Please? At least when we're alone."

"All right then, Miss Naya," Felicia said with a tentative
smile.

Close enough. "Thank you." Then, trying to sound casual,
Naya added, "We'll be setting off soon. Why don't you go
above to watch? I'll join you in a few minutes."

"Of course."

Once Felicia had left, Naya closed her eyes and reached out through the aether. She could sense Felicia walking down the hall. Unease and excitement mixed in her aether. She seemed earnest enough. Had Delence sent her to spy on Naya like he'd sent that other servant to watch the dungeons? That seemed likely, but it was also possible he thought she'd truly need a maid to keep her presentable at the Congress. Either way, Naya would have to be careful not to let Felicia discover her true intentions.

Naya checked her father's desk and found it empty. That wasn't surprising. Delence's people had likely searched the room for evidence connected to Valn's plots. If they'd found anything, they hadn't bothered to tell her.

No matter. Her father had rarely kept important records in the desk when he wasn't aboard the ship. Naya walked to the bunk. She crouched next to it, then carefully opened the two drawers set beneath the thin mattress. The drawers were empty, but after a moment she managed to free them from their tracks, exposing the boards beneath.

The loose board under the bunk was hard to find even if you knew where to look. Naya drew in more aether, then envisioned the runes for light. Slowly, a warm glow blossomed in the palm of her hand, illuminating the dusty space under the bunk. Her hand tingled as she held the image of the rune in her mind. Through trial and error, she'd learned that maintaining a soft light like this was far harder than creating a single bright burst as she'd done in Valn's cell. It was one in a long list of exercises Lucia had recommended she practice in order to gain a better understanding of how her reaper's binding worked.

After a few minutes' careful work, Naya found the loose board and worked it free. She reached inside the hidden compartment and smiled as her fingertips brushed worn leather. She drew out her father's logbook, followed by a heavy purse full of gold Talmiran stars and silver glints. She hefted the coin pouch thoughtfully, then set it aside. It wasn't much, at least not in the face of the costs Delence was already covering to sail the *Gallant* back to Talmir. Still, having the pouch made her feel less helpless.

Anticipation thrummed through her as she opened the logbook. The handwriting was achingly familiar. She couldn't read the cipher her father had used, though it looked similar to the one he'd taught her. Naya ran her fingers over the text, curiosity and horror warring inside her. Did she really want to know what he'd written? Did she have a choice? The logbook might contain clues about who Valn and her father had been working with. If she could find their allies, maybe they would lead her to the rest of Lucia's journals.

Naya glanced up at the door. She would read the logbook, but not now. She didn't want to leave Felicia waiting for long, and anyway it would be nice to be above deck to watch the sails catch that first breath of wind. She carefully put the board back over the hidden compartment and set the drawer into its tracks. The logbook and coin purse went to the bottom of the small bag of personal possessions she'd brought from Lucia's shop.

Naya climbed to the upper deck and found Felicia just as the tow boats pulled the *Gallant* away from the dock. Ahead the *Lady* was already underway, her massive sails unfurling like clouds against the summer sky. Felicia grinned, shading her eyes with one hand, and craned her neck to stare at the sailors in the rigging. Naya found a patch of deck by the starboard rail where they would be safely out of the way. She spotted Francisco standing near the bow, his arms crossed and his gaze fixed on the *Lady*.

For a moment Naya's eyes lingered on him. He stood with his feet planted against the gentle rock of the ship and his back perfectly straight. She tried to imagine what the last few months must have been like for him. He would have been resurrected only to learn that his father had been kidnapped by Talmiran agents. It wasn't a fate she would wish on anyone.

But at least Francisco had gotten his father back. And while Delence was a calculating bastard, he'd accepted his son after his resurrection. He hadn't tried to murder him in a blind rage.

Naya heard Captain Cervacaro call out and returned her attention to the glimmering blue horizon. The sails unfurled with a furious noise of flapping cloth, and the *Gallant* surged forward on the wind.

CHAPTER 7

NAYA

Once the ships left the mouth of Belavine Bay, they settled into a comfortable speed at a little over five knots. Francisco's face had gone sickly green almost as soon as the sails unfurled, and he'd retreated below. Naya stayed above, watching the crew work and trying to banish the sense of wrongness that came from seeing so many strangers on the familiar deck.

Captain Cervacaro stood at the helm talking with his first mate, a hard-faced Ceramoran woman called Pit. Sailors moved through the rigging, adjusting the sails as Cervacaro called out orders. Reial, the crooked-nosed young Silmaran who'd shown Naya to her cabin earlier, sat a little way away coiling a long stretch of cable and inspecting it for damage.

Naya kept her hands in her pockets as she watched the work around her. She'd hoped that once they got moving, the knot of anxiety inside her chest would ease. But even the soothing roll of the ship wasn't enough to unravel it. She ran her fingers over the runes of the simple rune disk concealed against her palm. With a slight twist, she activated the disk and felt the sharp tug as it pulled aether from its surroundings to convert into heat. She split her attention between watching the sailors and slowly forcing more aether into the disk, then drawing it back out before the runes could overload.

She had no idea what challenges she might face in Talmir, never mind what she might find on the other side of death. She needed every advantage she could get. That meant practicing as much as possible so she could learn to better control and manipulate the aether around her.

The disk grew hot, then cool against her palm. The wind set a spray of seawater stinging against her cheek as the *Gallant* crested a gentle wave. Despite his rough appearance, Cervacaro obviously knew his business. He kept a steady hand on the wheel, and his crew jumped quickly to obey his orders. Naya was torn between admiration and lingering unease. She could still feel her father's presence in every grain of wood, every stitch of sail. It made her feel like an intruder, or worse, a pirate.

But she wasn't an intruder. The *Gallant* was hers. If she was ever going to be a proper captain, she would need to learn the craft. She glanced around and spotted Felicia chatting eagerly with one of the sailors. Felicia said something and the sailor burst into a deep belly laugh. Naya smiled. Unlike Francisco, Felicia had taken eagerly to the voyage. She'd be fine on her own for a few hours. Naya started toward the helm.

"Miss Garth, your skirt!"

Naya turned to see Reial running toward her. "My skirt?" She looked down, then cursed. Smoke was drifting in thin wisps from a darkening patch of cloth just over where the rune disk sat in her pocket. Naya could feel the searing heat and the unsteady pressure as the metal warped and the runes began to break. She jerked the hot disk of metal from her pocket and threw it overboard. It flashed in the sunlight before disappearing into the rolling waves.

"What was that?" Reial asked.

Naya ducked her head, brushing at the scorched fabric to hide her expression. Stupid. She'd let her concentration slip for just a moment and nearly set herself on fire. "Just a rune disk.

I was fiddling with it and I guess I didn't realize how hot it had gotten."

"You're all right? Not burned or anything?" Reial asked incredulously.

Naya forced a laugh. "No, just my clothes. One of the benefits of being a wraith." She showed him her unburned hand as evidence.

"You should be more careful," Reial said, taking a step back. "You're lucky that thing didn't start a fire. Why would you even have something like that?"

Naya grimaced. Fire at sea, whether from a lightning strike or a careless cook, was one of the great dangers to a ship like the *Gallant*. She knew that. She also knew it was stupid to practice with her powers in such a public space. These last few weeks, she'd spent most of her time with people who already knew her secrets. Now that she was traveling, she had to remember to be more careful. "It was just an old heat disk a friend gave me," Naya lied. "I didn't even realize I still had it in my pocket. I must have turned it on by accident." She gave Reial what she hoped looked like a bashful smile. "Sorry to worry you. I'll let you get back to work."

"Wait. Where are you going?" Reial asked as she turned to leave.

"To speak to Captain Cervacaro. I was hoping he'd teach me about sailing."

"Now's probably not the best time," Reial said, glancing at Naya's burned skirt. "Wouldn't you rather go change or something? I'm sure he'd be happy to talk about all that later over dinner."

"I'm fine. And I'd rather have the chance to watch the captain at work," Naya said. Before he'd taken the helm, Cervacaro had asked her, Francisco, and Felicia to join him for dinner that night.

"Right. Well, thing is, the captain doesn't like interruptions, especially not when he's getting the feel for a new ship," Reial said, shifting so he was standing between her and the helm where the captain stood. "But if you want, we could go stand by the deckhouse. We'll be out of the way there and I can explain the maneuvers to you as we go."

Naya could sense the unease in his aether. She frowned. She guessed that his reaction was about more than just her accident with the rune disk. "Did the captain order you to keep me away?"

Reial looked away. "Not in so many words. But I was to keep an eye on you and make sure you don't come by any trouble."

Naya crossed her arms over her chest. "He does realize this is my ship, not his, doesn't he?"

"Of course. He didn't mean offense by it. It's just . . ."

"Just what?"

Reial sighed. "Look, Captain Cervacaro is a good man, but he's never been quick to trust, and lately he's been having a turn of bad luck. It's made him wary."

"It's not as though I'm going to grab the wheel out from under him," Naya said in exasperation.

Reial smiled. "I'm sure you wouldn't. Still, the captain's more likely to be amiable if you talk to him when he's off duty."

Naya hesitated, then nodded reluctantly and followed Reial to the side of the deckhouse. A moment later the captain shouted orders to move the ship to a starboard tack. The ship slowed as they turned into the wind, men running and hauling on braces to adjust the sails to the new heading. Through it all Reial stayed by her side, occasionally pointing out details of the maneuver.

Now that Naya thought about it, Reial had been nearby ever since she'd boarded the *Gallant*. Was Cervacaro really so worried that he'd order one of his crew to waste all his time watching her? Did it have something to do with her being a wraith? Cervacaro was Ceramoran, but sailors tended to be more superstitious than most, and even in Ceramor, not everyone was comfortable around the undead.

"You said before the captain's had some bad luck. What did you mean?" Naya asked.

Reial shifted uncomfortably. "I probably shouldn't have said anything about that."

"If there's trouble, I'd rather know about it. Does he think I'm bad luck?"

Reial squinted up at the sails, then shook his head. "It's not really about you. Just . . . well, the owners of the last ship we sailed on did him a bad turn, nearly got us all killed."

"What happened?" Naya asked.

"We used to serve together on the *Arabella*. She was a good vessel, but the investors who owned her were a bunch of landfeet who didn't know sails from bedsheets. We had a shipment go foul when we were running sugar from Banen to Ceramor. The owners were furious, blamed the captain even though it wasn't really his fault. After that the owners got it into their heads that the best way to make up the loss was to send us on a run out to Vesra Shark."

Naya's eyebrows rose. "Vesra Shark? Isn't that somewhere in Endra?"

"Yeah. North coast, near the mountains. One of the owners talked to a captain who got rich making the journey a few years back. He said Vesra Shark was a wealthy city, full of metalsmiths forging alloys better than anything here in the west. Guess this captain didn't mention that most ships that pass that way don't come back."

"But you went anyway?" Naya asked. "What was it like?"

Reial hunched his shoulders. "Cold seas. Storms. Can't tell you much about the city. The people wouldn't let us past their walls. Had to trade with whichever merchants rowed out to us, and the rates weren't near so good as the captain had hoped. We hit a bad storm on the way back, lost the foremast and the upper mainmast, along with a good bit of sail. When we limped back to harbor, the creditors decided the ship wasn't worth the cost of repairs. After all we'd risked, they sacked the whole crew and sold poor *Arabella* for scrap."

"I'm sorry," Naya said. Her throat tightened at the thought of the *Gallant* being so ill-used. She had a dozen questions she wanted to ask. She'd never met anyone who'd sailed round the northern edge of the continent. But she could tell by the look in Reial's eyes and the bitter tang of his aether that he didn't want to say any more about the trip.

They stood together in silence, watching the other sailors work. Wind snapped at the sails and the deck creaked softly. "Why is it you want the captain to teach you sailing anyway?" Reial asked.

"Because the *Gallant* is mine," Naya said. "If I'm going to own a ship, I ought to know how to sail her."

Reial frowned at that. "Forgive me for saying it, miss, but you don't seem the type that would make a good captain."

Naya faced him, anger rising in her chest. "Excuse me? What's that supposed to mean? You don't even know me."

"Maybe not. But back at port people said you were a spy, and that you started the uprising that took down Valn. Now here you are sailing with a bunch of diplomats to go make fancy laws and such."

Naya crossed her arms. "What's your point?"

Reial met her eyes, his gaze steady and cold. "Learning to captain a ship like the *Gallant* isn't something you do in a handful of days, and someone who goes brushing elbows with diplomats doesn't seem the sort to spend years learning the trade proper. And," he added, "captains can't let themselves get distracted when they're on duty. You about lit yourself on fire a minute ago and barely even noticed."

"Maybe I was simply focused on something else," Naya grumbled.

Reial gave her a disbelieving look and Naya scowled back at him. "I know it won't be easy," she said. "But I have to start somewhere."

Reial looked away. "True enough, I guess. Just don't be surprised if the captain isn't amiable to teaching you all he knows. We've all got our work to do, and seems to me yours is on land."

Naya wasn't sure what to say to that. Reial nodded as though silence was answer enough. Naya watched as he walked away and returned to checking over the length of rope. He was wrong. She could be a good captain. She'd always loved the ocean, always felt so free with nothing but open waves around her. She knew learning to be a proper captain wouldn't be easy. Still, with a few months at sea, and the right mates to offer advice, she could do the job. She was sure of it.

But . . .

Naya closed her eyes. All that would have to wait until after the Congress. Where would she find the money to pay the crew after it was all done? What about cargo? And if—no, when— she brought Corten back, would he be willing to sail with her? If not, would he wait for her while she traveled from port to port?

Naya opened her eyes again and looked up at the taut white sails, but the wind and open sky beyond offered her no answers.

That night the cook set the table in Naya's cabin for her dinner with the captain. Cervacaro sat at the head with his first mate, Pit, to his right and Naya to his left. Francisco and Felicia sat at the other end. They waited silently as the cook served spiced chicken and vegetables onto the polished silver plates Naya's father had always reserved for special occasions. Felicia eyed the food with interest, but Francisco was obviously still struggling with seasickness.

"I hope you've found everything to your liking so far," Cervacaro said as he cut into his chicken.

Naya nodded. "Yes, and thank you again for giving up the captain's cabin. You didn't have to do that." Her conversation with Reial was still sharp in her mind. She didn't intend to simply give up on learning to sail, but if she wanted the captain's help, she'd obviously have to be careful about how and when she asked.

Cervacaro waved her thanks away. "Think nothing of it. And you, Lord Francisco, I trust you've settled in?"

Francisco picked up his fork, then set it down with a clatter. "I'm hoping this trip doesn't take so long that we have time to 'settle in.'"

The captain chuckled. "If the winds hold, it shouldn't be more than ten or twelve days to Lith Lor. Don't worry, you'll find your sea legs before then." To Naya he added, "You have a good ship here, Miss Garth."

"Thank you," Naya said.

"Your father used her in the fruit trade, correct?"

Naya nodded, her shoulders tensing at the mention of her father. "We also carried wines from some of the northern vine-yards." And secrets for the Talmiran Embassy.

"Good markets for a fast ship," Pit said. She was leaning back in her chair, swirling the wine in her glass. Her plate was already empty, though they'd barely sat down a few minutes ago. "Imagine she'd also do well carrying tea or sugar from the Islands."

"No doubt," Cervacaro said. "It's a shame there wasn't time to fill her holds with something more useful than ballast before we sailed. You could have made a nice profit off this trip."

"This trip isn't about profits," Francisco cut in.

"True," Cervacaro said. "You travel for a higher purpose." He tipped his glass in a gesture of respect, though Naya thought she saw something mocking in the way he looked at Francisco.

"Ballast?" Felicia asked, glancing between Cervacaro and Francisco. "What is that?"

"Weights, essentially," Pit answered. "This trip we're using gravel. A ship like the *Gallant* isn't designed to sail with an empty hold. Without the ballast we'd be too light and risk bobbing about with our rudder clear out of the water."

Felicia's eyes widened. "Who would have thought a ship would need rocks to float?"

Pit chuckled. "The trick is not floating too much. If we're too light in the water, the ship's liable to tip over and send us all on a very unwelcome swim."

Cervacaro turned to Naya. "Speaking of cargos and such— tell me, have you thought about what you're going to do with the *Gallant* once all this is over?"

"I haven't decided yet. Why?"

Cervacaro gave her a smile that Naya guessed was meant to look fatherly. "I worry Lord Delence didn't fully consider the consequences when he passed the *Gallant* on to you."

"What are you talking about?" Francisco asked.

"Last I heard, the undead don't have any rights in Talmir," Cervacaro said. "And that includes owning property like this fine ship. It'd be a shame to see them try to seize her when we set into port."

"They won't." Francisco's tone was dismissive.

"Oh?" Cervacaro raised his eyebrows. "Well, maybe. Still, it wouldn't hurt to be careful." He turned back to Naya. "You'd do well to think on the *Gallant*'s future, Miss Garth. It's a burden having to take care of all those little troubles of managing a ship, and the cost can be terribly heavy." He took another sip of wine, examining the dark-red liquid through the glass. "If you weren't keen to deal with all that trouble, I could help. I've got some money stashed away. I'd be willing to buy her if you'd like.

That way the port officials won't have anything to complain about, and you won't have to worry yourself about what to do with her later."

Naya stared at him in shocked silence. "Maybe Lord Delence didn't tell you, but I trained for years, first at the Merchants Academy and then alongside my father. I know how much it costs to operate a trading ship. I know it won't be easy. But the *Gallant* isn't for sale."

Cervacaro frowned. "I meant no offense. All I wanted was to propose an option you might not have considered. You said yourself you didn't know what to do with her. And this way you needn't worry about disrupting your work at the Congress. We'd honor our contracts with Delence. We'd see you to the Congress, then wherever you want to go after that. You'd walk away with a fat purse, and you wouldn't have to risk losing the ship over some legal technicality."

Francisco snorted. "The *Gallant* won't be seized. My father wouldn't have brought it if he thought it was a risk. I—" The ship rocked against a wave, and Francisco snapped his mouth shut. Sweat beaded on his forehead. "Excuse me." He stood, then hurried from the room.

There was a moment of awkward silence, followed by the faint sound of Francisco heaving in the next room. Cervacaro shook his head. "Not much ocean in that boy, is there?"

Felicia glanced at the door, her face scrunched in sympathy. "Isn't there anything that can be done?"

"He'll be fine in a day or two," Cervacaro said, waving the comment away. "But back to the conversation. Why don't you give my offer some thought, Miss Garth?"

Naya stood, anger making her bones feel hot. Why was everyone on this ship suddenly so intent on telling her what she could and couldn't do with her future? "I said no. The *Gallant* isn't for sale."

Cervacaro's eyes narrowed. "I won't press you if you feel so strongly about it. Just think on what I said. The *Gallant* is a fine ship, but she'll be worth little more than scrap if you don't have the means to outfit her." He stood. "Come, Pit, we should go see to things before the watch changes."

"Aye, sir." Pit drained the last of her wine, then followed Cervacaro out of the cabin. A moment later the cook returned to clear away the dishes.

Naya's fists clenched and unclenched as she watched the cook leave. The captain might be a competent sailor, but he had all the subtlety of a dead rat. He hadn't even waited a day before trying to buy her ship out from under her.

He was likely trying to take advantage of her. Even if he'd been saving during his time aboard the *Arabella*, Naya doubted he had enough to afford a whole new ship. Perhaps he'd hoped she didn't know the *Gallant*'s worth. Or maybe he'd thought the prospect of future debts would be enough to scare her into selling it for cheap.

Well, even if he'd come to her with chests of gold, she would have turned him away. The *Gallant* might not feel like home anymore, but it was all she had left. She would no more consider selling it than she would selling her own bones.

Naya and Felicia sat in silence for a moment. "Do you think he'll be all right?" Felicia asked, glancing at the wall separating Naya and Francisco's cabins.

Naya followed Felicia's gaze. Unlike the question of the *Gallant*'s future, Francisco's seasickness was a problem she knew how to help fix. "I'd better get him to come outside. He'll only feel worse if he stays below like this." She would have liked to avoid Francisco if she could. But as Ceramor's two undead representatives, they'd have to work together once they got to the Congress. That would be easier if she could convince him she wasn't his enemy.

CHAPTER 8

NAYA

Naya knocked on the door to her old cabin. Back when she'd first joined her father aboard the *Gallant*, he'd had the carpenter put in a wall to divide the captain's cabin. The newly created room had only been big enough to house a narrow bunk and a sea chest, but Naya had loved it all the same.

"What?" Francisco's voice came muffled through the door's thin wood.

"May I come in?" Naya asked.

"Whatever you need can wait until morning."

"I just want to talk."

"Tomorrow." He was obviously trying to sound stern, but the note of misery in his voice ruined the effect.

Naya rolled her eyes. "If you want to spend your whole night sick, that's your business. But in case no one's told you, you'll feel a lot better if you go above deck. It will help your body get used to the waves. And if you'd like, we can ask the cook to make some ginger tea to settle your stomach."

Silence. Then Naya heard a rustle of cloth. Finally, Francisco opened the door a crack and peered out at Naya. She gave him a sympathetic smile, trying to ignore the smell of sick wafting from the small room.

"What do you really want?" Francisco asked.

"To help," Naya said. "It won't do anyone any good if you show up at the Congress half-dead."

"I doubt your people would even notice. What is it you call us, 'walking corpses'?"

"I don't call us that," Naya said. She had once, back before she'd come to Ceramor and had learned exactly how wrong her people were about necromancy and the undead. "Just come out for a bit, please? If you don't feel better, you can go back to stewing in here."

The ship rocked as they cut through a small wave. Francisco squeezed his eyes shut. "Please don't talk about stewing, or stew. I really don't want to think about food right now."

"Not another word," Naya agreed.

Francisco drew in a shallow breath. "Fine, let's go." He brushed past Naya on unsteady feet, and Naya followed him up the narrow stairs. The wind had shifted while they were at dinner, blowing more strongly from the west. Naya tucked her hair under the collar of her shirt to keep it from whipping in her face. If she concentrated, she supposed she could probably keep it from blowing at all, or will it into a braid, but the mental effort didn't seem worthwhile.

Francisco crossed the deck and stood by the starboard railing, holding on with a white-knuckled grip. "You said something about tea?"

Naya nodded, then walked to the deckhouse that served as the ship's galley. She found the cook looking over a provision list while a cabin boy of perhaps twelve scrubbed the night's dishes. He seemed unsurprised by Naya's request, and in a few minutes she was striding back across the deck with a steaming mug held carefully in both hands. Francisco stood leaning against the rail, his eyes fixed on the horizon.

"Here." She handed Francisco the tea. He took a careful sip, grimacing at the sharp taste before taking a larger swallow. The wind whipped the steam from his mug and toward the dark shadow of the coast before them.

"Thank you," Francisco said.

Naya nodded. They stood together in silence for a few minutes, watching the coast roll past. "Your father said we'll be working together at the Congress," Naya said cautiously. "He had me study with a tutor back in Ceramor, but I still don't feel like I've got a good grasp on what we'll be doing."

Francisco took another sip of the tea. "You're supposed to give your testimony at the trial and read the other delegates' aether, let my father know if anyone's acting especially guilty or suspicious."

Naya watched him out of the corner of her eye. "But the trial is just one part of the Congress. Delence said we're Ceramor's undead representatives. We're supposed to show the other delegates that the undead aren't monsters. I just don't know what we can do to make that happen."

"Do?" Francisco smirked. "I don't know about you, but I expect I'll be doing a great deal of standing in corners."

"How is that supposed to help?"

"Well, seeing as how most Talmirans take our mere existence as a personal affront against all of creation, I'd say standing around will be more than enough to act as a suitable distraction."

"You know, not all Talmirans are that bad," Naya said. "And—wait, what do you mean about a distraction?"

Francisco tensed, as though realizing he'd said more than he should. "I only meant that we're not the ones making any of the decisions. You'll testify at the trial, and they might let us watch a few of the meetings. Other than that, we're to attend the parties and smile and keep quiet to show all the nice delegates how harmless we are."

Naya drew in aether. She could feel the focused energy of the sailors at their tasks, and the mysterious swirl of life deeper in the ocean. Mixed with that, just faintly, was a bitter anger drifting off Francisco. She remembered the look in his eyes when the ships left Belavine. She doubted anyone who'd seen him there would ever make the mistake of thinking him harmless. "You want to do more," she guessed.

"It doesn't matter what I want." Francisco glared into his tea. "Thanks to you and your friends, I'm undead now. Under the treaty laws, I can't hold any sort of political office, and if Father tried to involve me directly in the negotiations, it would only hurt our cause."

"I'm sorry," Naya said. "I never meant for—"

"Stop!" Francisco said. "I see what you're trying to do here. I don't want your apologies. Apologies won't change what happened."

Naya had to clench her jaw to keep from snapping back at him. "You know, it will be a lot easier to convince people to trust us if we don't spend the whole Congress treating each other like enemies."

Francisco's grip on the mug tightened. He glared out at the darkened sea for a long moment before meeting her gaze again. "Let me make one thing very clear. My father might be willing to overlook what you did to our family, but I won't. I'll work with you if that's what he thinks is best, but I don't trust you and I don't forgive you. So stop acting as though we could be friends. It's a waste of time."

Anger and guilt warred in Naya's chest. Before she could untangle them into a reply, she heard the heavy tread of boots behind her. "Apologies for interrupting, but you two best get below," Captain Cervacaro said, raising his voice to be heard over the wind.

"Is there a problem?" Naya asked.

"Storm coming," Cervacaro said. "Shouldn't be too bad, but

we'll have to swing a little wider of the coast to avoid drawing too near the rocks round Bassil Point."

"Is there any risk?" Francisco asked.

"There's always risk," Cervacaro said with a hard smile. "But don't worry. These summer squalls blow themselves out quick."

Naya stayed on deck long enough to see that Cervacaro spoke true. The *Gallant* rocked as the waves rose, but she'd seen her father navigate worse without so much as a torn sail. Naya lingered a few minutes, watching carefully as Cervacaro turned the ship away from shore and ordered the larger sails trimmed to ease the strain on the masts. When the rain started, she reluctantly trudged below deck.

She kept one hand on the wall as she traversed the narrow hallway to her cabin. Her thoughts felt hazy and slow. It was the mental exhaustion of a long day spent battling too many questions with too few answers. She could draw aether to suppress it, but that was only a temporary fix. She needed to spend a few hours alone and give her mind a chance to rest.

When she opened the door to her cabin, she heard a sharp intake of breath and felt a stab of fear in the aether. Felicia was kneeling on the floor, stuffing something back into Naya's bag. Her father's logbook, Naya realized with a start. "What are you doing?" she asked, stepping into the room and quickly shutting the door.

Felicia stood, then grabbed the edge of the bunk to keep from falling. "I'm sorry! The deck started pitching and that bag wasn't tied down. Your things spilled out. I was only trying to put them back before anything got damaged."

Naya crossed the room, panic rising in her chest. She knelt next to the bag and opened it. Yes, there was her father's logbook near the top, and not far from it, the bag of coin. She pushed those aside and withdrew a velvet-wrapped bundle from the center of the bag. Bracing herself against the wall, she unwrapped it carefully, then breathed a sigh of relief when she found Corten's little glass bird inside still intact.

Felicia let out a startled yelp as the ship surged over a larger wave. "We aren't going to sink, are we?" she asked, her expression hovering somewhere between fear and excitement.

Naya refolded the covering surrounding the bird. "We won't sink." Was Felicia's fear just for the storm, or was it an act to cover what Naya had seen? Felicia wouldn't be able to read anything in the logbook, but if she reported it to someone, it could bring trouble. Naya tried to judge how long she'd been gone. It'd been at least a half hour since she had left to check on Francisco, more than enough time for Felicia to rummage through Naya's things.

Naya put the bird back in the bag, then secured it in the drawer below the bunk. "Come on, I'll help you into the hammock."

"I don't think—" Felicia began.

"Trust me," Naya said. "In this weather it will be a lot more comfortable than the bunk." And once she was up there she'd have trouble getting down without help until the storm passed. Naya wouldn't have to worry about Felicia sneaking off or trying to rummage through her things again.

Eventually Felicia agreed and let Naya help her up into the hammock. Once Felicia was situated, Naya settled into the bunk, gripping the wall to keep from sliding as the ship rocked. She whispered a prayer for smooth seas and fast winds. They were barely a day into their voyage and already it felt like the longest crossing she'd ever made.

CHAPTER 9

CORTEN

Corten's legs felt heavy as he trudged through death. The shadows around his feet had turned from grass to uncertain mist. Images flashed in the corners of his vision, faces or places he remembered, but he no longer fell into them. The memories felt somehow far away, like they had happened to someone else. In the distance he heard the howls of the creature that had chased him, but he no longer had the energy to run.

A strange glow caused him to look up from his shadow-wrapped feet. Ahead he saw a massive rectangle of pale-gray light. Brighter light shone around the edges, like illumination seeping through the cracks of a door. The sharp outline of the doorway was so different from the uncertain world around him that for a moment Corten assumed it was another hallucination. But no, the door wasn't anything from his memories. It felt more solid, more real, than anything else he'd encountered in this strange place. As Corten stared at the doorway, he noticed other figures in the dim light. Unlike the shadow man who'd confronted him before, these were obviously people, and obviously dead.

An old woman with sallow skin drifted past Corten. She walked out of the darkness like she was in a dream, apparently unafraid of the monsters lurking in the shadows. Everything about her, from her gray hair to her flowing dress, looked insubstantial, almost transparent.

"Excuse me," Corten said. But the old woman's eyes remained locked on the doorway, and her calm expression didn't change as she walked past him. When she reached the door, she raised her hand to touch the rectangle of light. Then she vanished.

Corten watched in growing horror as others streamed toward the doorway and disappeared. Most were like the old woman, calm almost to the point that they looked like they were sleepwalking. But there were a few people who didn't step through. They lingered around the edges of the light, sitting or lying down or standing and staring at the door as Corten did. Corten approached the nearest, a black-haired man who looked to be in his late forties. His cheeks were gaunt, and a deep gash surrounded by purple bruising marred the right half of his forehead.

"Excuse me?" Corten asked.

The man didn't seem to hear him. He rocked back and forth, muttering something under his breath.

"Sir?" Corten grabbed the man's sleeve.

The man cried out and jerked away. He took a step back, then glanced over his shoulder and whimpered before shuffling forward again. His eyes met Corten's, then seemed to look through him to fixate on the door. "Can't go forward. Can't go back. Can't go forward. Can't go back."

"Don't bother with him," said a voice from somewhere to Corten's right.

Corten spun. A young woman, perhaps in her early twenties, sat on the ground ten paces away, watching him through a single dark eye. The other eye was just an empty socket bisected by a nasty scar. The woman had dark skin and wavy black hair that suggested some mix of Banian blood. She wore loose trousers and a man's shirt and seemed somehow more solid than the people around her.

"Why not?" Corten asked.

"Cuz he's mad," the woman said with an unnerving grin.

Corten looked again at the gaunt man. "What's he doing here?"

"Same as all the rest of us. Standing in the doorway."

"The door to what?"

The woman tipped back her head and let out a laugh that shrieked like rusty iron. As though in answer, the shadows beyond the light seemed to writhe, and Corten heard a distant rumble that might have been a growl. The woman's laugh cut off abruptly and her eye narrowed. "Door to what. That's the question, isn't it? On the Islands they say death just leads you to another life, on and on and on again as we all follow the Way's Light. Might be that. Might be the realm of that Creator the Talmirans and Ceramorans are always yammering about. Might be the chambers of the Silmaran All-Judge and his whisper court. Or the world of the damned. Might be something else. Most people don't seem to ask any questions. They walk up to the door, and then they disappear."

They watched together in silence as more souls streamed toward the door. The souls looked to have come from all walks of life—rich, poor, young, old. Some wore the marks of their deaths plainly, the frailty of long illness or the ravages of a more violent end. The worst of these drifted forward with their hazy legs not quite touching the ground. Others looked so ordinary that Corten never would have guessed there was anything wrong with them if he'd passed them on the street. He even saw one man pushing himself forward in the ghostly image of a rolling chair, its form re-created from memory by the same strange magic that shaped Corten's fire-scorched clothes.

"What are those?" Corten asked, half to himself, as a few blobs of colorful light drifted playfully into view among the more distinct figures.

The woman's expression softened. "Babies, I think. There was a necromancer who came through here once and told me that the ones who die real young haven't had time to get attached to their bodies yet, so when they show up here, they look like that."

"Oh." Corten's chest tightened.

There was something both tragic and hypnotizing about the procession. And the longer Corten watched, the more he felt the subtle pull of the door on his senses. It wasn't anything so obvious as the wind and monsters that had driven him here. It didn't speak like the shadow man. But there was still something undeniably enticing about it, like the pull of a soft bed after a long day's work. Corten shuddered and took a step back. "Why haven't you gone through?" he asked the woman.

She took a long time answering, and for a moment Corten thought she hadn't heard him. He was just about to repeat the question when she pried her gaze from the door to give him a flat look. "Maybe I just don't want to," she said, sticking out her chin. "Don't see you hurrying to give yourself up."

Corten shoved his hands into his pockets. "I'm not ready to die yet."

The woman snorted. "Hate to tell you, but you're already dead."

"I've got friends," Corten said, hating how uncertain the words sounded. "They'll come for me."

"They won't. Even the necromancers can't touch this place. Nobody comes here but the dead, and nobody leaves unless it's through the door. The scavengers see to that."

"Scavengers?"

The woman pursed her lips. "Don't know what they are really, but they live in the dark. They've got a taste for people like you and me, the ones who try to hold on. There's something about that trying that clings to us."

"You seem to know an awful lot," Corten said.

"The shadow man told me," the woman said, looking away. "He comes by every now and then and whispers about how I've got to go through the door, how everybody goes through. He says, 'Go on, Servala, there's nothing left for you out there. Your family's gone through. Your crew's gone through. Don't you want to know where they went? Don't you want to rest?' Then the shadow man goes on about how if I tried to go back into the dark, the scavengers would tear me up. Wouldn't believe it if I hadn't seen it happen myself."

"So you've just been waiting? For how long?"

Servala shrugged. "No idea. Time's funny here."

Corten glared at the door, nurturing an irrational hope that if he just stared hard enough, it would give up its secrets. When nothing happened he sat down next to the woman. "You said your name's Servala?" he asked.

"That's me," Servala said.

"I'm Corten."

Servala gave him a curious look. "Well, Corten, you're better off going through that door. We all go mad out here, eventually."

"Thanks for the advice, but I think I'll wait a while." Some part of Corten knew he was being stupid. He was dead, and if anyone had ever managed to come back from this deep into death, he was pretty sure he would have heard about it during his training with Lucia. It would be better to give himself up to whatever lurked on the other side of the door than to go slowly mad waiting for a rescue that might never come. For all he knew, Lucia had already given up and boxed up his bones for transport to the family crypt.

Scraps of the Dawning Chant echoed through Corten's memory. People in Ceramor and Talmir both followed the guidance of the chant, even if the Talmiran keepers interpreted it differently.

Both sides agreed that beyond death peace and comfort waited for all those who had lived a good life. It was just the details of what those lives should look like that they quarreled over.

Had he lived a good life? The Talmiran keepers would say he'd damned himself by practicing necromancy. But he'd never understood their arguments. How could it be wrong to reunite a dead child with their family, or to call back the soul of a mother stolen away by some illness?

Go through, the door seemed to whisper. *All answers wait just beyond the threshold.*

Corten shuddered. Someday he would walk through that doorway, but not yet. Lucia might still come for him. And besides, he'd always hated being told what to do. Everything about this place, the wind and the monsters and the light peeking under the crack of the door, it all felt like one giant setup designed to drive him into taking that last step he could never retrace. He wouldn't go that way. Not yet.

CHAPTER 10

NAYA

The *Gallant* sailed for a week and a half before Naya spotted the white cliffs of Lith Lor rising from the eastern horizon. She stood on deck with Felicia in the late-afternoon light as the *Gallant* and the *Lady* navigated into the wide harbor. They'd gotten lucky with the weather after that first night. Though there'd been a couple of days of fitful winds, they'd had clear skies for the rest of the journey.

Francisco had eventually gotten over his seasickness, though he'd remained distant whenever Naya tried to speak to him. She'd spent her days watching Cervacaro at his work and her nights practicing at manipulating aether and puzzling through the cipher in her father's logbook. All the while she'd tried not to worry about the things she couldn't control, ignoring the voice in the back of her mind that whispered like a ticking clock.

No hope. He's gone. Too late. Too late.

Lucia had warned Naya that even if they managed to successfully perform the shadow walk ritual, there might be nothing left of Corten to find. No one knew exactly what happened to souls that weren't resurrected. Most necromantic theories agreed that death would somehow seek to claim a soul after it had been separated from its body. If a necromancer tried and failed to pull a soul back, it meant the soul was truly gone. Maybe that was what had happened to Corten. But Naya remembered those last seconds before Lucia's portal had closed. She was certain she'd seen Corten struggling to reach her. If something really did exist on the other side that tried to keep souls away from life's borders, then Naya had to believe Corten would fight it. Meanwhile, she would do everything she could to help him.

Naya squinted at the shimmering water of the bay as a rowboat broke off from one of the docks and started toward the *Lady*. That would be the harbormaster. She felt a shiver of unease as she watched the little boat approach. There'd been no turning back for her ever since the *Gallant* set sail. But with the city looming over her, everything felt more real than it had before.

Fabric rustled as Felicia leaned against the rail next to Naya. "Why did they build atop the cliffs like that?" Felicia asked. "It must be hard bringing anything up from the docks."

Naya forced aside her worries. Since the night of the storm, Felicia had seemed determined to prove herself. She'd sorted Naya's clothes, explaining the various fashions that were popular among the different courts, then helped drill Naya in the names of different ranking officials who'd be attending the Congress. Perhaps most importantly, she'd never hesitated when Naya asked to be left alone, and Naya hadn't seen any sign that Felicia had tried to go through her bags again. It didn't prove anything, but it did make Naya wonder if she'd read too much into what she'd seen.

Naya followed Felicia's gaze up to the white cliffs of Lith Lor. "They say the founders wandered for decades during the Chaos Years before the Creator sent Gaen Lus a vision of Lith Lor. He saw a city that would never fall, and then followed the vision's clues here. The cliffs make it impossible to take the city by sea. Anyone who wanted to assault Lith Lor would have to come from the east or the south, which means they'd have to bring their army over the plains, where they'd be vulnerable for miles."

"Still, it seems terribly inconvenient," Felicia said.

"That's what the freight lifts are for. The Academy of Magics has rune scribes find ways to improve them every year. The systems work so well now that it's barely any slower than loading at other docks."

Felicia squinted. "What about those people climbing?"

Naya looked where Felicia was pointing. After a moment she spotted the tiny figures. "There's a fee to use the lifts. The stairs are there for anyone who doesn't want to pay it."

"I hope they won't make us climb," Felicia muttered.

"Of course not," Naya said. But a thread of doubt twisted through her chest. Relations between Talmir and Ceramor were as tense as they'd ever been since the war. Whatever reception Queen Lial had planned for the Ceramoran delegation, Naya doubted it would be a warm one.

Her suspicions were confirmed as they were made to wait one hour, then three. Apparently, all the docks were either full or reserved for merchants carrying critical shipments for the city. Naya didn't get to hear the details of the argument between Delence and the harbormaster. But in the end, the *Gallant* and the *Lady* anchored off to the side of the main docks, and the delegation and their luggage were rowed ashore in smaller boats.

It was not an auspicious start.

Waves lapped against wood as Naya stepped from the rowboat onto the dock. The sun had set while they waited. The night air was cool and damp and rich with the scents of brine and rotting seaweed. The moon rose fat and yellow behind her, illuminating the sheer white cliffs looming just beyond the shoreline. Naya touched her mother's silver pendant.

"Welcome home," she muttered to herself.

At the edge of her senses, she could feel the city's pulse, aether churning with the mingled emotions of thousands of lives lived so close together. It was one more reminder of what she'd become. Naya shivered, imagining the person she'd been a year ago standing on the cliffs and glaring down at her. That Naya had known so much less about the world beyond her home. She'd been terrified of even meeting one of the undead, much less becoming undead herself. She'd trusted blindly and put all her faith in Talmir, and in her father. Both had betrayed her.

But I changed. Maybe the people here can change too. The Congress wasn't just an opportunity to return and search for Lucia's journals. This was also a chance to show her countrymen how wrong they were about the undead. She didn't know if that was even possible. But if things stayed the way they were, people like Valn and her father would keep pushing for war and more innocents would die in their pointless conflicts. If she could do anything to stop that, she had to try.

The dock where they disembarked bustled with soldiers, delegates, and sailors, but beyond that the well-lit shore was conspicuously still. Naya's eyes narrowed when she spotted a man in heavy shackles being half led, half carried by a team of nervous-looking Ceramoran guards. The man's back was stooped, and his head was covered by a black hood, but Naya doubted anyone on the dock could mistake his identity. The Ceramoran guards handed the former ambassador Dalith Valn off to a squad of Talmiran soldiers, who promptly escorted him toward the lifts.

The Ceramoran guards then retreated to the rowboats and started back to the *Lady*. The rules of the Congress dictated that the host nation was responsible for security. All others were forbidden from bringing their own armed escorts to the event. That rule was meant to stop arguments from escalating to violence. But the hostility Naya felt in the aether made her wish the Ceramoran guards were coming with them to the palace.

As soon as Valn was out of sight, the delegates were ushered forward by a tall, thin man in a formal uniform and shining black boots. "Welcome to Lith Lor," he said. "I am Grand Marshal Palrak, head of the Talmiran delegation and representative of Her Majesty Queen Lial, second of her name, ruler of Talmir, and protector of the true word of the Creator. My men and I have the honor of escorting you to the palace."

Delence returned Palrak's bow. "Grand Marshal, it's good to see you again. I trust Her Majesty is well?"

"She is," Palrak said. "She sends her thanks to you for returning the traitor Valn. We are eager to see him brought to justice."

"I'm surprised she didn't come herself to see him," the woman standing next to Delence said. Naya had never met her, but she recognized her by her description. King Allence's aunt, Dresdrie Briello, was an older woman with broad shoulders and narrow eyes. She was dressed in an elaborate gown that looked more suited to a ballroom than a dock.

"Her Majesty has entrusted me with the task of securing the traitor," Palrak said. "She sends her apologies that she could not greet you personally upon your arrival. If you'll follow me, the carriages wait above."

Lady Briello sniffed at that but made no further comment. Most members of the delegation were experts in something— trade or shipping or the legal systems of the Powers and the Congress. Lady Briello was listed as an expert on the history of the Ceramoran royal family. It didn't seem like the most important of roles. But by the way Lady Briello carried herself, one would think she was the heart and soul of the delegation and all the rest were mere scribes and hangers-on.

At Palrak's urging, the group started toward one of the waiting freight lifts. The servants had been sent ahead with the luggage while secure transport was organized for Valn and the delegation.

Lucia fell into step beside Naya as they walked.

"I never thought I'd be so glad to see land, much less that belonging to Talmir," Lucia muttered by way of greeting.

Naya smiled, more than a little relieved to see Lucia after the long journey. "I take it the ocean didn't agree with you?"

Lucia shook her head. "If I never set foot on another one of those floating death traps, it will be too soon. Honestly, I don't know how the merchants manage it, going back and forth like that all the time, spending weeks with nothing but a few layers of tarred wood between you and the depths."

"You get used to it after a while." Naya's smile faded as they waited for the lift. "I'm sorry I couldn't contact you." Short of stopping both ships and sending someone across, the only way to send a message would have been by the signal flags. As much as she'd wanted to speak to Lucia, Naya hadn't wanted her words spelled out for anyone watching to read. "I don't suppose you got a chance to see Valn while we were at sea?"

Lucia glanced around nervously, then shook her head. "No," she said very softly. "But let's not talk about that here."

"Move along," one of the Talmiran soldiers escorting them said. Emotions thickened in the aether. Impatience prickled the back of Naya's neck and anger settled like smoke on her tongue. Naya shuddered and hurried to join the others in the lift.

CHAPTER 11

NAYA

Naya steeled herself as she stepped from the cramped lift and onto the wide cliffside street. It was exactly as she'd remembered, and her throat tightened painfully at the familiar sights. The street in front of the lifts opened into a large plaza, allowing room for wagons to load or unload cargo. Beyond that taverns, inns, and shops lined the streets. Every building boasted the white-painted walls and red roofs required for structures in the cliffside and palace districts. Tall aether lamps stood in orderly rows, but the light spilling from nearby windows bore the yellow glow of candles and oil.

"This way." A soldier directed Naya and Lucia toward one of the five black carriages waiting by the lift. Naya walked quickly, hoping for a chance to speak privately with Lucia during the ride. That hope was ruined when she found Francisco already waiting inside. Naya tried to catch Lucia's eye as they took their seats. Lucia only shook her head before turning to stare out the window.

They rode in silence for a few minutes. Francisco sat across from Naya, his expression distant as he watched the city roll past. Again, Naya wondered what Delence had been thinking when he'd asked her and Francisco to work together. There were other undead who surely could have joined the delegation and who would have been more willing to work with her.

Something Francisco had said tugged at her memory. Naya frowned. "Back on the ship, you said that your father brought us here as a distraction. What did you mean?"

Francisco's shoulders tensed, but he kept his eyes fixed on the street outside. "Nothing. It was a poor choice of words."

"It sounded like more than that. If there's something else going on here, don't you think it would be better if you told me? Maybe I can help."

"I already told you. I'm not interested in—"

"I'm not asking you to be my friend," Naya cut him off. "I don't know about you, but I didn't come here to make friends. I came to help the undead and to protect the peace between Talmir and Ceramor." She was surprised by how true the words felt. Yes, she'd come to find a way to save Corten. But she also wanted to fight back against the hate and anger that had gotten him killed in the first place.

Francisco met her eyes. "Are you questioning my loyalty to our cause? You of all people?"

"No! But I'm tired of you treating me like we're on opposite sides. I'm sorry for what happened to your family. I wish I could take back that night, but I can't." She leaned forward, meeting Francisco's glare. "I understand if you can't forgive me. But your father invited me here because he thinks I can do some good for Ceramor. If you decide to cut me out, keep in mind it's his plans you're blocking."

Francisco looked away. Bodied undead like him were harder to read than the living, but this close Naya could sense the dark anger in the aether leaking off his tattoos. It settled against the back of her throat like the stench of burning pepper, bitter and sharp all at once. "Why do you care?" he finally asked. "You must know that anything we gain here will likely come at a cost to Talmir. And you already switched sides once. How am I supposed to trust you'd stay loyal to us now?"

Naya glanced at Lucia, who was listening to the exchange with obvious curiosity. "I switched sides because I realized what Valn was doing was wrong." She paused, the words sticking in her throat. "I was wrong about the undead. I was scared to question what Valn and my father told me, and because of that people got hurt. I want to make up for that, and I want to prove that Talmir and Ceramor don't have to be enemies."

Francisco let out a snort that might have been a laugh. "Is that all? You *just* want to make peace between two countries who've been at each other's throats for decades? I can't tell if you're an outrageous liar or just tragically optimistic."

"I'm telling the truth," Naya said, more than a little annoyed with his amused tone.

Francisco met her eyes, watching her for a moment. "In that case, I have a question for you. Do you think you would have changed your mind about the undead if you hadn't become one?"

Naya's first instinct was to snap at him. Of course she would have seen the truth. But something in the careful way Francisco had asked the question made her pause. She thought about the horror she'd felt when she first realized what she'd become, and about the cold and spiteful way she'd treated Lucia. Shame sent a rush of heat to her face. "I don't know," she said reluctantly. "But it shouldn't take dying to realize that sort of hate is wrong."

"It shouldn't," Francisco agreed. His expression was intense, somehow captivating. Then he looked away and slumped back against the seat of the carriage. "Maybe someday other people will see that too. But right now my father doesn't think necromancy is our biggest problem. Ceramor and Talmir fought each other even before the Mad King's War. So even if we could somehow agree about necromancy, we'd find something else to argue over. My father thinks the only true path to peace is to make the cost of war too high for any leader to risk."

"That sounds ominous," Naya said.

"It's practical. But strengthening Ceramor will mean making sacrifices."

"Sacrifices?" Lucia asked.

Francisco nodded. "My father brought us here because he knew the Talmirans would be furious about having to allow undead at the Congress. He wants them to think he's trying to revoke the bans on necromancy. That way when they block us on those issues, it will make them think they're winning. Meanwhile, my father will be working to convince the Banian delegates to forgive Ceramor's debts and to propose lifting the restrictions on our army and trade. If they agree, the Silmarans will follow. Talmir alone won't be able to stop the vote from passing, and Ceramor will be one step closer to regaining its former power."

"That can't be right," Lucia said sharply. "The Necromantic Council helped rescue Lord Delence and the king. They wouldn't throw our interests aside after that."

"My father will," Francisco said with blunt certainty. "Even if the other Powers don't hate necromancy as much as Talmir, they'll still be more comfortable working with us while the restrictions are in place. We have to prove to them that Ceramor is a trustworthy ally, and that they'll be safer and more prosperous if they help us thrive."

Naya clutched her mother's necklace. She'd known Delence had a reputation for cold calculation. But using his son as a distraction to further his own goals seemed especially cruel. She'd heard the ache in Francisco's voice when he'd said he could never hold a political office now that he was undead. From the way he talked, it was obvious he'd been studying to follow in his father's footsteps. Instead of fighting for the changes that would let him chase that dream, his father had chosen this. No wonder Francisco was bitter.

Before anyone could say more, the carriage jerked to an abrupt halt.

"What was that?" Lucia asked, one hand moving to cradle her plaster-wrapped arm.

Naya glanced out the window. Cold fear slithered through her. A crowd had gathered around the carriages. She'd been so focused on Francisco that she hadn't noticed the sharp-smoky taste of their aether.

"Go home!" someone shouted.

"Monsters!"

Francisco's brows drew together as he peeked out the window. "Where are the soldiers?" he asked.

Something shattered against the side of their carriage, and one of the horses shrieked. Francisco jerked away from the window, his eyes wide. The attack seemed to rally the crowd. Men and women surged toward the carriages, their faces twisted with a need for violence.

Naya flinched as bodies slammed against the side of their carriage, making it rock wildly.

The carriage wheels groaned. Naya forced her fear aside.

"Come on!" she shouted, grabbing Lucia's good arm. But before she could open the far door, the crowd shoved again. The carriage tipped, then crashed sideways onto the pavement. The world became a chaos of flailing limbs and splintering wood. The window shattered and Lucia screamed. Naya landed with her back pressed flat against one wall and her head twisted at an awkward angle against the roof.

Lucia was lying in a heap next to her, curled around her broken arm. Blood trickled from a cut on Francisco's forehead, and bits of broken glass glittered on his coat. He pulled himself to his hands and knees with a groan. The sounds of conflict outside grew louder. What was going on? Naya crawled to Lucia, fear tightening her throat. "Lucia?" she asked, touching the necromancer's arm.

"I'm all right," Lucia said, though the lines of pain in her expression told a different story. She sat up and looked Naya up and down, then turned to Francisco. "You're bleeding."

"It's not that bad," Francisco said. "We have to get out of here." He stood, his shoulders hunched against the side of the carriage that now faced up, and reached for the door latch. Naya drew in aether and listened. Outside, the crash of fists and feet against wood stopped, replaced by shouts of pain. Hopefully that meant the soldiers were driving the crowd back.

"As soon as you have a clear route, get Lucia to safety," Naya said to Francisco.

"What about you?" Francisco asked.

"I'll make sure no one comes after you from behind."

Francisco hesitated, then nodded. He shoved the carriage door open and Naya hauled herself up and out, trying to orient herself in the confusion.

Men in the blue-and-black uniforms of the Talmiran city guard frantically waved the other carriages through the palace gates while a score of soldiers in blue and gold tried to push the crowd away. Now that she had a clear view, Naya realized there couldn't be more than fifty people gathered in the shadows cast by the aether lamps atop the walls. A few in the crowd wielded improvised clubs or broken bottles, but the soldiers seemed reluctant to draw their own weapons. Naya heard a muttered curse behind her as Francisco helped Lucia toward the open door. Lucia's face was pale, but her jaw was set in determination.

Desperate rage surged like fire through the aether. Naya turned just in time to see a man in tattered clothes sprinting toward her through a gap in the soldiers' line. His eyes were wild and bloodshot, and something sharp gleamed in his right hand. Naya's own eyes widened in horror as she realized what it was. The blade was not so finely wrought as others she had seen, but the aether twisting into the runes along its length marked it as a wraith eater.

CHAPTER 12

NAYA

Naya's focus narrowed to the blade as the attacker ran toward her. Aether rushed into the runes in a sickening vortex. Such weapons were designed for only one purpose—destroying the undead. Her fists clenched, and the aether churning inside her begged for release. She could gather heat in her hands to burn the man, or she could dazzle him with a blast of light. But if she did that, she'd reveal the illegal modifications Lucia had made when she'd carved Naya's bones. Even a burst of unusual strength might risk drawing attention.

The man lunged, moving with the frantic energy of an untrained fighter. Naya twisted to the side, slapping his arm to direct the knife away from her. He stumbled, then spun and tried to jab the knife into her chest. The attack was clumsy, but wraith eaters weren't like ordinary blades. Just touching one would strain the runic bonds that kept Naya tethered to the living world. Again Naya avoided the blow, feeling the knife's pull strengthen as it brushed the front of her blouse. Why weren't the soldiers helping? She risked a glance to the side. Most were still occupied with holding back the crowd. But one soldier's eyes were focused intently on the knife in the attacker's hand.

"Help me!" Naya shouted. But the soldier didn't move. Naya clenched her teeth. She turned to evade another wild slash and managed to catch her attacker's wrist. She grabbed his elbow with her other hand and twisted his whole arm up and back over his shoulder.

The man cried out as he lost his balance and fell backward. His breath left him in a whoosh as his back struck the ground, and the knife clattered away onto the pavement. Finally, one of the soldiers stepped in, pinning the man down.

"Get inside the gates!" a soldier, the same one who'd been watching her so intently before, shouted. Naya saw contempt written plainly on his features. She bent to snatch up the wraith eater, but the soldier moved one booted foot to cover the blade. "Get inside!" he repeated.

A shudder crawled through Naya as she met the soldier's eyes. She wondered if the uniform was the only thing preventing him from joining her attackers. She turned on her heel, her skirt swirling as she ran toward the palace.

Past the gates, she joined Francisco and Lucia, who were hobbling toward the remaining carriages. A few members of the delegation stood outside their carriages while others poked their heads through the windows. Naya spotted Delence striding toward them, a furious frown visible under his gray mustache.

"Are you all right?" he asked Francisco.

Francisco stood a little straighter. The cut on his forehead was shallow and looked like it'd already stopped bleeding. "Yes, sir, just a few bruises and scrapes."

Delence nodded, then turned to Grand Marshal Palrak who stood with the soldiers by the gate. "What is the meaning of this?" he asked.

"You were warned, I believe, that including undead in your party would pose additional security risks," Palrak said.

"Are you telling me Queen Lial's command over her people is so weak that she cannot prevent them from attacking guests outside her own palace gates?" Delence asked.

Palrak's already stiff posture became rigid, and his aether took on the smoky stench of anger. "We will of course do everything in our power to protect the delegation. However, you should understand that many people are outraged at your insistence on bringing undead into Talmir. Our queen must walk a careful line between fulfilling her duties as Congress host and soothing the unrest your arrival has caused. Until moments ago, those people appeared to have gathered in peaceful protest. Attempting to disperse them earlier would have only caused greater anger and strife."

Nothing about the crowd had looked peaceful to Naya, and she could tell Delence felt the same. His nostrils flared as he drew a deep breath, salvaging some of his outward calm. Naya could feel tension building in the aether like the pressure before a thunderstorm. "I see," he said. Then without another word, he stalked back to the carriages.

Naya struggled to keep her expression blank as they rode the rest of the way to the palace. What had that man been doing with a wraith eater? Such weapons were rare even here in Talmir. For him to have one, for their carriage to be the last in the line, for it to be the only one attacked . . . It was all too much for coincidence.

Once past the gate, the carriages followed a wide road that bisected flower beds and tiny groves of well-tended trees. Here the sounds of the city were muffled, and the night air hung heavy with the scents of flowers. The main palace sat at the center of the garden. Five wings radiated out from the palace's domed center, their white marble walls gleaming in the moonlight. It looked strange from the ground, but from above the shape mimicked the starburst symbol of the Dawning, a reminder that the Creator was always looking down on those who ruled. Naya's unease grew as their carriages halted in front of the palace's main entrance, a wide doorway located between two of the building's wings.

A small army of servants waited on the staircase that swept up to the palace's main doors. They bowed in unison as the delegation approached. "Welcome to Talmir, my lords and ladies," said a long-faced man at the head of the gathered servants. "I am Chief Steward Neln. Our queen has charged me with arranging your accommodations. I apologize for the commotion outside, and for the unconventional nature of your arrival."

"Where is the queen?" Lady Briello asked. "She makes us come like thieves in the night, subjecting us to that rabble. And now she doesn't even have the decency to greet us in person? My royal nephew will hear of this insult."

Neln's bow deepened, his back and shoulders rod-straight. His expression of calm deference might as well have been painted on. "Forgive me, Lady Briello, no insult was intended. I will personally see that the delegation's guard is doubled to ensure nothing like this happens again. The queen did wish to greet you, but certain matters arose that required her attention. She will be most pleased to welcome you formally at the ball tomorrow night."

Naya suspected she wasn't the only one who saw through the obvious lie. Queen Lial had clearly never intended to be here tonight. She knew exactly what sort of message she was sending. *You are not welcome. You are not wanted here.*

"If you follow me, I will show you to your rooms." Neln gestured toward the double doors at the top of the stairs. He led them to a hallway on the third floor that ran the length of one of the palace's wings. The whole hall had apparently been set aside for their use, including studies and meeting rooms at one end and servants' rooms on the floor above.

As the delegates sought their rooms, Lucia placed a hand on Francisco's shoulder. "Come with me. That cut needs tending."

Francisco gave a small nod and muttered thanks under his breath. Unsure what else to do, Naya walked down the hall until she reached a door with a brass plaque bearing her name. It opened onto a lavish sitting room complete with two couches and a writing desk. A door to the left opened onto a bedchamber and a private water closet. Felicia stood in the bedroom, carefully plucking dresses from one of the two sea chests Delence had provided. The smaller bag with Naya's personal belongings lay next to the chests, seemingly untouched.

Felicia paused in her work as soon as she noticed Naya and dipped a shallow curtsy. "Sorry I don't have it all done yet. Things were a bit hectic when we first arrived, and it seems the palace staff had some confusion over whose luggage went where." Her apologetic smile fell away as she looked more closely at Naya. "Your clothes . . . what happened?"

Naya glanced down at her skirt and blouse. One sleeve was torn at the elbow, and there were smudges of dirt and wood splinters stuck everywhere. "There was an attack at the gates. Our carriage got overturned by a mob."

Felicia's eyes widened. "Really? What was it like?" She seemed to realize what she'd said and blushed. "I mean, is everyone in one piece?"

"It wasn't exactly fun, but everyone's fine," Naya said. Then after a moment's thought, she added, "But you should probably be careful. If anyone finds out you're my lady's maid, they might come after you. In fact, I wouldn't be offended if you wanted to ask Delence to reassign you."

Felicia shook her head. "And then what? Make one of the others take my place? Don't worry, I won't be scared off by a little mob."

"No one has to replace you," Naya said. "I don't need a lady's maid."

"But of course you do," Felicia said. "Who will help you with your clothes and your hair, and everything else?"

"I don't need help!" Naya snapped. "Practically everyone

here thinks I'm a monster. They're not going to care what my hair looks like."

Felicia took a step back. "I'm sorry," she said.

Naya realized her hands were shaking. There was a stink of fear growing in Felicia's aether. Naya looked away, embarrassed. "No. I'm sorry. I didn't mean to yell at you." Awkward silence settled between them. "Can we talk about this later?" Naya asked.

Felicia curtsied. "Yes, of course," she said, sounding relieved. "If you need me, there's a rune disk on the desk in the sitting room."

After Felicia left, Naya sat down on the bed and stared at her empty sea chest and the unopened bag beside it. The room was well lit, but Naya imagined she could feel the night pressing in. Her throat tightened, and for a moment she nearly called Felicia back, if only to have someone there to break the quiet.

Instead she opened the small bag. She checked that her father's logbook and purse were still secure at the bottom, then carefully extracted the velvet-wrapped parcel that sat just above them. The tips of her fingers seemed to tingle with energy as she unwrapped the little glass bird inside. She'd packed it carefully, but still it was a relief to see it had remained undamaged through the journey. The bird sat in her palm with its wings half-furled and the corners of its beak turned up in the suggestion of a smile.

Naya set the bird carefully on top of the nightstand. "Well," she said, staring at the bird's mismatched eyes. "We made it to Talmir." She pulled her knees to her chest. The bird didn't respond. Obviously. Still, Naya imagined the room felt a little less empty. "I'm not sure what I'm supposed to do now. I thought that maybe by the time I got here I would know, but . . ."

A knock came at the door, startling Naya from her thoughts. When she opened the door, she found Lucia standing out in the hall. The necromancer looked exhausted, but she smiled when she saw Naya. "May I come in?"

"Of course," Naya said.

Lucia strode into the room and dropped onto one of the plush couches. "Creator, I'm tired." She flexed her uninjured hand and Naya saw her fingers were trembling. "It's a good thing Alejandra wasn't here to see that," Lucia said. "She was already so furious at me for leaving. I told her a dozen times that she was being silly, that even the Talmirans wouldn't break the peace laws of the Congress. I didn't mean it to be a lie. I wasn't expecting . . ." She trailed off, then clenched her shaking fingers. "Well, we're here now, so I suppose there's no going back on it." Lucia blinked, then rubbed her eyes. "How are you feeling?"

"Fine," Naya said. "The wraith eater didn't get close enough to do any real damage to my bones."

Lucia's eyes widened and she sat forward. "A wraith eater? What happened?"

"A man in the crowd attacked me." The anger smoldering inside her flared. "And the guards just stood there watching it happen."

Lucia surprised Naya by giving an indignant snort. "I suppose we should be grateful they didn't try to tip our carriage themselves." She paused, then looked more closely at Naya. "Well, I'm glad to hear you weren't hurt. But when I asked how you were feeling, it wasn't your bones I was talking about."

Naya's throat tightened. In her mind she saw the twisted hatred in the face of the man who'd attacked her. That same hatred had echoed on the faces of everyone else in the crowd, and she'd sensed it in the guards and some of the palace staff as well. Logically she'd known something like this would happen. She'd told herself to expect it. But seeing it in person had felt like a punch to the stomach.

"I'm fine," she lied.

Lucia's eyes still looked worried behind her glasses. She reached out and patted Naya awkwardly on the hand. In the moment of contact, Naya could sense something warm and soft and sad in Lucia's aether. "I'm afraid I've never been much good with people," Lucia said slowly. "But if you need someone to talk to, I can at least listen."

Naya's eyes burned with tears she couldn't shed. She had the irrational urge to bury her face in Lucia's shoulder and sob like she had when she was small. Corten's death had left her hollow. Now the world felt so heavy around her that she feared any moment she would crumble into nothing. But Lucia wasn't her mother. It wasn't her job to take care of Naya. And if Lucia realized how shaken she was feeling, she might decide Naya was too weak to go through with their plan.

"Thank you," Naya muttered. "But I'm—I'll be fine." She drew in a deep breath of aether to steady herself. Then wanting desperately to change the subject, she added, "You said you couldn't talk to Valn during the journey? What happened?"

Lucia removed her glasses and cleaned them with a small white cloth. "Delence made sure no one got near him. And I'm afraid my constitution didn't agree with sea travel. I wasn't able to spend much time with the delegates." She frowned. "What little conversation we did have wasn't terribly fruitful. Delence has used the recent upheaval to move his friends into power. It's been mostly good for the Necromantic Council, but everything I heard fit with what young Francisco said earlier. The people his father chose for the delegation are more interested in achieving economic independence and rebuilding the Ceramoran Army than they are in expanding the rights of the undead. I doubt any of them would take kindly to our little quest."

"So we'll just have to make sure they don't find out," Naya said.

Lucia sighed. "Yes, we will. I only wish we had more to go by.

Valn's trial and the Congress negotiations should take at least two weeks. But if they conclude before we find what we need, we'll lose our only excuse for being in Talmir."

Naya crossed her arms, frustrated. "Valn had to have allies working with him from Talmir."

"Could you find a way to speak to him again?" Lucia asked cautiously.

"I don't know," Naya said. She'd managed to get to Valn in Belavine because she'd had the help of the Council. But here she didn't know anyone in the palace outside the Ceramoran delegation. And if she was caught sneaking into Valn's cell here, the punishment would be far more serious than a warning.

"Is there anything else I can do to help prepare the ritual?" Naya asked.

Lucia shook her head. "No, we've already done as much as we can without the portal runes. There are a few more steps but . . ." Lucia trailed off, flexing the fingers of her right hand. "Well, there's no point in worrying about them until we're sure we can complete the ritual. With what Francisco said, it sounds like we're going to have a hard enough time finding the freedom to search for my journals. If Delence means to use us as a distraction, then he'll be doing everything he can to draw attention to us. That's going to make it tricky to act discreetly."

"I know," Naya said, her frustration turning the words into a groan.

Lucia responded with a yawn. "I don't think there's anything more we can do tonight. Let's discuss this tomorrow. I am desperately looking forward to sleeping in a bed that won't tip out from under me."

CHAPTER 13

NAYA

After Lucia left, Naya glanced up at the elegant clock perched on the writing desk. It was late, but not ridiculously so. Delence might still be awake. She took a moment to compose herself, then slipped out into the hall. The aether on the other side of Delence's door lacked the soft haze that usually accompanied sleep, so Naya knocked.

Delence opened the door with a scowl. "I told you I don't want—oh, it's you. I thought it was that servant again."

"May I come in? There's something I need to talk to you about," Naya said.

"Is it important?" Impatience tinted Delence's aether. It itched against Naya's skin like the beginning of a rash.

"It's about what happened outside the gates," Naya whispered.

Delence scowled. "You of all people should know what to expect coming here."

Naya glanced down the hallway. "Can we talk about this in private, please?"

Delence eyed her for a moment before stepping back and letting her into the room. "You don't seem injured, so what about this incident was so important that it couldn't wait until morning?" He had shrugged off his jacket and loosened the buttons on his white shirt. Already the surface of his desk was disappearing under neat piles of paper.

"One of the men in that crowd attacked me with a wraith eater," Naya said, unnerved by Delence's callous response.

Delence's expression darkened. He ran two fingers over his mustache. "So they were armed. The Talmiran rune scribes made thousands of those weapons during the war. I'm not surprised a few people around here would still be holding on to them."

Naya shook her head. "I don't think it was blind luck that they targeted the carriage Francisco and I were in. And none of the guards made a move to help me until I'd already knocked the knife from that man's hand. It was like they were waiting to see if he'd succeed."

"What are you suggesting?" Delence asked.

Naya scowled. She couldn't believe Delence didn't see the connection. "I don't see how any of this could have happened unless some of the soldiers or city guards helped plan the attack. And I don't like knowing that the only people allowed to carry weapons at this Congress are trying to kill me. If they tried once, they'll try again." She could feel her control cracking. Her voice rose, and she couldn't keep the edge out of her tone. Logically she knew yelling at Delence wouldn't fix anything. But the cool, casual way he'd taken her news grated against her nerves like sand.

Delence turned away from her and walked to his desk. He uncorked a bottle of amber liquor and poured a generous few fingers into the bottom of an already wet glass. He took a slow sip before answering. "You're accusing the queen's guard of having conspired to murder members of a foreign delegation. That's a very serious claim."

"You don't believe me?"

Delence swirled the liquid in his glass. "I believe this little display was meant more to scare us than as an assassination attempt. I expected something like it, though I didn't think she'd act quite so fast."

Naya blinked. "You expected this?"

"I assumed we'd be attacked eventually, yes."

"And you didn't think to warn me? Why? Did you think my reaction would be more distracting if I didn't see the attack coming?"

Delence frowned. "I see you and Francisco have been talking. What exactly did he tell you?"

"Only that you have no intentions of actually helping the undead," Naya said. "I guess I can understand you being willing to risk my life, but what about him? He's your son."

Anger flashed in Delence's dark eyes. "I suggest you watch your tone."

Naya stepped closer. "My tone? I gave up everything to save you. Corten died rescuing you. When you asked me to come back to Lith Lor, I thought it was because you wanted to help the undead. But you're just as bad as Valn. You think you can use people however you want, no matter how much you hurt them." A small voice in the back of her mind whispered that she should back down. In Ceramor, Delence had warned her that he would send her home if she disobeyed him. But that voice was the same one that had told her to trust Valn. It was the same voice that had promised that if she could just be smart enough, good enough, she would earn her father's trust and love. That voice was fear, and it had made her a pawn too many times before. She was done listening to it.

"I am trying to stop a war," Delence said, the words falling in the air like heavy stones. "What were you expecting when you came here? That a few clever words on your part would be enough to end decades of hate? It's more complicated than that. My son understands that."

"Your son understands that you care less about him than you do your precious trade deals," Naya said.

Delence tensed. Then he drained the contents of his glass

and turned away from her. "It's late, Miss Garth. I suggest you retire for the night. We'll all have work to do in the morning."

Naya thought about trying to push further. But the tight lines of Delence's shoulders made her somehow warier than if he'd shouted. She turned and stomped out of the room.

Back in the hall, Naya closed her eyes and leaned against the wall. Her anger was draining away, replaced by a queasy sense of unease. Creator, why had she shouted at Delence like that? Corten was her reason for being here, not the Congress. She shouldn't let herself be bothered by the way Delence treated Francisco, or the way Francisco seemed to accept it willingly. And as much as she hated to admit it, Delence had been right about one thing. How could she really hope to make a difference when Talmir and Ceramor had spent decades hating each other?

What she needed to do was stay focused. Reaching into her pocket, she felt the reassuring crinkle of the torn page containing the key she'd constructed to decrypt her father's logbook. The pages she'd managed to translate so far hadn't revealed anything useful, but there were still plenty of entries left.

CHAPTER 14

CORTEN

The only way for Corten to mark time outside the doorway was by the endless flow of souls moving past. He tried to put aside his own fears and watch them with a clinical eye. The first time he'd observed Lucia performing a resurrection, he'd puked before she was even halfway through extracting the bones. He could still remember the glare she'd fixed him with. She'd told him he had to stop looking at the body as though it were a person, because it wasn't. To a necromancer, especially one who created wraiths, a body was just parts and those parts had to be reforged before they could be used to draw a soul back from death.

Now he looked for details: faces, clothes, age, and marks left by whatever injury or illness had caused the death. Cataloging those mundane details was less horrifying than looking at the door or thinking about the never-ending flood of souls. By focusing on the little things, he could almost make himself forget what he was watching. "You really have no idea how long you've been here?" he asked Servala when he found the doorway again tugging at his attention.

"I know it's been a long time," Servala said. She sounded tired. "You see Davious over there?" She gestured to the man Corten had first tried to talk to. "He was still sane when I got here. He's Silmaran, some fancy scholar from the capital. He used to go on and on reciting these terrible poems he said he'd written. I'd always tell him that if I ever went through the doorway, it would be just to get away from his damned poems." She grimaced. "Course now the only one who really talks to me is the shadow man, and he's not much of one for actual conversation."

Corten glanced around at the other souls who lingered by the doorway. "Are all of them insane?"

Servala shrugged. "Most."

"But not you," Corten pressed. "Why?"

Servala looked sideways at him. "What makes you think I'm not insane?"

For just a moment, Corten saw something dark lurking behind her single eye. It was like staring down a portal during a resurrection. His skin crawled, but he forced a laugh. "Just a guess. You seem more, I don't know, focused than the rest of them."

Servala looked back toward the door. "Why are you asking? You planning to stay a while?"

"Well, I'm not going back out there." Corten gestured at the darkness over his shoulder. "And I'm not ready to go through the door, not yet. So I guess the answer's yes, I'm staying a while."

Servala snorted. "See, I've got no idea if that's good sense, or if you're already mad." After a moment she added, "But you'd probably be better off just going through the door. Waiting out here isn't exactly fun."

In answer Corten crossed his arms and gave her a level look. "Really? I hadn't noticed. Everyone else looks like they're having so much fun. And the shadow man is a real joker. I'd assumed life out here would be one big, long party."

"Ha ha," Servala said drily, but Corten saw a smile tug at the edge of her mouth. This one wasn't the wide, slightly insane grin he'd seen before. It was soft, and sad, and it made her look much older than her features would suggest.

"All right." Servala heaved a sigh. "Well, I guess if you're going to be stubborn about it, there are a couple of tricks I know. But if I'm going to help you, you've got to do something for me."

"Like what?" Corten asked.

"I'll tell you what I know about keeping your head together in this place, and you tell me everything I want to hear about what's going on out there." She waved vaguely at the darkness behind them.

"Out there . . . ?" Corten asked, glancing uneasily over his shoulder.

"Out in the living world, yeah. Price of salt, who's king, what you ate for breakfast—whatever I ask about, you answer, deal?" There was something hungry in her voice, and as she spoke her focus wandered back to the door.

"Deal," Corten said. Talking cost him nothing. In fact, talking about the living world might even help ground him, keep him from thinking about the tempting whisper of the door's power.

Servala grinned, then shook Corten's hand. "Good. First question. Where are you from?"

"Ceramor," Corten said.

Servala nodded. "Figured that much. Mostly it's Ceramorans who come here expecting some necromancer will rescue them from death."

"Are you Ceramoran?" Corten asked.

Servala raised her eyebrows. "Do I look Ceramoran?"

"No, but you speak the language, so I thought maybe . . ."

Servala laughed. "I'm not speaking Ceramoran. I'm speaking Shalesh."

Corten stared at her, wondering if this was a sign of the

madness she'd mentioned. "Shalesh, what . . . wait, isn't that an old name for the Banian tongue?"

"It's not. Shalesh is the true language, spoken on Sures, the true home of the people," Servala said sharply. She looked away from Corten and glared at the door. "Least that was how it was before the islands unified and everybody started speaking that mouthful-of-seaweed dialect and calling themselves Banians."

"Okay," Corten said slowly. "But then how can I understand you? I don't speak Shalesh." He'd never met anyone who did. It had been more than a hundred years since the three warring tribes of the Banen Islands had unified under a single council of rulers.

Servala waved the comment away, seeming to shed her anger with the gesture. "Talking here isn't the same as it is out there." She paused. "This place isn't like the real world. I'm talking to you, but what you're hearing isn't really my words, it's the meaning behind them."

"Huh," Corten said. "I guess that makes sense. It's sort of like how wraiths shape their bodies."

Servala shrugged. "I don't know anything about that. But everything here works the same. It's all more about the meaning of things rather than just their shapes."

Corten wrinkled his brow, concentrating on her words. For a moment the sounds seemed to twist in the air, becoming strange in his ears. He could still understand her, but the words were all wrong. It made his head pound, and he quickly gave up the effort. Corten rubbed his temples. "Okay. So what's this trick of yours? How do you stay sane out here?"

"Well, like I was saying, this place is all about meanings. It isn't solid like things are out there, and it looks a little different to everybody. Take Davious. Back when he was still talking, he said he saw this place as a library with shelves that went on forever."

"That doesn't sound so bad," Corten said.

"Sure, on the surface. But he also said that all the books were blank and every time he tried to pull one out, the shelves would wobble like they were about to topple down on him."

"Oh." Corten winced, thinking about the unstable footing and grassy fields that had haunted him on his long walk through death. Just thinking about it seemed to summon the spectral voice of the wind and the tickle of grass against his legs. "What do you see?" Corten asked.

Servala's expression darkened. "An ocean. Getting to the door was like swimming through a storm. The whole way here, I kept thinking that if I could just get over the next wave, I'd find a rope in the water and be able to haul my way back up onto my ship. Except there never was any rope, and when I finally felt land under my feet, all I found was the door."

"So is that how you died? Drowning?" Corten asked.

Servala smirked. "Awful personal question, seeing as how we just met."

Corten felt his cheeks heat up. "Sorry. You're right, that was rude." In Ceramor most undead didn't like talking about how they had died. Who wanted to remember something like that?

"Eh, it's all right. And no, I didn't drown. Back in the real world, there was a rope. I caught it and managed to climb aboard. Course it took two days for us to sail out of the storm and no matter how many blankets my mates wrapped me in, I couldn't seem to get warm. Fever, I guess. I never made it back to port."

"I'm sorry," Corten said.

"It was a long time ago. Anyway, you were asking about how I survive here. Answer's simple, really. I found my rope."

"What do you mean?"

"Just what I'm saying. This place, however you see it, it's something that makes you feel unstable, uncertain. It wears you down and makes you want to rest. That makes the door seem awful appealing, and if you don't go through it, eventually there isn't enough left for you to be you. Once I figured that out, I started thinking. Back when I was living, I sailed aboard the *Crier Gull*. She was my refuge on the waves. I thought maybe if I had her here, I could survive even these waves, at least until I decide to go through the door on my own terms."

Corten realized what she was saying and smiled. "So you made her, didn't you?"

Servala answered his smile. "That I did."

"Can you show me?"

Servala's smile fell a fraction. "I can try. But I'll warn you fair, it might not work. I tried explaining all this to Davious and a couple of others before, but none of them could wrap their heads around it."

"Won't know until we try," Corten said.

Servala nodded. "Follow me." She led Corten a few steps away from the door to a spot where its light began to fade into the uncertain gray of the darkness beyond. Corten shivered, feeling the ground shift under his feet and the wind pick up again against his face. Whatever power existed in this place, it didn't want him to leave the light of the door now that he was here.

Servala gestured out into the dark. "Do you see her?"

Corten squinted, willing himself to see a ship instead of just twisting shadows. But as the seconds ticked by, his stomach sank. He shook his head. "I don't."

Servala chewed her lip. "Give me your hand," she said after a moment, extending her own toward him.

Corten hesitated, then took the offered hand. Servala's skin felt cool against his, and her palm was rough with calluses that probably came from her days sailing.

"Now close your eyes," Servala said.

Corten did. With his eyes shut, the darkness felt more imposing around him. He had to fight to keep from opening them and running toward the relative safety of the door. He felt Servala's grip tighten as though she sensed the impulse.

"Listen," Servala said softly. "The waves are crashing against the shore. The air's cool, and still damp from the morning mist that's burning off. Through the last white swirls, you can just see the *Gull.* She's a two-mast ship, square rigged, and twenty yards from fore to aft. Her sails are set and waiting for a wind, the cloth so white their tops seem to vanish in the mist. She's not a fancy ship, but she's sleek, and her sides are painted blue like sunlight glinting off shallow water. She's got aether lamps set all along the rails. They're beacons, set out so that no matter how dark it gets, her sailors can always find their way home." There was a catch in Servala's voice on the last words. She shifted until Corten sensed her standing in front of him, still holding his hand tight.

"Can you see her in your mind?" Servala asked, her voice a whisper.

"Yes." He could imagine the ship, her sides lapped by gentle waves he couldn't feel. Though he'd lived in Ceramor for years, he'd never spent much time at the docks. Despite that, there was a clarity and detail to the image that he suspected was somehow coming from Servala. He could almost hear the creak of wood and the snap of sailcloth.

"Good," Servala said. "Now take this." She pressed a thick rope into his open hand.

Corten opened his eyes in surprise and stared down at the rope. It was half as thick as his wrist, and dripping wet. His eyes followed it slowly through the water that now surged cool against his legs and up to the waiting ship. "Wow," he said softly.

Servala let out a whoop and dropped his hand. She grinned fiercely at the ship. "You can see her, can't you?"

"Yeah, what'd you do?" Corten asked.

"It's in the talking," Servala said, still grinning. "I had to find a way to get you to believe in the *Gull* like I do. I had to make you hear what she really means. You're the first one who's been able to hear it."

Corten looked back down at the rope. Memories of Naya rose up through his mind, the soft smile and the longing look in her eyes whenever she'd talk about the ocean and her father's ship. "I'd heard something like it before. I guess that helps," he said. His throat felt tight around the words. He looked up at the ship again and had to fight the disappointment as some irrational part of his mind expected to see Naya waiting for him on deck.

"Well, don't just stand there," Servala said. "Come aboard."

CHAPTER 15

NAYA

Took on four hundred crates of oranges from the west Belvales region before departure. Feels strange leaving without the girl, but it's time she saw the true nature of our work. Creator willing, Valn will find someone to continue her education. Must be getting soft, nearly called her back as she left the ship. But I've watched her grow. She's clever. She'll play her part when the time comes.

Naya slammed her father's logbook shut. She was getting faster at decrypting the new cipher. But after a night spent reading, she was starting to wish she'd thrown the cursed thing into the sea. Most days her father had written only a few notes on weather or prices, or what cargo the *Gallant* had taken on at various ports. But quite a few of the longer entries were about her. After everything that had happened, reading her father's praise made the back of her neck prickle.

Felicia arrived a few minutes later to help her prepare for the ball and Naya welcomed the distraction with relief.

"I know you said you don't need a maidservant," Felicia said, laying out a dress of blue silk and silver lace. "But the ties on this will be tricky without someone to help."

Naya ran her fingers over the smooth fabric. The skirt was long and flowing. The sleeves were lace, designed to flare at the wrist and drape over the backs of the hands. "This is beautiful," she said. The dress was far more elaborate than anything she'd ever worn.

Felicia smiled. "I've been thinking about what you said last night. It can't be easy having to be here with all these people who think you're a monster. But if you have to face them, you might as well look beautiful while you do it."

Naya stared at the dress and tried to imagine herself wearing it, striding with her head held high through a ballroom full of startled politicians and Talmiran nobles. There was something powerful about that image that reminded her of aether humming in her bones. A slow smile spread across her lips. "A beautiful monster. I guess we could try that."

Felicia returned her smile with a grin, then got to work. Naya stared at her reflection as Felicia wove the elaborate network of ribbon ties securing the dress. Her old face stared back at her— hazel eyes and a sharp nose surrounded by a tumble of brown curls. Studying and working for her father hadn't given her many opportunities to dress up, and she'd always thought herself plain. But tonight the curves of her dress seemed to hug her just right, the blue contrasting prettily with the rich brown of her hair. She looked like herself, yet somehow completely different.

Felicia met Naya's eyes in the mirror and gave her a satisfied smile. "You look perfect."

Naya walked into the hall, her feet feeling strange in a pair of silk slippers. Back in Ceramor, Corten had convinced her to give up shoes. A wraith's feet couldn't be hurt by cold or sharp stones, and going barefoot had given her a better grip when running along the rooftops of Belavine. Here bare feet would draw too many whispers. She didn't want to give the people of Talmir any more reasons than they already had to scorn her.

Naya found Francisco waiting in the hall wearing a fine black suit decorated with silver embroidery. His hair was slicked back in the latest style, and the gash on his forehead was obvious despite an attempt to cover it with powder. The formal clothes made him look older than he had on the ship, and his face was set in the carefully neutral expression of someone used to wearing a mask. But when his eyes met hers, they widened, then drifted down to take in the dress.

"You like it?" Naya asked.

Francisco's mask returned. He bowed. Naya noticed that his suit had been cut with a higher collar than was usual in Ceramor and that he wore a silver-and-red patterned cravat that hid the ring of tattoos encircling his neck.

"Felicia did a good job," Francisco said. "Are you ready? The rest of the delegation is gathering at the end of the hall."

Naya nodded, then followed him to where the others waited. Almost twenty people were gathered in the hallway, every one of them dressed in fine suits and gowns. Naya didn't recognize all of them, but from her lessons in Ceramor she knew most were scribes, translators, and assistants. Delence waited at the end of the hall with the five others that represented the core of the delegation. He spoke softly with Lady Marcel, a tall, silver-haired woman in an elegant purple dress who served as the delegation's expert on foreign law. Lord Vanissare, King Allence's master of trade, stood beside her, his puff of disheveled gray hair making an odd contrast to his sharp suit. To his left, Admiral Artello leaned against the wall, wearing a formal captain's jacket and fine blue trousers rather than a gown. She gave Naya and Francisco a curt nod as they approached.

Naya stepped sideways as she passed Lady Briello, who was gesturing animatedly while speaking with a middle-aged man with very thick eyebrows and a severe expression. That had to be Lord Falcasio, who represented the interests of the Ceramoran orchard owners—the backbone of Ceramor's economy after the war.

Once everyone was gathered, the tall steward from the night before escorted them to the central palace. Everywhere Naya looked she saw the sheen of gilt and fine carved wood. The carpet beneath her slippers was thick, and the walls were decorated with paintings of country life so detailed she imagined she could step through the picture frames to disappear among their fields of shifting wheat.

The hallway intersected with several others, and they joined the richly dressed crowd waiting outside the arched entrance to the central ballroom. Naya tried not to stare as a Banian delegate brushed past in a flowing cotton robe bound at the waist by an elaborate green sash. Near the front of the crowd a group of Silmaran delegates stood close together, speaking softly. The arms of their suits were covered in complex embroidery that served as a sort of public biography for those who knew how to read the colorful designs. Her own dress was more in line with Talmiran styles. Lace had come back into fashion in Talmir while she was away, and everywhere she saw it spilling from jacket cuffs and accenting colorful silk dresses. Unease tightened in Naya's chest as she felt the aether of the crowd pressing in on her. She'd been to parties with her father, but never anything so grand as this.

She tried to summon again that sense of power she'd felt back in her rooms. The people in this place wanted to dismiss her as something monstrous, but she would show them she was so much more than that.

Naya stood a little straighter. As she did, her eyes were drawn to a man and a woman near the edge of the crowd. They stood a good three inches taller than everyone around them and had light skin and strange hair that shone like burnished copper. Their clothing was like nothing Naya had ever seen. Both wore loose silk pants bunched into high boots and long shirts cinched with heavy belts studded in gems and silver. More gems gleamed from heavy bracelets around their wrists, and delicate black leather gloves covered their hands.

"Who are they?" she whispered to Francisco. He too was staring at the strange pair, as were many others in the waiting crowd.

"They must be the ambassadors from Endra."

"Endra?" Naya asked. "I didn't know they had ambassadors." Endra was the name for the lands east of the Blackspine Mountains. Naya knew little about them save that the region was populated by scattered city-states like the one Reial claimed his last ship had been sent to. It wasn't unheard of for merchants to try sailing the northern passage, or for caravans to attempt crossing Al Dras Pass to trade with one of the cities. But Naya had never heard of any of the city-states seeking formal contact with their western neighbors.

"According to my father," Francisco said, "they arrived a few days ago with an entourage of servants and performers. They've got a new queen who claims to speak for all the cities. She says she wants to build waystations and open up safer trade routes through the mountain passes."

"Why are they here tonight? They're not a part of the alliance, are they?"

"Not that I know of. I'm not sure why Queen Lial invited them," Francisco said.

Naya wanted to ask more, but before she could they reached the entrance to the ballroom. Up ahead someone called out, "Lord Salno Delence and the Ceramoran delegation."

As they entered the ballroom, Naya's eyes widened. She'd heard stories about the center of Queen Lial's palace, but she'd always assumed they were exaggerations. She craned her neck to stare at the vaulted ceiling—white plaster crossed by gilded beams in a repeated sunburst pattern reminiscent of the shape of the palace's five wings. The walls were shining white marble covered by fine tapestries displaying the history of Talmir, and the floor mirrored the patterns of the ceiling with inlays of blue and gold stone. Four massive tables had been set up in a half circle facing a raised platform in the center of the room. The chairs were arranged such that everyone seated would have a clear view of the platform.

A fifth table sat off to the right on an even higher platform. There, a squad of wary soldiers watched over Queen Lial and her two young children, the Crown Prince Gel and his sister, Princess Misa. The queen wore a gown of palest blue and gold lace, the bodice crusted with pearls and sapphires so it shone like sunlight on waves. It was a dramatic difference from when Naya had glimpsed her at the Gallows Day festival last year. Apparently, since then, the queen had completed her three years of public mourning over her husband's passing.

Servants appeared to lead the Ceramoran delegates to their table. Naya found herself seated at the right end of the table, with Francisco on her left. The position gave her a good view of both the platform in the center of the room and the royal table. She was more than a little surprised to see the two Endran ambassadors take seats beside the queen and her children. She glanced to the side and found Francisco watching them as well, a faint frown on his face.

The room's aether was thick with emotions, and Naya had to concentrate to avoid getting overwhelmed. Conversation swelled around them, and soon servants were moving between tables and laying out food. The first course was a soup, something bright green and fragrant with mingled herbs and vegetables. Naya breathed in the steam, then dipped her spoon and raised it to her lips. She couldn't eat, but by concentrating she could just taste the sweetness of the summer vegetables and imagine the soup's creamy texture.

"You don't have to pretend for their sake," Francisco said softly.

Naya opened her eyes and found him watching her. "It isn't about them," she said. She set the spoon down, feeling suddenly foolish. "Anyway, why do you care? Are you worried I won't be distracting enough if I try to enjoy myself a little?"

Francisco's forehead wrinkled in a scowl that disappeared an instant later under his polite mask. "I only meant . . . never mind."

Naya held the spoon but didn't raise it to her lips again. She could feel the gazes focused on them like a heavy cloud looming in the aether. She glanced sideways at Francisco, who was eating his soup with the mechanical determination of a marching soldier. Here she was, sitting at a feast she couldn't eat, next to a boy she'd watched die. All around them, the most powerful people in the world talked and schemed.

"What are you smiling at?" Francisco asked.

Naya shook her head. "Do you ever wonder if what we're trying to do here is completely mad?"

Francisco took another bite of his soup. "Every day," he muttered.

CHAPTER 16

NAYA

Servants came and went, carrying course after course of delicacies. Naya watched each one go with growing frustration. Once, in Ceramor, she'd tried eating a piece of cake in a fit of impulse. The results had not been pleasant, but watching the endless procession of flaky pastries, spiced vegetables, and buttered fish disappearing back into the kitchens almost made her want to repeat the unfortunate experiment.

It didn't help that the servant delivering her food shook with fear every time he set a plate in front of her. Naya tried smiling at him, but that only seemed to make things worse. The back of her neck itched as she sensed people from the nearby tables staring at her and Francisco. She distracted herself by focusing on the dancers and musicians performing on the stage in front of the delegates' tables. Women in flowing gowns twirled and dipped while men in jackets and loose trousers demonstrated the dramatic leaps and flips common in Talmiran folk dances.

When the dancers finally finished, Queen Lial stood, signaling that the formal entertainment was over, and invited the guests to enjoy the remainder of the evening.

"Come on," Francisco said as he and Naya stepped away from the table. Servants rushed forward to move the long tables to the sides of the room, while musicians with string instruments began playing softly next to the dance floor. "I want to find some of the younger members of the Banian delegation."

Naya nodded, preparing to follow him. But something out of the corner of her eye caught her attention. She turned, noting one of the servants helping move the table next to theirs. The woman's hair was more gray than brown, and the way she held her head down made it hard to see her face, but there was something familiar about her.

Shock hit Naya like a cold wave. "Celia?"

"What did you say?" Francisco asked, raising his voice to speak over the growing buzz of conversation and music.

"I'll be right back," Naya said.

"Wait—" Francisco made to grab her wrist, but Naya moved before he could reach her. By the time she managed to squeeze through the small crowd of guests gathering around the dance floor, the servants had already finished their task. An elderly man in a steward's uniform was giving orders while other servants draped the tables in fresh white cloth and set out a spread of drinks and sweets. Naya scanned their faces, but Celia wasn't among them.

Naya hesitated. A moment ago she'd felt certain of what she'd seen. But how many times had she imagined catching a glimpse of Corten, only to turn and see a stranger? It didn't make sense for Celia to be here. Unless . . . Naya drew in a sharp breath. If Queen Lial had been overseeing Valn's mission directly, then Celia could have returned to the palace seeking sanctuary. If Celia was here, she could be the key to proving a connection between the queen and Valn's plot.

"Do you smell something rotting?" said a woman to Naya's right, her voice loud and faintly slurred with drink.

Naya glanced over and saw two Talmiran women dressed in lace-draped gowns, one young, the other perhaps in her forties. The older woman was staring at Naya like she was something foul dragged in off the street. "Oh dear, it seems the rumors were true." She held a glass of wine in one hand and from the flush on her cheeks, Naya guessed it wasn't her first.

Naya felt heat rise on her own face. She was about to turn away from the pair when she recognized the younger woman. She looked about a year or so older than Naya, with dark eyes and brown hair spun up in an elaborate style to highlight her slender neck. "Sai?" Naya asked. "Sai Ayun? What are you doing here?"

The older woman looked at Sai. "You know this creature?"

Sai looked away. "No, of course not," she said quickly.

A small voice in Naya whispered that she should just walk away. But the older woman's insults and Sai's cowardly evasion were more than she could ignore. "Don't be silly, Sai, I'm Naya Garth, we shared classes at the Merchants Academy," Naya said in a tone that was perhaps only a little too bright to be taken as sincere. Sai had been a year above her at the academy and had come from a wealthy family just one step shy of nobility. Despite that, she'd been one of the few who'd never looked down on Naya for her parentage.

Sai shook her head. "I knew a Naya, but I heard she died in that unfortunate incident in Ceramor."

The older woman pressed a handkerchief to her nose. "Oh, poor Sai, how terrible to be confronted by the corpse of a dead friend."

"I'm not a corpse," Naya said, fighting the sudden urge to knock the wineglass out of the silly woman's hand. She took a step forward, and the woman recoiled as though attacked.

"Lady Elv, perhaps we should go," Sai said, sounding uneasy.

"Hush, Sai." Lady Elv leveled a glare at Naya. "Not a corpse? Creature, who are you trying to fool, us or yourself?"

"Excuse me?" A new voice interrupted before Naya could answer. "Lady Elv, Miss Ayun? Trade Master Galve wanted to speak to you."

Lady Elv turned and arched her eyebrows. Behind her stood

a tall young woman with a wide smile. She wore a Banian-style robe patterned yellow and red. Her skin was darker than Naya's but still lighter than most Islanders, and her black hair was curly rather than straight.

"Ah," Lady Elv said. "Mel, isn't it? I see that your mother decided to bring you along after all."

The newcomer, Mel, grinned. "And the trade master decided to keep you on his staff despite the rumors about that little incident at Mistress Brilla's salon last month. Surprises all around."

Lady Elv sputtered. "You—Come, Sai, it seems we're wanted in better company than this."

Sai nodded. "Of course," she said. She didn't so much as glance at Naya before following Lady Elv into the crowd.

"Sorry about that," Mel said. "I heard what they were saying and thought you might want a rescue."

Naya blinked, unsure what to make of the strange girl. "Thank you."

Mel smiled. "No trouble. Lady Elv has something of a condition where all her common sense drains out as soon as she enters a party. I expect she leaves it behind in hopes that the void will open more room for the queen's expensive wines."

Naya snickered, but the little bubble of humor popped when she looked back in the direction Sai and Lady Elv had gone. "It seemed like common sense wasn't the only thing she lacked."

"Very true." Mel looked around, seeming to notice the stares they were getting from other guests. "I'm afraid you'll find she's not alone in her opinions, though most people here will have more tact in expressing them."

"What about you?" Naya asked. Mel's abrupt arrival had startled her out of her anger, but that didn't mean she could let her guard down. She glanced again toward the side of the room and noted with frustration that most of the servants had retreated now that the tables were reset.

Mel shrugged. "I don't know. You're the first undead I've ever met. So far you seem perfectly decent."

"There you are!" Francisco squeezed through a gap in the crowd. His gaze darted between Naya and Mel as he straightened his cravat. He smiled at Mel and offered a low bow. "Sorry if I'm interrupting. I'm Francisco Delence."

"Well, hello there." Mel answered his bow with a Talmiran curtsy that looked only a little strange with her Banian robes. "Mel Jeden."

Francisco's smile lost its warmth. "Ah. Would you be the daughter of Ambassador Jeden?"

Mel grinned. "From your tone I can tell you've met my dear mother."

Francisco cleared his throat. "Not in person." He turned back to Naya. "Miss Garth, would you please come with me? There are some people we should speak to before the festivities wind down."

"All right," Naya said, glancing back at Mel.

Mel waved one hand in a shooing gesture. "By all means, don't let me keep you. I'm sure we'll see each other around later."

Francisco surprised Naya by offering her his arm. She took it, and he all but dragged her back into the crowd. "What were you doing?" he asked under his breath, his polite tone replaced by one of exasperation.

"Nothing. I thought I saw someone I knew," Naya whispered back. She tried to pay attention to the faces around them and not the surprising warmth of Francisco's arm against hers.

"Who?"

Naya hesitated. "Nobody. I was wrong." She didn't want to mention Celia until she was sure of what she'd seen.

Francisco gave her an irritated look. "Fine, but next time don't run off like that. Maybe this place just looks like a party to you, but trust me when I say the people here are every bit as dangerous as that crowd that attacked us outside."

"I know how to take care of myself," Naya said.

Francisco stopped walking and met her eyes. "You obviously know how to fight, but this is different." He glanced around. "Speaking of, what were you and Mel Jeden talking about?"

"Nothing. She just came over and introduced herself." Naya really didn't feel like explaining the entire conversation with Sai and Lady Elv.

"Well, stay away from her if you can. Her mother is the Talmiran ambassador to the Banen Islands. She's spent the past five years working to keep the Banians against us. If Mel sought you out, it was probably at her mother's request."

Naya frowned. She knew who Ambassador Jeden was, of course. But Mel had seemed completely different from the descriptions Naya had heard of her cold, calculating mother. "I'll be careful," she said. "But I'm not going to spend the entire Congress hiding in the corner."

"That would be an impressive feat, seeing as how this ball-room is round."

"You knew what I meant," Naya said, rolling her eyes.

"Did I? Maybe finding corners in round rooms is a trick they teach all the Talmiran spies."

"Careful," Naya said. "If I didn't know any better, I might think you were developing a sense of humor."

Francisco's shoulders tensed. "I have a perfectly good sense of humor, it's just this place that isn't funny."

"If you say so," Naya said. She watched Francisco out of the corner of her eye as he led her through the crowd. She thought she was beginning to see the boy hiding behind the mask of the politician's son. He was clever and passionate, and she found herself wanting to like him despite everything else. It made her wish they could have met under better circumstances. Perhaps in another life, they might have been friends.

Naya worked to keep her expression pleasant as she and

Francisco spent the next hour mingling among the lower ranked members of the Silmaran and Banian delegations. Francisco moved easily among the delegates, brushing off sideways insults and always working to turn the conversation back toward the advantages of stronger alliances with Ceramor and the harmlessness of the undead. He was clearly in his element.

Meanwhile, Naya's head throbbed from the effort of trying to sort individual emotions while answering the often-probing questions of the other delegates. She'd promised herself she would work to end the fear and hate her people had promoted for so long. Yet so far this night had been a harsh reminder of how difficult that task would be. Only Mel had treated Naya as a person rather than a curiosity, or something to be feared. And according to Francisco, even that might have been a ruse.

When the Silmaran delegates they'd been speaking with stepped away to get more drinks, Naya touched Francisco's arm. "I'm going back to the rooms," she said.

Francisco glanced around. His eyes were a little glassy and his cheeks flushed from the wine the Silmarans kept insisting he share with them. "I should stay here a while longer," he said.

"So stay," Naya said. "We don't both have to leave."

Francisco frowned. "I don't like the idea of you going back alone."

Heat rose in Naya's cheeks and she wasn't sure if she should feel amused or annoyed. Francisco was the one who looked like he might need an escort after all the wine he'd drunk. "I can take care of myself."

Francisco hesitated. "All right," he said finally. "But you should go straight back to the rooms."

Naya breathed a sigh of relief as she started toward the grand doors. She was nearly out into the hall when a heavily accented voice called to her in Talmiran. "Excuse me, are you Naya Garth?"

Naya turned and was surprised to see one of the Endran ambassadors hurrying toward her. The man's copper hair was unusually long, held back in a tail at the base of his neck, and the gemstones in his wide belt glimmered as he paused before her and bowed.

"I am," Naya said.

The ambassador smiled. "Then I am glad I have caught you. Forgive me. We were not introduced. I am Zultaren Bargal, emissary to Her Great Majesty Queen Alethen the first of the Sun Blessed Lands." His accent had a strange, almost singsong quality.

"It's an honor to meet you," Naya said, covering her confusion with a curtsy.

"The honor is mine. It is not every day that I find myself in the company of one who has returned from the far side of death."

Naya ducked her head. What in creation was she supposed to say to something like that? And how had the Endran ambassador known who she was? Despite his smile, there was something disquieting about the intensity of his gaze. "Do you not have necromancy in Endra then?"

"No," Bargal said, adjusting one of his thin gloves. "Our magic is different from yours. I had heard rumors that the people of Ceramor rediscovered the ancient secrets of necromancy. But when my queen asked me to investigate, I honestly expected to find nothing more than stories."

Naya blinked at that. Surely news of the Mad King's War had made it across the mountains. "It's more than stories. The people of Ceramor have been practicing necromancy for decades."

"That is what everyone here tells me," Bargal said. His smile sharpened. "Though from the rumors I hear, the Ceramorans are not the only ones."

Naya's arms prickled as though the temperature in the room

had just dropped several degrees. "What rumors would those be?" she asked carefully.

Bargal tilted his head to one side, looking bemused. "Why, the ones about this trial, of course. I heard it was a Talmiran traitor who resurrected you."

"Oh." Naya fought off a wave of disappointment. For a second she'd thought Bargal might somehow know about Lucia's journals. Rumors of Valn's role in the coup were a far more rational explanation for his comment, though the way Bargal spoke made Naya wonder what exactly people had been saying. "I'm not sure what you've heard, but the necromancer who resurrected me is Ceramoran. Valn only gave the orders."

Bargal's forehead furrowed. "I see. I apologize then. I must have confused what was said. Your language is rather tricky." Before Naya could respond, he bowed again. "I find the subject of necromancy fascinating, but few people here seem willing to discuss it. If you have time during the Congress, I would very much like to speak with you more about your experiences."

"My experiences?" Naya asked.

Bargal smiled. "Of course. You've been beyond death. Who wouldn't want to know about that?"

Naya stared at the strange man, trying to guess his purpose. She'd seen him sitting at the queen's table. Obviously, he'd come to make a deal with Talmir. Why then would he care about necromancy? "I'll have to talk to the head of my delegation," Naya said carefully. "But if I have time, I'd be happy to meet with you."

"Excellent." Bargal smiled, flashing a set of very white teeth. "Then I will look forward to seeing you again."

CHAPTER 17

NAYA

Naya stepped into the relative quiet of the hallway outside the ballroom. Several soldiers guarded the doors, but otherwise the hall was empty. Naya paused, considering the hush. With most of the delegates still at the party, the bulk of the palace servants and soldiers would probably be focused here. The rest of the palace was likely to be near-abandoned. She had meant to go straight back to her rooms as Francisco had suggested, but this seemed like too good of an opportunity to pass up.

Naya started down the hall at a leisurely pace. Delence had implied that Queen Lial was behind Valn's attempt to overthrow the Ceramoran throne, and Celia's presence here would support that theory. There was a chance, if a slim one, that Lucia's journals were hidden in this very palace. Naya couldn't hope to find them by wandering the halls, but it would help to get a better sense of the building's layout. If she was lucky, she might even figure out where they were keeping Valn.

Naya heard footsteps and glanced back to see one of the soldiers by the door moving to follow her. She fought down a grimace, then paused and smiled at the soldier. "Thank you, but I don't need an escort."

The soldier stopped, standing just out of reach. He was perhaps in his forties, with a thick, well-trimmed beard under a wide nose and very dark eyes. Now that she was away from the crowd, it was easy to sense the tension leaking through his aether. "Apologies," he said. "After last night's incident, the queen has ordered us to keep you guarded at all times."

It had probably been too much to hope that they'd let her go unwatched. The soldier was bound to get suspicious if he thought she was wandering the halls aimlessly. An idea came to her. "What's your name?" she asked the soldier.

The soldier blinked. "My name?"

Naya smiled, ignoring the way the soldier's hand rested on his sword. She tried to summon some of the warm patience Corten had shown back when he'd taught her to draw aether. "You already know who I am. It seems rude of me to not ask for your name as well."

The soldier was silent for a moment, wary. "Sergeant Norel Leln," he finally said.

Naya curtsied. "Nice to meet you, Sergeant Leln. I was hoping to look at some of the artwork in the palace before I go up to my rooms. Is that all right?"

Leln hesitated, then nodded his head. "So long as you stay on this floor, all unlocked areas of the palace are open to members of the delegations."

"Good," Naya said. A night spent surrounded by the aether of people who feared and hated her had left her nerves frayed. But while Leln was obviously cautious of her, his aether lacked the pungent hatred she'd sensed in some of the other soldiers. That gave her hope.

Naya continued down the hall, glancing over her shoulder to see Leln following. She searched her mind for some topic of conversation to break the uneasy silence. "The palace is very beautiful," she said. "It must be an honor to work here."

Leln made a grunting sound that might have been a yes.

"Have you worked in the palace long?" Naya asked.

"A few years," Leln said stiffly.

"Have you ever met the queen?"

"Yes."

"What's she like?"

"Regal."

Naya gave up, instead focusing on memorizing all she could of her surroundings. She wandered the palace, trying doors and occasionally stopping to stand in front of paintings or statues while she reached out through the aether. Most doors were locked, and those that did open revealed lavishly decorated sitting rooms or meeting halls. A few had bookshelves. Naya itched to browse through them, even though she knew illegal necromantic texts wouldn't be left out in so obvious a place. Instead, she noted the location of the locked doors and stairways she found. She would have liked to try some of the stairways, but each one was guarded by a pair of soldiers in formal uniforms. What would she have to do to get past them?

"You like Eloy Vasken's work?" Sergeant Leln asked.

Naya nearly jumped at the sound of his voice. She blinked. "Sorry?"

Sergeant Leln gestured at the painting in front of her. It showed a narrow street lined with wooden houses, some painted in mismatched shades of white, others bare. Laundry lines crossed above the heads of what looked like a market-day crowd dressed simply in muted colors. All of it was painted in a rough style very different from the detailed realism she was used to seeing in Talmir.

"Is Vasken the artist?" Naya asked. The painting was nice, but she'd only stopped here because she'd noticed a stairway leading down from the wing they'd just passed. There was something odd about the aether here, a faint mix of tension and despair that reminded her of the dungeons beneath the Ceramoran palace. But the source was too far away for her to sense more without getting closer. She didn't know if Queen Lial's palace had a dungeon, or if the queen would have ordered Valn locked away in the Barrow in nearby Justice Square.

"He is," Leln said. "The queen has a few more of his pieces on the second floor in the northwest wing."

Naya raised her eyebrows. "You seem to know a lot about artwork."

Leln cleared his throat. His discomfort seemed to have eased as they walked. "I have daughters. One of them is attending classes at the Academy of Arts. She's always talking about this painter or that when she's home. It rubs off on a fellow."

Naya smiled. "She must be very good if she's at the academy." There were five academies in Lith Lor, each training its students in a different specialization. The Academy of Arts was the smallest, and quite exclusive from what she'd heard. Naya had attended the Merchants Academy, which taught finances, geography, and various other skills to prepare the children of wealthy merchants and lesser nobility for the day when they would join their parents' enterprises. Beyond that were the Academy of Sciences, the Military Academy, and of course the Academy of Magics.

Leln stood a little straighter and gave Naya a hesitant smile of his own. "She is. Creator willing, her work will someday hang in these halls." He was quiet a moment. "I'd offer to show you Vasken's other works, but that wing is currently housing the Banian delegation."

"That's all right," Naya said. Warmth bloomed in her chest. Maybe changing the minds of other Talmirans wouldn't be as impossible as she'd feared. Clearly not everyone in the palace was as hostile as Lady Elv. She glanced down the hall. They'd nearly completed a full circle of the palace's central ring. The swirl of aether from the ballroom seemed to have lessened. It was late, and as Naya watched, a group of delegates in Banian robes rounded the corner, speaking softly among themselves. "I should be getting back to my rooms anyway," Naya said.

Once they got back, Naya slipped into her room and shut the door firmly behind her. She leaned against the wall and closed her eyes. Leln had seemed far less nervous, almost friendly, as they'd returned to the Ceramoran delegation's halls. But friendly or not, he still hadn't let her out of his sight. She was going to have to get creative if she wanted to move through the palace unwatched.

She crossed to her desk and sat. Servants had stocked the drawers with more writing supplies than Naya had ever owned. She pulled out a thick sheet of paper and a gold-tipped pen and ink, then did her best to sketch a map of what she'd seen. It would look suspicious if anyone found it, but she didn't trust herself to memorize all the details. The results mostly served to show how little she'd managed to learn wandering the halls. If she could get out on her own, maybe she could start filling in the gaps. Though with soldiers at every stairway, it would be slow and risky work to get access to the other wings.

"Assuming there's even anything to find here," she muttered under her breath.

A knock came at her door and Naya started, glancing at the clock. It was past midnight, late for anyone else to still be up, especially since the first meeting of the Congress was tomorrow morning. The knock came again and Naya reluctantly stashed her writing supplies and stood.

She opened the door to find Francisco outside. His cravat was loose around his neck and his face looked even more flushed than it had when she'd left the party. "Um, yes?" Naya asked.

"Where have you been?" Francisco demanded.

Naya's shoulders stiffened. "Here," she said.

"You're lying," Francisco said. "I told you to go straight back to the delegation hall."

"So? You're not my nursemaid. Creator, how much wine did you drink after I left?" All the tension of the evening came rushing back. When she'd left the ball, she'd thought Francisco's cautions were because he was still nervous after the attack. But the anger on his face now suggested there was more to it than that.

Francisco wrinkled his nose. "I am not drunk. Anyway, don't change the subject. I heard some soldiers outside talking. Apparently you were wandering around the palace for more than an hour. What were you doing?"

Naya winced. Creator. Whatever was going on, this was not a conversation she wanted to be having out in the hall where anyone could overhear. "Would you please keep your voice down?"

Francisco crossed his arms. "Why? Do you have something to hide? You've been acting friendly lately, but maybe that's because you don't want me to pay attention to what you're really up to."

Naya grabbed his sleeve and pulled him into the room, shutting the door behind him. With her hand on his arm, she could sense his aether. It made her head spin and her chest feel strangely hollow. Definitely drunk.

"Let go of me!" Francisco pulled his arm free, then glanced around the room. "What are you doing?"

"I'm trying to keep you from waking up the whole damned palace," Naya said, struggling to keep her voice even. "And in answer to your question, I was just looking at paintings. There was a soldier with me the whole time, so it's not as though I could have done anything."

"But you wanted to," Francisco said. He took a step toward her. "You're up to something. Tell me what it is, or I'll tell my father you're carrying coded documents."

"What?" Panic made Naya's chest go tight.

Francisco smiled. "Felicia is a very loyal Ceramoran. She told me she found a book full of coded messages in your bag."

"That's none of your business," Naya said, her thoughts racing. So Felicia had told Francisco about her father's logbook. Why hadn't he confronted her about it before now?

"Why? Were you hoping no one would find out you were still spying for Talmir?"

Naya's mouth dropped open. "That's ridiculous. Are you listening to yourself? Even if I wanted to spy for them, which I don't, they would never take me. I'm a wraith, remember? When we were attacked outside the gates, the guards didn't even bother to help. Why would they do that if I was on their side?"

"I don't know. Maybe it was all a setup to get us to relax our guard."

Naya's jaw clenched. This was so stupid. She couldn't afford to spend the entire Congress fighting off accusations like this. Somehow she had to convince Francisco to trust her.

Naya's thoughts turned back to her nights spent training with Celia. *Truths carefully shaped can be just as deceptive as lies,* Celia's voice whispered through her memory. Could she twist the truth into something less threatening? Maybe. "It's my father's logbook," Naya said after a pause.

Francisco blinked. "What?"

"The coded document Felicia saw—it's my father's logbook. I found it in his cabin on the *Gallant* and I've been translating it."

"Not possible. My father had the *Gallant* searched before he gave it to you. They brought all Garth's papers back for analysis weeks ago."

She'd assumed as much—still, it was infuriating. "Well, maybe if he'd consulted me I could have told his men where to look. My father wasn't exactly the most trusting person. He never kept anything important where he thought strangers might find it."

"Then you still should have said something sooner."

Naya shook her head. "I can read my father's ciphers faster

than anyone else. I wanted time to translate the logbook on the journey over. That way, if I found anything useful, I could take it to Delence."

"What did you think you would find?"

"I don't know. Maybe something that could expose Valn's other allies, or something that could explain what my father did to me. He acted like he loved me, but then he gave me over to Valn for his schemes. And when he found out I'd been resurrected, he looked at me like I was this disgusting thing he had to get rid of." Her throat threatened to close off around the words. The memories of that night still felt like a raw wound, one she wasn't sure would ever heal.

Francisco leaned back, and Naya saw curiosity and something that might have been sympathy spark in his eyes. He was still angry, still suspicious. But that curiosity was the hook she'd been hoping to land. "You want revenge," Francisco said.

Naya hesitated. "Not revenge. I want to make sure Valn and his allies don't hurt anyone else. None of them deserve to get away with what they tried to do."

"Have you found anything?" Francisco asked after a moment.

"No." Naya let frustration leak into her voice, another little truth. "It's just ordinary stuff so far."

Francisco sat on the arm of one of the room's overstuffed chairs. He rubbed his hands over his face, then stared at the floor, obviously trying to focus. "Valn's allies—assuming he even has any more—won't be easy to pin down."

Naya bit her lip. "If there was strong evidence of a connection, would the Congress act on it?"

"Maybe? But even if Hal Garth wrote down the names of his accomplices, his word alone wouldn't be enough."

"It would at least be a place to start." Naya met Francisco's eyes. "You said on the ship that your father only wants us here as distractions. But we could be so much more than that. Valn was training me to gather information. I know how his people operate, and I know this city. You obviously know all about the Congress. If I can find a lead in the logbook, then maybe together we can get the evidence we need." Naya leaned forward, trying to make the anxiety humming through her body sound like excitement. It was a risk. But if she could convince Francisco that all she wanted was to find Valn's allies, then maybe she could turn him from an enemy to an accomplice.

Francisco was quiet for a long moment. "We only have two days until the trial. And if we got caught doing anything illegal, it could ruin everything."

"So we should just give up?" Naya asked.

"I didn't say that. Just—my father has a plan. We can't mess it up. We need to be cautious."

"We might not have time for caution. Valn's facing execution. When he dies, all his secrets die with him."

"You're assuming he has any allies left to find," Francisco said. He sounded tired.

Naya could hear the frustration leaking back into his tone. She took a step back. "You're probably right. We should stick to the plan, be the good little distractions your father needs." She looked down at the carpet. "Just, please, let me keep translating the logbook. If I find something, I promise I'll bring it to you."

"Good little distractions," Francisco muttered under his breath. He sighed. "Do what you want with the logbook, just don't mention it in any of the meetings and I guess it won't really matter."

Naya heard the tread of his shoes on the carpet. When she looked up, she saw him standing with his hand on the doorknob. "I'm sorry," he said softly. "When I knocked on your door, I was not in a good state. I just . . . It's hard to know who to trust in this place."

"I know," Naya said.

CHAPTER 18

NAYA

Felicia arrived early the next morning, presumably to help Naya dress for the Congress meeting. She smiled as she stepped into the room, but her smile fell when she saw Naya's expression. "Miss Naya?" she asked, sounding uncertain. "I, ah, I see you've already gotten dressed. You never rang last night, so I wasn't sure if I should come down and . . ." She trailed off.

Naya crossed her arms. After what Francisco had told her, she hadn't felt up to facing Felicia last night. She'd spent a good half hour wrestling with the ties on the back of her ball gown before realizing she could simply make her body incorporeal and step through the fabric. She'd changed into a far more practical skirt and blouse of a modest Talmiran style, then spent the remaining hours of the night translating her father's logbook and trying to figure out what to do about Felicia. In the end she'd decided a direct approach was her best option.

"You've been spying on me," Naya said.

Felicia's eyes widened, and Naya sensed a jolt of icy panic slicing through the girl's aether. "I would never—"

"Would never dig through my bags and then report everything you found to Francisco? That sounds like spying to me, and I would know."

Felicia opened her mouth as though to object. Instead she

bit her lip and ducked her head. "I wasn't spying exactly. Your things really did fall out of your bag back on the ship and I . . ." She grimaced, then met Naya's gaze with obvious effort. "I did what I thought was best. When we left Ceramor, Lord Francisco asked me to look for anything suspicious. He said it could be important, so when I saw that strange book in your bag, I told him about it."

When put that way, it didn't sound so unreasonable.

Naya shifted uncomfortably. "You could have asked me about it instead of going straight to Francisco."

She could sense Felicia's fear and uncertainty like a heavy, sour fog in the aether. But underneath that she caught a glimmer of steely determination. "Is that what you would have done in my place?" Felicia asked.

"That isn't the point at all." Naya glared at Felicia. This wasn't how she'd expected this conversation to go. "I never wanted a maid, especially not one I can't trust."

"Then what would you have me do? Should I go sit on my hands and wait in the servants' quarters until the Congress is over?" Felicia asked.

"No, that's not—" Naya closed her eyes and let out a frustrated sigh. "Could we start over?"

Felicia looked away. "If that's what you want. But if you expect me to go around pretending I don't see things, or never asking questions, you'd be better off dismissing me."

"What if I asked you to come to me first if you do see something?" Naya asked.

Felicia hesitated. "I guess I could do that."

"Good." Naya felt her shoulders relax a little. "Because I'd appreciate having someone around who can run errands and carry messages for me." Felicia would likely have an easier time moving around the palace without guards following her every move.

Felicia's eyebrows rose. "Even if it's someone you don't trust?"

"I trust you a lot further than I do the palace servants," Naya said.

Felicia sniffed. "That's just common sense. From what I've seen, the queen hired a right mob of newcomers to handle all the extra guests. Half of them don't even seem to know their way around any better than I do."

Naya responded with a weak smile. Even with all the preparations she'd made before coming to the Congress, she still felt badly out of her depth. She needed allies, and she was starting to realize that there was a lot more to Felicia than she'd first assumed. Felicia must have heard all the rumors about what Naya had done in Ceramor. But when Naya had confronted her, she'd told the truth and defended her actions. Naya respected that. "What you saw on the ship was my father's old logbook. Francisco's agreed that I should be the one to translate it to see if it has any more clues about Valn's allies."

Felicia met Naya's eyes, as though looking for something there. Eventually she nodded. "Have you found anything?"

"Not yet," Naya said. "But I'll work on it some more after the meeting."

Felicia glanced at the clock on the mantel. "Speaking of, maybe we should do something with your hair before everything gets started?"

"What's wrong with my hair?" Naya asked. For the moment it hung in a simple braid down the back of her neck, the same way she'd usually worn it before she'd died.

"Well, simple styles like that aren't really in fashion right now," Felicia said. "I was talking with Lady Briello's maid Yenni up in the servants' quarters and she said she knew a girl who was maid to a lady wraith. Yenni said this girl would always do her lady's hair and makeup, even though the lady could twist her features any way she liked. The lady found it easier to hold the changes if she saw them done beforehand by ordinary means.

If you'd like, I can show you some of the new styles, then you can shift that way whenever you like."

"We could try that," Naya said cautiously. Felicia had done up her hair last night, but it hadn't occurred to Naya to try re-creating the look from memory.

Felicia grinned. "Excellent!"

A half hour later, Naya stepped into the hallway with her hair spun in an elaborate coil on the back of her head. She wasn't sure she could re-create the knot from scratch yet. But having watched Felicia create the style did make it easier to hold the image in her head and keep her hair from falling back into her usual braid or loose curls.

Most of the other delegates were already gathered near the stairs. Naya paused at the edge of the group, and after a moment Francisco came to join her. He was dressed in a fresh suit and walked with the quick steps of someone impatient to be elsewhere. Despite that, he looked exhausted. The skin under his eyes was puffy, and Naya saw him wince when a door slammed farther down the hall. "Good morning, Miss Garth," he said.

Naya smiled politely. She wasn't sure exactly where they stood after last night's conversation, but at least his tone wasn't as confrontational as it had been before. "Please, just call me Naya," she said.

"That wouldn't be very appropriate," Francisco said.

"Please?" Naya asked. "It's strange having so many people call me by my father's name." At first in Ceramor it had felt like treason to shed her old name. But in a way, it had also been freeing. As Naya Garth, she'd been a merchant's apprentice who'd kept her head down and done as her father said. But Blue had been so much braver. She'd danced across rooftops and fallen in love with a boy who shaped molten fire with his bare hands.

She couldn't be Blue anymore. Blue had died the day she told

Corten the truth. Naya wasn't sure exactly who she was now, but she knew *Miss Garth* didn't fit the person she'd become.

Francisco watched her, and for a moment the tense lines of his face seemed to soften. "Naya, then," he said.

Four soldiers waited at the end of the hall to escort the delegates to the first meeting of the Congress of Powers. "Excuse me, Miss Garth?" one of them said as Naya approached with the others.

Naya tensed. "Yes?"

The soldier stood parade-straight, staring at a point somewhere above her head. "The queen has requested you join her for tea."

Naya stared at the man, stunned. "Queen Lial wants to have tea with me?" Queen Lial was a devout follower of Dawning law. She wasn't as fervent as Naya's father had been, but the queen was still outspoken about the dangers of necromancy. Why in creation would she want to meet with a wraith?

"I am to escort you there now," the soldier said.

Naya heard murmurs from the other delegates. Delence clasped one hand on her shoulder. "Of course, Miss Garth would be delighted to join Her Majesty." He squeezed so hard Naya imagined it would have left bruises had she still been made of flesh and blood. She struggled to regain her composure.

"What about the meeting?" she asked. Regulations prevented any ruler from attending the Congress meetings in person. Since the other leaders couldn't abandon their lands to join the debates, Queen Lial would be represented by a delegation of advisers and experts, just as the other three Powers were. But though the queen wasn't expected to be there, Naya had certainly been planning to attend.

"Don't be foolish, girl," Delence said with strained cheer. "We wouldn't insult Queen Lial by ignoring such a request. We'll do well enough without you."

Naya searched the aether. With Delence's hand on her shoulder, it wasn't hard to pick his energy out from the crowd. He was obviously annoyed, though whether that was at her or the queen, she couldn't be sure. The soldiers were farther away and harder to isolate among the energy of the delegates gathered in the hall. Their aether felt sharp and cold against her senses. They feared her, but so did almost every Talmiran who knew what she was.

The soldier who'd spoken first gestured for her to follow. Naya scanned the aether as they walked but didn't find anything out of the ordinary as the soldier led her around the edge of the palace's central circle and then to what proved to be a miniature version of the huge dock lifts. Rich carpet covered the floor of the lift, and the ceiling was decorated in a star pattern that mirrored the one in the grand ballroom. The soldier followed her inside, then pulled a small lever. Runes drew aether, and soon the lift began its ascent.

They rose slowly until the soldier turned the lever back and opened the doors. Naya blinked against a sudden rush of sunlight, struggling for a moment to reconcile what she was seeing. A green-and-blue-tiled walkway wound from the lift's doors to disappear among lush foliage and bright flowers. The room's ceiling was made entirely of glass, the huge panels bounded by a metal frame that looked too insubstantial for Naya's comfort.

Faint, strange music sounded from somewhere beyond the lush greenery. Naya closed her eyes. The aether drifting from the plants felt cool and soothing after the flood of harsh emotions that had surrounded her ever since she'd returned to Talmir. Combined with the rich smells of damp earth and growing things, it made her want to curl up and doze in the sun. Reluctantly she pushed the urge aside. She couldn't imagine why Queen Lial would summon her. But whatever the reason, it would be best to keep her wits sharp.

She followed the soldier around the corner to where the path opened up. Fruit trees and beds of flowers formed a half circle around a delicate table laden with tea and sweets. The wall at the edge of the circle was made of the same glass as the ceiling, offering an incredible view of the city.

Queen Lial sat at the table with the two Endran ambassadors, who were dressed in simpler variants of the flowing pants and tunics they'd worn the night before. Naya recognized Ambassador Bargal from their brief conversation. His companion was a woman with short red-brown hair and striking features. She looked younger than Bargal and wore an impassive expression as she watched a trio of Endran musicians play next to the table. Their instruments were pipes of some sort, each one a slightly different length and shape.

Their music rose and fell in a slow, mournful melody. Naya paused at the edge of the clearing, not wanting to interrupt. Through the aether she could sense the sharp anticipation of soldiers standing guard somewhere nearby.

The song concluded and Ambassador Bargal turned to the queen. "What do you think of our people's music?"

"It is lovely," Queen Lial answered with a smile. "Truly. I think there is much we can learn from each other."

"I agree," Bargal said with a deep nod. "We've stayed separate for far too long." He glanced over as though noticing Naya for the first time. "But forgive me, you have another guest."

The queen turned to Naya, and her smile was replaced by a cool expression. "Ah, yes. Business calls. Ambassadors, I'm afraid I must speak to this young woman alone."

Naya stood awkwardly to the side as the musicians tucked away their instruments and the two ambassadors rose and bowed to the queen. Ambassador Bargal didn't so much as glance at Naya as he and the others brushed past her—strange after he'd been so eager to speak to her the night before.

"Please, have a seat," Queen Lial said.

Naya pushed Bargal from her mind and turned to face the

queen of Talmir. Queen Lial sat watching Naya over the rim of a porcelain teacup. She wore a high-collared gown of light green with a skirt cut to display its many silken layers. Tiny aether lights woven into the fabric highlighted the subtle color changes among the different skirts.

The queen's dark hair tumbled artfully from a twisting knot at her neck, and she sat with an air of casual elegance that made Naya feel homely and awkward by comparison. The bones in her hand throbbed as she fought down the sudden image of her hair exploding back out into a snarl of curls. Instead, she willed herself to be the calm, elegant girl she'd seen in her dressing room mirror that morning.

"Thank you, Your Majesty." Naya dipped a low curtsy, then sat in the ironwork chair across from the queen. She tried to keep her expression pleasantly neutral, even though a part of her wanted to sprint back to the rune lift. The woman sitting across from her could have her executed at a word. She could claim Naya had tried to attack her. Creator, she might not need any excuse at all.

Queen Lial took a sip of her tea. "You're wondering why I asked you here," she said.

"Yes, Your Majesty."

The queen's eyebrows rose a fraction. "How very polite. Though I can see from your eyes that you're not at all pleased to be here."

Naya blinked. "Your Majesty, I—"

"No. Please don't bother making excuses. I hear more than enough of those as it is. Your unease is understandable, so let me make a few things clear before we continue our conversation. I am aware of the circumstances that led you to be what you are. I know you were not a willing participant in Valn's schemes, and while Talmiran law makes it very clear you are no longer a citizen, I'm happy to leave any questions about your soul for the

Creator to sort out." She paused and looked intently at Naya as though expecting an answer.

"Thank you?" Naya said after an awkward silence. She wasn't sure if she should feel impressed or insulted by the declaration. On the one hand, many Talmirans would dismiss her as a monster. It meant something significant that the queen was willing to speak to her like this. On the other hand, she was the *queen*. She could change the laws about undead citizenship or speak in favor of peace and reconciliation between Talmir and Ceramor. She hadn't, which made her comments about Naya's soul little more than a condescending attempt to win her gratitude.

Anger won out and stirred like a hungry beast in Naya's chest. She drew in aether and fought to quash it. She didn't know what was going on here, but she couldn't risk doing anything rash, not if she wanted to leave the garden alive.

The queen watched her with a knowing smile, then selected a red-and-white cookie from the plate next to the teapot. She took a bite, the brittle sweet snapping audibly in the silence. "You're welcome. Now, let us speak about Belavine. As I understand things, you saw a great deal of the traitor's plans."

The queen's gaze was intent, her golden-brown eyes glittering with a focus that seemed to drill straight through her former subject.

Naya looked down at her folded hands. She didn't have a heart to pound, but the tension humming in her chest felt liable to shake her apart all the same. "I'm sorry, Your Majesty. Lord Delence made it clear I wasn't to answer any questions about that until the trial."

Queen Lial waved the comment away with a dismissive gesture. "Lord Delence isn't here. And quite frankly I am not convinced he's been entirely honest in his reports."

"But you think I will be?" Naya asked, unable to keep the disbelief from her voice.

"Perhaps. After all, he hasn't been honest with you either."

"What do you mean?" Naya drew in aether, trying to figure out if the queen was lying. But the little lights in the queen's skirt were sucking up her aether. Between that and the aether drifting from the plants, it was hard to get a clear read on her emotions.

"I wonder, did Lord Delence tell you I had been planning to withdraw Valn from his position shortly before the Belavine incident?"

"I—no, Your Majesty," Naya said.

"I thought not. And I assume he's told you that I am the true mastermind behind Valn's scheme?"

"He's never said that," Naya said. That much at least wasn't a lie. Though Delence clearly believed the queen was behind the coup, he'd been careful to avoid saying so outright.

The queen smiled thinly, as though she saw right through the avoidance. "Well, be that as it may, he has made it clear through his actions that he suspects me. He refuses to trust any evidence I offer to the contrary or to work with me in uncovering the truth."

"What truth would that be?" Naya leaned forward. She wasn't sure what game Queen Lial was trying to play here. But if the queen was willing to discuss what she knew of Valn, that wasn't an opportunity Naya could pass up.

Queen Lial set down her teacup. For a moment she seemed lost in thought. "Do you know what I love, Miss Garth? Numbers. Numbers are so much clearer and more honest than people. Often they reveal the little truths that people try to hide. I like to know the truth, so I make a point of always reviewing the kingdom's financial reports. And in those reports, I found certain numbers regarding Valn's expenditures that seemed a little too tidy to be real. I suspected something was going on at his embassy, but I had no idea of the scale until I heard the news from Ceramor."

Naya sat quietly and listened with growing unease.

"The bribes Lord Delence claims were paid to Ceramoran

officials represent a substantial amount of money, especially when you consider the added funds needed to supply and ensure the loyalty of Valn's spy network. I've searched my accounts but so far found no indication where that money might have come from. Do you know what that means, Miss Garth?"

"That you need better accountants?" Naya asked.

The queen's expression darkened and Naya cursed herself for not thinking before speaking. "It means," Queen Lial said sharply, "that someone is lying to me. If that money left Talmir, then my numbers should show some sign of its passing. They don't. So either someone inside my government or the guilds is working very hard to hide their traitorous donations, or the money didn't come from Talmir."

Naya realized her hands had curled into fists around the fabric of her skirt. She forced her fingers to relax. "Who else would pay to start a coup in Ceramor?" she asked.

"Who else indeed?" Queen Lial asked with a smile. "It seems strange that Delence is so insistent on ignoring my offers of help, especially given how much he has benefited from Valn's actions."

"That's—" Naya snapped her mouth shut. She could tell from the lines of tension around the queen's eyes that she'd already pushed her luck. Calling the queen a liar to her face did not seem like a good idea. "I'm not sure what all this has to do with me, Your Majesty."

"It has everything to do with you. After all that happened to you in Belavine, I believe you have very good reasons to want to see Valn's allies exposed. So why don't you and I have a nice little talk, and perhaps between your experiences and my numbers, we can find the truth."

Naya leaned back in her chair. She and Delence had both assumed Queen Lial had supported Valn's plans from the start. What if they'd been wrong? Valn's allies could be anyone. They might not even be in Talmir. Lucia's journals could be on the other side of the world.

Naya felt her thoughts spiraling toward panic as the queen stared at her. "I can't help you," she said, hating the waver in her voice. Even if Queen Lial was telling the truth, Naya wouldn't risk giving her any information. She had too many secrets. One wrong word could expose her as a reaper. And there was a chance this was all a trap, a way for the queen to probe and find out exactly how much Delence did or didn't know about her involvement with Valn.

The queen picked up another cookie and examined it. "That's a shame," she said. "Especially given your circumstances. I heard you had some trouble on your way into the palace."

Anger surged in Naya's chest. She had risen halfway from her chair before she realized what she was doing. When she did, she sensed a sharp pull through the aether as the guards hiding among the plants readied wraith eaters. Queen Lial continued to watch her, unmoving. Naya shuddered, then eased herself slowly back to a sitting position. Creator, what had happened to staying in control? "Some trouble?" she asked in a voice that was marginally calmer than she felt. "We were attacked. And your guards weren't exactly helpful."

The queen shrugged. "I am willing to overlook the details of your condition. Unfortunately, most of my people are not so open-minded. But . . . they might be more willing to accept you if you were seen helping clear the good name of Talmir."

"And if not?" Naya asked.

The queen took another bite of her cookie. She chewed thoughtfully, then dabbed at the corner of her mouth with a perfectly white napkin. "If not, then who knows what might happen."

CHAPTER 19

NAYA

Naya's hands shook as one of the soldiers escorted her out of the queen's garden. Queen Lial's threat still rang in her ears. Her chest burned with the memory of the small, confident smile the queen had given her—a smile that seemed to say she was certain Naya would bend to her wishes.

Well, she wouldn't. Queen Lial might think she was being generous by lowering herself to sit at the same table as one of the undead Talmir so despised. But her condescending attitude had almost been worse than the open hate in the eyes of the crowd that had attacked Naya.

After riding the lift back to the first floor, Naya asked the soldiers escorting her to let her into the Congress meeting. They refused, ignoring her arguments and insisting the meeting wasn't to be disrupted once it had begun. She considered trying to sneak in, but the risk and effort didn't seem worthwhile. The only part of the meeting she really cared about was the discussion deciding the final details of Valn's trial. She could get notes on those details from Francisco or Delence once they were done.

She was nearly back to the Ceramoran delegation's hall when a familiar voice stopped her. "Naya?"

Naya turned and was surprised to see Mel standing at the end of the hall with a folder tucked under one arm. "What are you doing here?" Mel asked. "I would have thought you'd be at the meetings."

Naya glanced at the soldier beside her. "I was planning on it, but the queen decided she wanted to talk with me and we only just got done."

"Queen Lial?" Mel asked, sounding surprised. "Why? I mean no offense, but I've heard she wasn't exactly keen on having you here."

"I—she was curious about me, I think," Naya said. Mentally, she cursed herself. The reason sounded implausible, even to her. But somehow it didn't seem smart to tell the daughter of a Talmiran delegate that the queen had threatened her. She probably shouldn't have even mentioned the meeting.

"Queen Lial curious about the undead. Now that is curious!" Mel smiled, then wrinkled her nose. "Sorry, that sounded much better in my head."

"What are you doing here?" Naya asked, eager to change the subject.

"Nothing exciting. Just picking up some documents that one of the Banian delegates wants my mother to look through later." Mel's expression brightened. "Anyway, you're lucky you missed the start of the meeting. From what I've heard, it's going to be hours of speeches and people arguing over the rules about who's allowed to discuss what when. And seeing as how you now have a perfectly excellent excuse to avoid all that, why don't you and I go out and find some lunch? I know a place a few blocks from here that has the best fried polle."

"Oh, um . . ." Naya's chest ached with a sharp sense of loss. Fried polle had always been one of her favorites, a mix of sweet potatoes, spices, and meat all wrapped in a crisp pastry shell. Before her mother had died, they'd gone together every year to the Founding Day celebration in the central square outside the palace. Naya remembered sitting at a table near the edge of a crowd of dancers, popping fresh pastries into her mouth. She'd eaten so many she'd felt sure her stomach would burst. There'd been a simple joy to the way taste and texture had blended together. That was one more thing she'd lost when Valn had decided she'd be more useful as a wraith than as a living girl. "Thank you," Naya said, struggling to hold back the tide of conflicting emotions. "But I don't eat."

Mel looked confused, then she covered her mouth with one hand. "I'm so sorry. I didn't mean to . . . I mean, I guess I forgot."

"It's okay," Naya said, not meeting Mel's eyes. "I should probably be going."

"Right. Of course," Mel said. "Well, I guess I'll see you around?"

"Sure," Naya said, feeling suddenly tired. Mel's reaction shouldn't have bothered her. Mel had been far kinder than she'd expected from any of the Talmirans. But good intentions couldn't change the sting of how badly out of place Naya felt in her former homeland.

The delegation's hall was near-empty when Naya returned, most everyone still out at the meeting. That was probably for the best. Delence would want to hear about her encounter with the queen, and Naya was not looking forward to reliving that particular conversation. She sat in her desk chair, running one finger along the smiling beak of Corten's glass bird. "Was I mad to come here?" she whispered.

Alejandra had called Lucia's plan a false hope. She thought what they were trying to do was impossible. Why shouldn't she? According to every record Naya had ever seen, no one had been brought back after a failed resurrection since the rediscovery of the necromancy runes more than fifty years ago.

Naya squeezed her eyes shut. Maybe she would fail. But Corten's absence was like a hole in her chest. She couldn't shake the feeling that she'd been somehow a better person when he was around. Corten had made her laugh when she'd felt like her entire life was over. He'd followed her into a burning building. Even after she'd lied to him so many times, he'd followed her, forgiven her. If she gave up now, it would be a betrayal far worse than any she'd ever committed.

Naya sighed, setting aside the glass bird, and retrieved her father's logbook and her notes on the cipher. Valn was still her strongest lead. But unless she got lucky, she wouldn't get the chance to speak to him until the Congress brought him forward for his trial.

After about an hour, her eyes caught on one of the longer entries in the logbook.

V says he found a solution to our funding problems. Good news. My accounts are running low and it seems every week V's requirements grow. Am relieved that the plan will not slow, but V's secrecy is concerning. Wouldn't reveal anything about our new ally. Whoever it is must be wealthy and very well connected. V thinks we can accelerate the plan, and tensions in the city suggest his influence is growing. Can see the hunger in his eyes when he speaks. Knew going in that his motives were tainted, but I fear this new "ally" has stoked his ambitions even further. Who else could have such an interest in our cause? Why does he keep their identity a secret? Does he doubt my loyalty?

Naya flipped forward and skimmed a few more entries.

Resurgence. Is it the code name of a person, or a group? Either way, suspect this is the source of V's new funding and confidence.

She found two more mentions of Resurgence, the second dated just a little before she and her father had last sailed to Ceramor. Whoever or whatever it was, it seemed to have been key in establishing the network of spies and bribed officials Valn had tried to use to take over Ceramor. There were more hints throughout the journal about her father's growing suspicions. He'd mistrusted Valn's new allies and suspected the ambassador was trying to isolate him from the core of the plan he'd helped build.

He'd been at least partially right. Valn had lied to her father about his plans for Naya, and her father's writings gave no hint that he'd known about the war runes or Lucia. Naya tapped her pen against the desk. *Resurgence.* Would Queen Lial recognize that name, or Delence? The queen had seemed certain that Valn's finances could be used to track his allies. If Resurgence was the source of those funds, then perhaps it also held the key to finding Lucia's journals.

Naya tucked the logbook away in her desk, then gathered up her notes and her satchel and headed back out into the hall. She had to figure out what the name meant.

The others still hadn't returned, but Naya could sense aether coming from the rooms assigned to Lucia. She wasn't surprised to find Lucia hadn't gone to the meeting. Even if the delegates would have welcomed the opinions of a necromancer, which Naya very much doubted, Lucia had no stomach for politics. She hadn't even attended the queen's feast.

Lucia opened the door at Naya's knock. "Is the meeting over already?" she asked as she stood aside to let Naya into her rooms.

Naya shook her head. "I didn't go. Queen Lial sent someone to summon me just before it started."

Lucia pushed her glasses up her nose. "Well, that's surprising. You seem to have come out of it unharmed at least. What did she want from you?"

"Information, I think. Anyway, that's not why I came." She quickly explained what she'd found in the logbook.

"Interesting," Lucia said, her voice musing. "I've never heard of anyone calling themselves Resurgence. But if such a group was funding Valn, then it suggests he really didn't have the support of the throne. Why go to them if he could draw funds from Queen Lial's treasury?"

"Maybe," Naya said, frustrated. "Or Resurgence was just a code name Valn used to hide the identity of his government contacts."

Lucia's brow wrinkled. "Hmm."

"What?" Naya asked.

Lucia shook her head. "I think we're looking at this wrong. I've been trying to imagine who in Talmir would have had both the means and the incentive to recover my journals. It would have been risky, and it wasn't as though they could have expected to use the runes for anything once they had them. Unless . . ." Lucia trailed off, her expression growing distant.

"Unless what?"

Lucia paced between the window and the door. "How much do you know about the creation of the wraith eaters?"

"Not much," Naya admitted.

Lucia nodded. "Wraith eaters only started appearing near the end of the Mad King's War. By then, the Talmiran rune scribes had been experimenting on captured undead for months, searching for a more effective way to kill them."

"That's awful," Naya said with a shudder.

Lucia's expression turned sad. "Yes. But maybe no more so than some of the things we did while searching for ways to resurrect more powerful undead." She was silent for a moment, her eyes distant and her aether dark.

Naya reached out and touched her hand, unsure what to say to offer comfort. Lucia had barely ever spoken of her time as an apprentice necromancer during the Mad King's War. But whatever Lucia had done or seen, she'd come out of it with a conviction to use necromancy for the good of others. Naya squeezed Lucia's hand, trying to convey through touch what she couldn't put into words.

Lucia started, then looked down at Naya's hand and offered her a strained smile. "But that was all long ago," she said with forced cheer. "Anyway, my point was that the Talmirans only learned to defeat the undead by studying necromancy themselves. And if you look at the bindings on a wraith eater, it's clear they rely on some of the same rune combinations we use for necromantic portals. Perhaps when the purges began, the Talmiran rune scribes decided to save some of the necromantic works they were supposed to destroy. There were plenty of people who thought the peace wouldn't last, and having access to those works would have made it easier to develop new weapons against the undead."

Naya grimaced. The wraith eaters were bad enough. She didn't want to think about what other weapons Talmir might have developed in secret preparation for another war. "If the scribes were involved, then any works they preserved would likely be somewhere in the Academy of Magics." The academy stood at the heart of all Talmiran magic. Only rune scribes trained and registered there could make and sell runic devices in Talmir. Naya's heart sank as she thought about the imposing walls that surrounded the academy's complex. "If that's the case, I don't know how we'll find your journals. It's not as though I can just show up at the academy gates and ask the scribes if they're hiding any forbidden texts on necromancy."

"Could you break in?" Lucia asked.

"I don't know. Maybe? Even then I wouldn't know where to start looking." She had no idea what sort of defenses the academy might have. And Delence had said the Talmirans would be watching her closely. They'd only grow more suspicious if she tried to leave the palace.

They sat in silence. Eventually Naya shook her head. "This

is all just speculation. I want to talk to Valn again before we make any plans. If I can ask him about Resurgence, maybe I can finally get some real answers."

Lucia pursed her lips. "Do you have a plan?"

Naya shook her head. "I'm still working on it. But wherever he is, they'll have to bring him out for the trial. I'll find a way to speak to him then."

CHAPTER 20

CORTEN

Corten sat on a stack of coiled rope with his back against the *Gull*'s mainmast. Beside him, Servala leaned on the port rail with her head tilted up and a smile on her lips. Darkness still lurked all around them, but the ship's aether lamps made it feel less oppressive than before.

Servala snapped her fingers. "Okay, next question. What'd you do for fun back in life?"

Corten shrugged. "I don't know. I used to study a lot."

"Studying is not fun," Servala said with a look of disgust.

Corten laughed. "It is if the books are interesting enough." He thought for a moment. "When I was younger, my brother and I would sometimes go swimming in a river by our house. After I moved to Belavine, I made friends with a few other necromancers and apprentices who would play cards together at the Bitter Dregs. And some nights I would climb up on the rooftops and watch the stars."

"I used to swim and play cards back with the *Gull*'s old crew," Servala said. "Stars are useful enough for navigating, but just looking at them doesn't sound like much fun."

"I guess it depends on the company," Corten said, remembering the soft smile that would spread across Naya's face as she stared up at the sky.

Servala leaned forward. "Company, eh? And who's this lucky lad or lass who's got you looking all dewy?"

Corten's face flushed. "Her name's Naya. But anyway, what about you? What did you do for fun?"

"Nope," Servala said with a grin. "My ship. I'm the one who gets to ask the questions, remember? So this Naya, you miss her, huh?"

"Of course I do," Corten said uneasily. Servala's questions were starting to sound more like demands.

"Well, maybe she'll show up here someday."

"Don't say that!" Corten snapped, surprised by the sudden heat in his voice.

Servala's eyes widened, then her expression hardened into anger. "You don't tell me what to do, boy, not here." The aether lamps flickered and the darkness surrounding the ship inched a little closer.

Corten shivered. "Sorry. Can we just talk about something else? I don't like thinking about her here." If Naya showed up here it would mean she'd died again. A part of him whispered that maybe that wouldn't be so bad. They'd be together. They could face the questions of the door together, just like they'd faced so many other dangers back in Belavine.

Corten clenched his fists, trying to drive the desire away. He didn't want Naya dead. He didn't want to see her again just to drag her through the door to that final death. He took several deep breaths, then looked up. Around him the aether lamps had brightened again, and Servala was smiling as though nothing had happened.

"Sure. Let's talk about something else," she said.

Corten tried to return her smile, but his unease continued to grow. He was beginning to suspect that Servala's ship wasn't the haven it had first seemed. Still, if she was mad, then her madness had to be better than that of the souls standing transfixed by the doorway. The conversation continued as Corten answered Servala's seemingly endless questions about the living world. Though she listened attentively to Corten's account of Valn's plots and the plight of the necromancers in Ceramor, her real interest clearly lay in the mundane details of day-to-day life. As Corten talked, he could feel the ship changing subtly around them. He described the bakery near Matius's shop, and a moment later the smells of fresh bread and cinnamon wafted across the deck of the ship. When he told Servala about the city's architecture, splashes of brighter color and carvings of vines appeared along the ship's railings.

The little touches of home bleeding into his surroundings should have been a comfort. Instead they left Corten feeling more unnerved than ever. The changes were a reminder that this place was little more than a fantasy.

"I'm running out of things to say," Corten said, trying to make the comment sound light. In truth, he felt as he had walking toward the door, as if something vital were trickling away from him with each story he told.

"I'm sure you can think of more," Servala said. "What about your brother? You've barely talked about him. Or this Naya girl. Tell me what she's like. Is she pretty? Did you two . . ." Servala trailed off and made a suggestive gesture with both hands.

Heat crawled up Corten's neck and into his face. "That's none of your business."

Before Servala could respond, a gust of cold wind blasted across the deck of the ship. The rigging creaked, and in the distance Corten heard the howls of the scavengers echoing through the endless dark. "Corten Ballera!" a raspy voice called from beyond the ship.

Servala turned in the direction of the voice. Her eyes narrowed. "Oh, him again."

Corten rushed to the ship's railing. The shadow man stood

just a few feet away, floating in the air above the dark waters. As Corten looked around, those waves seemed to blend into windswept grass, creating an impossible landscape that made his head ache.

"So," the shadow man said, "this is where you chose to hide."

"I'm not hiding," Corten said.

"No? Then what do you hope to achieve sitting here on the threshold with the mad and the lost? You have seen what this place does. Do you mean to become like Servala? Or are you just another fly for her web?"

Corten's grip on the railing tightened and a shiver of fear danced down his spine. "Don't listen to him!" Servala said behind him. "That old bastard only ever wants one thing, and that's to send us through the door."

"I'm not hiding," Corten repeated. "And I'm not going through the door. I'm going to find a way back to life."

The shadow man shook his head. "There is no way back."

"Then I'll make one!" Corten shouted. He felt something flickering inside him, a flame of determination that had all but gone out. His fear grew. Sitting here with Servala might feel safer than facing the darkness, but it wasn't getting him any closer to his goals. And somehow he knew that if he waited too long, the flame inside him would die. He would become like all the others standing around the door—a husk.

Corten turned and started walking across the deck. "Where are you going?" Servala asked, scrambling to her feet.

"I don't know yet," Corten said.

"You can't leave!"

Corten didn't see her move, but suddenly Servala was standing in front of him. "Stay," she said more softly, pressing her hand to his chest. "There's nothing left to you out there. They've all forgotten you by now. But I won't forget you. Stay with me, and we can make our own world." Her features flickered, her hair tumbling into brown curls and her face softening into almost familiar lines. *Naya?* Corten thought.

His heart stuttered in his chest. He slapped Servala's hand aside and stumbled away. "No!" The ship wavered and again he felt the crushing weight of darkness. But with it came realization. *Are you just another fly for her web?* "You said none of the others could see your ship," Corten said. "That was a lie, wasn't it?"

"I don't know what you're talking about." Servala's tone was still pleading. But now her eyes shifted with the desperate look of a cornered animal.

Corten edged backward as the pieces clicked together in his mind. He'd felt increasingly exhausted as he'd talked to Servala, even as she'd grown more animated, more demanding in her questions. "You've been feeding off of me," he said, and he knew from the flash of guilt in her eyes that it was true. Anger lent him a fresh burst of energy. "The others waiting by the door, how many of them are like that because of you? You've stolen something from them. Why? Just so you can keep waiting out here?"

Servala flinched. "It isn't like that!" she said. "I've only done what I had to. They were weak. I needed something to keep me going. You've felt the door's pull. There's something wrong with it. Everything about this place is wrong. I had to fight it. I had to keep myself strong."

Corten kept inching backward until he felt the press of the ship's railing. Something brushed his leg and he looked down in horror as a thick length of rope snaked tight around his ankles, binding him. Servala took a step toward him, one hand outstretched. "Please, stay with me," she begged. "You're resilient, and you're smart. I'll teach you how to draw the energy. Maybe together we can even do what you said. We'll sail the *Gull* away from here and find a way back into life."

Corten hesitated, feeling the allure of her offer twine round him like the rope. Escaping death wouldn't be easy. He was deluding himself if he thought he had the strength to do it alone. Maybe this was the only way.

"No," Corten said through clenched teeth. "Not like this." He didn't intend to give in to death, but he also couldn't let himself become like her. The rope around his legs felt like a band of iron securing him to the deck. Servala's face twisted with rage. She reached for him, and Corten was sure that if he let her touch him again, she would gobble up whatever spark of life was left in him. He reached down and grasped the rope, calling up memories of the relentless heat of the glassblowing furnaces he'd worked with for so many long hours. Curls of white smoke drifted up, then the rope burst into flames.

Servala screamed as though she were the one burning. The rope went slack and Corten kicked it away. Servala lunged for him. The tips of her fingers brushed his shirt as he shoved himself up and back, his whole body screaming with terror as he plummeted over the rail and down, down toward the rolling waves below.

CHAPTER 21

NAYA

Naya returned to her rooms after her conversation with Lucia. A few hours later, she sensed aether swirling outside her door and heard the murmur of excited voices. The meeting must finally be over. When she peeked out into the hall, she was surprised to find Francisco standing just outside with one hand raised to knock. He took a quick step back. "Good, you're here. My father wants to speak with you," he said.

"Now?" Naya asked. She'd expected him to summon her, just not so quickly.

"No, next week. Of course now."

Naya gave Francisco a flat look before following him toward his father's rooms. His clothes weren't so neat as they had been that morning, and his expression was distant.

"Did something happen at the meeting?" Naya asked.

Francisco shook his head. "Nothing unexpected."

"Then why do you look like you want to punch someone?"

Francisco stopped and scowled at her. Naya gestured toward his hands and the crumpled papers he held in a death grip. He looked surprised as he eased his grip and made a half-hearted effort to smooth out the papers. "Why is everything about violence with you?" he asked.

"That's not an answer."

Francisco sighed, then rubbed the bridge of his nose. "Nothing went wrong exactly. It's just been a long day. If you want the details, ask my father, or get the notes from one of the scribes."

Unease tightened Naya's stomach as Francisco knocked softly on Delence's door. "I've brought her," he said as he opened the door.

"Good, thank you. Why don't you go back to your rooms and rest," Delence replied.

Francisco's shoulders tensed. "Shouldn't I—"

"Rest," Delence repeated. "The Banians are hosting an after-dinner salon in two hours. I'll need you sharp for that."

"Yes, Father." Francisco stepped away from the door. Before leaving he met Naya's eyes. He had a strange look on his face, and for a second Naya thought he wanted to say something more. Then he turned and walked briskly away down the hall.

Naya stepped into Delence's room and shut the door behind her. Delence stood by the window on the far side of the room, his back facing her. "Tell me about your meeting with Queen Lial," he said without preamble, making the words a command rather than a question.

Naya felt something inside her snap at his tone. "Oh, the meeting was just lovely," she said, letting all her frustration and impatience leak out in exaggerated sweetness. "We drank tea and talked about numbers."

Delence glared at her. "I assume you're joking."

His tone was a warning, but Naya couldn't help a bubble of slightly hysterical glee that rose in her throat. She swallowed it with effort. "Well, I guess I didn't actually drink the tea, seeing as how I don't have a body to put it in. But the queen really did spend quite a while telling me how much she loves numbers. After that, she all but threatened to have me killed if I didn't help her track down Valn's real allies. Oh, and she also implied that you won't help her with the investigation because you're trying to set her up."

Delence's lip twisted in a scowl before he regained control of his expression. "Absurd, but not surprising. I suspect this was her way of trying to bypass the laws that keep her from participating directly in the Congress. She's no doubt hoping to manipulate your testimony. I trust you didn't tell her anything?"

"Nothing important, but she did tell me something interesting."

"What?" Delence asked.

"She said she'd been planning to replace Valn even before she heard what happened in Ceramor. Do you know if that's true?"

Delence shook his head. "She's made that claim before. It's an obvious fabrication to hide her involvement. Was there anything else?"

Naya started to shake her head, then paused. "One thing. The Endran ambassadors were there when I arrived. They seemed to be on good terms with the queen."

Delence's expression darkened. "Another threat then."

"What do you mean?" Naya asked.

"I suspect Queen Lial is hoping to make an alliance with the Endrans as an alternative to the Congress of Powers."

"You think she'd abandon the Congress?" The prospect was unsettling, but Naya couldn't see how leaving would benefit Talmir.

"I doubt she'll go that far, but she is making a show of her connection with the Endrans. She wants us to know that she's exploring other options, and that Talmir can remain strong even without the Congress."

Naya's brow furrowed. "She might be disappointed. I spoke to Ambassador Bargal after the feast and he seemed eager to learn more about necromancy."

Delence's eyes lit up. "Is that so? Tell me what happened."

Naya described her brief encounter with the ambassador, and the way he'd ignored her in the queen's garden. Delence paced back and forth across the room as she spoke. "This changes things. I want you to set up a meeting with the Endrans. Answer their questions about necromancy and try to figure out what dealings they've had so far with Queen Lial. If they're interested in you, perhaps we can use that to upset whatever Queen Lial has planned."

Naya stood torn between excitement and unease. "Why not have Francisco talk to them? He's been studying the Congress longer than I have, and I know he'd like to play a bigger role in your work." Also if Francisco was busy dealing with the Endrans, he was less likely to bother her while she searched for Lucia's journals.

"You can bring him with you, but you're the one they approached. Better that we not risk giving offense by sending someone else."

"All right," Naya said reluctantly. "I'll see what I can learn. Could you have one of the scribes send me their notes from today's meeting?" Those notes would hopefully contain any new details about the schedule for Valn's trial.

"Talk to Vanessia. She's coordinating records between the scribes, so she can get you whatever you need."

Naya nodded, then started for the door.

"One more thing," Delence said. "Francisco told me about the logbook you found on the *Gallant*. He convinced me that it will be fastest to let you handle the translation. But once you're done, I want you to hand over a full copy of everything you've found, along with the original book."

Naya fought down a grimace. It had probably been too much to hope that Francisco would keep quiet. "I'll give you the translation, but the book belonged to my father. I don't see why I have to give it to you."

"Because I'll want someone else to check your work. Also, it could prove useful as leverage in the future," Delence said.

"Leverage against who?" Naya asked.

"That depends on what you find," Delence said with a cold smile.

CHAPTER 22

NAYA

The chief scribe curtly informed Naya that copies of the meeting notes wouldn't be ready for a few hours yet. Naya returned to her rooms, nervous energy buzzing through her as she considered her next move. Her thoughts circled back to her earlier conversation with Lucia. Lucia's guess that someone at the Academy of Magics might have kept her journals after the Mad King's War made sense. The years following the war had been turbulent, and more than a few people had assumed the treaties would fail. Naya wouldn't be surprised to learn that the Talmiran rune scribes had continued their weapons programs in secret.

Naya crossed to her desk, then pulled out a fresh sheet of paper and a pen. Lucia had said Valn's supporters might not be a part of the Talmiran government. But runic magic was more tightly regulated in Talmir than in Ceramor. Someone powerful in the government, or at the Academy of Magics, must have been helping Valn.

Naya's throat felt tight as she thought about the cloud of unanswered questions looming over her. She closed her eyes and drew in aether, trying to smother her emotions under the hum of outside energy. She couldn't answer all those questions yet, but she had an idea that would at least let her get out of the palace for a few hours to gather information. She wrote two notes, one to Mel and one to the Endran ambassadors. Naya sealed the notes, then sent Felicia to deliver them.

"I spoke to Miss Jeden," Felicia said once she got back. "She seemed quite excited. Said she'd be happy to join you for an outing tomorrow and that she'd organize the transportation. You're to meet her by the front palace gates at ten o'clock tomorrow morning. If that's all right?"

"That's perfect," Naya said. There would be no Congress meetings tomorrow, giving the delegations time to finalize preparations for Valn's trial. "What about Ambassador Bargal?"

Felicia's smile fell. "I tried to deliver it personally like you asked, but the servant I talked to said the ambassadors were out." She wrinkled her nose. "He was rude about it too. I expect that from the Talmirans, no offense, but I don't see what cause some Endran servant has to be looking down his nose at me."

"Maybe he didn't mean it. I'd guess their ways are different from ours," Naya said, remembering her conversation with Reial back on the *Gallant*. He'd said when their last ship had traded in Endra, they hadn't even been allowed into the city.

Felicia shook her head. "Rude is rude. Doesn't matter where you're from. I'll keep an eye out to see if they send anything back. You're going with Francisco to the salon tonight, right? Do you want help getting ready?"

Right. Tonight would be the first in a series of social events hosted by the different delegations. "I think I'll be fine," Naya said, and then an idea struck her. Every delegation would send at least a few representatives to the salon. Would the Endrans be there as well? After the queen had shown them favor at the inaugural ball, everyone would probably be aching with curiosity to find out what they were doing in Talmir. This could be her opportunity to speak to them. "Actually, would you mind waiting here just a minute?" she asked Felicia.

Felicia tilted her head curiously. "Sure, but what—"

"Thanks. I'll be right back." Naya jogged across the hall and knocked on Lucia's door.

"What is it?" Lucia asked as she opened the door.

"There's a party tonight Francisco and I have to attend. Would you like to come with us?"

Lucia's eyes widened. "Why in creation would I do that?"

"Why not? It doesn't seem fair that you should have to spend the entire Congress locked up in here."

"Thank you, but after what happened at the gates, I'm happy to do exactly that."

Naya shook her head. "That sort of thing will keep happening if we don't show everyone here that we're people, same as they are."

Perhaps she was wrong, but Naya's instincts told her that Mel's kindness was more than half-genuine. She'd said Naya was the first undead she'd ever met. That would be true for most people who lived outside of Ceramor. They based their opinions on stories that still echoed with fear from the Mad King's War. But if the daughter of a Talmiran ambassador could break free from those fears, then others could too.

"Are you feeling all right?" Lucia asked, still looking dubious.

Naya smiled. "I'm fine, and I think this is an opportunity we shouldn't pass up. There's someone you should talk to and I think he might come to the salon." She gave Lucia a quick summary of her most recent encounter with the Endrans. As she spoke, Lucia's expression turned thoughtful.

"It would be fascinating to hear their opinions on necromancy. I've heard rumors of Endran magic, but never anything concrete," Lucia said once Naya had finished.

"Perfect," Naya said. "I'll go get Felicia."

Two hours later Naya and Lucia stood next to a visibly irritated Francisco, just outside the rooms appointed for the

Banian salon. At Felicia's suggestion, Naya wore a yellow dress decorated in geometric patterns, with ribbons of the same color woven in her hair. Lucia's dress was simpler, but that simplicity turned to elegance when paired with a few choice pieces of jewelry Felicia had selected from Naya's chests.

"I still think this is a bad idea," Francisco grumbled. He'd left his suit jacket behind in favor of a deep-blue vest and white shirt cut to hide his tattoos. Even tense and grumpy, Naya had to admit there was a lean elegance to the way he moved that reminded her of actors on a stage.

Lucia was staring into the room full of brightly dressed delegates as though eyeing a pack of hungry wolves. "I agree," she said. "Why did I let you talk me into this?"

"It's just a party. You'll be fine," Naya said, trying to infuse her voice with a sense of confidence and cheer that she didn't feel. A part of her wanted to flee back to the safety of her rooms, but back there she wouldn't be able to do anyone any good.

Naya stepped into the room, hoping the others would follow. The Banian salon was more subdued than the elaborate ball Queen Lial had hosted the night before. Low chairs were arranged in circles around the room, with tables along the edges offering a wide array of finger foods and drinks. There was no dance floor this time and the room hummed with conversation.

That conversation sputtered when people spotted them. Naya ignored the whispers and stood on tiptoe, and after a moment she spotted Mel in conversation with a pair of young scribes from the Silmaran delegation.

"Come on," she said, grabbing Francisco's arm and directing him toward the group. They would need to find the Endrans eventually, but before that Naya wanted to say hello to Mel.

"Where—" Francisco began. Then he spotted Mel. "Naya, no."

But it was already too late. One of the Silmaran scribes looked over and smiled. "Lord Francisco!" he called. The speaker was a young, sandy-haired man with only a few narrow strips of embroidery along the sleeves of his suit jacket, marking him as a low-ranking member of the Silmaran bureaucracy. Naya recognized him vaguely from the night before, but couldn't set a name to his face. Mel met Naya's eyes and Naya thought she caught a hint of cool relief in her aether. She didn't have time to wonder what had caused it before Francisco bowed to the Silmaran scribe.

"Leori Avase, good to see you again," Francisco said.

"And you. My associate here is the honorable Jelvi Serini," Leori said, motioning to his companion.

Jelvi bowed. He had a round, friendly face and an air of almost jittery energy. The braid on his sleeves was thicker than Leori's and marked him as having at least one relative in the Silmaran senate. "Charmed. I've heard so much about you, Francisco, and your father of course."

"Only good things, I hope," Francisco said with a smile that Naya wouldn't have questioned if she hadn't seen the way he was scowling only a moment ago.

Jelvi laughed. "Something like that. I think we can agree that a man like your father cannot exist without sparking at least a few interesting rumors."

"What rumors would those be?" Francisco asked, his politeness turning a few degrees colder.

"It seems Jelvi is a collector of rumors," Mel said. "He was just telling us in overwhelming detail how he heard that your father personally stormed the Ceramoran palace to rescue King Allence from Valn and his allies. It sounds implausible the way he tells it, but even my mother has had to admit Lord Delence handled himself bravely, so I'm inclined to believe there's some truth to the account."

"Implausible? I'm sure you mean exciting," Jelvi said, reaching out to touch Mel's arm.

Francisco raised his eyebrows. "Ambassador Jeden called my father brave? Really?"

"Technically she might have said he's a foolish, reckless showoff, but really it means the same thing coming from her," Mel said, shifting her weight to move her arm farther from Jelvi's reach.

Leori cleared his throat. "Uh, Francisco, you've met Miss Mel Jeden, yes? And I don't think you've introduced us to your companions."

Francisco nodded, then introduced Naya and Lucia to the others.

"It's good to see you again, Naya," Mel said. "Tomorrow should be fun."

"Tomorrow?" Francisco asked.

"Mel and I are going out together tomorrow." Naya tried not to sound like she was admitting a guilty secret. She hadn't broken any rules by inviting Mel to spend the day with her. But given Francisco's mistrust of Mel and her mother, Naya knew he wouldn't approve.

"Going out, or going *out*?" Jelvi asked with a sharp smile. "Why, Miss Jeden, I didn't realize you and Miss Garth were so close. Could it be that your tastes are so bold as to tend toward the necrotic?"

"That's disgusting," someone said from behind Mel. The others shifted and Naya saw Sai standing a little way away, carrying a drink in each hand.

Mel forced a laugh. "*Necrotic* really isn't a very appealing word, is it?" She turned and made a show of looking Naya and Francisco up and down. "But to answer your question, I'm afraid my tastes trend toward the, ah, masculine, regardless of undead status."

"Alas, then I'm still lacking an explanation for why you refused my offer of dinner," Jelvi said. He'd probably meant his tone to sound playful, but there was an edge under it that Naya didn't like.

Naya frowned. Jelvi reminded her of some of the younger men her father had occasionally invited over to drink and discuss business. The worst of them was a man only a few years older than her. He'd developed a fondness for seeking her out for private chats. He'd rarely touched her, but the way he'd loomed over her, or let his fingers linger on her sleeve, told her he would have done much more if he didn't fear her father's anger. She opened her mouth to tell Jelvi off, but Francisco beat her to it.

"So the only explanation you could imagine was that she refused you because she's attracted to the undead? Do you hear how conceited that sounds?" Francisco glared openly at Jelvi.

The relief in Mel's aether flashed brighter. She took a step closer to Francisco and gave him an appraising look. "Well, at least his lack of imagination is giving ample opportunity for your better qualities to shine."

Sai made a sickened noise. "Honestly, Mel, how can you joke about these things?"

"Who said I'm joking?" Mel batted her eyelashes in such an obvious display that Naya had to fight back a snicker.

Sai shook her head, then turned away. "Disgusting," she said again.

"Why?" Naya asked, her tone sharper than she'd intended. She could feel attention focusing on them. Color had risen in Jelvi's round cheeks, and he was scowling back at Francisco while Leori looked distinctly uncomfortable.

Sai turned to Naya. "Because it's unnatural. You're both unnatural. The Naya Garth I knew was a good Talmiran girl. She never would have let herself become something like this."

"Like what?" Naya asked. "A monster? Is that what you think the undead are?"

Sai shook her head. "You're not even that," she said flatly. "You're just a tool for Talmir's enemies. Unnatural, and pathetic."

The words hit Naya like a slap. "You're wrong," she said, but Sai had already turned away and disappeared into the crowd.

"I think we should be going," Leori said loudly.

"But—" Jelvi began, then cut off as Leori elbowed him unsubtly in the ribs. Jelvi gave Mel one last look, then sighed. "Fine. Have fun playing with the corpses, Mel. I'm sure your mother will be delighted to hear about the company you're keeping."

The two of them beat a hasty retreat, leaving Mel, Naya, and Francisco standing awkwardly. All around them people very deliberately turned away, pretending they hadn't been listening in on the conversation.

"Well . . ." Lucia said drily. "They all seemed like charming people. I can see why you were so eager to have me come to this delightful gathering."

"This isn't why we're here," Francisco said through clenched teeth. "Come on."

He turned and stomped away.

"Wait—!" Mel began, then trailed off, exchanging an uncertain look with Naya.

Naya wanted to scream in frustration. Instead she said to Mel, "Sorry. I'll see you tomorrow," then followed Francisco.

She caught up to him near the edge of the room and grabbed his arm. "Hey," she said. "We shouldn't have just walked away like that. Mel was—"

"She was baiting us," Francisco said.

"Sai and Jelvi were the ones being insulting. I think Mel was just trying to make the best of it."

Francisco shook his head. "Just stay away from her. Whether it's intentional or not, she's obviously a magnet for trouble, and I've had enough of that for one night. Let's just find the Endrans and get out of here."

"Fine," Naya said. She still didn't agree with Francisco's assessment of the situation, but this wasn't the right place to have that argument.

CHAPTER 23

NAYA

The Banian salon was spread through a suite of connected rooms, so it took several minutes before Naya finally caught a glimpse of Ambassador Bargal's distinctive copper hair. She squeezed past a knot of delegates who were listening while Grand Marshal Palrak, the head of the Talmiran delegation, and his husband discussed the expansion of the rail lines into eastern Talmir. On the other side of the group, Naya found the Endran ambassadors talking quietly together next to one of the food tables. Ambassador Bargal noticed her and his face broke into a warm smile. "Ah, Miss Garth. And this must be Lord Francisco, and . . . forgive me, I don't know your other companion."

"Lucia Laroke." Lucia's eyes were bright with curiosity as she looked at the two ambassadors.

"A pleasure to meet you," Francisco said with a bow.

"And you. My companion is Ambassador Noreth," Bargal said, waving at the short-haired woman who stood beside him. "We were just talking about how we hoped to find you here. Isn't that right, Ambassador Noreth?"

"Yes. Great hopes we had," Noreth said. Her accent was far thicker than Bargal's, and her cool expression seemed to contradict her words.

"You got my invitation then?" Naya asked.

"Invitation?" Bargal glanced at his companion with a raised eyebrow. She said something to him in a language Naya didn't recognize, and he answered in the same before turning back to Naya. "Forgive me, the servants had not notified me yet. We have been so very busy these past days. But this only makes it doubly good fortune to have found you here."

"Naya told me you were interested in necromancy?" Francisco asked.

"She is correct," Bargal said. "Our queen has great respect for the old powers. And I myself would very much like to know what it is like to travel back from the darkness of the other side."

Naya glanced around, trying to judge if anyone had overheard that. Even in Ceramor people were cautious in the way they spoke about necromancy. What one saw on the other side of death was considered deeply personal, and few undead spoke about the experience.

If Francisco was perturbed by the ambassador's curiosity, it didn't show on his face. "We're happy to answer questions. Madame Laroke is a necromancer, so she can provide more details than we can."

"A necromancer?" Bargal's eyes lit up. He turned to Lucia and bowed more deeply. "Forgive me, my lady, I did not realize. I have heard your kind call the dead with the strength of your voice and will alone. Such power is to be honored."

Lucia blinked, obviously startled by Bargal's reaction. "Well, it's more complicated than that, but the song is an important part of our rituals."

"Of course, all magic has its complexities," Bargal said. "If you ever wish to travel east, please know you would be warmly welcomed. My queen's scholars would be eager to exchange knowledge with you."

Naya felt a shiver of unease and turned her attention to the aether, trying to read the ambassador. His enthusiasm for necromancy seemed out of place compared to the way he'd acted around Queen Lial. What game was he playing? As she focused on him, she noticed the strange pattern in his aether. Energy concentrated around his wrists rather than drifting to mingle with the already-thick aether of the room.

"I'm sure if you wished it, my father could also arrange for you to visit Ceramor," Francisco said to Bargal, his eager tone drawing Naya's attention back to the physical world.

Bargal smiled. "We do hope to see all your fine western kingdoms soon." He turned his attention to Naya. "Tell me, Miss Garth. Did your meeting with the queen go well? We have been told that your lands are in conflict, but perhaps we misunderstood if she is inviting you to tea."

"Things between Talmir and Ceramor are complicated," Naya said cautiously. The last thing she wanted was to try and explain the tensions between the two countries. "But there's been peace for thirty years now."

"Ah, I understand," Bargal said. "Old feuds are many in our homeland, but all that is behind us now that Her Great Majesty Queen Alethen the first has united us."

"So all the city-states now follow one ruler?" Francisco asked.

"We do. Her Majesty is not one to be denied. What else could we do but bow to her will and set aside our differences?"

Naya exchanged a glance with Francisco. She wasn't sure how many city-states populated the Endran plains. But everything she'd heard made it seem unlikely they would unite so suddenly.

Someone bumped into Naya hard enough to make her stumble. Behind her a woman cried out. Naya turned to see Lady Elv, the woman she'd met at the ball, staring back at her in horror and clutching her arm. "Did you see that?" Lady Elv asked, her voice wavering. "That thing assaulted me!"

"What? I didn't do anything," Naya said. People all around them were turning to stare.

"It shoved me!"

"What are you talking about? You ran into me." Naya's anger flared. This was absurd. Surely Lady Elv couldn't think anyone would believe such an obvious lie. And yet Naya could feel something sharp building in the aether. People were murmuring behind their hands and while some looked amused, many others seemed angry.

Lady Elv flinched away from Naya. "Look at its eyes. Oh, please, keep it away from me."

"I didn't do anything." Naya threw up her hands in exasperation, and a few onlookers gasped and took a step back. Naya glared at them. What were they, a flock of frightened chickens?

Grand Marshal Palrak stepped out of the crowd, frowning. "Perhaps," he said softly, "you should apologize to the lady."

Before Naya could say anything, Francisco stepped up next to her. "We apologize," he said, his voice cold.

Palrak nodded curtly. "Your companions look tired, Lord Francisco. I think you should return to your rooms for the night."

Naya stared between Palrak and Lady Elv. "She's the one who should—"

Francisco grabbed her arm. "We were just leaving," he said.

Naya turned to protest, then paused when she saw the dark anger in Francisco's eyes.

"Perhaps we can continue this another time? I'd like to learn more about Endran magic," Lucia said to the Endrans.

Bargal nodded, his pale eyes fixed on Naya. "Yes, I would like that very much."

Naya let Francisco pull her toward the doors. The crowd parted around them as though they carried some foul plague. "Why did you let them push us out like that?" Naya asked Francisco once they were back in the hallway.

Francisco cast a wary glance at the soldiers by the door. "Because it only would have gotten worse if we'd stayed."

"And this is better? Now that we're gone, Lady Elv is free to say whatever she wants about us," Naya said.

"Francisco is right not to beg for more trouble," Lucia cut in. "At least we were able to speak to the Endrans. They do seem unusually interested in necromancy, more so than most Ceramorans even."

"I guess," Naya said.

Lucia smiled. "I admire your determination, but you have to realize that people won't change overnight. Many in that room have been fighting these battles since before you were born."

Naya knew that. Just like she knew she'd be better off not drawing attention to herself while she searched for Lucia's journals. But the more she saw of Talmir, the more she wanted to change things. Even if this country never felt like home again, she had to believe her people could be better than they were. She thought back over the encounter with Lady Elv and her brow furrowed. "Do you think they pushed us out because we were talking to the Endrans?" she asked.

"Why do you say that?" Francisco asked.

"I know Lady Elv has a reputation as a drunk, but don't you think the timing of her running into me was a little too convenient?"

Francisco gave her a sharp look.

"What?" Naya asked.

After a moment Francisco shook his head. "Nothing. You might be right."

They returned to the delegation's hall in silence, followed by a pair of Talmiran soldiers. Lucia bid them good night and returned to her rooms. Naya would have liked to follow her and tell her what she'd seen in the Endran ambassador's aether. Before she could, Francisco touched her arm. "Can I talk to you for a minute?" he asked.

"Sure," Naya said.

Francisco motioned for her to follow him to one of the now-empty sitting rooms near the end of the hall. "Have you found anything else in the logbook?" he asked. Now that they were in private, he let his shoulders droop. There were shadows under his eyes that Naya hadn't noticed before. Underneath the mask of confidence, he looked every bit as frustrated and unsure as she felt.

Naya hesitated. She'd meant to lie. But the note of desperation in his voice reminded her that, despite the secrets between them, they were on the same side. "Does the name Resurgence mean anything to you?" she asked.

"No. What is it?"

"I don't know. My father didn't either, from what I can tell. But he thought that name was tied to whoever was helping fund Valn's operations."

Francisco looked thoughtful. "I'll see what I can find out. I'll need more than just a name before I bring this to my father."

"Be careful," Naya said. "Whoever or whatever Resurgence is, they could have a presence at the palace. They'll be easier to catch if they think their identities are still hidden."

"I know." After a pause Francisco added, "You should be careful too. I know my father wanted us to draw attention here, but I'm starting to worry that he underestimated how the Talmirans would respond."

"You're thinking about the attack at the gates?" Naya asked.

Francisco nodded. "I get the feeling whoever staged that won't stop because of one failure."

CHAPTER 24

CORTEN

Corten fell from Servala's ship and plunged into the rolling, icy waves below. He gasped, kicking and flailing at water that felt somehow thick as mud. Clumps of grass sprouted from the crests of the waves and brushed against his fingers as his perception of the shadow world struggled against Servala's. He could feel her will in the waves rising higher around him, seeking to slam him against the hull of the ship. He didn't know if he could drown in death, but he had no intention of finding out.

Trying to swim only made the water feel more real around him. Instead Corten forced his fear aside and closed his eyes. He tried to dismiss the icy press of the water. He imagined fields of tall grass blowing in the wind and solid ground beneath his feet. The water flickered, becoming thick and slow like sucking mud. Corten clenched his jaw and concentrated harder. A sharp ache blossomed between his eyes, and for an instant he felt the grasses drifting around his legs twist into thick ropes like the one that had sought to bind him on Servala's ship.

Corten kicked hard and wrenched his legs free. Servala screamed in frustration from somewhere above him. Then the water vanished and Corten stumbled, landing on his hands and knees in a field of tall grass. His clothes were perfectly dry. When he looked back, he saw only a faint shimmer where Servala's ship had been.

"Not bad," the shadow man said. He stood nearby, and though Corten couldn't see his face, he thought he sensed grudging respect in the shadow's tone.

"Why didn't you warn me about her?" Corten asked as he got to his feet.

"I warned you not to linger," the shadow man said. "There are more scavengers here than those who hunt the deeper dark."

"Are you saying those monsters out there were once human souls?" Corten asked, his anger turning to horror at the thought.

The shadow man didn't answer, and Corten threw up his hands in frustration. "Fine, don't tell me." He started walking away from the door and Servala's ship.

"Where are you going?" the shadow man asked, keeping pace with Corten though his legs didn't seem to move.

"I'm not going to stand around here and wait for her to try something else, that's for sure," Corten said.

"Then you must go through the door," the shadow man said.

Corten turned to face the shadow man. "Why do you care? You keep hanging around, giving me vague warnings, but you didn't look interested in stopping what Servala was doing. And what about all the others here?" He waved a hand at the long procession of souls drifting toward the doorway. They were fainter, barely visible outside the radius of the door's light. "Shouldn't you be helping some of them?"

"I am not the only guide, and most of those who come through the fringe don't need our help. They pass on willingly and do not attract the attention of the scavengers."

"That still doesn't answer my first question," Corten said. "Why are you trying so hard to get me to go through the door?"

The shadow man didn't answer for a long moment. Finally he said, "We protect all those we can from the scavengers. We guard the fringe and the door to death."

That still didn't tell Corten anything more than he already

knew. He considered the shadow man, trying to put together what he'd learned to form a picture that made sense. "When I fell into my own memories before, was that you trying to protect me?"

The shadow man shifted, and Corten got the impression that he was somehow uneasy. "Memories hold strength here. Strong memories, and strong wills, can shape this place. The strongest can act as a barrier to hide you from the scavengers' sights."

"And you can see my memories?" Corten asked.

The shadow man didn't answer. Corten tried not to shudder at the way that dark face stared down at him, invisible eyes seeming to bore into him. Whatever the shadow man was, Corten didn't think he was human. Though he said his job was to guide souls to the door, he didn't seem able to intervene directly in any way other than forcing people to relive their old memories.

Everything here seemed to come back to the question of will. Maybe that was the key to fighting his way back into life. He had to harden his will, make it both armor and weapon, and carve a way out of the fringe. Corten smiled as a plan began to take shape in his mind. Servala's ship had been a false refuge, but the idea behind it had been sound.

"What do you intend to do?" the shadow man asked.

Instead of answering, Corten turned and stared out at the darkened landscape of death. He closed his eyes and imagined the front of Matius's shop—worn cobblestones under his feet and windows full of glass plates and bowls that glimmered in the sun. He'd been a mediocre glassworker at best, but that shop had been a refuge to him after his first resurrection. Matius had given him work and kindness, and a place where he could sit alone to come to terms with the future he'd lost.

He called to mind the feeling of quiet peace, the heat of the furnaces, and the beautiful, twisting shapes of Matius's statues. He remembered his own small room, the dusty smell of books, and the way the morning sunlight slanted across the polished wood floors. His throat tightened. Creator, he wanted so badly to be back there, to be alive again. He wanted to kiss Naya again. He wanted to fix the chasm that had grown between him and Lucia. He even missed his parents—and Bernel, for all that he could be an annoying brat. He'd been meaning to go home and visit them for ages. Now if he couldn't find a way out, he might never see any of them again, not on this side of the door anyway.

Bright pain flashed between Corten's eyes, growing by the second. He didn't let the pain distract him. He drew together all his need and pain and frustration. When it felt like his chest would explode from it, he let it out in a wordless shout of command.

His shout echoed as though bouncing off hard walls. The tinkle of rattling glass sounded around him. Corten stood perfectly still, barely daring to breathe for fear of having his hope shattered. When he finally got up the courage to open his eyes, a grin spread across his face. He was standing back in the shop. The walls were hazy, not quite as solid as Servala's ship, but still they were there. He'd done it.

Outside, the shadow man stood on the threshold of the open doorway. Corten crossed the shop's floor and peered into the swirling darkness of the creature's face. Before, he had entered freely into Corten's memories. But now Corten was the one in control. The shadow man leaned forward, and Corten felt something pushing against his will.

"Sorry," Corten said. "But we're done talking. I've got work to do."

Then he slammed the door shut.

CHAPTER 25

NAYA

The next morning, Naya left her rooms to meet with Mel. She was both nervous and relieved to find Mel waiting for her with a carriage at the palace gates. After what had happened at the Banian salon, she wouldn't have been surprised if Mel had canceled. Naya caught Mel's gaze, and the other girl smiled and waved.

"Hello," Mel said. "I'm glad you made it. I hope you don't mind that we'll have company." She pointed over her shoulder to two soldiers who stood stiffly by the carriage.

"This is Tren and Baz. Apparently my dear mother worries that I'll die if I go outside without them."

"The ambassador is rightly concerned," said Baz, the older of the two soldiers. He was a stocky, bald man with broad shoulders and a sour expression. "It isn't appropriate for a young lady to travel the city without an escort."

Mel's eyes slid past Naya to where two more soldiers stood behind her. They'd followed her from the delegation hall, presumably to keep her safe. "I know poor Baz has nightmares at the prospect of young ladies so much as breathing without a proper escort, but do we really need to take half the Talmiran Army with us? The carriage will be an awfully tight fit with six people."

The two soldiers exchanged a look and one shrugged. "I know Baz. If he'll be with them, then there's no reason we can't wait here for Miss Garth's return."

"Excellent!" Mel clapped her hands. "Then let's be off. You said you wanted to go see the gardens in Lestor Park, right?"

Naya nodded. "I know they're not as grand as the palace gardens, but I used to go there all the time as a girl." That was true, but she'd mostly chosen the spot because the Lestor Park gardens sat just next to the Academy of Magics. It would give her a chance to survey the academy in more detail without drawing attention to her search.

Mel smiled, apparently accepting Naya's weak excuse. "Well, I'm happy to go anywhere that's not here."

Francisco's warning echoed in Naya's mind as she got into the carriage. There were no angry crowds waiting outside this time, but still she felt uneasy as the carriage rattled onto the streets of Lith Lor. She hated that the morning sunlight felt like it carried the scalding heat of too many prying eyes. She hated imagining she could hear the angry shouts lurking just under the ordinary noise of market crowds. Most of all, she hated that it made her wonder if even Mel's kindness was an act intended to draw her out and leave her vulnerable to another attack.

Mel's guards rode in the carriage with them on the way to the gardens. Though they wore Talmiran uniforms, both had the darker features common among people of Banian descent. Baz stared straight ahead, his thick eyebrows drawn down in a glower that seemed more befitting of a man attending a funeral than one asked to watch over a pair of young women on a trip to the park. Tren was younger than his partner, and handsome in a rough sort of way. He was also more relaxed, often letting his attention wander to the view outside the window.

Mel seemed to pick up on Naya's unease, and they settled into awkward silence as they rode the short distance to the park.

After a few minutes, the carriage came to a halt and Naya followed the two guards out into the bright midmorning sunlight. They weren't the only ones who'd come to enjoy the park that day. All around, Naya saw families and couples strolling beneath the dappled shade of the trees. Mel hesitated, then smiled and linked her arm with Naya's. "Well, here we are. What did you want to see?"

Naya tensed. It wasn't uncommon for friends to walk arm-in-arm in Talmir. But Mel's simple gesture sparked faded memories of the school friends she'd had back before her mother died and her days became consumed by private tutors. Even after entering the Merchants Academy, she'd struggled to make close friends. In Ceramor she'd found allies in the Necromantic Council, but most of the people there were older than her. Those that were her own age had treated her with a strange mix of awe and caution in the weeks leading up to the delegation's departure. They didn't exclude her, but it was clear none of them were sure where she fit into their world. Naya wasn't sure either, and that feeling of drifting disconnected from everyone around her made her chest ache.

"Or I can pick something if you want?" Mel said, jerking Naya's thoughts back to the present.

Heat rose in Naya's cheeks, and she tried to push the feelings of melancholy aside. She had more important things to do than wallow in self-pity. "Sorry." She glanced around, then nodded to a path that followed the outer edge of the park. To her right, the outer wall of the Academy of Magics loomed. "Let's go this way. I think I remember there being a fish pond on the other side of the park."

Mel raised an eyebrow but didn't object. Naya heard the two soldiers fall into step several paces behind them. After they'd taken only a few steps, Mel said, "I'm sorry about last night."

Naya hesitated. "What do you mean?"

"All that stuff with Sai," Mel said with a scowl. "I was in a foul mood having to talk to Jelvi, and when Sai started looking down her nose at us like that, I just wanted to make her leave. I shouldn't have used you and Francisco to do that. Will you tell him I'm sorry?"

"It's not your fault Sai said all those things."

"Oh, I know. Sai didn't used to be so bad, but she's become a pompous brat ever since she started working for Lady Elv. Still, I could have been more diplomatic about how I handled it." Mel sighed. "With my mother being who she is, you would think I'd be better at dealing with people but . . ." She trailed off and shrugged.

"Why were you talking to Jelvi?" Naya asked.

"My mother wanted me to seek him out," Mel said. "Jelvi's uncle is important in the Silmaran senate, and Jelvi's started working as his aide recently. Mother thought it would be useful if we became friends. I didn't realize how much of an ass he is until we were already talking. We barely introduced ourselves before he asked me to dinner, and when I said no, he launched into the rant about all these great stories he knows. I guess he was somehow trying to convince me to change my mind about dinner."

"That does not sound pleasant," Naya said. "Why didn't you just walk away?"

"Because even if Jelvi's an ass, he's an important ass. My mother's already angry at me for what I said to Lady Elv at the ball. I was trying to follow her rules and be polite, but in hindsight I think even she would have agreed Jelvi wasn't worth the effort if she'd realized what he's like."

"Sai and Lady Elv aren't worth it either," Naya grumbled. "If more people talked to them like you did, maybe they'd stop acting so insufferable."

Mel laughed. "Sai, maybe, but I doubt Lady Elv will ever change. I can't remember a time when she wasn't involved in some scandal or another. It's one of the great mysteries of the Talmiran court why the trade master keeps her on as his secretary."

They walked in silence for another minute. Naya kept one eye on the academy wall as she mulled over Mel's words. The complex was one of the oldest in the city. Supposedly the walls had been built to fend off the bandits who had roamed these lands before the Dawning prophets brought stability back to the world. The walls certainly looked their age. The white stone blocks were streaked with gray, their edges worn down from years of rain and wind. The metal spikes that had once adorned their tops were mostly missing, leaving gaps like broken teeth. Over their tops Naya could see the red tiled roof of a tall building.

The walls wouldn't be hard to climb, but what then? The university grounds were huge. Without more information, she could probably spend days wandering among the buildings without finding what she needed. And that was assuming she didn't get caught.

"I'm getting the feeling that the gardens aren't really what you're interested in," Mel said.

Naya tensed and felt a flush spread across her cheeks. She glanced over and found Mel smiling at her. This close, Mel's aether seemed to wrap around Naya. She was plainly nervous despite her smile, and Naya tasted fear like metal on the back of her tongue. But overshadowing both was a bright current of curiosity that swirled and danced around her. Naya searched for another lie, another casual dismissal that would push Mel away from the truth. But her stomach twisted at the idea. Each new lie she told reminded her of the wall of secrets she'd built between herself and Corten, and the look of disgust on his face when he'd realized what she really was. "Why are you trying so hard to befriend me?" she asked instead.

Mel looked away. "Is that what you think I'm doing?"

"When we first met at the ball, you said you don't hate the

undead. Maybe that's true, but you also said your mother asked you to make friends with Jelvi. Maybe you're just doing the same with me." As Naya spoke, she tried to ignore the pressure of Mel's arm against hers, the song of the birds above, and the bright smells of plants overlying the less pleasant odors of the city. Instead she concentrated on the subtle flow of energy surrounding them. She didn't want it to be true, but she needed to know all the same.

The city's pulse swelled around her, heavier and more deliberate than what she'd sensed in Belavine. Within it she felt Mel's aether darken with shame, then flash with smoky anger. "All right, it's true I was talking to Jelvi because my mother asked. But this is different. I'm not her spy. And I certainly didn't start talking to you for her sake."

"Then why?"

Mel laughed, though there wasn't much humor in it. "I guess I thought you might be different from the others."

"What do you mean?"

Mel glanced at Naya. "I've seen the way everyone treats you."

"I'm undead. It's not surprising that they'd hate me." Naya tried to make the words casual, but she could hear the bitterness in her own voice.

"Well, believe it or not, it isn't so different from how they'd usually treat me."

"Why?" Naya asked, more than a little surprised. As the daughter of an ambassador, Mel should have had a place among the upper echelons of the court hierarchy.

"Because my father's from the Islands."

"That doesn't seem like much of a reason," Naya said. True, the people of Banen were unusual, and her father had always regarded them warily because of their refusal to follow Dawning teachings. But even he had admired their skills as shipbuilders and sailors, and the Banians had always been welcome in Lith Lor.

Mel responded to Naya's frown with a wry smile. "How much do you actually know about Banen?"

"Not very much, I guess."

"Most Talmirans don't. Life on the Islands isn't like it is here. I spent most of my time growing up there with my father. A few people knew who my mother was, but most didn't care." She tilted her head back as though savoring the dappled sunlight. "Then my mother decided it was time I came here and learned what it meant to be a proper Talmiran lady. I barely knew anything about court life when I arrived, and I guess I made it pretty clear that all I wanted was to go home. . . . Add to that the fact that someone found out about my parents, and well . . ." She shrugged.

"What do you mean they found out about your parents?"

"You mean you haven't heard yet?" Mel held one hand over her mouth in a look of exaggerated shock. "Even after he found out my mother was pregnant, my father refused to convert and marry her under Talmiran law. He loved her, and he was happy to be with her, but he wouldn't sacrifice his principles for her. The strangest part of it all was that my dear mother accepted his terms despite her good Talmiran upbringing. It was all a terrible scandal."

"Ah," Naya said, remembering her first months at the Merchants Academy. Her father had hired tutors to prepare her, but she'd been slow to master the courtly manners. Even when she had, the others hadn't forgotten where she'd come from. The Dawning taught that no romance could be pure without the blessing and commitment of a formal marriage. Children born outside that sacred bond were destined to be fickle creatures.

Mel nodded. "I'm not saying it's the same as being undead. But I do know what it's like to not be good enough for them. I know what it's like to be hated for something you can't change."

They walked in silence for a moment. Naya thought back to

the first night she'd met Mel, factoring in the new information. There had been something scornful in the way Lady Elv had greeted her. Mel had responded with such casual confidence that Naya hadn't given the interaction a second thought. But it made sense. Mel's dark features were distinctive enough to make her stand out, and her decision to wear Banian clothes was a statement of defiance given her mother's position. Mel seemed to identify closely with her father's people, but here she was stuck in Talmir surrounded by people who expected her to align with her mother's beliefs without question.

"I'm sorry," Naya finally said.

"It's all right. Makes sense that you'd be suspicious. Everyone comes here to play politics. They're always backstabbing and scheming. It's one of the things I hate so much."

"So it's different in Banen?" Naya asked.

Mel tilted her head to the side. "It is and it isn't."

They reached the end of the path and paused. Naya glanced right. The park curved around one side of the academy and from here she could just see the main gates. Guards in uniform stood watch as a few scribes in simple robes traveled in and out. The scribes entering the academy paused by the guards. Naya saw one hold up a silver medallion he wore on a chain around his neck. Metal flashed in the sunlight and the guard nodded the scribe through the gates. Another scribe passed wearing several medallions of various metals over a much finer set of robes. He didn't even look at the guards, who bowed respectfully as he strode by.

Through the open gates, Naya could see the edge of a cobbled plaza, and beyond that a tall building, the roof of which was visible even above the crumbling walls. Perhaps if she could get her hands on one of those medallions and a robe she could walk right past the guards and the walls. That still wouldn't help her find Lucia's journals once she was inside, but it was a place to start. When Naya looked back at Mel, she saw the other girl also staring at the gates. Mel met Naya's eyes and offered her a weak smile. "What now? Do you still want to look for that fish pond?"

Footsteps crunched on the path behind them as Baz and Tren approached. "Don't mean to interrupt," Tren said. "But we should be getting back to the palace. Don't forget your mother wanted you to join her for lunch."

Mel gave a dramatic sigh. "Of course, wouldn't want to keep dear Mother waiting." She flashed Naya a grin that seemed to defy the unease that still hung in the air between them.

Naya could feel that unease echoed in the aether. But she returned Mel's grin in spite of it. She still wasn't sure how far she could trust Mel. But the pain and anger in Mel's voice when she'd spoken of the other Talmiran nobles had felt too real to be a ruse.

They spoke of inconsequential things on the ride back to the palace. As Mel stepped out of the carriage, Naya caught her hand. "I want to change things," she said, fear and excitement rising in her. "Talmir and Ceramor don't have to be enemies. We can be better than we are. I don't know how yet, but I want to prove to people that it's true."

Mel met Naya's eyes and whatever she saw there made her smile. "Let's do it."

CHAPTER 26

NAYA

Francisco came knocking at Naya's door barely a half hour after she had returned to the palace. "I heard you and Miss Jeden went out into the city together."

"I was careful," Naya said smugly. "And as you can see, it worked out fine."

Francisco looked her up and down. "Well, it seems you at least managed to avoid getting attacked by any mobs."

Naya scowled. Not even Francisco's grim caution was going to smother the hope Mel's support had given her. "You know, not all Talmirans form mobs the second they see one of the undead."

"Right. I guess they usually call them armies. Did you at least learn anything useful?"

"I did. And Mel asked me to apologize to you about last night."

Surprise flashed across Francisco's face, and then the mask returned and he shrugged. "Probably just another trick to sucker you in and gather information for her mother."

"It wasn't! Mel's a better person than you give her credit for."

"I'm sure she's perfectly decent, but—"

"But what? You saw the way other people were treating her just for talking to us. How much proof do you need before you're willing to give someone a chance?"

Francisco looked away, and Naya thought she saw a flush of color darkening his cheeks. "Fine. You can tell her I accept her apology."

He sounded more grudging than sincere, but Naya let the subject drop. "Good. There was one more thing. Mel said some interesting things about Lady Elv. I think we should keep an eye on her. There's something about that woman that doesn't make sense to me."

"What do you mean?"

"I'm not sure exactly. I just get the sense that she's more than what she seems."

Francisco's expression grew thoughtful as he watched her.

"What?" Naya asked.

"You really don't know?" He sounded surprised.

Naya glared at him. "Okay, yes, you caught me. I know exactly what you're talking about, it's just that I so love round-about conversations."

Francisco shook his head, then glanced down the hall. "Sorry. I just assumed you would have known since you worked for Valn." He lowered his voice. "Trade Master Galve, Lady Elv's boss, is Queen Lial's spymaster in Talmir."

Naya's eyes widened. "You're sure?"

Francisco glanced down the hall again. "We shouldn't talk about this out here. Can I come in?"

Naya stepped aside and Francisco hurried into her room, shutting the door behind him. "My father's suspected him for years, but he found proof during his investigation of Valn. He only told me last night because he wanted me to be careful around the trade master and Lady Elv."

"She's a spy?" Naya asked.

"Think about it," Francisco said. "As Galve's secretary she has the access she needs to keep tabs on anyone trading in Talmir, and her reputation means people underestimate her."

Naya crossed her arms. Why hadn't Delence told her any of this? "Is your father planning to accuse Galve at the trial?" As trade master, Galve would certainly have had the access and the means to funnel money to Valn's network. He might even be able to keep that information out of the accounts the queen had searched. His name wasn't on Lucia's list, but he was certainly old enough that he could have also been involved in the purges.

"No," Francisco said, his expression darkening. "We don't have any proof that he knew about the plot. Until we do, it's better to act as though we don't suspect him. Don't talk to anyone about this, okay? My father doesn't want the information spreading."

"Then why did you tell me?" Naya asked.

"Because if you started looking too closely at Lady Elv, you might risk spooking Galve. And . . ." He pressed his lips together, as though tasting something bitter. "I'm starting to realize I misjudged you earlier. We have a job to do here, and I shouldn't have let my personal feelings over the past get in the way of that. I'm sorry."

Guilt twisted at Naya's stomach. "I'm sorry too. I wish I had seen what was really going on in Ceramor before Valn went after your family."

Francisco nodded, not meeting her eyes. "I should get back to work. Let me know if you want to go over anything before the trial tomorrow."

After he left, Naya went to her desk and skimmed through the notes the scribes had left from the Congress meeting. Valn would be brought over from the prison early tomorrow morning for the trial. He'd be held in a secure room near the Congress meeting hall until the trial began. Naya had to figure out a way to get to him so she could ask in private about Galve and the names on Lucia's list. She pulled out the map she'd drawn of the palace halls. She had a few guesses about where they'd put Valn, but she didn't know exactly when he'd be moved or how she'd get past the soldiers guarding him.

Creator, she didn't even know how she was supposed to get out of the delegation hall without being followed. So far she hadn't managed to go anywhere without one of Queen Lial's soldiers tailing her. Naya tapped the map in frustration, then she froze.

Naya Garth couldn't leave without being followed, but what if they thought she was someone else? Naya grabbed the rune disk on her desk and activated it, waiting impatiently until Felicia arrived.

"Did you need something?" she asked as Naya let her into the sitting room and shut the door.

"Yes. Did anyone follow you when you went to deliver those letters for me yesterday?" Naya asked.

Felicia blinked. "I . . . I don't think so. Why? There wasn't any trouble with your outing, was there?"

"No," Naya said. "But I'm going to need your help with something. Is there any chance you could get access to a palace servant's uniform?"

"I wouldn't know where to look. The palace staff have made a point of keeping themselves separate from us, which is frustrating because there's this one boy in the kitchens who has the prettiest eyes. I caught him watching me when I went to help Yenni get Lady Briello's dinner. I bet he would have come over and talked to us if the head cook hadn't smacked him with her cleaning rag for slacking." Felicia sighed, as though describing the end of a tragic romance instead of some chance encounter in a sweaty kitchen.

Naya smiled. "He probably doesn't speak Ceramoran."

Felicia winked. "He might. Even if he didn't, I'm sure we could find some other way to . . . communicate," she said suggestively.

Naya's cheeks flushed. "Felicia!"

Felicia laughed. "Sorry. I forgot how Talmiran you still are—you're all so proper. What did you want a servant's uniform for anyway?"

Naya chewed her lip. With a servant's uniform and a new face, she could have slipped beneath the notice of the ever-watchful palace guards. There was another option, but it would mean trusting Felicia with something much bigger than carrying messages. "There's something I need to look into, but I need to be able to leave my rooms without being followed. Will you help me?"

"Help you how?" Felicia asked hesitantly.

"You don't have to do much. I'm going to call you back here in a few hours. All you'll have to do is wait in my rooms while I'm gone. Oh, and I'll need to borrow your clothes."

Felicia's eyes widened as she seemed to realize what Naya was implying. "I—wait. You want to pretend to be me? Is that it? Can you even do that?"

"I think so. I'll need to practice some first."

Felicia looked away, and Naya could feel the unease washing off her. "I'm not sure this is a good idea. What if they catch you?"

"They won't. Please. I swear I wouldn't be asking if this wasn't important."

"What do you plan to do?" Felicia asked.

"I need to talk to someone without worrying about Talmiran soldiers following me around."

"Who?" Felicia asked.

"You'll be safer if you don't know."

Felicia shook her head. "No. I'm sorry but if you want to use my face, then I have a right to know who you'll be using it to talk to."

Naya hesitated. Revealing her plans to find Valn was too dangerous. Could she convince Felicia without telling her the whole truth? "I thought I saw someone at the ball who shouldn't be here. She's a spy I worked with back in Belavine." Naya saw Felicia tense and continued quickly. "If she's really here, then she might try to do something before Valn's trial."

"So you mean to go looking for her?"

Naya nodded. "I don't want to bother Delence until I know what's actually going on. Will you help me?"

Felicia remained silent, staring at the floor. Naya's throat tightened as the silence stretched. She was about to say something when Felicia looked up. "All right," she said. "I'll do it."

Naya grinned. "Thank you."

She and Felicia spent the next three hours working on the transformation until Naya was confident she could mimic Felicia's features well enough to fool the guards. Learning the new face felt easier than it had in the past. Naya wondered if that was due to all the practice she'd had at manipulating aether, or if she was slowly losing her attachment to the way she'd looked before she'd died. It was a disconcerting thought.

"You're sure this is right?" Felicia asked as Naya let go of the transformation.

Naya shook her head. "I'm not sure how else I can get out of here without being followed. I'm sorry, I know I'm asking a lot of you."

"It isn't that." Felicia smoothed her skirts. "Like you said, all I have to do is wait here for you to come back. It just gives me the shivers seeing you look exactly like me. You could go out there and kill someone, and people would think I'd done it."

"I'm not going to kill anyone," Naya said.

"Oh, of course I know that," Felicia said, though the fear in her aether seemed to counter her words. "I've just never done anything like this before." She smiled weakly. "When Lord Delence offered me this position, I was hoping for adventure. But I was thinking more of catching the eye of some pretty messenger boy who'd turn out to be a long-lost prince or something, not so much of lending out my face to hunt spies."

Naya's eyebrows rose. "I seriously doubt any of the messenger boys here are princes in disguise."

"You're right," Felicia said seriously. "Princes are far more likely to hide in the kitchens. Maybe I should sneak back down there tonight."

"Please tell me you're joking," Naya said.

Felicia laughed. "I am. Still, you never know. That sort of thing happens all the time in the stories, and stories have to come from somewhere, don't they?"

They spoke for a few minutes more. After that Felicia left to get some rest before they set their plans in motion. Once she was gone, Naya went back through her notes, looking for anything she might have missed regarding Trade Master Galve. So far as she could tell, Galve had never so much as traveled to Ceramor. If he had been working with Valn, it would have been through intermediaries.

A knock at the door startled Naya from her contemplations. She glanced at the clock. Almost midnight. How had it gotten so late?

The knock came again, quiet and precise. Naya frowned, then stood and checked the aether. There was something odd about the energy on the other side of the door. It felt too thin to be someone living. Francisco, perhaps?

She opened the door to find a palace servant standing on the other side, her face set in a polite smile. A spark of anticipation danced through the woman's thin aether.

Before Naya could ask what was going on, the servant leapt forward. Her shoulder connected with Naya's chest, sending them both stumbling into the room. Naya's leg collided with the arm of the couch as she struggled to put more distance between herself and the servant. The door clicked shut.

"What are you doing?" Naya asked, panic rising in her throat. The woman before her had sharp features and black hair pulled back in a tight bun. Her aether flowed strangely, as though drawn into a rune device near her hand or wrist.

The woman met Naya's gaze. Her eyes were unusually pale, more gray than brown. They narrowed as she drew a slender knife from a hidden sheath against her leg. Runes ignited as the wraith eater's blade drew from the servant's aether. She attacked.

Aether roared through Naya's bond, eager to be unleashed. The woman advanced with a fighter's grace. She slashed at Naya's chest so fast that the knife in her hand seemed to blur, the glow of the wraith eater's runes seeming to wrap around her wrist.

Naya ducked and twisted, trying to put furniture between herself and her attacker. What was going on? Was the palace under attack? Naya sidestepped another slash, searching for an opportunity to move inside the woman's guard. The tip of the knife grazed her arm and icy pain shot through the limb. Darkness wavered on the edges of her vision as the hungry blade sucked at her energy.

Naya clenched her jaw and aimed a punch at her attacker's face. She concentrated aether in her right arm, imagining the runes for force as she did. Her fist seemed to leap forward, connecting with the woman's jaw and sending her reeling back. Naya's lips pulled back from her teeth in a snarl. "Who are you?" she asked.

The woman smiled, revealing bloody teeth. Too late Naya saw the woman's hand slipping behind her back. She threw something, another knife. Naya flung herself sideways. Fabric tore and an icy chill wrenched her shoulder as the knife passed harmlessly through her. Then the woman was on top of her.

Naya caught the woman's wrist, stopping her just before she plunged the wraith eater into Naya's chest. This close she could feel the blade's pull. It was like a gaping maw, trying to suck her back into the dark tides of death.

The woman grunted with effort, and the tip of the blade dipped lower. The glow around her wrist brightened. Were those runes encircling her arm? That didn't make any sense. Naya could feel her own reserves fading. Almost without conscious thought, she reached out through the aether, searching for the bright source of energy at the woman's core. Her soul. If she could pull that brilliant glow toward the wraith eater, she could separate it from the woman's body and send it into death. But even as she reached, her will faltered. Her father's empty eyes loomed before her, and she remembered the sickness that had filled her when she'd drawn away his soul and sent it screaming to the other side.

The knife dipped lower, the tip pressing a dimple in the fabric of Naya's dress. Fear crawled up Naya's throat, pushing out her anger. She gasped as the tip of the knife pressed into her skin. Ice radiated from the tiny puncture and pain throbbed through the bones of her hand.

"Help!" The word sounded inhuman as it slid past Naya's lips. She couldn't die here. She tightened her grip on her attacker's wrist and saw pain flicker in the woman's eyes. Wood splintered and the hall door burst open. "Stop! Drop the knife!" a man shouted.

The woman glanced up. Naya rallied the last of her strength and managed to shift the knife a couple of inches while her attacker was distracted. Then something tugged hard at the aether behind her. She heard the crack of a rune pistol and blood exploded from the woman's shoulder, spattering hot drops across Naya's face and chest. The woman toppled sideways, dropping the knife.

"Don't move," a man said.

A young Talmiran soldier stood in the doorway. He fumbled with something on his pistol and the weapon's second rune plate clicked into place. Blood pumped from the hole in the woman's shoulder where the heavy slug had penetrated. She glanced between Naya and the soldier, then sprang to her feet and ran toward the window.

Naya flinched as the second shot tore through the room, this time hitting the woman in the leg. She collapsed with a cry of pain. Behind Naya the soldier cursed and dropped his spent pistol, drawing his sword with a ring of metal on metal. Naya was more than a little relieved when she didn't feel the renewed tug of a fresh wraith eater. Her bones ached from the brief contact with the woman's knife, and she doubted she could fight the soldier if he decided to finish what the fake servant had started.

Naya dragged herself to her feet. The soldier advanced, his eyes flickering between her and the woman on the floor. Sweat trickled down the side of his neck and his eyes were wide enough that Naya could see the whites all the way around. The woman rolled over, something clutched tight in one hand.

"It's over," Naya said. "Tell me who you are—and who sent you."

The woman raised whatever she held to her lips. Naya realized what she was about to do and lunged forward, but not before the woman could tip the contents of the tiny vial down her throat. "Get a doctor!" Naya shouted at the soldier as she fell to her knees beside the woman.

The soldier hesitated, still holding his sword at the ready.

"Now!"

He left. Naya grabbed the woman's shoulders. Her muscles began to twitch and bloody foam dripped from her lips. For an instant her eyes locked on Naya's, the pupils so wide they showed only a faint hint of lighter color around the edges. "We are the flood," the woman said, the words coming out in a choking gurgle. "We will wash you away."

"What does that mean?" Naya asked. But she could feel the woman's aether fading. She reached out for the soul. Maybe she could catch it before it passed to the other side, hold it somehow and stop the woman's body from dying. But the light faded from the woman's eyes, and then there was simply nothing left for Naya to catch.

Naya rose to her feet, swaying. The bones in her left hand throbbed like a heartbeat. She reached the door as the soldier returned with a white-haired man carrying a doctor's satchel. Naya shook her head. "Don't bother," she said. "It's too late."

The doctor gave her a startled look, then glanced at the soldier. "Yes . . . er . . . I'll just double-check, shall I?"

Naya moved out into the hall and let the two men into the room. Her thoughts felt sluggish and disconnected as the woman's words danced circles through her mind. *We are the flood. We are the flood.* What had she meant? Was it just the ravings of a madwoman, or something more?

"Excuse me."

Naya blinked as another soldier pushed past her, headed to an open door on the other side of the hall. She became aware of the sound of voices, and a mix of half-dressed delegates and guards moving through the hall. Naya's throat tightened. The other door was Francisco's.

CHAPTER 27

NAYA

Naya slipped through the crowd gathering around Francisco's room. There she found Lucia crouched next to Francisco's prone form. His white nightshirt was stained with blood from a wound near his stomach. His eyes were closed and his breathing ragged. Naya's chest lurched. "Is he alive?" There was so much blood. His skin was turning gray and the tattoos around his neck and wrists somehow seemed faded.

"Yes," Lucia said simply. She held her hands pressed against Francisco's wound and didn't bother looking up. "Has the surgeon come yet?" she asked over her shoulder.

"On his way, madame," a man said behind Naya.

Naya turned to face the man, an older soldier in a crisp uniform. "What's going on? Is the palace under attack?" she asked.

The soldier's aether hardened like ice around him. "We don't know, but I've ordered reinforcements to protect the royal family and the other delegations. My men were stationed at the end of the hall. They heard screams and found Lord Francisco under attack by a man wearing palace livery. They discharged their weapons, but the attacker escaped through the window."

Naya ran to the open window. The wooden ledge was splintered where an iron hook had been lodged. A narrow rope dangled from the hook, almost invisible against the white stone wall. Naya squinted but couldn't make out any sign of movement in the dark gardens beyond.

A commotion rose behind her and she heard Delence shout, "Where is my son? Get out of the way!" He stormed into the room, somehow managing to look imposing despite his hastily donned clothing and unkempt hair. Dark blood soaked the knees of his pants as he dropped to Francisco's side. "Francisco?" He reached down gingerly and squeezed Francisco's hand.

Francisco's eyes fluttered and he let out a soft groan, but otherwise he didn't stir.

"It was a wraith eater," Lucia said with a hard edge in her voice. "The contact wasn't long enough to fully drain him, but I'll need to re-ink the runes as soon as possible if he's going to recover."

Naya tried to keep her attention focused on the physical. Splintered wood under her fingers. Cool night air. But still the room's aether pressed against her senses, a nauseating mix of panic and anger magnified by the all-too-physical smell of blood. Lucia was a genius necromancer—if anyone could help Francisco, it would be her. "We need to go after the assassin before he escapes," Naya said.

"I've raised the alarm," one of the older soldiers said, directing his words at Delence. "The gates are locked, and in a few minutes we'll have three squads out to search the grounds."

"Good. Keep me informed." Delence stood, his eyes falling on Naya. He seemed to take in her torn sleeve and exhausted expression. "You were attacked as well?"

"Yes, by a woman. She was also dressed like a servant."

"Where is she?"

"Dead."

Delence's expression tightened into a look of frustration before smoothing again. He turned to the soldier. "Explain how two assassins managed to saunter in here without your men so much as noticing them."

"Sir," the soldier said, his spine straightening. "I don't know, but I swear by the Creator's grace I intend to find out."

Naya was surprised by the note of sincerity in the man's tone. She couldn't pick out any details of his emotions from the foul backdrop, but he seemed genuinely angry about the attack, nothing like the soldiers she'd encountered during the attack outside the palace gates.

The surgeon arrived then with a team of assistants carrying a stretcher. He grew pale when he saw who his patient was. "Are you sure you need me? I don't have any experience tending to dead—"

"He isn't dead yet," Lucia snapped. "Treat the wound as you would any other of its type. When you're done, I'll reapply the tattoos and handle the rest."

Delence stepped aside as the surgeon and his assistants loaded Francisco onto the stretcher. "Come with me," he said to Naya. He led her out into the hallway, shooting a sharp look back when one of the soldiers sought to follow him. Other members of the delegation stood in the doorways of their rooms.

Delence stopped near the end of the hall, then turned to Naya. "Tell me exactly what happened."

Naya crossed her arms. Her fingers shook and her aching bones made her feel dizzy and tired. For once she wasn't angry at Delence's commanding tone. It was something familiar at least. "A woman wearing a servant's uniform forced her way into my rooms and attacked me with a wraith eater. She was obviously trained to fight. And she moved faster than anyone I've ever met," Naya said.

Delence's expression darkened. "Did you recognize her? Did she say anything to you?"

Naya hesitated, focusing on Delence's aether. "She did, but it didn't make any sense. She said, 'We are the flood, we will wash you away.' Do you have any idea what that means?"

Delence's frown deepened, and Naya sensed genuine confusion mixing with the fear and anger in his aether. "That's all?"

Naya nodded.

Delence slumped, running his fingers over his mustache. "The flood . . ." he muttered, then shook his head. "It could mean we're dealing with insane radicals, or something else entirely."

"It's hard to imagine this isn't connected to the attack at the gates," Naya said, keeping her voice low. "You said yourself that they'd try to kill me. If the palace soldiers are involved, we can't just wait around and—"

"Enough," Delence said, raising a hand to cut her off. "Whatever is going on, the attack failed, and I doubt they'll make another attempt tonight."

"But—"

"I need to see to my son. I don't like the idea of him alone with all those Talmirans. It would be too easy for someone to arrange an accident while he's weak." He glanced down the hallway. "I'm sure Queen Lial will try to lock down control of the investigation soon. I'll have to make sure someone examines the assassin's body before her soldiers can remove it." His voice dropped and his eyes unfocused as though he were talking to himself. Then he blinked and focused back on Naya. "It won't be practical for you to use your rooms tonight. I'll have someone send for Felicia. She can help you get settled in one of the extra rooms at the end of the hallway."

"I could help with the investigation," Naya protested. "The second assassin is still out there somewhere." She lowered her voice to a near whisper. "After everything that's happened, I don't think we should trust Queen Lial's soldiers."

"I am aware," Delence said. "But there's little we can do about it tonight." He shook his head. "Stay here. Avoid answering any questions if you can. I need to think about how best to respond."

Naya glared as Delence walked away. Did he really expect her to just sit around and wait? The bones in her hand still ached from the contact with the wraith eater. She didn't think she'd cracked them again, but that didn't make the ache any less irritating. Tension hummed through the palace's aether, prickling the back of her neck and filling her with the need to do something. She waited until Delence had disappeared around the corner, then headed for the stairs that would take her to the palace's main level.

No fewer than six Talmiran soldiers had been stationed at the base of the stairs. Two of them promptly moved to block her path. "I'm sorry, Miss Garth, but we'll have to ask you to remain in your rooms until the situation is resolved," one of them said gently. After a moment Naya recognized Sergeant Leln, the soldier who'd spoken with her about art after the inaugural ball.

"Have you caught the second assassin yet?" Naya asked.

Leln frowned. "Our men are still searching. That's why I'll have to insist you return to your rooms. It isn't safe for you here."

Naya struggled to maintain a polite expression. "Apparently it wasn't safe for me up there either. Let me through and I might be able to help. I'm a wraith. I can sense things your soldiers can't." If she opened her senses, she might be able to pick out the assassin's aether and find him before he could escape.

Reminding them what she was only served to heighten the unease and mistrust in their aether. "You won't be doing any such thing," the soldier next to Leln said. "Return to your rooms, Miss Garth, or we will have to escort you there." The way he said the word *escort* made it clear he didn't intend that process to be pleasant.

"That's enough, Ralen," Leln said. "Miss Garth, if you would please—"

"No!" Naya said. "I'm not just going to sit around and wait

198

while you let him get away." Leln didn't seem like a bad person. But Naya remembered all too well the way the other soldiers had reacted the last time she and Francisco had been attacked. What was to stop them from letting this assassin slip away now? They might not even consider what the assassin had done to be a crime, not when the people he'd attacked were already technically dead.

Naya tried to slip between Leln and Ralen, but the lingering ache and exhaustion from the previous fight made her slow. Ralen grabbed her arm in an iron grip. "Stop!"

"Don't touch me!" Anger flared hot and strong through her. How dare he grab her! Naya twisted, reversing Ralen's grip and wrapping her fingers around his forearm. Aether rushed into her bones, and this time she didn't hold it back. The rune for force shone in her mind as she squeezed Ralen's arm. Pain flared through her hand, but it was nothing compared to the satisfying sound of Ralen's bones snapping like dried twigs. He screamed. Naya shoved him away and spun to face the other soldiers. The anger that had been locked inside her for so long felt like an inferno. Had she really thought she could change anything here? She was a fool. These people hated her. Queen Lial could have organized this whole attack for all she knew. She had to get out of here. A soldier behind Leln began to draw his sword, and Naya felt the tug of a wraith eater activating.

Her lips curled in a sneer.

"Naya?"

The voice wasn't loud, but it hit Naya like a blast of icy water. Mel was standing in the hall, a little behind the group of soldiers. Her eyes were wide and she held her hands over her mouth in obvious fear. Fear of Naya.

Naya stepped away. "Mel? What are you doing here?" She darted a glance around the gathered soldiers. The one whose arm she'd broken had retreated behind his allies. The others were watching her with a mix of fear and anger. Leln stood directly in front of the injured soldier with his hand on the hilt of his still-sheathed sword.

"Step away, Miss Garth," Leln said in an icily calm voice. "And think carefully about what you do next. The Congress protections do not give you the right to harm my men."

Shame rose like ashes from Naya's anger. She backed away from Leln. "I only wanted to help," she said. She glanced at the faces around her. "He grabbed me. It wasn't my fault."

"That damned corpse broke my arm!" Ralen snarled.

"What's going on?" Mel asked, her voice a little higher with the edge of panic. "Naya, what happened?"

"I was just trying to help." Naya tried to hold on to the anger, tried to summon back the inferno that had made everything feel so right and clear just a moment ago. All she found was the bitter taste of ashes, the hate and fear reflected in the eyes of those around her.

Corpse. Monster. Murderer.

Naya turned and ran back up the stairs, ignoring Mel's cry to wait.

CHAPTER 28

NAYA

Naya bolted up the stairs and squeezed past the soldiers and delegates still lingering in the hall. She muttered a vague excuse in response to their questions. At the end of the hall, she found one of the unoccupied rooms and slipped inside, locking the door behind her. The room was a mirror of the one she'd been assigned before. The only difference was that the furniture here was upholstered in golden yellows and pale creams instead of shades of green and brown.

Good thing I didn't get this room. They never would have gotten the bloodstains out.

Naya let out a sound that was part laugh and part sob at the gruesome thought. Her legs collapsed until she was sitting on the floor with her back to the door. She stared down at her hands, feeling the snap of the soldier's bones in her grip. All she'd wanted was to help find the assassin. He shouldn't have gotten in her way.

She thought about the look of mingled confusion and fear on Mel's face, the ice in Leln's voice that was so different from the hesitant kindness he'd shown her before. So much for proving she wasn't a monster. Her eyes burned, and not for the first time, she wished she could still cry.

How could she have been so stupid? Even if the soldiers had

let her past, the assassin would probably be captured or gone by the time she could get outside and join the search. And if Queen Lial or her soldiers were involved in this somehow, she'd just given them the perfect excuse to condemn her publicly.

Maybe worse, after what she'd just done, Delence could decide that keeping her here wasn't worth the risk.

A knock came at the door and Naya tensed. Her eyes went first to the window. She could pry it open and escape. The palace grounds would likely still be full of soldiers searching for the assassin. If she was clever, then maybe she could sneak past them. Once out in the city, she could change her face, find a way to keep away from the queen's soldiers and the city guard. Finding Lucia's journals would be harder on her own, but not impossible.

She'd taken two steps toward the window when the knock came again.

"Miss Naya? Are you in there?" Felicia called.

Naya hesitated, logic catching up to the panicked spin of her thoughts. She squeezed her eyes shut and drew in aether, trying to calm herself. No. If she ran, she would almost certainly be caught.

"There you are," Felicia said when Naya opened the door. "Are you all right? What's going on?" Behind her a soldier stood next to Naya's door, very carefully not looking at her. So they'd had someone follow her.

More questions brimmed in Felicia's eyes, though it was obvious she didn't want to ask them in front of the soldier. "Come in," Naya said. She saw the soldier's mouth twitch, but he didn't object as Felicia stepped into the room and Naya shut the door behind her.

Felicia reached out to touch the torn sleeve of Naya's dress. "Are you all right? I heard there was an attack. People are saying Francisco was stabbed, and Delence's man told me I needed to make up a new room for you because there's a dead body in your old one." Felicia was obviously trying for a casual tone, but her eyes were too wide to pull it off.

"I'm—" Naya tried to say *fine*, but the word wouldn't come out. She swallowed and started over. "Francisco will be fine, I think. Lucia and the surgeon are with him now. They haven't caught the man who stabbed him though. He could be any-where. He could be one of the queen's servants for real." She was babbling, breathing hard even though her body didn't need the air. She tried to stop herself but somehow the words kept spilling out. "I'm trying. I'm trying so hard. But I'm not fine. I just killed someone. And I broke a man's arm. And Mel saw it, and Delence's going to be furious, and everything is broken. I don't know what I'm doing here or why I'm even telling you any of this." She pressed her hands against her eyes in a futile effort to make the whole world disappear.

"Did they deserve it?" Felicia asked after a pause.

"What?" Naya looked up, confused.

Felicia stood with her hands clasped in front of her, not quite meeting Naya's eyes. "The people you hurt, did they deserve it?"

"I . . ." Naya took a deep breath and let it out slowly. "I don't know. The woman was one of the assassins. I guess I didn't really kill her, she took something so she couldn't be captured. I'm not sad that she's dead. I don't know if that makes me a bad person. The man whose arm I broke . . . I don't know. I guess he was just trying to do his job, but he grabbed me and I was angry, so I hurt him."

"Well, that's not so bad then," Felicia said, flopping down on one of the chairs. "I've done all sorts of stupid things when I was angry. When I was nine, I stole my big brother's birthday cake because he and his friends wouldn't let me play pirates with them. I hid under my bed and ate the whole thing out of spite, never mind that it was strawberry and I hate strawberries."

Naya smiled at the absurdity of the image. Somehow it wasn't hard for her to imagine Felicia with grubby knees and a wooden pirate sword sneaking into a kitchen to take revenge by cake. "What kind of person hates strawberries?"

"Anyone with good taste," Felicia said with exaggerated affront.

"You must have made yourself sick."

"Horribly so," Felicia agreed. "But I think my brother was more impressed than angry. He let me tag along with him a few times after that."

"That sounds nice." Naya blinked hard, trying to force away the burning in her eyes and the shaky hiccup feeling in her throat. She sat down in the chair across from Felicia. They stayed that way in silence for several minutes.

"Do you think this has anything to do with that spy you told me about?" Felicia asked abruptly.

"Spy? Oh, that spy." Naya tried to force herself to think clearly. She'd all but forgotten about the plans she'd made with Felicia. Had that really only been a few hours ago? "I don't know."

"Do you still want to try to sneak out?" Felicia asked quietly. "It's going to be harder with that soldier at your door, but I think we could still figure something out."

"You still want to?" Naya asked, not hiding her surprise.

Felicia met Naya's eyes, and Naya was impressed by the force behind her gaze. "I didn't really before, but now I want to know who attacked us. I know most people who look at me don't see anyone important, but I'm not stupid. I know how to look and how to listen. It doesn't take much of that to realize there's something very wrong going on in this palace."

"You're right," Naya said. She considered the idea for a moment, then shook her head. "But I don't think we should try anything tonight." Much as she hated to admit it, the attack had ruined any chance she might have had to go after Valn tonight. Security would be tight all over the palace, and after what she'd done to Ralen's arm, Leln and the other soldiers would be keeping an especially wary eye on her. If she disappeared now, it would only cause more trouble.

"Then what are we going to do? Should we tell Delence?"

"No!" Naya said. She tried to soften the refusal by adding, "He'll want to be with Francisco, and I'm sure he's got more than enough to deal with right now."

Felicia stayed with Naya a while longer, filling the silence with talk of inconsequential things. It helped. Eventually Felicia's eyes began to droop and Naya pushed her off to bed.

Dawn was just rising when the aether in the hall outside Naya's borrowed room abruptly boiled with distress and anger. A door slammed, and someone spoke, their voice quickly lowering to a bare murmur. Naya roused herself from the semi-sleep she'd settled into and peeked into the hall. She was a little surprised to find the soldier gone from her door. Vanissare, the Ceramoran master of trade, stood nearby, speaking with Lady Briello. They went silent as Naya approached.

"What's going on?" Naya asked. Vanissare's shirt was buttoned unevenly and his suit jacket wrinkled as though he'd dressed himself in the first thing on hand without bothering to call a servant. Lady Briello by comparison looked ready to attend breakfast with the queen herself.

Vanissare licked his lips. "We've just gotten word. Dalith Valn is dead."

The world seemed to go still. Naya stared at him. "What?"

"Apparently," Lady Briello said, her voice heavy with scorn, "they brought him over from the prison for today's trial just before the assassins attacked here. During the chaos someone killed Valn and the soldiers watching him. It's a disaster."

Naya's legs felt suddenly weak. "Did they catch the assassins?" she asked.

"Of course not," Lady Briello said with a snort. "Honestly, I told Salno something like this would happen. Talmirans think they can get away with anything. They'll claim to be investigating, and they'll make all sorts of noise about what an outrage this is. But secretly they're all laughing at us behind their hands. I heard from my maid this morning that the two who attacked here were wearing palace servant uniforms. The audacity of it is outrageous! You would think that if Queen Lial wanted us dead, she'd at least have the decency to send someone more subtle to do the job."

"My lady," Vanissare squeaked. "Perhaps we shouldn't make accusations until we know more. We still don't know for certain if the culprits were actually members of the staff or impersonators."

Lady Briello opened her mouth as though to begin a fresh rant, but Naya cut her off. "Where's Lord Delence?"

"In his rooms. He stormed off as soon as we got the news."

Naya's knock at Delence's door was met with silence. She knocked again, louder, and was rewarded by stomping footsteps. When Delence finally opened the door, his features were set into a stern mask. "Miss Garth, go back to your rooms. I'll deal with you later," he said.

Naya ignored the smoke of his anger. "Is it true? Is Valn dead?"

She expected him to brush off her question or shout at her. Instead he rubbed one hand over his face and let out a deep sigh. "I only heard an hour ago," he said. "But yes, it seems to be true."

Weight settled into the pit of Naya's stomach. Valn was

dead. Just like that she'd lost her best lead on the location of Lucia's journals. "Lady Briello said the Talmirans are responsible."

Delence's jaw tightened as he glanced down the hall. "Lady Briello would do well to learn some discretion."

"So you think it was someone else?"

"Did you come here for a purpose, or were you just looking for gossip? I've got too much to do to waste time with this right now."

"What are you going to do? What's going to happen to the Congress with Valn dead?" Naya asked.

Delence was silent for a moment. "I don't know. The trial has been canceled for obvious reasons. It's possible the Congress will be suspended until the culprit behind the attacks is determined. Even if the others don't blame Talmir, they'll still lose face over failing to provide a safe environment for the negotiations. I'm sure Queen Lial's delegates will blame us for inviting unnecessary strife by bringing you, but that can be managed." Delence shook his head. For the first time, Naya noticed the rumpled state of his clothes and the sallow hue of his skin. "I'm sending Francisco and Lucia back to Ceramor aboard the *Gallant*, but I'll need you to stay."

"Really?" Naya asked. Her knees went weak with relief. She'd been certain he'd try to send her away.

Delence's eyes narrowed. "Unfortunately. If it were up to me, I would send you back as well. I told you last night to return to your rooms. Instead you went and broke a soldier's arm."

Naya looked down, feeling a flush rising in her cheeks. "I didn't do it on purpose," she said.

"That's not how the soldier saw it. I've spent half the morning already trying to control this."

"If it's such a big problem, then why aren't you sending me away?" Naya asked.

"Because the Council still wants to hear your testimony

regarding the Belavine incident, and no doubt they'll also want to question you about the assassination attempt. I don't know when exactly those meetings will be scheduled, but in the meantime you'll be confined to your rooms. You won't leave this hall unless it's to attend an interrogation at the invitation of the queen or the Congress."

"What? That isn't fair!"

"You broke a man's arm!" Delence said, his voice rising to just below a shout.

Naya bit her cheek to keep from shouting back at him. "So I'm a prisoner now?"

"Officially? No, the law still protects you. But that will change if you keep acting like this."

Naya fought her anger. She couldn't go looking for Lucia's journals if she was locked up. She might get out for a few hours with Felicia's help, but even that would be far riskier now. "You said you're sending Francisco and Lucia back to Ceramor. Shouldn't Lucia stay? What if something happens to my bones?"

"You'll just have to be careful. Francisco is badly injured. I need Lucia to tend him on the journey, and I won't risk keeping him here. Not after last night."

Naya tried to come up with an argument that would change Delence's mind, but she could sense the steel of his resolve in the aether. Bleak despair welled up inside her. With Lucia gone and her every move watched by the queen's soldiers, she'd be trapped. She'd have no way to save Corten. Creator, she wasn't even sure she could save herself.

CHAPTER 29

NAYA

Naya walked slowly down the hall. Frustration and uncertainty churned in her stomach. She paid little attention to where she was going until her footsteps slowed outside the door to her rooms. She ran her fingers over the letters etched into the brass plaque, then opened the door. Part of her expected to find blood and the stench of death. But the servants who'd cleaned the room had done their work well. New carpets lined the floor and one of the low tables had been replaced. Otherwise the room looked exactly as it had before the attack.

Naya shivered as she remembered the way the poison had made the assassin's body twitch. The woman hadn't hesitated in killing herself to avoid capture. That wasn't the sort of loyalty a person could just buy.

As Naya looked away from the spot where the assassin had died, her attention caught on the ornate desk in the far corner. One of the drawers was partway open, marring the smooth contour of the desk's front. She took a step closer and spotted a corner of paper sticking out. Strange. She didn't remember storing anything there.

Naya opened the drawer and extracted a thin strip of folded paper. She opened it, frowning at the single line of spidery script.

Seamstress Talia wishes to discuss Blue tablecloths. 8th evening hour at the captain's house.

Naya's fingers went numb with fear. She recognized that phrase. It was the same code she'd used to contact Celia after they'd kidnapped Delence. Asking about tablecloths meant she wanted information. She glanced around the room, then stuffed the note into her skirt pocket and carefully shut the drawer.

What was this? An invitation? A trap?

She leaned against the desk, remembering the familiar figure she'd glimpsed at the ball. She'd half convinced herself that the woman she'd seen couldn't have been Celia. But the wording of the code was too specific to have come from anyone else. The message even included the reference to Naya's old identity—Blue.

Why in creation would Celia be trying to contact her now? A trap seemed the most obvious explanation. If Celia was in the palace, then it meant she was working for the queen. The assassins who'd attacked Naya had worn palace uniforms. They'd killed Valn, the one person who might expose any connections between the throne and the plot in Belavine. They'd tried to kill her, maybe because they weren't sure how much she could expose of Valn's connections and organization. But they had failed. So now they were trying to lure her away somewhere where they could finish the job.

Naya paced. Something about the theory didn't sit right with her. Celia was smart and subtle. She'd trained Naya. She had to at least suspect Naya would see the risk behind meeting with her. The note didn't offer any obvious threats or other incentives for Naya to come to the meeting. It didn't even demand her silence.

Naya reread the note, trying to puzzle out the meaning of the second line. The time was obvious enough. The codes she'd learned required her to subtract three hours if the time was written out in full, or add three if it was given in numbers. Celia wanted to meet at eleven, but the location wasn't one Naya recognized. All the codes she'd memorized had been specific to Belavine. There'd never been any reason for them to speak secretly of locations in Talmir. So what was the captain's house?

She racked her memory for anything Celia had said during their training that might expose the meaning behind the words. Celia wouldn't have used a code she didn't think Naya could understand. There would be no point. So she had to be missing something.

Naya drew in a sharp breath when realization struck her. What if the location was just a reference instead of a proper code? If that was the case, then Naya thought she knew where the meeting was meant to take place. The question was what to do about it.

By the time Lucia returned, exhausted, from her work with Francisco, Naya had drawn together the bits and pieces of a plan.

"I'm sorry I didn't check on you earlier," Lucia said as she shut the door. Her dress was stained with spots of blood and ink, and dark bags stood out under her eyes. "It's been ages since I worked with ink and flesh, so fixing Francisco's tattoos took longer than I thought it would."

"How is he?" Naya asked.

"He'll live. The surgeon knew his business and I've repaired the fading on his runes. He got very lucky. The wound alone could have killed a living man, and if those soldiers hadn't intervened when they did, the contact with the wraith eater would have broken the bindings on his soul."

"So resurrected who keep their bodies are more durable than the living?" Naya asked. She'd experienced the power of wraiths for herself, but she'd always assumed the bodied undead were more normal.

Lucia grimaced. "Yes. It's part of what gave the Mad King the idea to start his war. The tattoos binding bodied undead to this world can help sustain them even through wounds that would kill the living. They also tend to heal more quickly. That said, they still die if enough damage is done to their tattoos. And wraith eaters of course can strain the binding magic and eventually send their souls back to death." Lucia sighed, then stretched her shoulders. "Let's have a look at your bones before I collapse."

Naya shook her head. "If Delence asks you about them, I need you to tell him they're cracked."

Lucia blinked. "Well, I'll have to assess the damage first."

"No. I mean I need you to tell him my bones are cracked even though they're fine." Naya flexed her fingers. They still ached a little, but the pain was fading.

"Why?" Lucia asked.

"Delence plans to send you and Francisco out to the ships as soon as he can be safely moved. You still have my spare bones on the *Lady*, right?"

"I do."

"Good," Naya said. "I need an excuse to get out of the palace for a few hours without anyone following me around. There's no way I can do that if I'm locked up here. But if I can convince Delence to let me go back to the ship now and stay there until you can repair my bones, I think I can slip away." Delence knew Naya had been resurrected with an illegal reaper binding. But Lucia had managed to keep secret the extra modifications she'd made that allowed Naya's bones to heal. If Delence thought her bones were cracked, then he'd have no choice but to let Lucia stay long enough to fix the damage.

Lucia's eyes brightened. "Have you figured out where my journals are?"

"Not exactly, but I have an idea."

"What is it?"

Naya chewed her lip. "I think I know who Valn was working with, and I think Celia is back in Talmir."

"What?!" Lucia asked in a barely suppressed whisper.

"I'm still not sure of all the details. But help me get out of the palace unwatched for a few hours and I think I can finally get us some answers." If she was very, very lucky, she might get more than answers. But Naya didn't want to doom that luck by speaking her hopes aloud.

Lucia sat back, rubbing her face with one hand. "Creator. This is dangerous, isn't it? I should probably try to stop you. You're so young. You shouldn't have to be doing any of this."

"I'm not that young," Naya said. "I can do this. And when I do, we'll finally have a way to bring Corten back. We can expose Valn's allies and put an end to all of this." She felt like her chest was expanding as she said the words. It was a desperate sort of hope. Still, she would gladly take it over the despair she'd felt before finding Celia's note. She would make this work. She had to. If Celia's note was a trap, then Naya would find a way to slip it. She would get her answers, one way or another.

Lucia met Naya's eyes, then nodded slowly. "Perhaps you can. Just please, promise me you won't do anything too rash."

"I'll try. And you should take a nice long rest before you come to the *Gallant*. You look ready to fall over."

"How much rest?" Lucia asked, obviously catching on to Naya's meaning.

"At least until after sunset. In fact it would probably be best if you waited until tomorrow to come to the ship," Naya said. "You look *really* tired."

Lucia yawned. "Now there is a request I am more than happy to fulfill. You're sure you'll be all right?"

"I'll be fine." Naya smiled, then hurried away. She found Delence near the end of the hall, looking like he was about to leave.

"I need to speak to you," she said. He tried to brush past her, so she fell into step beside him. She let her shoulders slump and held her left hand protectively against her chest.

"Not right now. I've got a meeting to attend," Delence said.

"This will be quick. Lucia examined my bones, and one of them is cracked. She said it would be dangerous to leave it alone. I have to go back to the *Gallant* if she's going to replace it before they leave for Talmir."

Delence stopped and gave her a critical look. "Why didn't you say anything about that earlier?" he asked.

"I didn't want to complain unless I was sure there was a problem."

"Fine," Delence said, after a pause so long it left Naya feeling like she would explode with impatience. "I think I can convince the queen and the other delegates to allow that much. Once Francisco is stable enough for the journey, you can go across with them."

"If it's all right, I'd like to go to the ships now. I worked as Lucia's assistant for a while. If someone sends my bones and the rest of her tools from the *Lady*, then I can get everything ready while she rests. That way we won't cause any more delays than we have to." Naya lowered her eyes and tried to look meek rather than eager. Lucia would need very little help, but she hoped Delence didn't know that.

"I'll see if I can get approval," he said with a nod. "Wait in your rooms until I send for you."

Naya returned to her rooms. She made a quick survey of her belongings, then stuffed everything she thought she might need into a small bag and summoned Felicia.

"I'm going back to the *Gallant* for a day or two," she said once Felicia arrived. "Could you carry a message to Mel for me before I go?" She didn't know if Mel would accept a letter from her after what she'd seen last night. But she wanted a chance to explain herself, and she wasn't sure when else she'd get it.

"Of course," Felicia said. "After that I'll pack my things. Do you know how we'll be getting to the docks? I can see about arranging for a carriage if you haven't done it already."

Naya shook her head. "I appreciate everything you've done for me, but you don't have to come with me. I'll just be there until Lucia replaces my cracked bone."

Felicia looked down. "I'd rather come if it's all the same. There won't be anything for me to do here while you're gone."

"There probably won't be anything for you to do on the ship either. It's not as though I'll need new hairstyles while I'm waiting for Lucia to carve my bones."

Felicia let out a very unladylike snort. "Well, there's nothing wrong with looking nice even if there's nobody else to see. But even if you want to wear nothing but shifts and keep your hair a tangled mess, I'm sure I can still find some way to be useful."

"Are you sure that's what you want? I wouldn't mind the company, but someone did just try to kill me. You'd probably be safer staying away."

"I'm sure. I've been thinking, and since I haven't had much luck finding any lost princes, I've decided I'll have to look for adventure elsewhere. Following you seems like a good way to find it."

Naya raised her eyebrows. "What about that boy in the kitchen?"

Felicia waved the comment away. "Oh, I've decided anyone who can be dissuaded from talking to me by a cook with a cleaning rag isn't worth the effort."

Naya laughed. "I see. Felicia, has anyone ever told you you're a little odd?"

Felicia smiled. "It's been said once or twice. Now, I think you said you had a letter you wanted sent?"

Naya crossed to her desk and wrote a quick note for Mel,

then handed it to Felicia. "Delence said he'd call for a carriage. Once you've delivered this, get together whatever you need and come meet me at the palace's front steps."

Delence didn't waste any time keeping his promise. Barely an hour later, Naya received word from another servant that her carriage was ready. She tried to keep her head high and her expression calm as a squad of seven soldiers arrived to escort her out to the waiting carriage. With the clank of their weapons and the thump of their boots surrounding her, she almost didn't hear Mel call out, "Naya, wait!"

Naya's chest tightened. She turned and saw Mel standing just past the ring of soldiers, clutching a piece of paper in one hand. Baz, the older guard who'd been with them on their outing, stood behind her wearing a worried scowl.

"Hi," Naya said. "I, uh, guess you got my letter?"

Mel smiled weakly. "Yeah. I tried to get up to see you earlier, but the guards on the Ceramoran wing wouldn't let me through. They said it was too much of a risk."

Naya winced. "I'm sorry."

"I know." Mel waved the slightly crumpled letter as evidence. "Pretty sure you wrote that about four times."

"We should get going," one of the soldiers escorting Naya said.

"Wait!" Mel's brow furrowed. "I just . . . what's really going on here? My mother's been shut up with the Talmiran delegates since last night. Everyone's talking about assassins and some of the delegates are already planning to leave. They're saying the peace has been broken. Is it true?"

Naya tensed. Delence had said the Congress talks would be delayed, but Mel's description seemed to imply a deeper fracture between the Powers. "I don't know. Hopefully everything will calm down in a couple of days."

Mel nodded, though she looked uncertain. "And you're not

leaving for good, right? You'll send me a message when you get back?"

"If you want, but—"

"Good." Mel smiled. "Dead or alive, we bastards have to stick together, right?"

CHAPTER 30

NAYA

Felicia arrived at the carriage a few minutes after Naya. Her cheeks were flushed and she sounded out of breath as she slid onto the seat across from Naya.

"Sorry," she said. "At first the soldiers at the Talmiran delegation's wing wouldn't send anyone up to get Miss Jeden, and then everything was so hectic up in the servant's hall, what with everyone still being so upset about the attack."

"It's okay," Naya said. "Though you do realize we'll only be at the ship for a day or two, right?" She nodded to the over-stuffed bag Felicia was carrying.

Felicia blushed. "I know. But I couldn't pick what to bring, so I decided it would be faster to just put it all in. Things being as strange as they are, you never know what might be useful."

"Are you ready?" one of the three soldiers standing next to the carriage asked. They would be accompanying Naya and Felicia to the docks, presumably to ensure they arrived safely.

Or to ensure you disappear along the way.

Naya shivered and pushed the thought away. Still, she kept a part of her mind focused on the aether, alert for any sudden shifts in the soldiers' emotions. "Yes, let's get going."

The ride to the lifts seemed to take an eternity. As they bounced along the crowded streets, Naya's doubts grew. She imagined the note like a burning ember in her pocket. She knew she was taking a risk by seeking Celia out. If she got herself killed or captured, there would be no one to help Lucia find Corten's soul. But she no longer had time for caution. Celia had worked closely with Valn. She would know his allies. Naya had to take this chance.

It was late afternoon when their carriage finally reached the cliffs. Naya and Felicia stepped out into the golden sunlight to find the streets above the docks still bustling. Sailors and merchants came and went from the taverns nearby, and a crowd gathered by the edge of the cliffs, waiting to use the lifts. Farther north along the curve of the cliff face, Naya knew those without spare coin would be descending one of the precarious stairways carved into the rock.

Naya reached into the aether, feeling the city's pulse swell around her. Belavine had been a chaotic place of bright citrus and swirling colors. Its pulse beat time in children's running footsteps and the rattle and shriek of the trams. Lith Lor's pulse felt ponderous by comparison. The march of heavy boots on old stone vibrated in her chest, somehow harmonizing with a distant murmur of song and the sharp salt smell of the ocean breeze as it darted through the city streets.

"Hurry up," one of the soldiers muttered.

Naya returned her attention to the physical world and realized they'd reached the front of the line for the lifts. Felicia already stood inside, peering down to the docks below. From this height the cargo being unloaded from the various ships looked tiny.

Naya stepped into the lift and felt the tug of the runes as it descended. Once they reached the shore, the soldiers escorted them to one of the smaller docks, where a rowboat waited to take them out to the *Gallant*.

The ship looked to be in good condition, but as Naya

stepped aboard she felt sour unease wafting through the aether. Sailors lounged on deck, some working half-heartedly at small tasks, others throwing dice.

"Miss Garth," Captain Cervacaro said as he strode across the deck. "Lord Delence sent a message this morning that we were to take young Francisco back to Belavine, but he didn't say you'd be joining us."

"I won't," Naya said, though it pained her to think of the *Gallant* sailing without her. "I'll just be here for a day or two while Lucia fixes my bond."

Captain Cervacaro ran his fingers through his scraggly beard. "And our Talmiran hosts won't take issue with her performing necromancy in their waters?"

"It won't be a problem," Naya said, hoping she was right. At least nobody had balked when Lucia had gone to fix Francisco's tattoos.

"Very well. I suppose you'll be needing your cabin then?"

"I will."

Cervacaro glanced around, then snapped at one of the sailors throwing dice nearby. "Jeverin, go clear out Miss Garth's cabin."

The sailor scowled, then nodded. "Yes, sir."

"Why would my cabin need to be cleared out?" Naya asked, trying to keep her tone light.

Cervacaro shrugged. "You know how it is. This Congress was supposed to last for weeks yet. It seemed a shame to leave such a pleasant room empty, so I've been using it."

"I see." Naya gritted her teeth. It wasn't unreasonable. Still, it felt invasive that Cervacaro had so quickly moved into the space, as though he were the ship's true master and she just a guest.

Cervacaro looked around the deck. "Truth be told, I'm glad we're being sent back early. Never did much care for Talmir, and it seems things have gotten worse than usual with this Congress business going on. Half the taverns in dockside are refusing to serve anyone who's got even so much as a hint of a Ceramoran accent. I'll be glad to get back to friendlier waters." His gaze settled on Naya. "Don't suppose you've given any more thought to my offer?"

Naya shook her head. "I already told you, the *Gallant* isn't for sale."

"So you say. But once we reach Belavine, our contract with Lord Delence will be complete. Your ship will have no crew, and you'll be stuck out here for who-knows-how-long dealing with this Congress business. You'll have to find a proxy to hire you a new crew, or pay your docking fees. Either that or she'll be scrapped."

"I know," Naya growled. "And she won't be scrapped."

Cervacaro's expression softened. "Look, girl, I can tell you love this ship. She's an easy ship to love. And Creator knows, if it had been up to me, I would have given just about anything to keep the *Arabella* afloat. I'm not trying to take what's yours out of spite. I'm trying to save you the sorrow of losing her to decay and port taxmen."

Naya hesitated. In truth, the *Gallant*'s fate had weighed heavy on her mind ever since they'd set sail. And things had only gotten worse since then. Given the severity of Francisco's injuries, she couldn't deny him use of the ship to get home. And they couldn't send the *Lady* back since the *Gallant* didn't have enough space to get the rest of the delegates home once their business here was done.

But even though a part of her knew selling the ship would be the simplest option, she couldn't bring herself to do it. She shook her head. "I don't have time to deal with this right now."

Cervacaro scowled. "Well, you'd best find time soon. Once we get back to Belavine, me and my crew will have to find other work. My offer won't stand forever."

Naya and Felicia remained on deck for several tense minutes before the sailor Cervacaro had sent below returned to report the cabin was ready. Once inside, Naya shut the door and drew in aether to make sure nobody was lingering on the other side, or in the cabin next door.

"Well," Felicia said. "What should we do while we wait? I brought my embroidery kit. I also have a couple of novels. I've heard cracked bones can be painful, and I always find reading about someone else's troubles is an excellent distraction."

Naya shook her head. "My bones aren't actually cracked."

"I—sorry?"

"I needed a reason to be out of the palace and away from all those soldiers for a while. I'm going out tonight."

"I see." Felicia's expression brightened. "I'd hoped it was something like that but I didn't dare ask back at the palace. How can I help?"

"I'm afraid it won't be very exciting," Naya said apologetically. "I'll just need you to stay here with the door locked, and if anyone comes by tell them I'm resting and shouldn't be disturbed."

"You're right, that isn't very exciting." Felicia sighed dramatically. "But in truth the sort of excitement you get involved in is probably too uncomfortable for my tastes. I will stay here and nobly defend the cabin. But in return I expect you to tell me tales of your grand adventure when you return."

Naya smiled. "It's a deal."

Later, Naya opened the bag she'd brought from the palace and began sorting through the contents. Before she'd left, she'd cut out the oilcloth lining her sea chest. Now she spread the cloth out and set on it a change of clothes and a knife with a blade a little shorter than her hand. Last, she added the bag of coins she'd taken from the hidden compartment in her father's cabin. She wasn't sure if she'd need those, but it seemed better to have them than not. She wrapped the bundle tight and tied it with a pair of belts, trying not to think too hard about what she was about to do.

"Will you be leaving now?" Felicia asked.

Naya gave the belts a final tug, then examined her work. The bundle wouldn't be completely waterproof, but it was better than nothing. "Not yet. I have to wait until nightfall."

She stood and paced across the narrow cabin. Now that she had a plan, she itched to be going. Waiting only seemed to make her doubts scream louder. But there was no point in leaving now. In the daylight she'd almost certainly be spotted, and anyway Celia wouldn't be at the meeting spot for hours yet.

Naya sat on the bunk. She glared at the patch of sunlight coming through the cabin windows. "You said something about a novel?" she asked Felicia.

Felicia grinned. "Oh, yes. I'm not sure if it will be to your tastes. My sister always used to make fun of me for reading them. But I've always loved them."

"How many siblings do you have?" Naya asked, smiling as she remembered Felicia's story of stealing her brother's cake.

"Four—three brothers and one sister," Felicia said as she dug a book from her bag. "My brother Lukan is the oldest, he works for the city guard in Belavine. Next is Jekorio, he helps my dad in one of the warehouses by the docks. My sister, Cerria, is a nursemaid for a nice family in Riorrica, and Olli, my little brother, is still living at home. What about you? Do you have any siblings?"

"No," Naya said. "It was just me and my mother. After she died, I moved in with my father."

"That sounds lonely," Felicia said.

"It was," Naya admitted. She took the book Felicia was holding to keep from having to say anything else. Her eyebrows rose as she read the title.

"*The Count of Ceramor?*" she asked. "What is it? Some sort of history?"

Felicia laughed. "Ah, no. It's more of a romance. Though there are some very exciting sword fights too."

Naya felt heat rising in her cheeks. "Oh. It sounds very, uh, distracting?" She'd loved stories when she was a little girl, but between her studies at the Merchants Academy and her work with her father, she'd had little time to read for pleasure. She couldn't imagine the look her father would have given her if he'd found her wasting time with something like this. Somehow, trying to imagine his scowl made her all the more curious. She glanced out the window again at the sunny afternoon. Well, she did have hours before she could go anywhere. She ran her fingers over the cover, then flipped the book open. She would read a few pages, just to humor Felicia and give her mind a chance to rest. After that she would do something useful.

When Naya next looked up, the sky outside was dark. She snapped the book shut and jumped to her feet. At some point she'd curled up on the bunk. Felicia must have activated the cabin's rune lamps, because the space was bathed in a soft blue-white glow. How had she not noticed that? "What time is it?" she asked Felicia.

Felicia looked up from her needlework. "A little before eight? Sorry, you looked like you were really enjoying the book and I didn't want to interrupt."

Naya relaxed slightly. For a moment she'd worried that she'd somehow missed the meeting. But no, she still had enough time to get there and look around before the appointed time. She ran her thumb along the corner of the pages. Without realizing it, she'd read through nearly the whole book. "I guess I do like it. Though I thought it was stupid how Julet killed herself just because she thought the Count died."

Felicia smiled. "Really? But it's so romantic. After all, he was the only necromancer who lived nearby. There wouldn't have been anyone to bring him back, and she didn't want to live without him."

"She could have at least tried to find another way, or you know, checked to make sure he was actually dead?" Naya shook her head, then stood up. "Anyway, I should get going."

Felicia followed Naya's gaze to the darkened windows, nervous energy prickling through her aether. "You're really going out there?"

Naya reached into her bag and pulled out her father's logbook. "I have to." She held the logbook out to Felicia. Inside were her notes on how to translate the cipher. In the end she hadn't found anything more than the cryptic references to Resurgence. Maybe Delence and his scribes would have better luck. "If I'm not back by morning, I want you to give this to Francisco. Tell him I went after Celia and something went wrong." Hopefully it wouldn't come to that.

Felicia took the logbook hesitantly. "All right. But how do you intend to get off the ship without anyone noticing you?"

Naya smiled. "Watch."

Naya stripped down to her shift and grabbed her bundle of clothes. She crossed the room and opened one of the panels in the cabin's windows. The opening was too small for an ordinary person to squeeze through. But she wasn't ordinary. She drew in aether, letting go of the idea of her body as something solid and unchangeable. Her limbs compressed as she squeezed through the window. It was an unpleasant sensation, and like changing her features, she could feel the extra strain as the runes of her binding struggled to hold her soul to the less-familiar body.

Once through, she clung to the window's ledge, her bare toes pressed against the ship's side. She pulled her bundled clothes through next, then glanced up to see if anyone on the deck above had spotted her. The night was dark and so far it looked as though luck was on her side. Just to be sure, she extended her senses out into the aether. A moment later she felt the swirl of aether from the sailors standing watch above. Concentrating on it made her head feel suddenly too light. Perhaps Captain Cervacaro was using extra liquor rations to counter the cold reception they'd received on shore. Regardless, they didn't seem to have noticed her. She glanced back into the cabin and saw Felicia watching her with wide eyes.

Naya smiled, but the expression quickly turned into a wince as the night breeze cut through her thin shift. She tried not to think about how exposed she was, dangling from the side of the ship. She glanced down at the water and nearly scrambled back to the warm safety of her cabin. The drop had to be fifteen feet, but in the dark it looked far longer. Naya licked her lips, then let go with one hand to shove her arm through a loop she'd made with one of the belts.

"I can do this," she whispered. Then she let go of the ship.

Cold sea air whistled past as she fell. Naya clutched the bundle to her chest and pointed her toes straight down as her father had taught her. With a splash icy water enveloped her, sealing like a tomb over her head.

Naya's eyes opened wide as the cold and dark pressed in all around her. Fear squeezed her chest like a vise, and she had to remind herself that she didn't need to breathe. The dark waters couldn't kill her. Still, it was hard to keep the panic from grabbing hold. She looked up, focusing on the wavering glow of a ship's lantern where it reflected off the surface.

She tried to swim, but the lights might as well have been distant stars. The water felt heavy against her. It slid uselessly around her, and the surface grew no closer despite her frantic efforts. The ocean was a trap, gripping her stronger than death's tides ever had.

No. She couldn't die here. After all she'd been through, she wouldn't let a little water stop her. Naya forced herself to stop flailing. She drew in aether. The energy was more diffuse here, but the ocean was full of life and soon it swirled cool and ponderous up to meet her. She concentrated on her limbs, willing them to be solid, imagining the water churning as she forced it aside with each powerful stroke. When her head finally broke the surface, she found she'd drifted almost twenty feet from the *Gallant*'s side. The lights of the shore looked tiny compared to the vast darkness of the open ocean beyond the harbor.

Naya turned away from that darkness. Her father had ensured she knew how to swim before he'd allowed her to join him aboard the *Gallant*, and soon her arms and legs fell into the familiar rhythm. The moon had fully risen and the activity on the docks quieted by the time Naya reached the shore. She crouched on a narrow strip of pebbled beach in the shadow of the cliffs, searching for any sign that she'd been spotted. When no cry of alarm went up, she unwrapped her bundle and got dressed.

Despite her careful work, the clothes she'd brought were damp and rumpled. Hopefully the damage wouldn't be too noticeable in the dark. Once dressed, she stood quietly with her fingertips pressed to her face. Her skin softened and her features shifted subtly—broader cheeks, darker eyes, hair a little less curly than her own. It was tricky without a mirror, but by blending Felicia's features with her own, she could give herself a face she was sure no one in the city would recognize. She smiled to herself, imagining that this face belonged to a girl who could have been Felicia's sister in another life. That girl was bold and joyful, with a big family she knew she could trust. She was the kind of girl who would walk the streets at night unafraid, not because she knew how to fight but simply because nothing bad had ever happened to make her afraid.

Naya's smile faded as the reality of what she had to do settled back in. Still, as she started walking, she held on to that image of a life that might have been, wrapping it around herself like a warm cloak. She stuck close to the cliffs, trying to seem small and inconspicuous. A young woman in rumpled clothes riding up the lifts at this hour was bound to draw attention. Instead she turned onto one of the narrow stairways that zigzagged up the cliff. She took the steps two at a time, barely touching the safety rope that protected travelers from a deadly fall onto the rocks below.

From the top of the stairs, it took only a few minutes to reach her destination. Even in the dark, the route was eerily familiar.

The captain's house.

Captain Hal Garth's house stood on a street corner in one of the city's nicer neighborhoods. The houses here were grand, but they lacked the sense of stately age that surrounded the palace districts. Naya felt a chill as she approached the building. The windows were all dark behind drawn shutters and the hedges framing the front steps were more ragged than she remembered. She hadn't thought about what might have happened to the place since her father's death. He would have surely filed death papers, but Naya had never seen them. And somehow she doubted such documents would be respected given his status as a traitor to the Crown.

Naya glanced up at the stars. She still had more than an hour before the appointed time. She closed her eyes and reached out into the aether. Most of the street had the quiet, hazy feel of people sleeping. She couldn't sense anything coming from her father's house. Good. If this was a trap, then it seemed Celia hadn't arrived to set it yet.

Naya crossed the street cautiously. The front door's frame had been cracked, and a new lock was bolted onto it. She glanced around to make sure no one was watching, then slipped the tip of her finger into the lock. After a moment of wiggling her finger up and down, she felt the tumblers fall into place. She twisted, ignoring the uncomfortable pressure of the lock's metal against her finger as it clicked open.

Stepping into the front hall was like stepping back into a nightmare version of her childhood. Light from the streetlamps leaked through the cracks in the shutters. It gave just enough illumination for her to see that the house had been ransacked. Overturned and broken furniture cluttered the front hall, partially blocking the stairs to the second floor. Had robbers done this, or was it the work of overeager city guards hunting for evidence against a traitor? She crouched behind an overturned chair and drew in more aether, waiting. The house remained silent, and no new emotions swirled through the aether. After a moment she stood and began picking her way farther inside.

The air felt heavy, and there was a thin layer of dust on the floor. Whatever had happened here, it had been some time since anyone had been in the house. Slowly, she walked through the rooms on the ground floor, trying to make sense of the mess. In the kitchen, smashed dishes lay scattered outside empty cupboards. Someone had pulled the books off the sitting room shelves and left them lying about with pages torn and spines broken.

Miss Vani, the middle-aged woman her father had kept on as housekeeper and cook, would have been aghast to see the place like this. What had happened to her? Naya hoped that she'd been able to find new work and that the stain of Hal Garth's treason hadn't spread to her as well. Miss Vani had always kept herself apart from Naya and her father, but she'd also made sure to leave out a honey cake or some other treat for whenever Naya came home from her classes. Naya felt a stab of guilt that she hadn't given any thought to the woman's fate before now.

She headed upstairs and was just about to open the door to her old bedroom when she felt something stir in the aether below her. She crouched down and breathed in more aether. Closing her eyes, she sensed a sharp, nervous prickle that mingled with a heavy shroud of weariness. Underneath those was a cool thread of focused calm.

Celia had come.

CHAPTER 31

NAYA

Naya crept partway down the stairs, her bare feet silent on the dusty wood. She heard a soft click and then a creak as someone opened the back door into the kitchen. Her impression of the aether outside the house was fuzzier, but it didn't seem there were any other people out there. Strange. Had Celia come alone?

Naya drew her knife, then descended the rest of the stairs. She heard a *tink* as something disturbed the mess of broken pottery in the kitchen. She tightened her grip on the knife, then rushed through the kitchen doorway. A figure leapt back, shoes crunching on a broken plate. Naya could feel the shards under her own feet, but they couldn't cut her.

"Don't move!" Naya ordered.

The figure slowly raised two empty hands. The kitchen window was behind her, leaving her features in shadow. Still, Naya recognized the same lean frame and confident stance that had caught her eye at the ball. Celia wiggled the fingers of one hand and then reached slowly toward her side.

"I said don't move!" Naya took a step forward, brandishing the knife.

"Relax, girl," Celia said. "I'm just getting us some light."

Naya hesitated, and Celia pulled something small and round from her pocket. She gave it a twist and light blossomed from the runes around the edge of the disk. In its blue-white glow, the lines around Celia's mouth and eyes looked deeper than ever. Her cheeks were sunken and her skin pale, as though she hadn't been eating well. Still, her dark eyes glimmered with the same cool intelligence Naya remembered from her time in Belavine. "Blue, I presume?" Celia asked.

Naya nodded, then let her disguise slip away. A confusing tangle of emotions tightened her chest. Anger at the woman who'd betrayed her. Fear at what Celia's presence here could mean. And, strangely, relief that Celia hadn't died that night in the tunnels. Naya already had enough blood on her hands.

"You're early," Celia said, setting the light disk on the counter next to her.

"So are you." Naya glanced at the door behind Celia.

"I'm alone," Celia said, following her gaze. "Don't worry. There won't be any Talmiran soldiers barging in to interrupt us."

"There'd better not be. I've got half the *Gallant*'s crew waiting just a block away. They'll come if you try something."

Celia's eyes narrowed, and a hum of tension rose in her aether. Then she seemed to relax. "No. I don't think you do. I taught you better than this, girl. Don't tell lies that are too big for you."

"I'm not lying."

"Of course you are. You're a decent spy, but you don't have the money or the presence to inspire that kind of loyalty."

Naya clenched her jaw. "What are you doing here, Celia? Did Queen Lial order you to contact me?"

"Queen Lial? Hardly. She doesn't know I'm back in Talmir, and I hope to keep things that way."

Naya snorted. "Haven't you heard? You shouldn't tell lies that are too big for you. I saw you hiding among the servants at the ball."

Celia pursed her lips. "I was there. But the queen doesn't know as much as she thinks she does about what goes on in her palace."

Naya shook her head. "I almost caught up with you at the ball, but then Lady Elv blocked me so you could escape. I know you're working with her and the rest of the spies under the trade master."

"You know that, do you?" Celia asked, bitter scorn seeping into her aether. "In that case you know things I do not. Because so far as I know, Lady Elv and her ilk have no idea who I am. I didn't even know who they were until recently."

"That's impossible."

"Hardly. The branches of the Talmiran spy network are kept separate. It's a safety measure intended to keep disasters like what happened in Belavine from undermining all our resources. Even if a spy is captured and tortured, they can't expose information they don't have. Valn recruited me directly, so I never had any contact with other spies in Talmir."

"Then why did Lady Elv interrupt me right as I went looking for you?"

Celia lifted one hand in an uncertain gesture. "My guess? She probably had orders to watch you—and to coax you into lashing out if she could. Anything you do to embarrass the Ceramoran delegation only strengthens Talmir's position."

Naya stared at Celia, trying to judge if she was telling the truth. The timing had seemed too convenient for coincidence. But perhaps Lady Elv had seen an opportunity when Naya had moved away from Francisco. It was the first time she'd been alone in public. Taken in that light, Celia's explanation made sense. Queen Lial could have also meant for Lady Elv to unsettle Naya, perhaps hoping it would make her more susceptible to the queen's threats and demands for information. Games within games. Creator, she was getting sick of these politicians and their schemes. "If you're not working with the queen, then why did you call me here? What are you even doing in Talmir?"

"I invited you here because I have an offer to make. Information about Valn's death."

"Did you kill him?" Naya asked.

"No. But I know who did, and I fear what they might be planning next."

Naya felt a chill as she thought back to her father's logbook. His suspicions about Valn. Who else but Valn's allies would want to kill him? In Talmir at least, the dead couldn't share their secrets. "Does this have anything to do with Resurgence?"

Celia's face went suddenly, and carefully, still. "How do you know that name?"

"How do you?" Naya asked.

Perhaps it was the sight of her father's house torn apart, one more part of who she'd been destroyed. Or maybe it was the sharp salt smell on her clothes, the act of having to sneak into a place she'd once called home. But something inside her stirred, fanning the sense of reckless courage that had driven her from the ship. She met Celia's eyes. "Whatever information you think you have, I know you don't plan to just give it to me for free. You need something, and I don't think you would have contacted me unless you were desperate. So you'll be the one answering my questions."

Celia's lips tightened in a knife-thin smile. "If only Valn had known you had such spine, he never would have dared bring you back."

Naya waited, refusing to look away. Finally Celia glanced down. "Fine. You're right. I'll tell you what I know, but in return I need you to do something."

"What?"

"I want asylum in Ceramor."

Naya almost laughed at the absurdity of the request. "Everyone knows you worked for Valn. Why would Ceramor grant you asylum?"

"Because I have information they need. I know what would happen if I tried to go to the Ceramorans directly. I'd be dead or imprisoned within the hour. But you saved Delence's life. He might listen to my request if it came through you."

The aether surrounding Celia was heavy with exhaustion, and with a bone-deep fear that made the back of Naya's neck prickle. Celia had always seemed so calm and confident before. Whatever had happened to her since Belavine, it had shaken her. "Why should I trust you?" Naya asked, shifting her grip so her knife flashed in the dim light.

Celia held her hands palm up as though to emphasize her own lack of weapons. "I know what you are, girl. You can tell I've brought no one with me. If I wanted a fight, I wouldn't have come alone, and I wouldn't have let you see me coming. Not after last time."

Naya stretched her senses as far as they would go. Nothing in the sleepy aether surrounding the house suggested Celia was lying. "Is Trade Master Galve part of Resurgence? Was he funding Valn?" Naya asked.

"Galve? No. I doubt he would have approved of Valn's plans. He doesn't have the vision for that sort of thing."

"Then who or what is Resurgence?"

Celia shook her head. "First tell me where you heard that name."

Naya hesitated, then decided there probably wasn't much Celia could do with the information. "My father wrote about them. He didn't find much more than a name before he died, but he thought they were funding Valn in secret."

"He was right. Resurgence is a shadow organization funding agents spread through Talmir and Ceramor. From what I've seen, their goal is to stir up conflict between those two countries. I think they were already supporting Valn before he hired me. I helped expand his information network, gather blackmail, and pass along bribes to various officials among the guard and the Ceramoran elite. From the amount of money he gave me,

I always assumed we had the support of the throne, but I was wrong."

"You really expect me to believe all this?" Naya asked.

Celia leaned forward, her eyes on Naya's. "I am telling you what I know. What you believe is up to you."

Where else could all that money have come from? Naya thought back to her meeting with the queen. At first she'd assumed the queen's questions about Belavine were just for show, an excuse to threaten and intimidate her. But Naya had sensed curiosity in her aether. If Celia was telling the truth, that would make more sense. If Valn wasn't working for the throne, then he really was a traitor, and the queen would be just as eager as everyone else to uncover his allies' identities.

"When you were in Ceramor, did Valn ever tell you who was paying for everything?" Naya asked.

"No. I didn't learn about his source until later. After you and I fought, I used the embassy tunnels to flee the city. I knew I wouldn't be welcomed back in Talmir. I didn't have any illusions that my country would protect me after such a conspicuous failure. I planned to head south toward Silmar. But I was stopped by a stranger in one of the smaller towns two days out from Belavine." A bitter note entered Celia's voice. "He knew who I was and apparently knew exactly how to find me. He told me he represented Valn's superiors and that they still had work for me. He gave me money, and instructions on where to cross the Talmiran border and who to meet when I got there."

"Why did he make you come back?" Naya asked. "Why risk having someone recognize you here?"

"He didn't say. He just told me that the plan was nearing its conclusion and that I was to return to Talmir and await orders. I have family here, a brother. This man knew his name. He promised that so long as I followed orders, no harm would come to him.

"Once I got to the border," Celia continued, "they arranged for me to enter the palace with the extra servants hired to assist with the Congress. I was told to report anything I learned about the delegates and the status of the negotiations. They've given me other tasks as well, mostly minor spy work. Meanwhile I've been trying to figure out what's really going on. Between the attacks on you and Valn's death, I think the ones who hired me are trying to sabotage the Congress."

We are the flood. We will wash you away. Naya shivered as the assassin's words echoed in her mind. "Did Resurgence order Valn's death?" she asked.

"Yes."

"Who are they?"

Celia smiled grimly. "Trouble. I'll be happy to share every detail I have as soon as you get a promise of asylum for me and my brother."

"Fine. I'll ask." Something here still wasn't adding up. Even if Naya trusted Celia's word, she wasn't at all sure she could convince Delence to grant her asylum.

Naya drew in aether. The energy around Celia prickled with nervous fear. That certainly fit her story. She'd have to be desperate to ask Naya for help. Maybe Naya could use that. "There's one more thing I want to know first though. Who gave Valn Lucia's old journal?"

Celia raised one eyebrow. "He never told me."

"But you knew about it?"

"I'd seen the journal and I had my suspicions about how Valn had used it. An ordinary wraith wouldn't have been able to push past the salma wood plate in Delence's door. Before that, Valn had talked about his plans to create something 'special' that would give us an edge the Ceramorans would never expect. Why do you care where he got the journal?"

Naya paused. "I want something specific I can bring to

Delence. He's more likely to believe me if I give him details he can confirm." Even if Celia was trying to trick her, she might tell the truth if she thought this was a test. She could prove her good intentions by giving away a small piece of information here, in order to plant a greater lie later.

Celia's expression turned thoughtful. "It's only a guess," she said slowly, "but Valn has an aunt named Ela Hest. She's a scribe in the Academy of Magics. Valn spoke of her on and off. Apparently they were quite close when he was a child. Hest is old enough that she would have been active during the war. Valn made a trip to Talmir about a year before you joined us. I think he mentioned visiting his aunt then. If she didn't give him the journal herself, she's likely the one who told him how to find it."

Ela Hest. The name was one of the ones Lucia mentioned in her notes on the purges. "What else do you know about her?"

"Not much. I've never had much cause to deal with Talmiran rune scribes."

"Do you think she's connected to Resurgence?"

"I don't know. It's possible. But even if she is, I'd be surprised if she was involved in what's going on at the Congress. The scribes don't have a presence there."

"But she might know something."

"Perhaps. You should be able to confirm her family connections to Valn through the birth records in the Book of Lords. His last trip to Talmir is likely on the records as well. Anything else will be harder to track." Celia's brow furrowed briefly. "I don't know where Hest lives, but all the high-ranking scribes have private offices inside the Academy of Magics. That would be where I'd start if I was looking for a connection."

Naya had scouted the Academy of Magics. Only the outside, but that was enough to tell her the place was hardly a fortress. She was sure she could find a way inside if she had to. Finding Hest's office and getting back out unnoticed would be another challenge entirely. But that challenge would be worth tackling if her suspicions about Hest were right.

"I'll talk to Delence," Naya said. "How do I contact you?"

"There's a bronze statue at the end of the west hall just past the main entrance to the palace. It has a gap under its pedestal. Leave a note in the usual code there. I heard a rumor that you've been confined to your rooms. But given that you were able to meet me here, I'm assuming you won't have a problem planting messages inside the palace." Celia hesitated a moment, then added, "And, if you do try going to the academy, be careful. Any guards there will probably be equipped to handle the undead."

"Why?" Naya asked. "There haven't been any undead in Talmir since the war."

Celia smiled humorlessly. "You weren't alive back then, so you never saw the way fear spread when the Mad King's army was on the march. The academy fancied itself a bastion of hope against the corrupted hordes. As soon as they perfected the wraith eaters, they made a point of arming their own people. After the war ended, it became tradition for the academy guards to carry wraith eaters as a reminder of the academy's contributions and their dedication to using runic arts to defend Talmir."

"Perfect," Naya said grimly. "Are there any other defenses I should know about?"

"I don't know," Celia said, sounding irritated. "If you want my advice, forget Ela Hest and bring my offer to Delence. We don't have much time before Resurgence makes their next move."

CHAPTER 32

NAYA

Naya stood by a row of hedges one block from her father's house and drew in aether. Celia had claimed she'd come alone, but she could have placed someone with a signal rune on the nearby streets to follow Naya once she left. Naya waited a minute, then two, but didn't sense anything beyond the haze of people sleeping in the nearby houses. She wrinkled her nose. She was probably being paranoid. But better that than to allow Celia to draw her into a trap. She'd trusted the old woman once before, and Celia had returned that trust with lies.

Naya glanced toward the cliffs. She had hours left before dawn. If she returned now, she'd have plenty of time to get back aboard the ship before anyone could notice her absence. If she told Delence about her meeting with Celia, she might convince him to play along and extend an offer of asylum. He wanted to know who was behind Valn's death and Celia was too valuable a resource to ignore.

But returning now would put her back under the control of the queen and her soldiers. It would mean giving up what might be her last chance to explore the city freely. If Celia had told the truth, then Ela Hest fit Lucia's theory perfectly. And if she was the one who'd given Valn Lucia's journal, then tonight was

Naya's best chance to go after her. Thinking of it that way made the choice seem obvious.

For ten minutes she wandered randomly, darting around corners and drawing in aether to check for anyone who might be following. When she was reasonably sure Celia hadn't sent anyone after her, she turned her steps toward the Academy of Magics. Even then she didn't let her guard down. Carriages still traveled the main streets, and three times she had to change direction to avoid patrolling city guards. It seemed there were far more of them than the last time she'd been in the city. She didn't want to give them the opportunity to stop and wonder why a young woman was skulking around alone in salt-stained clothes.

She turned a corner and the white mass of the academy's walls rose in front of her. The iron gates were shut, and two guards stood by them. Naya paused in the shadow of a darkened restaurant across the street. The guards wore more elaborate uniforms than those she'd seen on the city guards or the soldiers in the palace. Their jackets were cut longer, with gold braid running along the shoulders and the academy's black-and-white crest stitched across the front. At their hips, each guard carried a sheathed sword on one side and a rune pistol on the other.

One of the guards yawned, rubbing his eyes. The other glanced over and said something, then both men laughed. They obviously weren't expecting trouble. Still, Naya doubted they'd let her in if she walked up to the gates without any sort of iden-tification. She didn't have one of the fancy medallions she'd seen the last time she'd been here, and she didn't know enough about the academy's inner workings to lie her way in.

Naya walked farther down the road. Across the street from the academy was a row of small shops and restaurants. Every-thing was closed except for two restaurants that looked like they were still doing brisk business despite the late hour. Most of the customers wore the robes and metal medallions of rune scribes.

She watched them, some talking and laughing in groups, others eating distractedly while reading or scribbling notes.

Naya brushed at the front of her dress. Her body still hummed with nervous energy. Perhaps she could learn something here. If Ela Hest worked at the academy, then surely some of the students would know her.

Naya ran her fingers over her face, checking that her disguise was still in place. It was, but maybe a different face would serve her better here. She concentrated, then felt her features shift to those of Blue. Her hair darkened to black, forming smooth, elegant curls. The lines of her face grew sharper and though she didn't have a mirror to check, she knew her eyes would have brightened to a striking true green. She pulled back her hair, as though tying it in a tail. She concentrated again, then lowered her hands carefully. Her hair stayed up, held in place by her will.

Most of her work as a spy had involved making herself inconspicuous. But Celia had also said there were times when it could be useful to attract attention. A part of Naya wanted to curl up at the thought of what she was about to do. She squashed it, drawing on Blue's confidence. If she could find the courage to jump fifteen feet into the ocean and meet with an enemy spy, then she could find enough to manipulate information out of a few scribes.

Naya walked past the first of the open restaurants. The crowd there was older, subdued. The second restaurant seemed more promising. It reminded her a little of the Bitter Dregs back in Belavine. Yellow light glowed from oil lamps, and the atmosphere around the place was one of cheerful familiarity. Most of the people inside looked like young students. They wore blue and gray robes and talked loudly over drinks and shared plates of food. Naya hesitated in the doorway. The restaurant's aether was thick and bright with an undercurrent of jittery weariness that made her think of hot tea and long nights spent studying in the comfort of her room.

Someone jostled Naya's shoulder. "Whoops. Sorry there," a male voice said.

Naya stepped back, then turned to see a young man with curly, dark hair and spectacles struggling to balance two heavy mugs of beer. "Sorry," Naya said quickly.

"Ha!" someone said behind the young man. "Isn't your fault Rask has two right feet." Another young man stepped up behind the first. He had a friendly, open face with a prominent nose, and his robes seemed to be of a finer cut than his companion's. He offered Naya a courtly bow. "Really, miss, may I apologize for my companion's rudeness by buying you a drink?"

Naya took another step away from them, smiling as politely as she could. "You don't have to do that."

"Ah, but I insist," the well-dressed young man said.

She couldn't drink. Did they suspect what she was? Were they testing her? No. She couldn't sense any suspicion in the aether around her. She relaxed and gave them what she hoped looked like an inviting smile. "All right, I guess a cup of tea would be nice."

"Tea? Are you sure? I know this place doesn't look like much, but the house beer is really something excellent," the well-dressed young man said.

"Come off it now, Dav," the young man with the glasses, Rask, said. "Not everyone likes to drink like you." He smiled at Naya. "If he's bothering you, we'll go."

"No, it's okay," Naya said. "I was the one standing in the doorway like a country girl who's never seen the city before."

"Is this your first time in Lith Lor?" Rask asked.

Naya shook her head. "Not the first, but I haven't been here in a long while, and I've never gotten a chance to really explore it." She let eagerness seep into her voice. "Tell me, are you two students at the academy?"

"What gave it away?" Dav asked, gesturing at his robes and

the copper medallion hanging from his neck. Up close, Naya could see the disk was scribed with a circle of runes.

Naya blushed. "Sorry. I guess that was a silly question, wasn't it? My ship just got into port. I had a bit of free time this evening, and I thought maybe I'd come see the famous rune scribes' academy."

Dav's brow furrowed. "Then I'm afraid you'll be doomed to disappointment. Nobody but scribes allowed in after sunset."

"Even during the day, you need an invitation from someone who's earned at least their third disk to be allowed inside," Rask said, sounding apologetic.

"Oh, that makes sense," Naya said, not having to feign her disappointment. She'd expected something like that, but searching the academy would have been so much easier if she could find a legitimate reason to be there. "Well, um, maybe I could trouble you for that cup of tea?"

Dav smiled. "We'd be delighted, Miss . . . ?"

"Jesale Ilvakal," Naya said. It was a Silmaran name to match Blue's pale eyes. Her dark hair would suggest some sort of mixed blood, but that was common enough in the port cities. When these scribes remembered her, it would hopefully be as a pretty young Silmaran merchant girl, someone with absolutely no connection to Naya Garth or the Ceramoran delegation.

"Well, Miss Jesale, we'd be happy to have your company."

Naya followed them to a table near the back of the room. As they walked, Naya pieced together what she hoped was a likely story. Rask set down their mugs of beer while Dav ordered her a cup of tea.

"You said you just got into port. Where did you sail from?" Dav asked when he returned with a cup of strong black tea.

"From Silmar," Naya lied.

Dav raised his eyebrows. "So far? Well, I must say, your Talmiran is excellent."

"Thank you. My mother was from Talmir originally. She taught me the language growing up." Should she have given herself a Silmaran accent? No. It was too late for that now. Best to keep things simple.

"And what brings you to our fine city, other than a fascination with the academy?" Dav asked.

Naya pretended to take a sip of her tea, then winced.

"Something wrong?" Rask asked.

Naya shook her head. "No, it's just a bit hot. I'll let it cool a while. I came here with my father. He's a merchant. Ever since I finished my schooling, he's been letting me sail with him to learn the business." She was surprised to feel her chest tighten at the half truth.

"And he let you go out into the city alone?" Dav asked, frowning with concern. "I don't mean to speak ill of our fair city, but I heard the Ceramorans brought trouble with them when they came for the Congress. If I were a father, I wouldn't feel safe knowing my daughter was walking the streets alone at night. Especially," he added with a wink, "if I had a daughter as pretty as you."

"You? A father?" Rask shook his head. "There's a laugh."

"I know how to take care of myself," Naya said, smothering a smile at the irony of Dav's warning. "Anyway, I told my father I was going into the city to visit my aunt, which is true, but . . ." She rotated her teacup in her hands and ducked her head. "Well, I may have misled him a little into thinking that I'd had a letter from her telling me she'd meet me by the lifts. See, I do have an aunt in the city—a great-aunt, really—she's from my mother's side. I've heard stories about her, but I've never gotten to meet her since my mother moved down to Silmar after she married my father." The two young scribes were leaning forward now, obviously curious. Naya's chest felt like a knot of anxiety, but she forced herself to go on.

"I know my great-aunt works at the Academy of Magics, but I wasn't sure how to get a message to her to ask if we could meet. I thought I could just come to the academy and ask after her, but then I got lost on my way here, and by the time I found the academy, the gates were shut and those guards were standing out there. I . . . I guess I lost my nerve, so I decided to come in here and get something to refresh myself, and you know the rest."

Rask nodded. "If you come back tomorrow, you could give your aunt's name to the gate guards and they could pass a message along to her, I'm sure."

Naya shifted in her seat. "I doubt my father will let me go back out again tomorrow. If you're right, and there's trouble in the city, he'll have heard about it by now. Do you know if there's any way I could leave a message for my aunt? I think my mother said she's important among the scribes. Might she have an office, or an assistant or some such?"

Dav took a deep pull from his beer. "Only scribes who've earned at least their fifth disk get private offices. What did you say your aunt's name was?"

"Ela Hest," Naya said, watching the scribes' faces carefully. It was clear immediately that they both recognized the name. Rask's eyebrows went up, and Dav snorted into his beer.

"Hest?" Dav asked. "Didn't know that one had any family."

"We're somewhat distant relations. But my mother had fond memories of her from when she was a child," Naya said, hoping the words didn't sound too forced. "Do you know how I could contact her?"

"Hest does have an office up on the top floor of Main," Dav said. "But . . ."

"But what?" Naya asked.

"Are you sure you're remembering the name right?" Dav asked.

Naya felt a chill. She'd said something wrong, but she wasn't sure what. "Why do you ask?"

"Hest is . . ." Rask glanced at Dav, then shrugged. "She's an odd one. Obsessed with her research."

"And cold," Dav said with a shudder. He blinked. "No disrespect to your family intended, but I wouldn't wait too long expecting a response from her."

"Oh." Naya leaned back in her chair, trying to look disappointed instead of relieved. For a moment there she'd thought they'd somehow seen through her lie.

"Maybe she'd be different with family," Rask said, his voice bright with false cheer.

Naya smiled. "Maybe." She glanced around. "Either way, I should get going before my father has a fit. Thank you for your help, and the tea."

Dav stood. "Wait! Are you sure you want to go so soon? I could walk you back if you'd like? A young lady like you really shouldn't be wandering the city alone at night."

"I'll be fine," Naya said, perhaps with a little more force than was necessary. The last thing she needed was to be stuck walking half the city with him.

"But you said you got lost on the way here. I would be happy to show you the way back to the docks," Dav said, holding out his hand and giving her a charming smile.

"Really," Naya said, "I've taken up enough of your time. In fact, let me buy your next round as thanks for helping me." She pulled out her father's purse and set a couple of coins on the table. As their eyes went to the coins, Naya stood and began making her way quickly toward the door. She heard Dav call something else, but she ignored him, weaving through the crowded tables. As soon as she was outside, she ducked around the corner and quickly changed her features back to the ones she'd used earlier that night. She let her hair fall around her shoulders just a moment before Dav stepped out of the restaurant. He glanced left and right, his eyes stopping on her. His brow furrowed. "Did you see a young woman come out of here? Black hair, pretty green eyes?"

Naya dipped her head to hide a smile at his look of utter confusion. "No, sir," she said, pitching her voice higher than usual. "Sorry, sir." She hurried away before he could ask anything else. Her body hummed with tension, and she imagined she could feel eyes on the back of her neck until she crossed the street and rounded the corner into Lestor Park. There she stopped under the shadow of the trees. Through the aether she could sense a couple walking somewhere deeper in the park, but it didn't seem anyone had followed her.

Naya sat down at the base of the tree, considering her options. At least Celia had been telling the truth about Ela Hest having an office at the academy. Dav had said the office was on the top floor of something called Main. She hadn't dared risk making the two scribes suspicious by asking for more details. The cover story she'd given them would only have gotten thinner the longer the conversation wore on.

Naya turned her attention to the academy walls. She closed her eyes and reached out through the aether. Here and there it swirled with eddies of emotion. From this distance she couldn't judge how many people were inside the complex, though she guessed the number was small. She sat frozen by indecision, drawing in aether until the bones of her hand seemed to buzz with pent-up energy.

Eventually she stood and started cautiously toward the wall. She might not get another chance like this. She would get in, search Hest's office, and get back to the ship. Even if the journals weren't there, perhaps she could find something else that would confirm Hest's connection to Valn. Naya paused by the wall, double-checking that no one was watching, then began to climb.

Chapter 33

NAYA

Naya pressed her fingers and toes into the cracked white stone of the academy's wall. Her body felt light and strong as she moved from one handhold to the next. It reminded her of all those nights spent up on the rooftops of Belavine. Those rooftops had felt like a secret world only she and Corten shared. As she climbed the tension slid from her shoulders. For the first time since she'd arrived in Lith Lor, the world felt simple again. In the dark she didn't have to worry about what other people thought of her. And it didn't matter if Celia was right and the guards carried wraith eaters. No one here knew who she was. If she did this right, they wouldn't even know she'd been here.

At the top of the wall, she paused, crouched between a pair of rusted iron spikes. Her eyes were drawn to the largest of the buildings spread across the grounds, a massive four-story structure set in the center of the academy. Dav had said Hest's office was in Main. That was probably short for Main Building. Talmiran institutions were never known for creative naming, and the building in the middle of the academy certainly looked important. If Naya were a high-ranking scribe, that was where she'd put her office.

She wrapped one hand in her skirt to keep it from billowing as she jumped off the wall. Her feet slapped against cool paving stones, the vibration humming up her legs and into the bones of her hand. As soon as she had her balance, she ran toward the nearest building, pressing her back against the wall. She checked the aether again. No spikes of alarm nearby. She hadn't been seen. Good.

She peeked around the corner just in time to see a guard leave the central building. He locked the door behind him, then started walking along the building's edge. Naya waited until he rounded the corner and disappeared, then she hurried across the twenty feet of open ground between her and the building. There were lights on in some of the windows. Just in case anyone happened to look out, she kept her head down and tried to move like someone who had important places to be.

No cries of alarm rose as she reached her goal. Naya wanted to laugh with relief when she made it into the shadow of the stone walls. After all the uncertainty she'd faced getting here, this felt almost easy.

Before her stood a large wooden door carved with flowing patterns that almost looked like runes. It was locked, but that was no trouble. Naya checked to make sure there wasn't anyone on the other side, then picked the lock and slipped inside. She found herself in a hallway with polished floors and doors leading off to either side. Naya checked the doors, all of which led to what looked like empty classrooms. At the end of the hall, she found another door that opened onto a dimly lit spiral stairway.

She climbed the stairs, ignoring the doors leading to the lower floors. She could distantly sense other people in the building. But from the mingled frustration and exhaustion in their aether, it seemed clear they were all focused on their own tasks. When Naya reached the fourth floor, the stairs ended and she found a locked door barring her path.

A sharp prickle of apprehension came through the aether on the other side of the door. Tension coiled in her stomach. Had someone noticed her? No, that couldn't be it. The emotions felt distant, like they were coming from a long way down the hall. Naya brushed her finger against the lock. Instead of opening it, she concentrated, then pressed her head through the doorway. The wood felt icy as she pushed past it, and then she jerked back quickly before anyone lurking on the other side could have a chance of noticing her.

The glimpse had shown her a long, empty hall with doors along each side. Whoever was there must be inside one of the rooms. Naya slipped her finger into the lock. This one was more complex than the one on the front door, but after a few minutes she felt the tumblers slide into place. She eased the door open and peeked into the hallway. Still empty.

Every door was marked with a name, and Naya found Ela Hest's office halfway down the hall. Excitement and fear warred inside her. The tension she'd felt in the aether was coming from the other side of the door. Someone was inside.

Should she find somewhere to wait until the person left? Naya considered the idea for a moment, then reached for the door handle. She didn't know where she could safely hide or how long she'd have to wait. It was easy enough to move around the academy now, but that would change when morning came. She couldn't risk getting trapped. Besides, no one in Lith Lor would recognize the face she now wore, and they shouldn't have any reason to expect she was a wraith.

Naya opened the door.

The office looked like someone had already ransacked it. The walls were lined with bookshelves, save the back wall, which held a large window. Gaps showed like broken teeth where books had been torn out of place. They were strewn across the floor, papers scattered, and a large pack sat atop the desk, half-stuffed with more papers. A broad, gray-haired woman stood frozen behind the desk, glaring at Naya. She wore fine-cut robes now rumpled and stained with sweat, and around her neck hung five heavy medallions scribed with runes.

The woman reached for something next to the pack. "Who are you? Get out of my office!"

Naya stepped into the room and shut the door behind her. She felt strangely calm as she surveyed the office, then met the eyes of the woman standing before her. "Ela Hest?" Naya asked. The woman didn't answer, but from the way she twitched, Naya knew she'd found the right person.

Naya's body tensed with excitement as she tried to make sense of the scene before her. Jagged anger spiked Hest's aether, but under it she stank of fear. She looked like she was packing to leave. The disarray all around her spoke of desperation. Why would someone obviously important not have a servant here to help her? Maybe because she didn't want anyone to know she was leaving?

"You were planning to run," Naya guessed.

The fear grew stronger in Hest's aether, stinking like sour sweat and bile. "I don't know what you're talking about. Whoever you are, you're not supposed to be here. Leave this instant or I'm calling the guards." She gestured toward a rune disk sitting on her desk.

"I don't think you will," Naya said, her mind racing. "I'm guessing you heard about Valn's death, and now you're scared someone is going to come after you. So you were trying to slip away quietly in the night." If Hest called the guards, then it would be much harder for her to get away unnoticed.

Hest's hand settled on the rune disk, but she didn't turn it. Instead she glanced at the bag. "My nephew's death has nothing to do with me."

"Of course it does. You're the one who gave him the secrets behind the reaper binding."

Hest's eyes widened just a fraction and her grip tightened

on the rune disk. A cold thread of determination mingled with her fear.

"Wait!" Naya said, sensing Hest was about to act. "I didn't come here to kill you. Those runes came from a journal, part of a set. Give me the others and I'll let you leave."

Hest stared at Naya. "Who are you?" she asked.

"Resurgence."

Hest shuddered at the name, though strangely the determination in her aether only seemed to grow stronger. "Were you the ones who killed him?" she asked.

Naya didn't answer, and Hest drew her lips together in a thin line of anger. "He wouldn't have talked, you know. Dalith had his faults, but he wouldn't have said anything at the trial."

"He told you," Naya guessed.

Hest shook her head. "He told me he'd found a way to finally end this conflict for good, to make Talmir safe. His views on the undead might have been too soft, but at least he was more of a patriot than all those sniveling politicians who've named him traitor. They all lost their stomachs after the war. At least some of us here at the academy haven't forgotten who our real enemies are."

There was a light in Hest's eyes that bordered on madness. It reminded Naya of her father, and she had to fight down a shudder. "Do you have the other journals?" she asked again.

"Why should I give them to you?" Hest asked.

"Because I'll let you live." Naya filled her voice with as much venom as she could muster.

Hest laughed bitterly. "What proof do I have of that?"

Naya tried to channel some of Celia's ruthless calm. Her thoughts raced to put together a lie Hest might believe. "We value silence over needless killing. Valn had to die because he was stupid enough to get caught. But you've managed to avoid any official suspicion. If you call the guards, I'll kill you. If you refuse to give me the journals, I'll kill you. But if you hand them over quietly and speak to no one about what you know, I'll let you live."

"And I'm supposed to do all this on your word alone?" Hest asked.

"What other choice do you have?" Naya forced herself to meet Hest's gaze. If Hest was like her father, then her hate might be enough to blind her to other risks. "You said you haven't forgotten who your real enemies are. You should be smart enough to see that Resurgence's goals align with yours. Valn's failure wasn't the end of our plans. Isn't it better to live on and see those plans fulfilled?"

Hest's lips drew together in a thin line as she seemed to consider the offer. "The journals are in a compartment in the floor, under that rug by your feet."

Naya held back a sigh of relief. "Show me."

"Look yourself," Hest said. "I won't go down on my knees before one of my nephew's killers."

Naya watched Hest for a tense, silent moment. Then she reluctantly crouched to push back the rug. Under it, she could just barely see the outline of a trapdoor hidden by the grain of the wood. "How do I open it?" she asked.

"There's a keyhole, hidden in a knot in the wood," Hest said. "The key is in my desk. One moment."

Naya brushed her fingers over the trapdoor until she found the keyhole. It was cleverly hidden, barely visible even after she knew where to look. She heard a drawer open, then close. When she looked up, Hest was pointing a rune pistol at her.

"This is for my nephew," Hest said. Then she pulled the trigger.

The crack of the pistol's rune plate was deafening in the small room. The room's aether twisted toward the weapon and something pierced Naya's chest like a jet of ice water. Wood splintered as the bullet wedged itself into the door behind her. Naya looked down at the round hole in the front of her dress. The bullet had come nowhere near the bones in her hand, and already the cold of its passing was fading.

"How?" Hest whispered. She stared at Naya, then her eyes narrowed. "You're one of them. A wraith. You tried to trick me!"

"Wait!" Naya began.

Hest lunged across the desk and activated the rune disk sitting there. "Wraith!" she shouted. "Spies! Intruders!"

Naya cursed, then slammed her finger into the keyhole on the trapdoor. No sense in looking for the key now that Hest had realized what she was. The disgust and anger in the woman's aether surrounded Naya like putrid smoke. She tried to ignore it, concentrating on the feel of the lock's tumblers.

Naya heard pounding footsteps from somewhere below. She felt the first pin catch, but the second one slipped before she could get it into position. She clenched her teeth. Somewhere to her right she could hear Hest moving. The footsteps outside were getting louder.

Naya closed her eyes and blocked it all out. The pins were the only thing that mattered. She had to focus. After what seemed like a lifetime, she felt the second, then the third pin click into place. She wrenched the lock open and hauled up the trapdoor. Old books were stacked inside, along with several sheets of loose papers covered in rune diagrams. Naya shoved aside books until she saw two with the same thin black covers as Lucia's journal. She pulled them out and flipped them open. Yes. The handwriting was the same.

Naya stood, clutching the journals to her chest. Hest had extracted a strange metal cube from her desk and there was something eager in her aether now. Whatever that cube was, Naya wanted nothing to do with it. She ran into the hallway, then froze as a man in the uniform of the university guard burst through the doorway to the stairs. His face was red and he was breathing hard. But as he saw her, he drew his sword. Runes glowed along the length as aether rushed into the wraith eater's blade.

Naya glanced over her shoulder. There were more office doors behind her, but after that was a dead end. Could she get past the guard to the stairs? The hall was narrow and the guard held his sword as though he knew how to use it. The journals felt like hot glass against her chest. She clenched her teeth. She refused to be trapped here, not when she was so close. She ran back into Hest's office.

The window. If she couldn't get down the stairs, she'd just have to take a faster route and hope it didn't do too much damage to her bones.

As she stepped into the room, something wrenched at her aether. Naya stumbled and gasped. She felt like she was drowning. Her whole body was burning with the need for air—no, for aether—but no matter how hard she tried, she couldn't pull any in. Hest was holding the small metal cube, and the runes covering it now blazed with aether. The air around it writhed like the edges of a necromancer's portal.

What in creation was that thing? Naya could hear the roar of the tides of death filling the office, could feel the icy water rising around her legs.

She stumbled toward the window. Her body faded in patches as her aether reserves drained. She had to concentrate to keep her hold on the journals as the tips of her fingers threatened to fade away. The bones in her hand burned with icy fire.

Naya reached for the window, fumbling with the latch. She distantly heard Hest shout something, and the sound of footsteps behind her. Naya willed every last scrap of energy into her arm, forcing the window open. It felt so heavy. She opened a gap a few inches wide before the window stuck. It would have to do.

Naya half jumped, half fell toward the gap. She kept her hands tucked in close to her chest, holding on to the journals.

Her shoulder went cold as it passed through the window and her body jerked as her dress tore. She had a brief sensation of falling, then everything went black.

CHAPTER 34

NAYA

The world returned with abrupt and painful clarity as Naya's back slammed into the ground. She gasped and aether rushed into her body. Her hand burned with the pain of cracked bones. The night swirled around her, burning stars above and cold paving stones below. Somewhere people were shouting. She wished they would stop. She wished they would all stop and just let her lie here and rest a while and—

The journals. Naya sat up with a groan. The right sleeve of her dress was badly torn, but she'd managed to hold on to the journals through her fall. More lights were coming on in the building behind her, and she could hear someone shouting from above. The guard in Hest's office couldn't follow her out the window, but there might be more coming. She had to get away.

She drew in more aether despite the throbbing in her bones and ran toward the academy's wall. Her head spun with the first few steps, but soon she was sprinting. Once she got to the wall, she stuffed Lucia's journals down the front of her dress and climbed. It was nothing like the easy climb earlier that evening, and Naya felt a bitter pang at how confident she'd been only moments ago. Her vision went wavy around the edges. She could feel her fingertips fading in and out, making it harder to grip the cracks between the stones. When she finally reached the top, she slid through the spikes, then dropped down to the other side.

Outside the academy, Lith Lor's pulse rose to meet her. Its steady thrum was the sound of soldiers' boots as they marched after her. Naya ran, darting through alleys and hiding in doorways or behind trash piles whenever anyone drew near. By the time she reached the stairs leading down to the docks, she wanted to weep with exhaustion. She half expected to find soldiers blocking the way, but this part of the city was quiet.

Despite the quiet, Naya didn't have any illusions about the consequences of what she'd just done. Hest had realized what she was. In Ceramor that might not have been so bad. But this was Talmir. So far as Naya knew, there was exactly one wraith in Lith Lor. Her. The city guards and palace soldiers knew that too. So did Queen Lial. If Hest or the guard reported what they'd seen, it would only be a matter of time before someone came after Naya.

Stupid. Naya had assumed that, like her father, Hest would be willing to sacrifice anyone for the chance to aid in Ceramor's downfall. But either Hest had seen through Naya's lies or her anger at her nephew's killers had been stronger than any desire to work with Resurgence. Naya shouldn't have taken her eyes off Hest like that. If not for that pistol, she could have gotten out without Hest ever realizing what she was. Naya pushed the thought to the back of her mind. She didn't have time to worry about what could have been. She had the journals. She would deal with the consequences later.

She made her way back down the cliffs to the isolated patch of rocky coast where she'd hidden her square of oilcloth. There she stripped down to her shift and wrapped her torn clothes carefully around Lucia's journals. She'd lost her knife at some point during the escape, but she added her purse of coins to the bundle, then wrapped it in the oilcloth and tied it tight. She briefly considered stealing a rowboat to get back to the *Gallant*, but what she'd gain in speed would be far offset by the risk of getting caught. Dawn was approaching and already a few sailors and dockhands were arriving to begin the day's work.

Naya tied the bundle to her chest, then slipped into the water so she floated on her back. She rowed with her arms, careful to avoid submerging the precious bundle and the journals inside. The eastern sky glowed with the first hints of dawn by the time she completed the grueling swim to the *Gallant*'s side.

Getting back into her cabin proved trickier than getting out. The ship's side was smooth and slick with moisture. Even with her light body, her fingers ached from trying to grip tiny grooves and bits of ornamental carving. She felt ready to collapse when she finally reached the windows of her father's cabin.

Someone gasped as she opened the window and tumbled onto the cabin floor. When she looked up, she saw Felicia and, surprisingly, Lucia standing over her. "You're back!" Felicia said. Then she lowered her voice so it wouldn't carry through the ship's thin walls. "Are you all right?"

"You're fading," Lucia said before Naya could respond, her tone more accusatory than worried. "You said your bones weren't cracked."

Naya sat up, leaning against the cabin wall. "They weren't." She drew in a breath of aether and concentrated on keeping her body stable. "How long have you been here?" she asked Lucia. "I thought you were going to rest."

Lucia pursed her lips. "So did I. I would have preferred to keep Francisco at the palace a while longer, but as the soldiers hadn't found the second assassin yet, Delence decided to move us early." Lucia glanced at Felicia. "Once I had Francisco settled, I came here. Felicia said you were . . . out. I thought it would look odd if the sailors saw me lingering on deck when I'm supposed to be replacing one of your bones, so I waited here."

"I hope that's all right," Felicia said. "I made up the bed when she came in so that if anyone else was outside the door it would look like you were resting."

Naya looked to where Felicia pointed and saw that she'd stuffed her bag under the bunk's blankets. She doubted anyone looking closely would mistake the lump for a person, but it would probably do to fool a sailor glancing into the room. Naya felt touched by the gesture. "Thank you. You were perfect." She hesitated. "Do you think you could give Lucia and me some privacy?"

Naya saw disappointment flash in Felicia's eyes. Her shoulders slumped even as she smiled. "Of course. If you don't need me anymore, I'll just be outside."

"Wait!" Naya said as Felicia turned to go.

She drew in aether, sensing the bittersweet mix of hope, disappointment, and fear in Felicia's aether. She wasn't sure if she was making a terrible mistake. "I promised you a story."

"It's all right," Felicia said. "I can't really blame you if you want to keep your secrets. After all, I'm just—"

"It's not all right," Naya said. "I found the spy I told you about, but she wasn't the only reason I had to get out there tonight. I'm not sure what stories you've heard about what I did back in Belavine. But . . . through all those stories, there was someone else with me, a boy named Corten." Naya's throat went tight around the name and she felt Lucia tense behind her. "Corten is one of the best people I've ever known. He is kind and good and strong, and he paid a terrible price for helping me. He died."

"Naya, are you sure—" Lucia began.

"It's fine," Naya said. "She deserves to know." Felicia had sat with her through the long hours after the assassin's attack. She'd helped Naya, and whenever Naya had confronted her, she'd been honest. Her father would have told her not to trust

Felicia. Valn and Celia would have called her a fool for giving anything away that could be used against her. But they weren't here, and they weren't her. If she was ever going to be more than the monster they'd tried to make her, then she had to stop doing things the way they would have wanted. She had to find her own way, even if that meant making mistakes.

"Corten died," Naya said with more conviction. "But I believe there's still a way to bring him back. That's why Lucia and I really came here. We thought someone in Talmir was hiding secrets we could use." She let herself smile. "And we were right."

Felicia stared at her, eyes wide. Then slowly her lips spread into an answering smile. "That is a very good story."

"Thank you," Naya said. "Will you help me figure out how to give it a happy ending?"

Felicia's smile spread into a grin. "Oh, yes."

A few minutes later, she left Naya and Lucia alone. She carried Hal Garth's logbook and a note from Naya containing everything she'd learned regarding Valn's allies. Felicia would keep watch over the door while Lucia was working and dissuade anyone from interrupting them. And if something went horribly wrong, she would take all the information they had to Delence.

"Based on all that, I take it you found my journals?" Lucia said as soon as Felicia was gone. The aether around her practically glowed with eagerness. "Where were they? Do you have them now?"

"I have them," Naya said. "But I was seen getting them. I'm pretty sure Queen Lial will send someone looking for me soon. Do you have everything you need for the shadow walk?"

Lucia's smile fell. Naya could feel her questions like a subtle pressure in the aether. "If you have the runes for the circle, then yes. I checked the supplies they sent over from the *Lady* and everything is there. There's still one more bone I need to carve. It's simple work, but I'm not sure it's a good idea to attempt it now. You seem to have cracked one of your bones since we last spoke."

"It happened while I was at the academy. Hest had a weapon I've never seen before." Naya saw the questions forming on Lucia's lips and cut her off. "But that doesn't matter. If Queen Lial locks me up, then you'll have no one who can go into death and find Corten. We have to do this now."

Lucia hesitated, then set her jaw. "You do realize that if you get yourself killed crossing over, Corten will still be just as dead. That doesn't serve anyone."

"I know what I'm risking," Naya said, forcing herself to stand straight. "Please, Lucia, this is why we came here. Even if the queen doesn't send anyone after me, who knows how long I'll be stuck here?"

"We've waited weeks already. A few more might not make a difference."

"Or it might make all the difference. Do you really want to risk Corten's soul on that?"

Lucia looked away. Naya could see her caution warring with eagerness. Despite her words, Naya knew Lucia was eager to try the ritual. Part of that was her desire to bring Corten back, but the rest had to be pure curiosity. Naya had seen that curiosity growing in the weeks before they'd left Belavine. Corten had once told her that it was the mysteries that drew him to necromancy. But while he had felt wonder at those mysteries, Lucia was hungry for them. Even persecution at the hands of the Talmiran Army and years spent hiding under a false name hadn't been enough to kill that hunger. "Will you at least look at the journals?" Naya asked. "Let's make sure the runes for the ritual are really there. After that we can decide."

Lucia nodded. "Very well."

Naya unwrapped the oilcloth bundle. Her clothes were damp, but the journals were thankfully unharmed. Lucia's hands shook as she took them. She scanned the contents of the first, then opened the second, flipping about halfway through. She stopped on a page that showed a complicated rune circle. A soft sigh escaped her lips as her fingers traced one of the runes. "This is it."

"Will you try it?" Naya asked.

Lucia stared at the page. Naya could feel the seconds ticking by. How long would it take for word of her presence at the academy to reach the palace? Impatient as she was, she forced herself to wait in silence. Finally, Lucia nodded. "Very well. But first I want to see your bond. Depending on how bad those cracks are, I may need to carve you an extra bone to help reinforce the damaged sections."

Naya took a step back. "I'm fine. Anyway, we don't have time for that."

Lucia glared at her. "This is not a negotiation."

Naya glared back, but she could sense the determination in Lucia's aether. "Fine."

Lucia retrieved her reader, a metal rod scribed with various runes, from a sturdy-looking chest by the door. Naya clenched her teeth and held out her hand. "Hmm, only one crack," Lucia said after a moment. "It's thin at least. Given sufficient aether and rest you could probably heal it in a few days."

"We don't have a few days."

Lucia twirled the reader in her hands, her brow furrowing. "You're sure they'll come for you?"

"Not completely," Naya admitted. She wasn't sure how many people knew Hest had kept those journals. And she was almost certain now that Queen Lial hadn't been involved with Valn's plot. Hest might want to avoid any royal investigations that could reveal her role in the treason. But to keep the secret, she'd have to silence the guard, and anyone else who'd heard the commotion. It could be simpler for her to just insist she had no idea why Naya had broken in. "We can't risk it. If the queen hears that a wraith broke into the academy, I doubt she'll wait for me to come back to the palace on my own for questioning." The thought left her insides feeling like ice. Even worse was the prospect of facing that and knowing that the risks hadn't been enough to save Corten.

"If that's true, then shouldn't you be focusing on escape? Could we convince the captain to sail now?"

Naya hesitated. "I . . . I don't know." She thought a moment, then shook her head. "No. Even if we got out of the harbor, they'd send ships after us. The *Gallant* is fast, but she can't out-run the entire fleet. And if I'm caught fleeing on the ship, Queen Lial will accuse Delence of hiding me from justice." She pressed her lips together. "I don't want to be the excuse she uses for another war."

"If she finds us performing illegal necromancy here, we might give her just that," Lucia said.

"She won't find out. This ship will be sailing in just a day or two. I'll tell the captain to give you my cabin. Corten can hide here and you can get him safely back to Ceramor."

Naya felt the eagerness spreading in Lucia's aether. "I suppose your bond with Corten will give you the best chance of finding him," she said. "The only other wraith who comes close is Matius, and he . . . well, he has a family." Lucia's expression pinched, as though she realized how the words must sound after they'd already come out. "Sorry."

Naya's throat tightened, but she ignored the feeling. "It's okay. Are you saying you'll do the ritual?"

Lucia pushed her glasses up her nose, her expression growing distant. "Creator forgive me if this doesn't work, but yes, I'll do it."

CHAPTER 35

NAYA

Lucia examined the diagram for several minutes, then directed Naya to clear the floor between the table and the desk. Once that was done, she pulled a jar of black paint from her supply chest and began to paint the runes across the cabin floor. She used a thin brush, laying down the runes with slow, precise strokes. Naya sat on the bed and watched. She tried to relax, turning her attention to the aether. She drew on the energy of the sailors and on the deep, rich pool of life lurking in the ocean below. Drawing in so much aether hurt, but she thought she could almost feel it flowing into the damaged bone, knitting the crack back together.

An hour passed, then two, before Lucia stepped back to examine her work.

"Is it ready?" Naya asked.

"This part is. As I said, I'll still need to carve another bone."

Lucia's eyes shone behind her glasses. Her aether felt sharp with apprehension, excitement, and guilt. She looked down at her hands, as though considering her words carefully. "As I mentioned before, there are three components to the ritual. The first is the portal. This version will allow you to step physically into death. I should be able to hold it for at least six hours. I've lasted longer in the past, but any more than that and others may wonder why it's taking so long to make a simple repair to your binding. If I'm interrupted and the portal closes, I'm not sure I'll be able to guide you back, shadow walk or no."

Naya nodded. She didn't know if they'd have even that long. "Before, you talked about a compass and an anchor."

"Yes. The compass I have ready. For that I'll be incorporating one of Corten's bones into your bond. Back during the war, one of the research groups experimented with linking wraiths' minds by adding bones from one to the other's bond. The hope was to allow them to communicate over long distances and make wraith squads more effective when operating behind enemy lines."

"Did it work?" Naya asked.

Lucia licked her lips. "Their successes were mixed. Necromancy is more complicated than the arts other rune scribes practice. The will of the bound soul affects how the runes in a binding interact. Our researchers found that wraiths with strong emotional bonds could use each other's bones, but the connection was never as powerful as we'd hoped, and the mental side effects proved to be too detrimental to justify the slight advantage."

Naya didn't like the hesitance in Lucia's tone. "When we left Belavine, you said you'd figured out how to make the compass and anchor work. You said the only thing left was to find the runes for the circle."

"I do have it figured out," Lucia snapped. "Your ties to Corten should be enough to let you accept one of his bones, and your connection should be stronger on the other side."

"And the side effects?"

"Shouldn't matter. I don't intend to permanently link you. After you come back through the portal, I'll remove the extra bones."

"Okay, then what about the anchor?"

"That's the one I still have to carve. But before that we'll need to extract it."

"Extract?" Naya asked. Then her eyes widened. "You don't mean . . ."

"The anchor bone must come from a living body. That connection is what will allow you to navigate back to the portal, just like the connection with Corten's bones should lead you to his soul. I believe one of the bones from my pinkie will be sufficient, but I may need your help with the process."

Naya shuddered. "Won't that . . . Are you sure?"

Lucia smiled. "I knew this would be necessary when I proposed the idea. Really, it's a small price to pay."

Lucia's casual air couldn't hide the fact that there was nothing simple or clean about what they had to do. Naya had fought before, had seen blood flow from cuts or broken noses. But still her mind recoiled as she held the knife over Lucia's outstretched finger. *A small price to pay.* Naya's grip tightened on the knife. She met Lucia's eyes and the necromancer gave her a tiny nod. Naya returned the nod. She'd made a promise to get Corten back. She cut.

Lucia's breath hissed as the knife bit into her flesh. She squeezed her eyes shut, and though the muscles in her arm twitched, her hand remained steady. Thankfully the knife was sharp. As soon as Naya felt it bite through to the wood of the desk, she grabbed the ointment-smeared bandages Lucia had set aside and wrapped the wound tightly.

Lucia drew in a deep, shuddering breath. "Let's finish this."

Despite the grayish tint in her skin and the pain pulsing through her aether, Lucia worked quickly. Naya helped wherever she could, retrieving tools and cleaning whatever Lucia no longer needed. In between the work, Naya sat on her father's bunk, drawing in aether and trying to will her injured bone to heal.

All too soon, the anchor bone was ready.

Naya sat in the center of the runic circle with Lucia in front of her. Two bones lay between them, Corten's rib and the small bone from Lucia's finger. "Remember," Lucia said, "you'll want to touch both bones at the same time. There's going to be dissonance. The runes I've carved should serve as a bridge, allowing you to form a connection with the bones. But it's your will that stabilizes that connection."

"I'm ready," Naya said. It felt like a lie, so before she could lose her courage, she reached out and touched the two bones. Lightning flashed up her arms and the world turned white with pain. She could feel her energy rushing into the bones, but it was nothing like when Jalance had tried to repair her bond. That had been like a wound reopened, old pains renewed as she tried to fit the pieces of herself back together. But these bones weren't hers. They resonated like sour notes from an off-tune violin, the shrieking vibrations threatening to rip her apart. Naya tried to force the bones to settle, but the dissonance only got louder, the pain magnifying. She gritted her teeth, or tried to. The resonance was swallowing her whole body. Lucia had said her will would stabilize the connection, but it seemed the harder she tried the worse things got.

Force wasn't working. She felt like she was being torn in three. There was no way to force the bones to become a part of her, because they simply weren't. Her soul had no way to shape itself around them. But even as she had the thought, she realized it wasn't quite true. In a way her life was already twined with Lucia and Corten. Lucia had brought her back from death. She'd shared a cell with Naya and given her the strength to fight when Naya's will had faltered. And Corten. Corten had changed everything. She wouldn't be here if not for him.

The darkness around her ebbed and flowed, and for a moment Naya thought she could see the way Lucia's and Corten's lives wove into hers. She felt the loneliness and uncertainty that had haunted Lucia since the war. The weight of secrets that had only doubled when Valn appeared like a specter from her bloody past. Emotions and memories flashed by, and Naya gasped as she felt Lucia's anger and fear of her transform to grudging respect, and then a sense of kinship and pride that made Naya's chest ache.

Meanwhile Corten's life wove around and through theirs, tying them together more tightly even as his threads became hopelessly entangled with Naya's. For an instant she saw herself as he must have seen her when they first met—a pretty girl, uncertain and stubborn and mysterious in her contradictions. Anger at her betrayal hit him like a physical blow. Forgiveness grew slowly as he watched her fight against Valn's plots. Then wonder exploded as her lips brushed his, as they imagined a future together. The lines of their lives spun together until they wove so tight Naya couldn't tell them apart. There was another flash of light and a single, bright burst of pain.

Then all at once the pain was gone, transforming to an uncomfortable hum in the back of her mind. Naya blinked and realized she was still kneeling in the center of the runed circle. Lucia stared back at her, eyes wide and one hand clutching her chest. Her breath was shallow and fast. As Naya recovered her senses she realized the dissonance had resolved itself into a rapid beat, almost like a pulse. She met Lucia's eyes. Lucia swallowed, closed her eyes, and made an obvious effort to calm herself. The pulse in Naya's mind slowed, focused until it beat steadily from the new bone in her pinkie. Naya reached up to touch her chest, felt the rib that rested there, just over her own heart, silent.

"Do it."

And just like that, Lucia began to sing. The words wrapped around Naya, strange and incomprehensible. The air shimmered, and something brushed against her arms, her back, her face, like tiny hands grasping her. Naya closed her eyes and fought a surge of fear as the roaring of death's tides dragged her under.

CHAPTER 36

NAYA

Naya opened her eyes to a world defined in shades of black and gray. Something that was not quite water and not quite mist rushed around her legs, tugging her deeper into death. Behind her, Lucia's image shimmered as if Naya were seeing her through the waters of a windswept lake. The necromancer's song echoed around her, urging her back toward the portal. Adding to the song's pull, a tenuous cord of light drifted from the bone in Naya's pinkie finger, binding her to life. The cord thrummed with each beat of Lucia's heart. Naya pressed her hand to her chest where Corten's rib lay, searching for another beat. An echo. Anything.

There was no beat. No string of light to guide her. But after a long, terrifying moment, Naya felt something stir. It was ethereal. The half-caught scent of orange soap on singed clothes. A brush of heat like breath from an open furnace. The memory of a kiss. The sensations were there and gone so quick they left her wondering if she'd imagined them. But as she stood, they seemed to pull her forward. Naya started walking.

Wisps of pale-blue aether steamed off her with each step, disappearing into the air. Unnerved, she tried to draw the energy back in. She felt nothing. It was like tipping back a glass and expecting cool water but instead finding only air. The bones in her hand glowed faintly through her skin, but a sliver of darkness marred her thumb where the cracked bone lay. What would happen if she ran out of aether here? Naya gritted her teeth and forced herself to keep moving. Lucia's song grew fainter, but the thread of light pulsed strong and steady. The tide pushed against her legs. Its roar twisted in her ears until Naya thought she could hear words among the noise.

Turn back.

Come.

Die.

Naya clutched the front of her blouse, following the ghostly sensations from the compass. Her thoughts grew fuzzy. They seemed to twine with the voices of the tide, making it hard to tell which came from the dark and which belonged to her. Noise rose around her until she felt like she was surrounded by a crowd of people. She could feel eyes on her, someone, no *something*, lurking behind her.

Naya took another step and the world exploded with color. Cobblestones appeared beneath her feet. Streets rolled outward while leaning shops rose in blocks to frame a strip of bright blue sky. Naya's head spun as she stared at the faded wooden street signs. Belavine. She was in Belavine. But how? She turned and—

"Watch—!" Something slammed into her. Naya fell, then looked up to see a heavyset woman in a flowing green skirt and black vest standing over her. A shopping basket lay next to Naya, its contents scattered over the paving stones. The woman pursed her lips as she bent to collect her things.

The thick smells of the Belavine market swirled around Naya. Horror rose in her stomach as she watched herself grab her document folder and stand. She was two people at once. One was the naive living girl with bloodied hands, eager to get her contract signed and please her father. The other was the real her, the girl who'd died and returned and fought and killed her father and—

"They're both the same, both you," a soft voice whispered.

No. No they weren't the same. Naya had become someone better, stronger. This other girl had been a fool who couldn't see the evil all around her. Her old body stood, and Naya experienced an echo of revulsion as her younger self realized the woman before her was undead.

The hairs on the back of the living Naya's neck prickled, but when she looked behind her, there was no sign of the man she'd noticed following her. Her hand throbbed, and for an instant she thought she saw something else there, something dark and writhing. Then her body started walking up into the hills, toward her own death.

With every step she tried to turn away, tried to pick a different path. But no matter how hard she fought, her legs wouldn't obey her commands. This wasn't right. She wasn't supposed to be here. She had to find Corten, had to save him.

"Are you strong enough?" the soft voice whispered again. "Are you really here for him? Or is it just your own guilt that drives you? You came back because you know your life is wrong. You should be dead. You should have died right here."

Naya felt the sting of the dart in her neck, the burning as the poison began to spread. More voices joined the first, forming a cacophony of whispers that seemed to come from everywhere at once.

Give up.

Rest.

You are not strong enough for this.

"I am," Naya snarled. She reached up and pulled the dart from her neck with trembling fingers. She could feel her limbs going numb. But that sensation couldn't be real. Maybe once she'd died like this, but now she had no flesh, no blood to carry the poison. This was just a memory, and she would not let it keep her from what needed to be done.

Naya took a step. Her legs steadied even as a deep ache blossomed in her hand. She took another step and the walls of the alley faded, a gray-and-black world peeking through. Naya clutched her chest and tried to find the thread of emotion that had led her this far. Corten was out there somewhere. "I will find him," Naya said.

A snarl of rage cut through the air behind her.

She spun and saw something dark and huge rise from the tidal mists. Arms and legs stuck out at odd angles, writhing against the darkness, making it impossible to judge the shape of the thing. It had far, far too many limbs, and claws, and mouths. Primal terror flooded her mind, burying logic and thought under the all-consuming need to flee.

Naya stood frozen, staring back at the monstrosity. The tides surged against her legs and every inch of her body shook with fear.

"Run," the soft voice whispered urgently.

"No," Naya said. This thing couldn't be real. This place was just trying to frighten her away. "No!" she screamed. She had no weapon, no way to fight if she was wrong. She planted her feet as the creature charged.

"You fool!" This time the voice was a shout.

Naya raised her hand in a warding gesture. Then bright sparks whirled around her. The ground vanished, sending her plummeting even as the creature's claws slashed forward with terrible speed.

Naya let out a startled cry and squeezed her eyes shut.

Instead of rending claws, she felt herself land gently on something soft and cool. Cautiously, she opened her eyes and blinked against the sudden brightness of afternoon sunlight. For a moment all she could do was stare in shock at the grassy hillside that had materialized around her. Down the gentle slope, she could just make out the red rooftops of Lith Lor in the distance. She scrambled to her feet. Her attacker was nowhere to be seen. The only sounds on the hilltop were the song of birds and the quiet shushing of wind playing in the leaves of a nearby tree. What was this place? Another memory? Was she still in death?

"Come sit on the blanket, Little Bird. You're going to stain your dress."

The voice was soft and kind, and it cut through Naya like a knife. She spun. A woman sat on a blanket behind her, pulling a loaf of bread from a picnic basket. She was in her thirties, though the lines on her face made her look older. Her brown curls were pinned up to show a slender neck, and she was smiling. Healthy.

"Mother?" Naya whispered.

Her mother's smile turned sad. "No, Naya, I'm not really her. But I thought talking this way would make you more comfortable."

Naya stepped back. "Who . . . What are you? Where am I?" This was worse than reliving her death. The wrongness of the scene made her head spin even as her heart cried out for her to fall into her mother's arms and weep with joy.

"Don't you remember?" the stranger who was definitely not her mother asked. "We're outside the village of Vel Dar. Your mother was born here, and when you were six, she brought you to visit."

She remembered. It was just a few months before her mother got sick. Naya had spent hours collecting flowers and rolling down one of the grassy hills with the village children. "This can't be real. How did I get here? And what was that thing?" she asked. She tried again to draw in aether, but still there was nothing.

The stranger flicked one hand in a gesture of irritation.

"That thing was a scavenger. They feed off the energy of life that seeps through with the newly dead. That one's been stalking you ever since you stepped through your portal. I've managed to hide you for now, but eventually more scavengers will come. They will find you, and they will consume you."

Naya shuddered. There were more of those monsters? "What are you? Why are you helping me?"

The stranger smiled again. "Think of me as a messenger. Your coming has sent ripples through the world's energy. Certain powers have taken notice. They sent me to deal with you."

Naya wrapped her arms around her shoulders. The rib in her chest still thrummed softly. She was beginning to wonder if she'd made a mistake charging so blindly into death. Somehow she'd convinced herself that once they had the ritual, finding Corten would be if not easy, then at least simple. Either his soul would be waiting for her on the other side or he would have passed on to someplace she couldn't reach. "Deal with me how?"

"First," the stranger said, "tell me of the one who sent you here. That portal she scribed is old magic, a sort we have not sensed for a very, very long time."

"She's a necromancer. She sent me to find someone," Naya said.

"That much is obvious. But where did she get such knowledge?"

Naya hesitated. "Does it matter?"

The stranger's eyes narrowed in an expression of cold anger that Naya was sure she'd never seen on her mother's face. "It matters a great deal."

Something in the stranger's eyes told Naya that any lie she told would be spotted immediately. "We got the runes in Talmir. One of the scribes there kept a book with notes on this ritual after the purges in Ceramor. I'm sorry, but I'm not sure where the knowledge came from before that."

The stranger tilted her head as though listening to something far away, then nodded. "We have seen memories of this purge." The stranger's eyes focused on Naya again. "It's interesting how she's bound you. You're like a bead on a string held taut, your path fixed between two points. Not the most elegant way of walking the fringe, but effective enough for what you seek."

Naya took a step toward the stranger. "If you know why I'm here, can you tell me where Corten is?"

Again the stranger paused as though to listen, though all Naya could hear was the distant song of birds and the whisper of the wind. A wrinkle creased the stranger's brow, then smoothed away. "We have watched the one you seek. He is stubborn, and his mind is strong enough that he has not yet broken, though he still refuses to pass through the door."

"The door?" Naya looked around, some part of her half expecting to see a door appear on the hillside. "Where is he? Can you bring him to me?"

The stranger held up one hand. "Peace, Little Bird."

"Don't call me that!" Naya snapped. Little Bird had been her mother's nickname for her. How did this stranger even know it? For that matter, how had she known what Naya's mother looked like, or about the day they'd gone to Vel Dar?

The stranger's expression darkened. "Watch your tone, spirit. You have no idea of the forces you're dealing with. Your necromancer is a child playing with magics she barely understands. You are far less than that."

Naya shivered at the sudden ice of the stranger's tone. There was something off about her, something old and inhuman. But whatever she was, she knew where to find Corten. "I'm sorry," Naya forced herself to say.

The stranger nodded. "Better. Now, I respect your courage in coming here. For that we will ensure you make it safely back to the living world, but you will be going back alone."

"No!" Naya cried. "I came here for Corten. If you won't help me find him, then let me go and I'll find him myself!"

"You will fail," the stranger said. "You have two options. Accept my offer and return to the living, or continue on to your true death. You might find the one you seek waiting near the door. But if you go that far, then not even the magic anchoring you will be enough to let you return."

"What about your magic?" Naya asked, following a hunch. "You said necromancy is only at the edge of the old magics. If necromancy can take me this far, there has to be something else that will let me walk the rest of the way."

The stranger's eyes darkened with anger until they no longer resembled anything remotely human. "No. That magic is not for you."

"Then I'll find my own way!"

"You'll die," the stranger said.

A voice spoke from behind Naya before she could reply. "You know there's another option."

Naya turned to see a shadowy figure standing on the green hilltop. Darkness wisped around him almost like aether. As Naya watched, the darkness solidified until she was looking at a man in strange robes with a long beard and dark, piercing eyes. "Who are you?" Naya asked.

"Someone who should not be here," the woman said. "Go away. I am dealing with this one."

The man shook his head. "I have watched the boy she seeks. He has strength. If we guide him back from the door, this could be the opportunity we've been looking for."

"So there is a way?" Naya asked. She looked between the man and the woman. "Please, I'll do anything."

"It won't work. I see no reason to waste the scraps of power we've gathered on this," the woman said. "He's no better than all the others you've suggested. Eventually he will break."

"So we keep waiting?" the man asked. There was scorn in his voice now. "You've heard the same whispers I have. You know what is coming. Make the boy our agent. At the least he will bring more information than we gain from the ordinary dead."

The woman shook her head. "The risks—"

"The girl seems willing enough to take them, and I believe the boy will be as well."

"What are you talking about?" Naya asked, frustration coloring her voice. "What do you mean you'll make Corten your agent?"

"Yes," the woman said. "Tell her exactly what you are suggesting. Tell her what it will cost and see if she is still so eager."

The man turned to Naya and she shuddered. On the surface there was nothing obviously wrong, but just like with the woman, she got the impression that something old and unknowable was staring out at her from behind the mask of that human face. "Our ties to the living world are thin. But we feel ripples, watch memories. We know someone has gone into the bone swamp and brought out secrets that should have been destroyed long ago. We have seen the image of a queen gathering armies in the east. The knowledge she has discovered could cause great suffering if used in the wrong ways. We need an agent in the world to find this queen, learn her intentions, and stop her if necessary. If the boy agrees, we will grant him what tools we can, and he will be bound to our task. If he fails, there will not be enough of him left to fight the door a second time."

"And if he succeeds, he gets to live out the rest of his life, right?" Naya asked.

The man and the woman exchanged a look. "If he succeeds," the man said, "then the power we lend him will become permanent."

"That is not the full price," the woman said. "The boy has been at the door too long. The energy we have will not be enough to make him what he needs to be. The rest will have to come from you."

"How much energy?" Naya asked. A shiver of fear ran through her.

"Five years should do it," the woman said. "What will it be, girl? Will you give up five years of your future for one who is already dead?"

Five years. What potential would she be signing away? How much time would she have left when it was gone? She couldn't know, and that thought was terrifying. Then again, she might die tomorrow at the hands of Queen Lial, or some madman with a wraith eater. Creator, she'd already risked a lot more than five years coming here. How was it that gambling everything could feel less terrifying than this finite cost? Naya swallowed her fear and forced a smile. Everything in life had a price. "Yes. If Corten agrees, then I'll pay the cost."

The woman gave Naya a disappointed look. For a moment her face looked so much like Naya's mother that Naya felt her throat closing around a sob. "If this is your choice, I will not stop you." She turned to the man. "Go. See if the boy is willing."

CHAPTER 37

CORTEN

Corten squinted against the heat of the glowing furnace runes. His arms were tired. His head ached. But the walls of the glass shop stood solid around him. Twice he'd felt them shake as something, or someone, tried to force its way inside. He'd pushed back those attacks and for the moment all was quiet outside.

He had no idea how much time had passed since. His only measure was the slow and steady drain of his own strength. If another attack came, he wasn't sure he could hold it off. But soon that wouldn't matter anymore.

He hadn't created this place just to hide, after all. When the shadow man left, Corten had gone to work. His arms moved in smooth arcs as he ran the blade of the glass sword one more time across the grindstone. He held it up and grinned, admiring the way the light gleamed off the polished surface and the glow of the molten core running through its center. It had felt like madness when he'd begun. Who made a sword out of glass?

Him, apparently.

Corten didn't know how to hammer steel. He had no memories to craft a forge from the darkness. Besides, glass had felt somehow right. This place didn't follow the same rules as the living world. So he'd poured all his frustration into the blade's glowing core. The edge was anger-sharp, tempered by memories of dusty books and long days spent studying the secrets that separated life and death. He wasn't a warrior. But if he was going to explore the darkness of the fringe, he needed the means to defend himself.

His shoulders hung heavy with the leather vest he'd always worn when working in the furnace. Instead of metal rune plates, it now glimmered with disks of dark glass. Into each piece he'd forged a happy memory—his mother humming off-key while he lay in bed sick, the day Lucia accepted him as her apprentice, that first time Naya looked at him and really, truly smiled.

Corten set the sword down and massaged his temples, wincing at the pain that had taken up permanent residence in his head. He was about to pick the sword back up and continue honing the edge when the pain intensified. Corten gasped. He planted one hand against the wall and braced for another attack.

But the blow didn't come. Instead, someone knocked on the shop's outer door. Corten snatched up the sword and waited. The knock came again. He stood and cautiously stepped from the forge into the main shop. While he'd managed to hold on to the memory of the forge, the rest of the shop was fading. His re-creations of Matius's statues looked eerie against the backdrop of near-transparent walls. Only the front door remained solid.

Corten tightened his grip on the sword. Then he crossed the room and opened the door. The shadow man stood outside, his face unreadable as ever. "What do you want?" Corten asked.

The shadow man looked him up and down. "Well," he said drily. "It seems you've been busy."

A flush crawled up the back of Corten's neck. There were no mirrors in the shop, and he hadn't bothered to dream one up. He'd hoped the smoky glass armor and glowing sword would look intimidating. But for all he knew, he looked as silly as a child playing warrior with oversize clothes and scraps of old wood. "What do you want?" he asked again.

"I come with an offer," the shadow man said.

"I already told you. I'm not going through your door."

"I know. That is why I have come to guide you back to life."

Corten tensed. "Just like that? Sorry, but I find that hard to believe."

"There is a price," the shadow man admitted. "We see darkness looming in the future. You will be our agent in the fight against that darkness. If you succeed, your life will be yours again."

Corten wanted to say yes so badly he could almost taste the sweetness of the word on his tongue. "Why me?" he asked instead.

The shadow man gestured to the glowing sword. "Because your will is strong. You have a chance to succeed. Also, someone has come looking for you."

"Who?" Corten asked, barely daring to hope.

"A girl. She came to barter for your soul."

Naya. So she and Lucia hadn't given up on him. Corten closed his eyes. He'd made the sword and armor out of a vague notion of fighting his way into the darkness in search of a path back to life. To have one handed to him now felt too good to be true. "If I say yes, then what? I'll be your slave?"

"You must join our fight, but your actions will be your own."

"Will you order me to kill anyone?" Corten asked.

"Yes, if there is no other option."

He didn't trust the shadow man. Perhaps he only wanted to lure Corten back out into the darkness so he could drag him to the door. But that didn't fit with the way he'd acted before. And if the offer was genuine, Corten would be throwing away his best chance to escape this place. Could he really risk giving that up? He hesitated, then slid his sword carefully into the sheath at his side. "I'll do it."

"Good. Then I will show you what we face, and I will carry

you as close as I can to the border. The last steps will be up to you."

Before Corten could respond, the shadow man grabbed his arm and the world vanished in a swirl of howling wind. His voice sounded in Corten's head. *"Look, and see the danger of what has happened, and what may yet happen again."*

Something slammed into Corten, as though the wind had condensed into a solid wall. Then light, and sound, and life materialized around him. He was standing at the edge of a courtyard paved with uniform slabs of gray stone. The air was hot and muggy, and above him clouds churned around a perfect circle of blue sky. Corten gaped. The edges of the world shimmered like the memories he'd fallen into. Except this couldn't be a memory because he was sure he'd never seen this place before.

He heard voices and turned to see a circle of strangers. They wore loose, vestlike shirts that exposed arms covered in spiraling runic tattoos. A muscular man stood in the center of the circle, his body covered in tattoos that glowed with aether. The runes were strange, and the man was speaking in a language that sounded both familiar and frustratingly incomprehensible. Even so, there was something powerful in the words that made the whole world pulse in time to their rhythm. The man called out and his followers echoed him in a rising, singsong chant.

Aether churned around them, creating a vortex more powerful than anything Corten had ever felt. As the energy built, the man in the center drew a long dagger. Corten watched in horror as he pressed the blade to his chest and carved a new rune into his flesh. The man spoke again, and though the language did not change, the meaning of the words echoed in Corten's mind. *"I name us gatekeepers! From this day on, the doors of death will be ours to command."*

Energy exploded from the circle and hit Corten like a punch. The man in the center grinned triumphantly. Then his face twisted as the rune on his chest burst into flame. The ground cracked and the howl of the wind rose to a scream. Something dark leaked into the aether. Corten braced himself, but the power flowed harmlessly around him. Everything else it touched died. Flesh withered and color leached from plants and stone alike. The people in the circle screamed, the runes on their bodies burning black as they crumpled to the ground.

There was no sense of movement, but suddenly Corten could see the destruction spreading. The plaza sat at the center of a vast city. As Corten watched, the ground sank. Buildings fell and thousands upon thousands died before the rising wave of darkness.

"*Remember*," the shadow man whispered. "*It must not happen again.*"

Corten flinched from the vision. Darkness swallowed him and through it he heard a familiar voice calling. Lucia's song. The notes wrapped around him and Corten ran, letting them guide him through the dark.

He saw the portal up ahead, but before he could reach it, a scavenger came screeching out of the dark. Clawed limbs slashed toward him. One cut his arm, drawing a bright line of pain down his biceps. Another bounced harmlessly off the glass disks of his vest.

Corten stumbled back and drew his sword. He slashed wildly and connected with one of the creature's limbs. The impact jarred his shoulder as the blade sliced deep into ethereal flesh.

The scavenger shrieked and reeled back. Corten saw his opportunity. He lunged to the side and sprinted. He could hear the scavenger chasing, but the glow of the portal was bright ahead. A claw scraped along his back and Corten leapt forward, his fingers stretched out and straining toward the glow of life.

CHAPTER 38

CORTEN

The world exploded with light and for a terrifying moment Corten felt nothing. Then, slowly, he became aware of pressure against his back and the brush of air moving against his cheek. A knocking sounded from somewhere nearby, sharp and urgent.

"Corten?"

That voice.

"What happened? Did it work? Is—"

He opened his eyes. At first everything was a blur of light and color. He blinked and the colors resolved themselves into the aged brown of a low wood ceiling. A soft weight settled over him, a blanket probably. When a wraith reformed their body after a resurrection, they always came back naked. *That voice. Naya.* Naya had called out his name. Which meant Naya was here. Which meant she'd seen . . . everything. Corten sat up, pulling the blanket in close.

Someone gasped. It took a moment for Corten's vision to fully clear. Lucia was sitting in front of him, just inside the edge of a rune circle he didn't recognize. When he turned, he saw Naya staring at him, her eyes wide and her lips parted as though about to speak. Her hair was a wild tangle of curls and beneath her joy, her eyes were shadowed by exhaustion. For a split second, the room was silent. Then the knocking began again.

"Naya? Lucia? What's going on? Are you all right?" a man's voice asked through the door.

"I told you, you can't go in there!" a woman's voice said, also from outside, sounding slightly frantic.

Corten looked around. He was in a wooden room, sitting on the floor between a long table and a small desk. Strangely, the legs of the table were bolted to the floor. "Where are we?" he asked. Was this real, or was it just another one of the shadow man's illusions? The edges of his vision didn't waver like they had before. His sword and armor were gone and everything around him looked solid and gloriously, wonderfully real. When he touched his arm, he found a thin white line, like an old scar, where the scavenger had cut him.

He tried to bask in the relief of finally being back, but all he felt was a sort of hollow fear. The shadow man's words echoed through his mind and the back of his neck itched with the conviction that the darkness lurked somewhere right behind him.

"Who is that? Damnation, someone, open this door!"

The unfamiliar voice snapped Corten back to the present. He tried to stand but fell back when the floor rocked gently beneath him. Wherever he was, it definitely wasn't Lucia's shop. The room smelled like wood and pitch, and something musty and sharp he couldn't identify. Lucia leaned forward, staring at him with an intensity she usually reserved for books.

"Everything is fine," Naya said, holding up her hands in a calming gesture. "You're safe." Her voice shook. She turned to glare at the door and seemed to steady herself before calling out, "Give us a moment, Lucia's still recovering." More quietly she added, "Please, Corten, I'll explain everything, just stay quiet and stay out of sight."

The banging on the door stopped. "Naya? Did something happen? One second I was asleep and the next my tattoos were burning with aether."

Quiet was the last thing Corten wanted to stay. His body thrummed with aether and his head was full of images of crumbling cities and beasts of shadow and claw. "Naya, I—"

"Please, Corten. We can't let anyone find you here."

That did not make him feel better. But he could hear the fear in her voice, so he nodded his agreement. Naya gave him a brief, tired smile, then slipped around the table and unlocked the door on the other side of the room. She opened it a crack. "Everything's fine, Francisco. Why don't you go back to bed? You look awful."

"That is exactly what I told him," the female voice from before said. "But he wouldn't listen."

"I said I'm fine," the male voice—Francisco, apparently—answered. "Is someone in there with you?"

"Only Lucia. She just finished adding the new bone to my bond."

"I thought I heard a man talking," Francisco said.

"Then maybe you were dreaming. I'm sorry we woke you." Naya's tone was soothing despite the rigid grip she held on the door.

"It definitely wasn't a dream," Francisco said, suspicion growing in his voice. "Who are you trying to hide in there?"

"Nobody!"

"Naya," Francisco said, now sounding exasperated. "You asked me to trust you, but you are making it damned hard."

"You're the one—"

This wasn't working. "Naya, stop," Corten said, bracing himself against the table so he could stand. "Whatever you're trying to hide, just stop." She'd said it was too dangerous for him to be seen. But Francisco didn't sound like he intended to go away, and if they kept on like this, their argument was bound to draw more attention. Besides, the tone of Naya's voice reminded Corten too much of those days in Belavine before he'd found out who she really was. He wouldn't sit quietly while she spun more lies.

"Who's there?" Francisco asked again.

Corten stepped carefully over the painted lines of the circle, noticing with a shudder that the wood looked pale and warped around the edges of the runes. He kept the blanket wrapped tight around his waist as he approached the door. A sallow young man about his own age leaned against the doorframe as though it were the only thing keeping him upright. His rumpled shirt hung half-unbuttoned and bulged where thick bandages had been wrapped around his stomach. Necromantic tattoos circled his neck and wrists, still rough with scabs from the needle's work. When Corten drew aether, he could feel the pulsing thrum of pain leaching off Francisco. A pretty Ceramoran girl with curly hair and soft features stood behind Francisco, staring at Corten with wide eyes.

"My name's Corten. Who are you?"

Francisco blinked, then his brow furrowed. "Francisco Delence. Wait. Did you say Corten? Corten Ballera?"

Naya made a small noise in the back of her throat. Corten glanced at her. She looked like she wanted to slam the door shut. "You know who I am?"

Francisco shook his head. "You can't be Ballera."

"Why not?" Corten asked.

"Because he's been dead for weeks."

Corten took a step back. "That can't be right." He tried to remember everything that had happened since he'd died, tried to track the time moment by moment. Days, maybe a week, no more than that, surely. He met Naya's eyes, hoping she'd deny it.

"I can explain," Naya said quickly. "Lucia and I found a ritual to bring you back. But we had to sail to Talmir to get a journal with the right rune diagrams."

"Did you say Talmir?" Corten asked.

"That's right, you're in Talmir," Francisco said. His voice was hard, and his eyes narrowed as he looked at Naya. "Creator, I can't believe this. Are you trying to start a war? And you." He turned to Lucia. "What did you do, exactly?"

"I, ah, I'm not actually sure." Lucia looked at the center of the ritual circle. Corten followed her gaze to a pile of broken bones. "I would very much like a few minutes to speak in private with Naya and Corten."

"If we're going to talk about this, could we please not do it with the door open?" Naya asked, casting a furtive glance down the hallway behind Francisco.

Francisco swallowed, looking like he might be sick. "I'm going back to the palace. My father needs to hear about this. He'll know what to do. He'll know how to hide what you've done."

"Wait!" Naya said. "I'll go with you, but I'm not leaving until I'm sure Corten is all right."

"No. Stay here," Francisco said. "I made the mistake of trusting you once. I won't do it again."

Naya flinched and Corten almost did the same. Those words sounded all too familiar. What had happened since his death?

"Fine," Naya snapped. "If you think you can convince your father and the Congress to let me leave with the *Gallant*, then be my guest."

Francisco glanced around, then stepped into the cabin and shut the door. "Tell me one thing. Why in creation would you risk this? Do you care at all what this could do to Ceramor's reputation if anyone finds out?" Francisco turned to the round-faced girl who'd slipped in behind him. "And what about you, Felicia? Don't tell me you were in on this as well. You should have come to me immediately as soon as—"

"This isn't her fault!" Naya snapped. Corten felt a tug in the aether as Naya drew energy. "Contrary to what you might think, we're not the ones you should be worrying about right now. I need your help keeping this secret if we're going to stand any chance of stopping the people who killed Valn."

Francisco's eyes narrowed. "What are you taking about?"

"Resurgence. They've got agents in the palace. They killed Valn, and I don't think they plan to stop there."

"And who, or what, is Resurgence?" Francisco asked.

Naya looked away. "I still don't know exactly. I have a contact who can give us more information, but she won't talk until I can make a deal with Delence."

Francisco shook his head. "Even if I could trust you on that, we don't have time to be organizing deals with a mystery contact. We have to get this situation under control." He turned to Corten. "I don't know what your role in this was, but unless you want everyone on this ship dead, I suggest you keep out of sight." He didn't wait for an answer before storming from the room.

Naya exchanged a look with Felicia. "Could you keep an eye on him?"

Felicia nodded. "I'll try." Her eyes lingered on Corten for a moment longer before she turned and followed Francisco toward a steep stairway at the end of the hall. As soon as she was gone, Naya shut the door.

Silence followed. Naya stared at the door, her face a mask of worry. Worse, now that he looked closer, Corten could see patches of her skin flickering between pale brown and translucent blue. She must have damaged one of her bones again.

Without thinking, Corten closed the gap between them. Whatever she'd done, whatever trouble she'd set in motion getting him here, didn't matter right now. He'd deal with what the shadow man wanted from him in the future. Right now he was just glad he and Naya both had a future to deal with. He felt Naya shiver as she stepped into his arms. "It's okay," he said. "We'll figure it out."

Her lips found his in answer. Her kiss was hot and insistent, like she was trying to make up for all the lost time stretched out between them. Corten leaned into her. He let the feel of her body against his burn away the hollow cold of death. For a brief, glorious instant, the world became simple and perfect.

Lucia cleared her throat. "I hate to interrupt, but would one of you please tell me what happened on the other side? What did you see?"

Naya stepped out of the circle of Corten's arms. A dozen emotions seemed to play behind her troubled expression. "I'm not sure where to start," she said softly.

Corten cast his eyes toward the ceiling. Images of writhing shadows and death flashed through his mind, too tangled to put into words. Better to start with something simple. "Are we really in Talmir?" he asked.

Naya nodded. "The ship's anchored in Lith Lor Harbor."

Corten drew a slow breath of aether. "Okay. Then first there's something I need to know. You said something about a journal. What did you do, Lucia?"

Lucia shook her head. "The real question is how did it work? This is impossible."

"What do you mean it's impossible?" Naya asked. Though she didn't look at him, Corten felt her fingers extend to brush against his. He took her hand in his, relishing the warmth of her skin.

Lucia gestured at the pile of bones in the center of the ritual circle with her bandaged hand—they had been carved as though for a bond, but every one of them had been snapped or cracked beyond use. "When Naya came through the portal, I thought I saw someone just behind her. I tried to hold the way open, but then the portal imploded and something forced me back against the wall. I heard bones breaking. When my vision cleared, Corten was lying in the circle. But those bones are the ones I meant for his binding. If they're here, broken, then what in the Creator's grace is keeping him bound to life?"

All three of them stared at the bones as Lucia's words sank in. Corten touched his chest. "It's a mistake," he said. "It has to be."

"I don't make mistakes," Lucia snapped. "Not in this." She pulled a reader from the small bag of tools by her feet, then touched it to Corten's arm. His skin turned transparent, and Lucia gasped. Corten looked down at his arm. There were no bones there, but the aether beneath his skin swirled in a way he'd never seen before. It looked almost like the wind that moved through the grasses on the other side of death. Runes formed in the glowing aether—there one moment, gone the next.

"It's impossible," Lucia repeated. She touched the reader to his other arm, then his chest. Each time the result was the same, swirling aether, dancing runes, no bones.

"It doesn't matter," Naya said, sounding like she was trying to convince herself as well. "You're back."

"Am I?" Corten asked, looking at Naya and Lucia in turn. "How can I be here without anything to bind me? This isn't how necromancy works." A soul couldn't exist in the physical plane without a binding that held it to its former body. Corten thought back to the deal he'd struck with the shadow man and wondered what he'd gotten himself into.

With an effort of will, he turned the skin of his hand transparent, displaying the same swirl of aether and runes. "This has to have something to do with the shadow men," he said, half to himself.

"The what?" Lucia asked, leaning forward. She glanced at Naya. "Do you know what he's talking about?"

"There were things on the other side that looked like people," Naya said in a tone barely above a whisper. "The ones I spoke to didn't look shadowy, but I got the impression that the faces they showed me were just masks. They offered us a deal. They would help bring Corten back, and in exchange we have to help them."

Corten pressed one hand to his forehead. His memories of the other side were already starting to feel fuzzy, like years had passed instead of only a few minutes. That was normal—few undead remembered details from their time on the other side. Corten squeezed his eyes shut again, as though that could lock the memories inside. Slowly, he told Naya and Lucia about his journey through death. Lucia snatched up a book and pen to take notes as he described the door, the shadow men and scavengers, and his encounter with Servala.

Naya's eyes widened when Corten described his desperate sprint to the portal. "You fought one of the scavengers?" she asked.

"You don't have to sound so surprised," Corten muttered.

"No, it's just . . ." Naya blushed. "I'm impressed."

"Oh." Corten felt a grin tugging at his cheeks. "Well, by all means, feel free to be impressed."

Naya laughed. Then Lucia cleared her throat and gave them both a hard look. "I want to hear more about this deal and the people you made it with."

Naya glanced at Corten. "I don't know much. The woman I met said something about a queen in the east who was tampering with old magic. She said we had to stop her, or something terrible would happen. But I've got no idea how we're supposed to do that."

"Me either," Corten said. "The shadow man who talked to me said something similar, but he was vague on the details." And of course, genius that he was, Corten hadn't bothered to ask. He met Naya's eyes again and saw his own questions echoed there.

Lucia continued to pepper them with questions. Corten's unease only grew as each one revealed more gaps in their knowledge.

"What I don't understand," Lucia said with obvious frustration, "is who these shadows are. And, if they intended for you to help them, why give you so little information?"

It was a good question. Someone knocked on the door before either Corten or Naya could come up with an answer.

Naya muttered a curse. She turned toward the door and Corten felt her draw aether. Her eyes widened, then her face went carefully blank. "Hide," she whispered to Corten.

"What is it?" he asked.

Naya shook her head. "Trouble."

Corten wanted to ask for more, but something in her voice stopped him. "Where should I hide?" The sparse room wasn't exactly brimming with options.

Naya scanned the small room, then pointed to a spot next to the door. "Stand there. They shouldn't be able to see you."

"What if they come inside?" Corten whispered back.

"I'll make sure they don't." Naya squeezed his hand once, then let go and turned to face the door.

The knock came again. "Miss Garth?" a man's voice asked. The speaker sounded older than Francisco. When Corten drew in aether, he could sense a prickle of unease mixed with steely anger. Whoever was on the other side, it didn't seem he'd come for a friendly conversation. Corten crossed the room to stand beside the door. Creator, he wished he had a pair of pants. It was bad enough to be hiding on a ship in Talmiran waters with no cursed idea what was going on. Having to stand there with nothing more than a blanket wrapped around his waist while Naya answered the door was somehow so much worse.

Naya opened the door partway, putting it between Corten and whoever was on the other side. "Captain Cervacaro," she said. "What can I do for you?"

"Miss Garth," Captain Cervacaro said, "I came to inform you that three squads of Talmiran soldiers are rowing toward our ship. They raised signal flags declaring their intention to come aboard. I also couldn't help but notice three Talmiran vessels have pulled anchor and are readying cannons in our direction. Lord Francisco is up above and seemed to think all this has something to do with you. You wouldn't happen to know what's going on, would you?"

Naya tensed. "I don't know. Give me just a minute and I'll join you on deck."

"Be quick about it. Those soldiers don't look happy."

Naya nodded, then shut the door. Lucia rose, clutching the table. "You don't think . . . " she began.

"He's right," Naya said. "They're here for me."

"Then we must hide you quickly," Lucia said, looking between Naya and Corten. "I saw you come in through the window last night. Could you and Corten go out that way? Maybe hide under the water until they're gone?"

Naya hesitated, and Corten used the opportunity to cut in. "Anyone want to tell me what's going on here?"

Naya looked at him. Exhaustion shone in her eyes, and for just an instant he thought he saw her lip tremble. Then she clenched her hands into fists and seemed to steady herself. "Those soldiers are here to arrest me."

"Why?" Corten asked.

"Because I broke into the Academy of Magics and stole some of the books of forbidden necromancy they were secretly hiding there."

Corten stared at her. From anyone else it would have sounded absolutely insane. But Corten had watched Naya escape the executioner's platform by using one of her own bones as a bomb. There was a force to her that somehow made the impossible seem normal. "Oh," he said. "And now I guess we have to jump out a window so they don't kill us?"

"We can't," Naya said. "There are too many ships in the harbor. If someone sees us go over, they'll just keep searching until they find us. We'll be putting everyone else on the ship in danger."

"What choice do you have?" Lucia asked. "You can't let them take you."

"Yes, I can," Naya said. "If I don't resist, then hopefully they won't have any reason to search the ship. You two will be safe."

"And you'll be locked up in a Talmiran cell waiting for execution," Lucia said.

"Not necessarily." Naya smiled, though Corten could still see the worry in her eyes. "I doubt Queen Lial wants the Congress to know about her secret weapons program. Those journals I brought back are proof that Talmiran scribes kept some of the works they were supposed to destroy during the purges. I saw more in Hest's office, and I saw one of the new weapons they designed. We can use that information against them. I'm still technically under the Congress's protection. She's sent enough soldiers that she can't just make me disappear and pretend she had nothing to do with it. And if she formally accuses me of breaking into the academy, there will have to be a trial."

"You think you can convince her to let you go if you keep her weapons program secret?" Corten asked. It sounded weak, far too weak to risk her life on.

Naya hesitated, then nodded. "I think I can make a deal with her. I'll offer to leave Talmir. Delence won't like it, but at this point my being here will only cause more trouble. Regardless, I need you two to stay free. You can protect the journals, and I gave Felicia a description of the weapon I saw. Get a copy from her if you can. If this goes badly, then someone has to warn the Necromantic Council that Talmir's been designing new ways to destroy the undead."

"I don't like this," Lucia said.

"Neither do I. But it's the best chance we have of everyone getting out of here safely. I'm the one who pushed to come here. If anyone has to face the consequences, it should be me," Naya said, glancing at Corten.

"No," Corten said. He stepped forward and grabbed her hand again. "Naya, I may not know everything that's going on here, but I know enough about Talmir to be sure that giving yourself up to their soldiers is a terrible idea. We'll come up with something else."

"There's no time!" Naya snapped. "Didn't you hear him? The soldiers are on their way. Any delay when they get here will only make things worse."

Corten faced her, his own anger bubbling up despite his best efforts to keep it down. "I did not come back from the dead just to watch you face another execution."

"And I brought you back because you were never supposed to die for me!" Naya said. "If those soldiers take me, at least I have a chance of talking my way out of it. I have permission to be here. You they'll kill on sight as soon as they realize what you are." Her voice broke around the words. Color had flooded her cheeks and she looked away. "Besides," she said more softly, "this is about more than just us now. I don't know what those things in death were, but I know they didn't send you back out of kindness." Naya met his eyes. "If the threat they saw is real, then someone has to be around to stop it."

"That isn't fair," Corten said. He squeezed her hand tighter, some irrational part of him whispering that if he could just hold her there, then somehow everything would stop going so wrong.

Naya looked up at the ceiling. Corten drew in aether, but he couldn't stretch his senses far enough to detect whatever it was she'd felt. "They're here," she said. "I have to go."

"Naya—"

He expected her to pull away from him, but instead she stepped closer. He froze, looking into her eyes—somehow bright and sad at the same time. She tilted her head up and kissed him.

This kiss was softer than the first. Corten leaned into it, wrapping one arm around Naya's waist. Her lips parted, and her tongue touched his, hesitant like a songbird leaping between branches. In that touch he could taste her sorrow and her uncertainty. He drew her closer, wanting to hold her there, to make her see that she didn't have to do this.

But as his grip tightened, she broke from the kiss, stepping smoothly to one side and out of his grasp. Her eyes met his. "Wait for me?" she asked.

Corten opened his mouth to answer, but he couldn't find any words. His chest was a tight knot of turmoil. He felt like he'd been dumped headfirst into a mire of politics and magic. He stumbled blindly while Naya strode confidently ahead. He hated that he couldn't find the path. He hated that part of him wasn't sure he could trust her enough to follow hers.

Naya didn't wait for him to find an answer. Instead, she gave him one last smile before slipping out the door.

CHAPTER 40

NAYA

Naya stood on the deck of the *Gallant* and tried not to flinch under the stony glares of the nine Talmiran soldiers standing before her. Her lips still burned with the memory of the kiss. It had felt so impossibly good to hold Corten again, and she'd sensed his eagerness when he'd kissed her back. In that moment she'd wanted to give up everything and flee with him. The only thing that stopped her was a gut-deep certainty that once they started running, they'd never be able to stop.

The aether around her carried the pepper-smoke tang of anger and anticipation as the soldiers formed ranks before her, keeping their hands close to the hilts of their swords. Naya had no doubt those swords were wraith eaters. In addition, two more squads waited in rowboats below, and three nearby ships had pointed their cannons at the *Gallant*, ready to fire broadside if she tried anything.

Naya supposed she should have felt proud that they thought her enough of a threat to deserve such an overwhelming show of force. Instead she just felt sick.

"Naya Garth, you are hereby charged with trespassing and the attempted murder of a Talmiran citizen." The soldier who spoke was a short man with a bushy brown beard that might have looked silly if not for the icy disgust in his aether.

Captain Cervacaro stood to the side of the soldiers and Naya saw his face pale at the accusation. Tension thickened in the aether, making her skin prickle. Naya met the soldier's gaze. "I don't know what you're talking about."

The bearded soldier's eyes narrowed. "I am referring to the attack at the Academy of Magics last night."

Naya did her best to look confused. "What attack? I was here on the ship all night."

"Several reliable witnesses reported your crimes. If you are innocent, then you have nothing to worry about coming with us to defend yourself in the courts." The soldier's lip curled into a sneer, as though he found the prospect highly unlikely. "If you refuse, we are authorized to take you by force."

Naya shivered at the bright thread of eagerness in his aether. She was innocent, at least partially. She hadn't tried to hurt anyone at the academy, though Hest had certainly done her best to kill her. She doubted her guilt or innocence would matter much to these men. "I'll come with you," she said quickly. "And I hope you'll send someone to tell Queen Lial that I've reconsidered her offer. I have information for her." It was a gamble. But if Naya was right about the queen's role in all of this, then it should be enough to get her to hear Naya out.

Something that might have been doubt or disappointment flickered across the soldier's features. "Restrain her," he said. Two more soldiers stepped forward, one of them pulling a complicated set of wooden cuffs from a pack on his back. Naya clenched her teeth at the icy touch of the salma wood. The chill of it radiated through her limbs as the soldier locked one set of cuffs around her wrists, then clasped a collar around her neck. Another set of cuffs bound her ankles, all of it held together with heavy metal chains.

"Is this really necessary?" Naya asked. The throb of the cracked bone in her hand seemed stronger amid the cold pain of the salma wood, and the chains around her ankles were so short that she'd have to shuffle rather than walk. She was glad that at least the compass and anchor bones weren't there anymore to add to the dissonant sensations, or worse, to somehow translate her pain back to Lucia or Corten. Both bones had cracked and fallen away as she'd stepped back into life.

The bearded soldier offered her a thin smile. "We know what your kind are capable of."

The soldier who'd cuffed her pulled out a salma wood club and prodded her toward the edge of the ship. There they hooked a rope onto her cuffs and lowered her down to the waiting rowboats like a sack of grain.

Panic tightened in Naya's chest as they secured her to a heavy iron loop on the rowboat, then started back toward shore. She flexed her wrists against her restraints but stopped when the soft clink of chains earned her a look from one of the soldiers watching her. Instead she turned her gaze toward the shore, trying to appear calm.

She told herself she would be fine. This wasn't anything like the last time she'd been locked in chains. She had a plan, and she had at least some allies back at the Congress. She just had to convince Queen Lial that dismissing the accusation was the smartest course of action.

If that failed, at least Corten and Lucia would be safe.

Naya's thoughts fuzzed in a fog of pain as the soldiers rowed her to shore, then escorted her up the lift to a waiting carriage. Despite her efforts to reassure herself, the carriage ride reminded her all too much of the ride to the executioner's platform back in Belavine. How was it that she kept getting herself into these situations? Less than a year ago, she'd been a merchant's daughter. The biggest danger she'd ever faced was that of shipwreck, and even that hadn't been much of a risk in the routes her father usually sailed. Now here she was facing the prospect of imprisonment and execution. Again.

A cruel voice in the back of her mind whispered that she never should have come back to Talmir. Everyone would have been better off if she'd just stayed in Belavine. Well, everyone except Corten. The memory of him standing whole and alive on the *Gallant* silenced that voice. She hadn't told him about the five years the stranger had demanded as part of the price for bringing him back. The choice had been hers, and knowing about it would probably only make Corten feel guilty.

The carriage doors opened and Naya stumbled out. "Where are we?" she asked, the panic rising fresh in her chest despite the numbing chill of the salma wood cuffs. The carriage had stopped in a dark stone chamber. Soldiers guarded an iron-bound door on the far wall. A boom came from behind her, and Naya looked back to see a larger set of doors being latched shut.

"Your new residence, until the queen decides what to do with you," the bearded soldier from the ship said.

"I thought you were taking me to the palace," Naya said.

The soldier sneered. "The palace? No. You'll be staying in the only part of this land where one of your kind belongs."

Naya looked down the dark hallway with a sinking feeling. "I'm a member of the delegation. You can't just lock me up like this."

But apparently they could, because one of the soldiers hit her across the shoulders with a salma wood club, forcing her to stumble forward. Between the effects of the salma wood and her cracked bone, she didn't have the strength to fight them. She'd hoped the soldiers would take her in for questioning immediately. Instead they'd brought her to the Barrow, the prison in Justice Square where the worst of Talmir's criminals were held. Did Queen Lial have more evidence than Naya had assumed? Or had she decided she didn't care about angering the Congress by locking Naya away down here?

The soldiers dragged her down and down, past cells with

heavy barred doors. The upper levels of the prison were loud with clanking metal and the cries of prisoners. As they descended the shouts were replaced with silence broken only occasionally by a quiet sob or a burst of hysterical laugher. Through the ice of the salma wood and her own dread, Naya could feel the darkness of the prison's aether seeping into her. The air tasted thick and heavy with despair, a sickly-sweet stench like something long dead. It made her shackles feel heavier and her doubts and fears multiply.

The soldiers finally stopped at a heavy door of dark salma wood. The bearded soldier unlocked the door and opened it to reveal a windowless cell little bigger than a closet. *Or a coffin.* Naya's throat went tight and the last of her courage left her. "No," she whispered, trying to push away from the dark opening. "No!" Her bare feet slid against the damp stone floor as she struggled to scramble away. She tried to push her wrists through her cuffs, but the shackles held fast.

A club slammed into the back of her head once, twice. Dazed, Naya stumbled into the cell. Her shoulder hit the wall and the freezing touch of more salma wood greeted her. Before she could even turn around, the heavy door boomed shut behind her, sealing her in darkness.

CHAPTER 41

CORTEN

Corten paced back and forth across the ship's cabin. This was wrong. He shouldn't have let Naya go like that. He should have said something, done something.

"Corten, please, sit down," Lucia said, her voice taking on the faintly exasperated tone he'd heard so often back when he was her apprentice. When he drew in aether, he could sense the sour mix of her fear and guilt, neither one strong enough to overshadow a bright thread of urgent excitement.

Corten turned to face her. "Sit down?! Is that really all you have to say? 'Sit down, Corten. Be quiet, Corten.'" He reached up, tugging at his hair, trying to let the sharp sensation ground him. "How can you be okay with letting her go like that? How are you okay with any of this?"

"I'm not," Lucia snapped. "But I see no point in acting rashly. One thing I've learned about Naya is that telling her not to do something she's set on is an exercise in futility. We'll have to trust her to take care of herself for a while until we can figure out how best to help. In the meantime, I would very much like to get back to our previous conversation."

"Of course you would," Corten muttered. Lucia had always been fascinated by necromancy, sometimes maybe too fascinated. After what he'd seen on the other side of death, Corten was starting to think that there were some secrets better left alone. Lucia narrowed her eyes and remained silent, waiting. Corten looked away, but he could still feel her gaze on the back of his neck. "I don't know anything else, all right?"

"Think, Corten. You know as much about our art as any fully trained necromancer. You must have some theories about what you saw."

Our art. Corten braced himself for the pain of that reminder but was surprised to feel only a soft ache. After his first death, nearly every conversation he'd had with Lucia had ended in an argument. She'd asked him to stay on with her and help carve runes, and he'd hated her for it. He'd wondered how she could be so blind as to why he didn't want to live surrounded by reminders of the future he'd lost.

Maybe it would have been different if his death had meant something. But he'd died so stupidly. With one wrong step, he'd lost his place as the family heir and his chance of becoming a true necromancer. When he'd told Lucia he wouldn't waste his time carving runes for her, she'd called him a spoiled child, claiming he was throwing away his talents just because he didn't want to face what had happened. And maybe in a way she'd been right. He'd spent years focused only on that loss, all the while avoiding the question of what he wanted to do with the life he had left.

"I'm not sure why the people Naya spoke to wore faces, and the one I met was only a shadow, but it seems obvious they're all part of the same group. The vision they showed must be connected to the ancient magics they told Naya about. I saw people who could have been necromancers performing some sort of ritual. Most of it I couldn't understand, but one of them talked about becoming gatekeepers and commanding the doors of death."

"Gatekeepers," Lucia muttered. "What do you suppose they meant by that?"

"I'm not sure, but whatever they were trying to do, it went wrong. Very wrong."

"Well—" Lucia began.

She was interrupted by the sound of the cabin door opening. Corten barely had time to take a surprised step back as a girl in a servant's dress hurried in and shut the door behind her. For an instant he hoped the girl was Naya, wearing a different face and somehow having already escaped the Talmiran soldier. Then he recognized her as the girl from earlier, Felicia.

"Sorry for barging in," Felicia said. "They've taken Naya and I wasn't sure what to do. I mean, when she said someone would come for her, I didn't think she meant—"

"Slow down," Lucia said. "We were just talking about what to do about that."

"You were? Good. Because Lord Francisco is up on deck preparing to go ashore, but he really does not look well. Naya gave me all these documents to give to his father, but given how angry Lord Francisco is at us, I wasn't sure I should give them to him. In fact, I'm not sure he should be going ashore at all. Even Captain Cervacaro tried to stop him."

"Well, of course he shouldn't be going, not unless he's trying to court a second death," Lucia said with a scowl. She shook her head. "Give me the documents, and go tell Francisco that I must speak to him before he considers leaving. If he still won't come, tell him I have an urgent message for his father that I cannot possibly entrust to anyone else."

"Right. What about . . . ?" Felicia's eyes darted to Corten and then quickly away. The look on her face made Corten painfully aware that he was still naked aside from the blanket around his waist.

Lucia followed Felicia's gaze, then shook her head. "If anyone asks you about him, tell them this is Matius. He's a sailor from the *Lady* who will join us to act as Francisco's footman on the journey back to Talmir. He'll be needing to borrow a set of clothes from Francisco, unfortunately, as he accidentally fell in the ocean on the way over and managed to drop his own bag in the water."

Felicia smiled. "Matius. Of course. I'll go tell Lord Francisco then."

"What was that?" Corten asked as soon as Felicia was gone. "No one's seriously going to believe I'm a sailor from the *Lady*. They'll have seen you come over without me."

"It was the best I could come up with," Lucia said irritably. "Anyway, a sailor nobody noticed is a good deal less likely to draw attention than a young man who simply appeared out of nowhere."

"And what do you mean to do with Francisco when he gets here?"

"Stall him," Lucia said. "Felicia is right. Francisco has a four-inch hole in his stomach and we'll all be better off if he stays here."

Francisco clearly didn't agree. He barged into the room a few minutes later. "What's this message you have for my father?" he asked. "And what was Felicia talking about when she said you'd need to borrow clothes for some footman? I don't have time to—" His eyes fell on Corten and he seemed to make the connection. "No," he said. "Find someone else's clothes to steal."

"There will be fewer questions if you just give him some," Lucia said. "As you may recall, we all have a vested interest in keeping his presence here a secret. Once Corten is properly clothed, we can all sit down and discuss what to do next."

"There's nothing to discuss," Francisco said. "You're staying here, and I'm going back to the palace to help my father fix this mess."

"You can barely walk," Lucia said. "You are in no condition to be going anywhere, and even if you did manage to make it to the palace alive, I expect your father would send you right back here."

"I'll go with him," Corten said.

"What?" Francisco asked.

"No," Lucia said, shooting him a glare. "That's a terrible idea."

"And sitting on our hands waiting for something to happen is better?" Corten asked. "You told Felicia that I was supposed to be Francisco's footman. So I'll do that. I can help him get to the palace and keep him safe." And maybe, while he was there, he could figure out some way to help Naya, or at least find out whether she was still safe. Anything was better than waiting here.

"Absolutely not," Lucia said. "If anyone out there finds out what you are, they'll kill you."

"I'm not some newly dead. I know how to hide," Corten snapped. "Nobody in Talmir is going to know what every sailor on the *Lady* looks like. Out there people aren't likely to give me more than a second look. If anything, I'll be safer than if I wait around here until someone starts asking questions." He turned to Francisco. "And Lucia's right, you can barely walk. Like it or not, if you want to get back to the palace, you're going to need help."

It took a few more minutes, but eventually Corten wore down their arguments. Francisco returned with a set of black pants, along with a shirt and vest in a more formal style than Corten was used to. They were about the same height, but Francisco's shoulders were narrower, leaving Corten's chest feeling strangely tight as he squeezed into the clothes. Still, he felt far more relaxed with pants on.

Francisco had covered his bandages with a fresh shirt and a crisp black jacket. It made him look less like someone who'd crawled their way out of a hospital, but he couldn't disguise the grayish tint of his skin or the careful way he moved. "So, I'm to call you Matius?" he asked Corten.

Corten nodded. He felt foolish using a fake name. Unlike Naya, he'd never been good at pretending to be someone he wasn't. He couldn't even change his face for more than a few minutes without feeling the wrongness of it as an ache in his bones. Would that be different now that he didn't have bones? A part of him wanted to experiment, but any mistakes he made would risk exposing him as a wraith. Better to keep things simple.

When they reached the ship's deck, Corten had to fight to keep from gawking. It had been one thing to reconcile himself to the fact that they weren't in Ceramor. It was something else entirely to see the vast ocean spread out on one side and the white cliffs of Lith Lor on the other. More than a dozen ships were anchored nearby, all of them decked out in bright flags. Inside the *Gallant* had felt cramped and damp. Now when Corten looked up, he saw huge masts rising to a dizzying height. Sailors were everywhere. Some lined up with bowls outside a little house on the other side of the deck where a man sat next to a cookpot. Others lounged or worked at tasks Corten couldn't identify.

Francisco earned a few odd looks when he ordered the sailors to let him down in one of the rowboats so he could go ashore. The captain, a bearded man with broad shoulders and dark eyes, pulled Francisco aside and the two argued in harsh whispers. Eventually it was agreed that they'd go ashore with two other sailors from the *Gallant*, who would wait with the rowboat in case they needed a prompt ride back to the ship.

Corten stood to the side while the debate went on, then helped Francisco into the rowboat. The white cliffs loomed over them as the sailors rowed for shore. He'd heard of Lith Lor, but he hadn't given the city much thought as anything other than a distant place he'd never see. Now it struck him as somehow appropriate that the Talmirans had decided to build on top of an imposing cliff. From up there they could look down on anyone who came to visit, forcing them to climb stairs or take a lift if they wanted the privilege of seeing the city itself. It was nothing like the welcoming bustle of Belavine's harbor.

When they reached the shore, they were greeted by a group of stern Talmiran soldiers. Francisco approached them and said something in Talmiran. One of the soldiers shouted what sounded like an order, and another jogged away down the docks.

"What's going on?" Corten asked Francisco in a low whisper.

Francisco gave Corten an appraising look. "You don't speak Talmiran, do you?"

"Of course I don't. Why would I?"

Francisco shrugged. "They're going to arrange for a carriage for us."

"They don't seem happy about it," Corten noted.

"In the past two days, there've been multiple assassination attempts, and now there's this mess with Naya. Even if the whole Congress weren't collapsing around us, these men know what I am and hate me for it."

"You sound surprisingly unworried about that," Corten said. Just standing next to these soldiers made him feel uneasy. They were part of a force that sought to wipe out everything he was. Their predecessors had hunted Lucia and her companions like wild animals.

"They won't do anything to me, not here at least. We'll see what rumors have spread at the palace, but if Queen Lial had decided to go after our entire delegation, then we wouldn't have made it even this far."

Corten wasn't sure whether he should be impressed with Francisco's confidence or annoyed. As they waited, he turned his thoughts to the question of what he was going to do once they reached the palace. He didn't have anything even remotely resembling a plan.

But if Francisco was going to speak to his father about what Naya had done, Corten wanted to be there. Francisco, and maybe also Lucia, seemed to have the idea that the safest course would be to keep him locked away on the *Gallant* until they could quietly ship him back to Ceramor. They saw him as an inconvenience and a risk. At least maybe if he spoke with Delence, he could regain some control over his own fate.

CHAPTER 42

NAYA

Naya imagined she could feel the walls closing in around her. The cell they'd locked her in was so small that she couldn't even sit or lie down comfortably. The floor was bare salma wood and the chill of it radiated up her legs, adding to the discomfort of the shackles around her wrists, ankles, and neck. There was no light, no sound, nothing to distract her from her pain and growing panic. In the dark it was so easy to imagine the press of death's tides against her legs. What if her return to the ship had only been another illusion? What if Lucia's portal had closed and all this time she'd really been trapped in death?

Naya forced that thought away. None of the visions she'd seen on the other side had felt real in the way the *Gallant* had. Surely she would know if she was still dead. She reached out and pressed her hand against the icy wood of the door. Its touch was uncomfortable but reassuringly solid. How long did they intend to keep her here? It felt like hours had passed already, but that couldn't be right. Delence would have heard of her arrest. He would remind the others that she was still a member of the delegation. He wouldn't leave her to rot in this place without even a trial to determine her guilt.

Will he really risk his own position to speak on your behalf? Even if he does, the queen and the other delegates might not listen.

Naya sank into a crouch, trying to make herself small. She thought she saw movement out of the corner of her eye and jerked to one side, crying out as her shoulder bumped into the wall. Nothing. Her mind was just playing tricks on her. She squeezed her eyes shut and reached with numb fingers to clasp her mother's pendant. She reminded herself that Corten and Lucia were both free and safe. She would survive this. And when the guards came for her again, she would find a way out of whatever charges they threw at her.

She didn't know how long she huddled in the dark before a noise caused her to look up. At first she thought it had only been in her head. Then the sound came again, a soft scraping like metal on metal. A crack of light appeared around the edge of the door and Naya lunged toward it before she had time to question the impulse. They could try to kill her if they wanted, but they would have to do it outside this cursed cell. Her shoulder connected with the door and it swung open a little farther, eliciting a grunt of surprise from the other side.

The chain between Naya's ankles went taut and she sprawled onto the stone outside the cell. She rolled over, readying herself for blows from salma wood clubs or the draining touch of a wraith eater. No attack came.

Naya blinked, staring at the man who stood holding the door to her cell open. He was tall and dressed in strange clothes. His copper hair was tied back in a tail, and he carried a bloody knife in one gloved hand. She recognized him with a start. "Ambassador Bargal?"

The Endran ambassador flashed her a smile that was all white teeth, then bowed in the formal Talmiran fashion. "Miss Garth, a pleasure to see you again. I do wish the circumstances were better."

"What are you doing here?" Naya asked. She forced herself to her feet. Her cell was set in a short hallway lined with five salma wood doors on each side. Two more doors of the same material guarded the ends. One was slightly ajar, and Naya thought she saw dark liquid seeping around its edges.

Bargal pulled a cloth from his pocket and wiped his knife clean, then snapped it into a sheath hidden somewhere in his sleeve. "I was dining with the queen when she told me of your capture. She was eager to brag of it. She seemed to think her circumstantial evidence and your unique nature are adequate justification for your rough treatment." He paused, his lip curling briefly in a look of disgust. "I disagreed."

There was something chilling about his casual tone—and that knife. "So you came down here to find me?" Naya asked, stunned. "That doesn't make any sense. There would have been guards. If the queen finds out, you'll have no hope of an alliance with Talmir."

Bargal smiled again, then pulled the key out of the keyhole on her cell door. It was attached to a heavy ring along with a dozen or so other keys. Bargal hefted the ring thoughtfully, making the keys clink. "After many meetings, my partner and I have decided this Talmiran queen is not suitable as an ally. We've chosen to pursue other options. Since we were leaving anyway, I thought I ought to give you the option of coming with us. I think you'd find our lands far more welcoming to one such as you."

Naya remembered the long descent through the Barrow. Salma wood and despair made it hard to focus, but she thought they'd passed at least three checkpoints, all guarded and locked. She drew in aether and examined the strange way the energy flowed around Bargal, concentrating at his wrists and blocking her from reading his emotions. She'd seen something like that before, hadn't she? "How did you get down here?"

Bargal shook his head. "An explanation for another day. Now my companions and I have a schedule to keep, and it will not go well if we tarry. I will unlock your shackles. Will you come with me?"

"What happens if I don't?" Naya asked.

"Ah," Bargal said, tilting his head to one side as though he found the question odd. "Where else would you go?"

"I . . ." Where indeed. If she fled, she'd be giving up any chance to claim her innocence. Queen Lial would use her disappearance against Delence. If she was very lucky, she might find her way out of the Barrow and back to the *Gallant*, but then she'd be stuck hiding on the ship until they could figure out how to get out of port. The prospect of returning to the palace and throwing herself on the will of the Congress was hardly more appealing. That left her with either accepting the ambassador's offer or refusing and letting him lock her back in the cell.

Naya glanced at the dark coffin-like space and shuddered. "I'll come with you."

"Good. Before we go, was the necromancer brought here as well?" Bargal asked.

"No." Naya's throat tightened with fear. "She's still on the *Gallant*. At least I think she is. Did the queen say something about her?"

Bargal's expression shifted briefly to annoyance and he said something in his own language that sounded like a curse. "I'd hoped they would take her with you. If she's still on the ship, then we'll have no time to retrieve her."

"Why do you need Lucia?" Naya asked.

Bargal smiled again. "I'll explain everything later. For now we must go."

It took him four tries to find which among the heavy ring of keys fit the locks on Naya's shackles. When they finally fell away, Naya gasped in relief. Warmth flooded into her limbs, and when she drew in a deep breath of aether, some of the ever-present ache in her hand faded. Bargal motioned for her to follow him toward the partially open door.

On the other side of the door, a solider lay dead in a pool of blood, his throat slit. Bargal stepped over the corpse as if he were dodging a puddle on a muddy street. Naya paused. "You killed him?"

"He got in my way," Bargal said. "Please keep walking, Miss Garth. We are in a hurry."

Fresh unease tightened around Naya's chest as she followed Bargal through a series of halls and up a short set of stairs. They passed by more cells. Some, like the one she'd left, looked like they'd been designed to hold wraiths. Others were more ordinary. The aether here felt thin, as though even the cells intended to house living prisoners were unoccupied. Despite that, the hall was clear of dust and lit by the pale glow of aether lamps.

Bargal finally stopped at a heavy iron door. He opened it cautiously, revealing two more dead soldiers lying in a low, dark tunnel. "Ah, good," Bargal said. "We should have a few minutes before the guard changes and these are discovered."

Naya stared at the bodies. Bargal barely seemed to notice them. He'd killed these men to get to her. They were Talmiran soldiers and no doubt scorned her very existence. But seeing their bodies left behind like garbage made her feel sick.

Bargal turned to look at her. His expression was calm, but there was something intense in his pale-gray eyes. "Tell me," he said, "is it true your kind can change the way they look?"

Naya wanted to run from his calculating stare. "If I have to," she answered cautiously. Something was very wrong here.

"Good, do so. From here on we'll risk running into others, and it won't do for you to be recognized."

Naya drew in aether. There wasn't much of it down here, which only made the strange pattern in Bargal's aether stand out even more. With a shock, she finally realized where she'd felt it before—in the assassin who'd tried to kill her in the palace.

When she'd first opened the door a few nights ago, she'd noticed the oddness in the assassin's aether. In all the confusion, she'd dismissed it as an effect of the wraith eater the woman had wielded. But Naya had sensed the pattern before the woman had activated the runes on her knife, hadn't she?

Naya closed her eyes and pressed her fingers against her face, hoping to hide the realization behind shifting features. She imagined Blue's face, feeling her skin grow soft as it shifted to take on the new shape. With a cracked bone, the familiar features would be easier to hold on to. She didn't think anyone in the palace would recognize her. Besides, wearing Blue's face had always made her feel braver and more daring, and right now she could use as much courage as she could find. When she opened her eyes, she saw Bargal staring at her with that same look of uncomfortable intensity.

"Perfect," he said. "Let's hurry now."

"Where are we going?" Naya whispered.

"The palace," Bargal said. "This tunnel will take us to one of the basement levels. Once inside, we will meet my companions at the stables, where we will take a carriage out of the city."

Naya had never heard of a tunnel connecting the prison to the palace. It made sense though. Anyone whose crimes required a ruling from the throne would see their trial carried out in the palace. The tunnel offered a discreet way for prisoners to be moved. But how would Bargal have known about it, much less known how to find it and when the guards would change?

"What happens when we get out of the city?" Naya asked, trying to sound eager rather than horrified.

"Back to Endra," Bargal said. "You don't have to worry about the details."

A chill ran down Naya's back. "Oh, of course," she said. Her smile felt more like a grimace, but Bargal seemed to accept it, turning and leading her down the tunnel.

She followed him, her thoughts racing. She didn't know what was causing the pattern in the aether, but she couldn't ignore the link between Bargal and the assassin. On top of that, Valn had been killed on his way to the palace for trial. This tunnel seemed the most likely route the soldiers would have used to take him there. Bargal's knowledge of the tunnel and the guard rotations was too much for coincidence. But what reason could the Endran ambassador have for being involved in Valn's murder? Why try to kill her, then rescue her from prison a few days later? It didn't make any sense.

Was Bargal part of Resurgence? Naya thought through everything Celia had said. Resurgence had funded Valn's efforts, then had him killed after he'd failed to spark a war between Talmir and Ceramor. They'd pulled Celia from Ceramor and snuck her into the palace among the glut of extra servants hired for the Congress. She'd said that she thought Resurgence was working to disrupt the Congress. What could the Endrans gain from all that?

Something Ambassador Bargal had said when they'd spoken at the Banian salon echoed through her memory, the words taking on new context. *Her Majesty is not one to be denied. What else could we do but bow to her will and set aside our differences?* He'd been talking of the new Endran queen. Naya had assumed the Endrans were exaggerating when they claimed their queen had united the warring city-states.

There were supposedly dozens of independent cities spread across Endra. It would take a potent mix of ambition and skill to convince the cities to abandon their independence and unite under a common ruler. If this Endran queen had made all the city-states bow before her, perhaps she hoped to do the same in the west. The woman Naya had met in death had warned her about an eastern queen who was tampering with dangerous old magic. Could they have been talking about the same person? It was a terrifying prospect, but the more Naya thought about it, the more she feared it was true.

CHAPTER 43

CORTEN

After nearly an hour's wait, the soldiers finally let Corten and Francisco ride the lift to the city proper. The streets above were busy, Talmirans hurrying between rows of oddly uniform shops and houses. Corten wasn't given the chance to see more as he and Francisco were escorted into a waiting carriage. The interior was plush, the seats covered in red velvet and the walls carved artistically in a way even Corten's wealthy parents would have approved of.

Corten stared out the window as the carriage started forward, trying to imagine what it would be like to grow up in a place like this. After a minute he let the curtains fall closed. He'd heard the ache in Naya's voice when she'd spoken about never being able to return home. There had to be something good out there, something worth missing. But right now he couldn't see it.

Glancing over, Corten saw Francisco staring at him. "What?" he asked.

Francisco shook his head. "Just wondering. Do you even know how much she risked bringing you back?"

Corten tensed. "She walked back into death. I know what that must have cost."

"No," Francisco said. "That's not what I'm talking about. I can't pretend to understand whatever magic Lucia uncovered to make this possible. But I know politics. We came here with a real chance at forging a strong peace. Naya knew that, and despite the risks she's taken, I think she really did want to see a better future for Ceramor and the undead." Francisco paused. "She's not stupid. She knew that if she got caught, she might be throwing all that away."

Francisco's words sent an uncomfortable shiver down Corten's back, followed quickly by anger. "What's your point?"

Francisco hesitated. "She didn't have the right to risk all those lives and plans. But she did it anyway. I can't tell if I'm furious at her or just incredibly jealous. Not many people would go so far, even for someone they care about."

"Everyone has a right to make their own choices," Corten said.

"Not everyone," Francisco said forcefully. "Naya came here as part of the delegation, and she used the power and access that gave her for her own selfish reasons. Having power means taking responsibility for more than just yourself. It means sacrificing your own goals for the greater good. My father taught me that. And now all the sacrifices that I—that we all made might be for nothing just because Naya decided to put your life before the safety of an entire country."

Corten felt his hands curling into fists. "If you're asking me to feel guilty for being alive, I won't."

Francisco slumped back in his seat. "That's not what I meant," he muttered. "My father—no. Never mind."

There was a bitter undercurrent to Francisco's words. Corten let the matter drop. This whole business with the Congress made him uneasy. Naya had spoken of the Congress of Powers and their treaties as though they were the only thing holding the world together. But those bonds she and Francisco so admired had always looked more like chains to him. True, the Congress alliance technically promised to defend Ceramor's borders. But they wouldn't need that protection if not for all the restrictions the treaty imposed. It didn't seem fair that everyone in Ceramor should have to keep suffering because the Mad King had been a monster and the Dawning keepers in Talmir were too scared to accept necromancy.

They rode on in silence until the carriage reached the palace gates. Corten didn't need to be able to sense Francisco's aether to tell he was growing more nervous as they approached the looming Talmiran palace. Corten felt his own body tensing as well. He didn't see any crowds or execution platforms at least. In fact, the limited view from the window suggested the grounds were all but deserted. There weren't even any gardeners moving among the flower beds, though it must have taken an army of them to maintain the expanse of perfectly trimmed lawns and hedges surrounding the palace.

Francisco's face looked pale by the time the carriage finally stopped. His expression was tight with pain, and he needed Corten's help to manage the step down from the carriage. At the bottom of the stairs leading up to the palace's massive front doors, they were met by a squad of Talmiran soldiers and a tall, thin man wearing clothes that looked something between a formal suit and a servant's uniform.

The man in the suit greeted Francisco in Talmiran and the two launched into a rapid conversation in the same language. Corten looked back and forth between them as they spoke. Neither one had raised their voice or altered their polite tones, but he could sense the animosity simmering in the air around the man in the suit and the soldiers. The man said something and gestured at Corten. Francisco dismissed the comment with a casual wave and then responded with what was obviously an order.

Finally, the man in the suit bowed stiffly and stepped aside. Francisco leaned on Corten's arm to steady himself as he climbed the stairs. "Translation?" Corten asked under his breath, trying not to let his frustration show. He'd never had reason to learn to speak anything other than Ceramoran. Now he badly wished he had Naya's easy talent for languages.

"Apparently my father is in a meeting with the queen and nobody knows when they'll be done. Steward Neln insisted I should go back to the ships to wait, for my own health, of course." The scorn in Francisco's voice was obvious. "Like every other Talmiran here, he'd rather not have me in the palace if he can avoid it. I told him my health was none of his business and that we would go to my father's rooms and wait for him there."

Two of the soldiers split from the group to walk before them, with two more walking behind. Together they passed into a wide hallway that branched left and right around what Corten took to be the center of the palace. Like the grounds outside, the hallways looked strangely empty. The heels of the soldiers' boots thudded on the marble floor and the only other people they passed were a group of servants carrying cleaning supplies. When Corten drew aether from them, he was met by a cloud of fear. The servants didn't so much as look up as the soldiers drew near, instead retreating quickly through an inconspicuous side door.

"What's going on?" Corten muttered to Francisco.

"I told you there were attacks," Francisco said, sounding troubled. "Everyone's probably afraid the assassins will strike again."

They passed a branch in the hall, connecting one of the palace's wings to the central hub. Here there was more activity. Four soldiers stood at attention guarding a stairway. They watched warily as the group walked by them. Corten's neck itched and a part of him longed to return to the relative safety of the ship. But if Naya was trapped somewhere in here, he had to find a way to help her.

After perhaps another minute they came to a second branch. More soldiers stood at attention here. A dark-skinned young woman dressed in a Banian robe stood before them, her expression impatient as she argued in Talmiran.

She cut off, her eyes widening as she noticed them. "Francisco? Way's Light, what are you doing here?" she asked in heavily accented Ceramoran.

"Hello, Miss Jeden. I might ask you the same question," Francisco said, raising one eyebrow.

"I came to find out what was going on. There are rumors that Naya's been arrested, but nobody will tell me anything." She shot a glare at the soldiers.

"That part of the rumors is true," Francisco said.

Corten looked more closely at Miss Jeden. She looked like she might be Banian, though her hair wasn't straight and her features had a vaguely Talmiran cast. Her robes were made of fine material but rumpled in places, and when he drew in aether, he could sense the worry and anxiety clinging to her like a dark cloud.

"Why did they arrest her? Do you know what's going on?"

"I don't—" Francisco began, but he was cut off by a sudden shout from farther down the hall.

The shout sliced through Corten's chest. He turned toward the sound, seeing Miss Jeden do the same out of the corner of his eye.

One of the soldiers barked an order.

Corten paused, realizing he'd started walking toward the source of the cry. "That sounded like Naya," he said.

The soldier who was apparently in charge of Francisco and Corten shouted something else while gesturing sharply with one hand. Corten couldn't understand the words, but he could guess the meaning of the gesture. *Stay here.*

Miss Jeden ignored the soldiers and ran down the hall. The

lead soldier said something else in an obviously exasperated tone, and three others followed him as he started after Miss Jeden.

Corten glanced back at Francisco. "Come on," he said, then ran to follow. He heard Francisco curse, then footsteps behind him and shouts of protest from the guards by the stairs.

CHAPTER 44

NAYA

Naya followed Bargal out of the hidden tunnel and into a dimly lit room. A small cell stood empty in one corner with a table and chairs set a little away from it. Two soldiers sat slumped at the table. Naya froze, but Bargal walked past them with barely a glance. When Naya checked the aether, she found the energy around them thick with the fog of deep sleep. Drugged, perhaps?

One more hallway and a climb up a narrow stair led Naya and Bargal abruptly into the opulence of the palace proper. Naya glanced around and realized she recognized the spot from her explorations. They were near the painting Sergeant Leln had shown her, not far from the Ceramoran delegation's wing.

Bargal continued down the hall, then stopped when he realized Naya wasn't following. "What are you doing?" he asked.

Naya drew in aether, trying to gather her courage along with the energy. "Thank you for your help, but I can't go with you."

Bargal frowned. "Why not?"

"I can't go to Endra. I have business here, and people I can't leave behind."

Bargal's frown deepened. "That is not a good idea."

Naya started to reply, then hesitated when she heard footsteps approaching from down the hall. A servant appeared a moment later, relief showing on his features when he spotted

Bargal. He was dressed in a palace uniform, but his aether wrapped strangely around him, pooling at his wrists just as Bargal's did. "Sir, there you are. Everything is taken care of. The carriage awaits you and your guest."

"And the other matter?" Bargal asked, apparently unsurprised by the servant's presence.

The servant cast a sideways glance at Naya. "Progressing as we speak. So I advise we move quickly." He spoke Talmiran clearly, but Naya caught a hint of the same accent Bargal had.

Bargal nodded. "Miss Garth, I am afraid we have no time for delay." He reached out to grab her.

Naya snatched her arm away. "No! Stay away from me!" she shouted. She felt certain now that the Endrans were the ones Celia had meant to warn her about. Resurgence's work had sown chaos and instability at every turn. She couldn't guess the full scope of their plans, but she could feel the hunger and urgency in Bargal's aether.

The Congress of Powers had never feared attack from Endra. Not only were the Endran city-states divided, but the Bone Swamp and the long ridge of the Blackspine Mountains left only a few narrow passes where an army could march west. United, the Powers could mount a formidable defense at the choke points. But if the Congress failed and if Talmir and Ceramor fell to war, there would be no united front. Talmir's army would sweep south into Ceramor, leaving Lith Lor and the rest of the northern cities largely undefended.

Terrible certainty welled inside Naya. War was coming, and it would be so much bigger than everyone imagined. She had to warn them. She glanced between Bargal and the servant, or rather the Endran spy dressed in servant's garb, for that was what she was sure the man was. He stood like a trained fighter with his weight on the balls of his feet, his posture loose but ready. "Help!" she shouted.

The servant lunged forward, then froze when the tread of booted feet echoed from farther down the hall. "Sir," he said to Bargal. "Please go. I will deal with this one." There was a glimmer of steel as he pulled a dagger from a sheath hidden somewhere in his vest. The blade was scribed with runes, and though they weren't yet active, Naya guessed the knife was a wraith eater.

"You forget yourself," Bargal snapped.

"No, you do. Ambassador Noreth made it clear that the girl was only to be pursued if she would come quietly."

Naya turned to run but made it only three steps before feeling the pull of the wraith eater activating. A blur of motion from the corner of her eye was the only other warning she had. She dove to the side, barely avoiding the slash of the spy's knife. How had he moved so quickly? Aether glowed through his clothing, a strange pattern of runes spiraling up his legs and across his arms, seeming to flow outward from the bright sources at his wrists.

"That's enough!" Bargal said. "I have tried to be polite, but we are out of time. You will come with us."

The sound of footsteps grew louder and a figure in Banian robes came running around the bend of the hallway, stopping when she saw them. Mel? Naya barely kept herself from speaking the name, her confusion quickly replaced by fear. What was she doing here? Four Talmiran soldiers appeared just behind Mel. Naya had never felt so happy to see them.

Two more people ran up behind the soldiers, one limping and clutching his side. Francisco. And was that . . . ? Naya drew in a sharp breath. For an instant she hadn't recognized Corten, dressed as he was in what looked like an extra set of Francisco's clothes. He froze when he saw her, Francisco drawing up sharp beside him and grabbing his arm for support. What in all of creation was Corten doing here? He was supposed to be back on the ship, safe. Two more soldiers came up behind them, their hands on their weapons and their eyes darting between Francisco and the larger group before them.

"Goodness," Bargal said evenly. "I am sorry to cause such alarm. This man merely bumped into the girl. She was startled, but no harm has come of it."

Fear burned in Naya's chest. Corten and Francisco both obviously recognized her based on the way they were staring. The soldiers still looked more confused than anything else, but that would change soon. She met Corten's eyes and willed him to understand as she mouthed a single word. *Run.*

Then she focused on the lead soldier, a handsome man with a few flecks of gray peppering his brown hair. "Don't listen to him. Ambassador Bargal ordered Dalith Valn's assassination. You can't let him leave the palace. He—"

"Enough!" Bargal interjected, the anger in his voice cutting through the air like a knife. "I'm sorry, sirs. She is not well."

Naya sensed the man beside her reaching for his weapon. Soldiers were staring at her, but they made no move to stop Bargal.

"Who are you, girl?" the handsome soldier asked.

Naya clenched her teeth, then let her disguise drop. The soldier's eyes went wide, and Mel gasped.

"I'm not the one you should be afraid of!" Naya said. "You have to run. Warn—"

Ice plunged into Naya's side as the Endran spy stabbed her with his wraith eater. Her words turned into a scream as pain flared in her hand. Her vision grew hazy as the weapon consumed her aether. Death's tides seemed to roar around her legs.

"No!" Corten shouted.

Naya latched on to his voice. She concentrated on the aether, forcing what scraps she had left into the bones of her hand and pushing. With a gasp she stumbled away from the knife. Her legs seemed barely solid enough to support her and the bones of her hand throbbed with fiery pain. The soldiers were shouting, drawing their weapons, and Naya thought she saw Corten trying to push through them to get to her. Through the darkness at the edge of her vision, she saw the handsome soldier draw his pistol and point it at the Endran spy. Then Bargal stepped behind the soldier so quickly he seemed almost to blur. He'd peeled off his gloves, exposing a dizzying pattern of glowing runes tattooed across his skin. More runes glowed from beneath his clothes, their light somehow more real to Naya's wavering sight than the bodies of the men around him.

The soldier pressed his finger to the trigger. Before he could fire, Bargal wrapped his hands around the soldier's neck and twisted. The soldier's head jerked to the side with a sickening snap. Even as he fell, Bargal snatched the pistol and turned it on another soldier. The bullet caught the woman in the throat and she collapsed, blood pouring through her fingers as she tried frantically to hold back the flood.

There was a moment of stunned silence, then the hallway exploded into chaos. Mel shouted as a soldier stepped forward to shield her. He drew his rune pistol and fired at the Endran ambassador. Bargal stumbled, red blossoming across one shoulder.

Naya struggled to understand what she was seeing. Runes glowed all across Bargal's body, aether flowing through patterns too complex to follow. The wound in his shoulder barely seemed to slow him down. He lunged forward and kicked the soldier in the chest before the man could fire his pistol's second shot. Bones crunched and the soldier stumbled, gasping like a fish thrown to shore. Bargal reached down and snapped his neck as casually as he had the first man's.

Meanwhile, the Endran spy advanced on Naya, forcing her to retreat until her back was against the wall. She drew aether, but what energy she could grasp flowed to heal the cracked bone in her hand. It was taking everything she had just to stay upright. From the corner of her eye, she could see Bargal surrounded by the four remaining soldiers, all of whom had drawn swords. Bargal was unarmed and blood dripped from his wounded shoulder. He was smiling.

The runes on Bargal's body flared. When he moved it was like water surging down a hill after a thunderstorm. Swords that should have cut him swung into empty air, and bones snapped wherever his fists struck flesh.

Naya was so focused on the horror of the assault that she didn't notice Corten sneaking toward her until she heard the crack of the rune pistol. The bullet caught the Endran spy in the leg. He stumbled, his eyes wide.

Corten stood behind the man, holding a rune pistol in surprisingly steady hands. Naya screamed for him to move, but he only looked up at her, blinking. Then the Endran spy spun, throwing the wraith eater toward Corten.

"No!" Naya screamed, moving too late. The blade flashed through the air, the runes glowing with cold fire. For a fraction of a second, Naya thought she could see Corten's aether pulling toward the blade.

Then he was simply gone.

The blade thudded into the wall on the far side of the hallway. "No!" Naya screamed again. The Endran spy rolled out of the way as she stumbled forward. Not even a scrap of clothing remained where Corten had stood.

"Don't move!" Bargal snarled.

Naya looked up and saw him standing farther down the hall, holding a knife to Mel's throat. The bodies of soldiers lay spread around him, and for the first time Naya noticed the sudden quiet.

Mel's eyes were very wide, and a thin trickle of blood dripped from where the knife's edge had caught her skin. Francisco lay on the ground beside them, panting shallowly and holding a bloody hand to the wound in his side.

"Sir. We have to go, now," the Endran spy said. The glow of aether around his wrists had gone almost entirely dark and the runes along his arms and legs were fading. Still he stood, ignoring the blood dripping from the wound in his leg.

"Secure the boy," Bargal said to him. "As for you," he said, turning his gaze on Naya. "These ones died because of you. Would you like me to kill the girl as well, or will you come quietly?"

Mel's eyes met Naya's. "Don't," she whispered.

In her mind Naya saw Corten vanishing. A chasm had opened in her chest, making her feel like the blade had struck her instead. It was impossible. After all she'd done, she refused to believe she'd lost him again so quickly.

Naya tried not to look at the corpses. She tried not to think about the look of frozen surprise on the first soldier's face as Bargal had so casually ended his life. Rage made Naya want to throw herself at Bargal, but exhausted and injured, she knew she couldn't get to him before Mel's body joined the corpses on the floor.

"Let her go and I'll come with you. She doesn't have anything to do with this," Naya said.

"And have her run to tell everyone what she's seen? No, I think I'll keep her here to make sure you behave." Bargal opened a small door that looked to lead into a servant's hall. "All of you stay quiet and move quickly. If you try to call for help, I can assure you it won't go well."

CHAPTER 45

NAYA

Ambassador Bargal forced them into the nearby servant's hall-way, then shut the door. The Endran spy took the lead, followed by Francisco, then Naya. Ambassador Bargal went last, holding the knife against Mel's spine.

Francisco stumbled after only a few steps. Naya moved on instinct to catch him and was rewarded by a sharp stab of pain in her bones. "I'm fine," Francisco said under his breath.

"Neither one of us is fine," Naya whispered back. "Come on, maybe together we can at least stay upright."

Francisco looked like he wanted to object, but instead he nodded wearily. "Do you know what they want?"

Mel gasped in pain behind them. "I believe I asked for quiet," Bargal said.

Anger and fear burned in Naya's chest. She started to turn, but Mel's voice stopped her. "I'm fine! Just keep moving."

Naya exchanged a look with Francisco and found her anger mirrored in his eyes. She tried to think how she could get the knife away from Bargal, but every scenario she imagined ended with the blade plunging into Mel's back. So she kept walking, waiting for anything that might provide an opportunity for escape.

The Endran spy led them confidently through the narrow

halls. Naya heard a shuffle and a gasp and looked up to see a serving woman coming from the opposite direction. "Out of the way, there's been another attack," the Endran spy shouted before the woman could ask what they were doing.

The woman pressed her hands to her mouth, then turned and fled. She was gone before Naya could decide if calling out to her was worth the risk. Probably not. She didn't want to get anyone else tangled in this.

"Sir, should I . . . ?" the Endran spy asked.

"Ignore her," Bargal said. "We'll be gone soon enough."

Naya clenched her teeth. The wraith eater had worsened the damage to her bones and it was a struggle just to keep her body solid and to keep walking. As for Corten . . . her mind kept replaying that instant when he'd vanished. Nothing about it made sense. She could have almost sworn he'd vanished before the wraith eater touched him.

Through the aether Naya could feel panic radiating off Mel behind her. Beyond that, the aether of the palace thrummed. Ever since Bargal had brought her up from her cell she'd felt the heavy fear of the palace's residents, but now fresh panic was spreading. The bodies had been found, or perhaps the servant was already spreading word of the attack. Of course, the woman wouldn't know what was going on. She'd probably seen the Endran spy's uniform and his wounded leg and assumed he was a victim. Any reports she spread would only add to the confusion, maybe even making it easier for Bargal and his companions to escape.

Reluctantly, Naya shoved aside her questions about Corten's fate. She couldn't do anything about it right now. She just had to trust and hope that he was somehow all right. She was certain that Ambassador Bargal's work in Talmir was the beginning of some larger attack. What she couldn't understand was why he'd risked so much to retrieve her from her cell. "Why are you doing this?" she asked. "Your people tried to have Francisco and me killed. Why work so hard to capture us now?"

Bargal was silent for a moment before answering. "You are obviously much more than you appear. My queen will be very interested in the magic that sustains you. It could prove the key to unlocking the secrets her scholars seek."

"What secrets?" Naya asked.

"The oldest and deepest known to man. Her answers may be yours as well if you only shut your mouth and cooperate. If we do this right, we can all get out of here safely and no one else will have to get hurt."

Naya clenched her teeth against a fresh wave of fear. Old magics. So, it seemed the warnings the strange woman had given her were true.

"You don't have to do this, you know," Naya said to Bargal. "Let Mel and Francisco go and I'll help you escape. I'll come with you to Endra. You can't really expect to get out of the city with hostages. Someone will have found those bodies by now and the palace guards will bar the gate."

"I think our chances are better than you know, and your friends here will all find they are safer with us than left behind. In a few hours, the news will spread, and this city will grow even less hospitable to your kind and to anyone who might be suspected of befriending you."

That sent a chill through Naya. "Why? What have you done?"

Bargal didn't reply. The hall they'd followed ended at a door. The Endran spy tried the handle, then muttered a curse in his own language.

"What is it?" Naya asked.

"He said the door is locked," Bargal said.

Naya sensed the beginning of a plan and worked to keep the hope off her face. "I can open it," she said, glancing back. She met Mel's eyes briefly before looking at Bargal. Mel stood very still, her mouth set in a thin line and her hands clenched into fists. Naya prayed she wasn't about to get her killed.

"Do it," Bargal said after a pause.

Naya let go of Francisco's arm and slid past him. She ducked her head so that Bargal and his spy couldn't see her lips move and whispered, "When I tell you, run." She didn't wait to see if Francisco would respond, didn't even dare to look at his face. The Endran spy made room for her, his eyes narrow and his aether prickly with suspicion. Naya kept her own eyes down and tried to look meek, not hard given her condition. She crouched next to the lock and slid her finger into it. Eyes closed, she felt her way through the tumblers. Long seconds ticked by and Naya heard footsteps coming from somewhere else in the hall.

"Hurry up," Bargal said.

Naya clenched her teeth. "I'm trying." The last tumbler clicked. Naya stood and opened the door, revealing a stretch of carefully trimmed lawn already shadowed with twilight, and beyond that a large wooden building that looked like it must be the stables Bargal had mentioned. Naya stood to one side as the Endran spy stepped out, followed by Francisco. She drew in aether and felt her bones ache in protest. "Go," Bargal said, jerking his chin to motion Naya through the door.

Naya shuffled outside, then stumbled and pressed herself against the wall as though it were the only thing keeping her upright. The Endran spy gave her a scornful look, but didn't move from where he stood guarding Francisco. The last ones through the door were Mel and Bargal. Naya pushed off the wall and leapt at Bargal, converting some of the energy in her bones into force to grab his knife arm and shove Mel away from him.

The runes on Bargal's body flared to life more slowly than before. The attack had obviously taken him by surprise, and Naya guessed the dimming glow around his wrists meant that whatever magic he'd used earlier was at least partially expended. Naya managed to keep one hand wrapped around the arm that held the knife, even though her own fingers now burned as though she'd stuck them in a fire. Aether was seeping from her arm in an alarming way, as though bits of her soul were drifting free from her cracked bones.

Still, she didn't let go as Bargal tried to twist free of her grip. She didn't know what Bargal was, but the runes tattooed on his body had to be tied to the impossible speed and strength he'd shown before. If there was one thing Naya had learned about magic, it was that all runes could be broken. She forced the aether in her bond down through her arm, trying to push it into Bargal.

The runes around her grip pulsed with sudden brightness. Bargal's eyes widened and an instant later Naya felt something else pushing against her, another will trying to force her aether out and away. In a flash Naya remembered the exercises Lucia had made her practice. Overloading a rune binding wasn't the only way to deactivate it. Naya stopped fighting the force, reversing the direction of her will and instead pulling Bargal's energy toward her.

Energy rushed into her. Bargal's hand spasmed and the knife fell from his grip. The runes on his arm dimmed. With a snarl Bargal swung at Naya with his free arm. Naya let her head turn transparent as Celia had taught her. Bargal would overbalance when his blow didn't meet resistance and she could use that to—

The fist slammed into her cheek, sending her stumbling back. Naya was so shocked she lost her grip on his wrist. Her hand went to her cheek as the force of the blow seemed to ripple through her body. Bargal hit her again, this time punching her in the stomach. The runes on his arm flashed and his fist connected with all the force of a cannonball.

Naya stumbled. She saw the bright glow of the runes flying

toward her again and barely managed to throw herself out of the way. From the corner of her eye, she saw Francisco grappling with the Endran spy. Francisco's face was deathly pale and his teeth clenched in pain, but he'd managed to get his arms wrapped around the man's chest. Mel was crawling toward him, her expression furious as she tried to reach the fallen knife. Naya heard someone shouting, then running footsteps. Bargal looked away from her. For an instant rage burned in his eyes, then his expression shifted to one of exaggerated fear. He stumbled away from Naya, clutching his shoulder and gasping for breath. "Please, help me! It's the wraith! She's trying to escape! Stop her!" he cried out.

"What?" Naya took a step back.

"Run!" Francisco shouted.

Naya looked at him, then back over her shoulder to see a pair of soldiers running toward them from the direction of the stables. Meanwhile a black carriage pulled into view just beyond the commotion. "What about you?" Neither Francisco nor Mel looked like they were in any shape to flee.

"We'll be fine. Run, damn you! Warn my father," Francisco shouted again.

"Please help! They're trying to kill me!" Bargal shouted. He'd fallen to the ground and was backing away from her. All signs of his supernatural strength and speed were gone, and with the bullet wound in his shoulder he looked exactly like the victim he was pretending to be. It wouldn't be hard to convince a few Talmiran soldiers that Naya was the enemy here, and by the time she got the chance to argue otherwise, it might already be too late.

In a few hours, the news will spread, and this city will grow even less hospitable to your kind.

CHAPTER 46

CORTEN

Corten saw the gleam of metal as the knife flew toward him, felt the wraith eater runes pulling at his bond. No. Not this again. He was not going to die again. He threw himself sideways and the world tore around him. Darkness and cold poured in and howling wind drowned out the sounds of fighting.

Corten fell back into the shadowy grasses of death.

"No!" He stood, his hands balling into fists. The knife hadn't even touched him. How—

"Peace, spirit," a raspy voice said behind him.

Corten turned and saw the shadow man standing among the grasses. "Peace?" he said. "Peace?" A humorless laugh tore from his throat. "Was this some sort of joke? Sending me back just so I could die again?"

"You are not dead," the shadow man said.

"I—what?"

"Did you think we would invest so much in your return and not offer you any protection? We would not waste our power so. You did not die. You merely stepped into the fringe."

Stepped? Corten looked down at his hands. He was still wearing Francisco's borrowed clothes. Over the shirt he once again wore his vest of glass plates, and he could feel the weight of the sword tugging at his hip. Interesting. Had they somehow persisted in this place? Or had his mind re-created them upon his return?

So far as he knew, there were only two ways for a soul to enter death: either by traveling through a necromancer's portal or by being thrown there by trauma great enough to separate it from its physical form. He had no body left to break from, and he was pretty sure he would have noticed if someone had opened a portal to death in the middle of the Talmiran palace. "How?" he asked.

"The details are beyond you," the shadow man said. "My people have spent long in the fringe. We know it and have used our knowledge and our power to bind you here. The magic of the binding acts as its own portal, allowing you to slip between this place and the living world."

Corten gaped as he tried to imagine the complexity of such a binding. "That's impossible. How can I be my own portal? And what do you mean I'm bound to the fringe? Spirits have to be bound to a part of their body. You can't just bind someone to a place, especially not this," he said, waving at the gray-and-black expanse around them.

"I told you the details were beyond you," the shadow man said blandly. "You should return to the other world now. If you stay here too long, your glow will draw the scavengers."

"No," Corten said. "I'm not going anywhere until I get some answers."

"Then ask your questions quickly."

"You said before that I was to be your agent. What did you mean? And what are you?" Corten asked.

The shadow man was silent for a moment. "It will be easier if I show you." Before Corten could protest, the shadow man strode forward and placed one hand flat against his chest.

A flood of images filled Corten's mind, flashes of runes, faces, voices. It was all chaotic and none of it felt as real as that first vision of the ritual. He stumbled away with a gasp. His head hurt. He felt like he had the first time he'd drawn too much aether, his body brimming with energy that threatened to tear him apart if he didn't set it free. "What did you do?"

"I have given you what I know, and what my people have seen in the memories of the dead who pass through here. The one you hunt calls herself a queen. She seeks to claim sovereignty over all realms, even death. If not stopped, she will attempt the gatekeeper's ritual. She will fail, just as those who tried before her failed. You saw the consequences."

"What if she succeeds?" Corten asked, remembering the darkness that had spread in his vision of that ritual, withering flesh and cracking stone with the force of its passing.

"She won't. The ritual is flawed at its very core. No mortal can control the doors of death. Trying warps the very fabric of reality."

"What am I supposed to do about any of this?" Corten asked.

"We cannot touch the living world, so you must go in our stead. Find this self-proclaimed queen and stop her."

"But if you can bind me like this, then why not do the same to yourself?"

"We have tried, but we are too deeply a part of the fringe now. We cannot pull ourselves back through the barrier." A snarling roar sounded somewhere in the distance and the shadow man looked around. "You must go."

The growl sent fear shivering through Corten. He had more questions but none he wanted to ask so badly that he would risk facing another scavenger. Besides, he had to make sure Naya and the others were all right. "How do I get back to the living world?" he asked. His head ached with the strange jumble of memories the shadow man had shoved into it.

"I have given you the answer. Think."

"What? I—Oh." One of the foreign memories flowed to the surface. Corten saw a set of runes in his mind, a binding that twisted around itself, echoing the patterns that now flowed through his own body. With it came an understanding that was more intuition than anything else. Corten raised one hand and focused his aether to draw a series of runes in the dark. Light trailed from his fingers to outline the shape of the runes in the air before him.

The runes felt familiar even though he was sure he'd never seen them before. As he traced the last line, he clenched his hand into a fist, as though to grab the last threads of energy and hold them tight. The darkness hummed with potential and Corten shivered at the sense of power. The energy he held didn't feel like aether. It was almost as though he could sense it straining against his will, trying to break free.

Something was moving in the dark. It crawled on a dozen arms with joints in all the wrong places. No time. Corten tore his gaze away from the scavenger, then pressed his closed fist against the center of the floating rune binding and pushed. The runes burned brighter. They drew energy from him almost as fast as the wraith eater had.

For a moment it was as though he were straining against a heavy door. Weakness seeped into his limbs, but some part of him knew that light and life existed just on the other side of that door. He had to get back. He thought of Naya, of Lucia, of that terrible killing darkness the vision had shown him.

The door shifted—not by much—but enough to open a crack. Enough for him to slip through. Corten pushed forward. He felt himself stretching, straining against the pull of the fringe. Then he stumbled into a blood-soaked hallway and gasped in a breath of aether.

The floor was covered in corpses and the energy he absorbed stank of fear and death. But he was back. He glanced down.

Though his sword and armor were gone again, he was relieved to see his clothes had remained. While they were talking on the ship, Lucia had mentioned creating a portal that let someone step physically into death. It seemed the shadow men had done the same with his new binding somehow.

Corten surveyed his grim surroundings. Soldiers lay broken across the hallway. He should have been horrified by the violence of the scene, but he felt only a sort of clinical detachment. Among the bodies he saw no sign of Naya or Francisco or the men who'd been fighting against the soldiers.

Those men. Another memory surfaced, this one of runes carved in flesh, glowing with aether. The runes on the arms and legs of the red-haired stranger and his companion weren't exactly the same as the ones in the memory, but they were close.

Enhancement magic. Crude, but effective.

Corten blinked the scraps of memory away before they could distract him. Someone shouted from beyond the curve of the hallway. Corten looked around and spotted a small servant's door. It had been left partway open and there was a smear of blood on the handle. Without giving himself time to question, Corten slipped through it and into the narrow hall beyond.

CHAPTER 47

NAYA

Naya ran, ducking back the way they'd come into the servant's hall. She'd made it more than halfway to where the fight had taken place when she rounded a corner and ran into someone.

Naya stumbled back, then gasped. "Corten?!" His eyes had a strangely distant look when they met hers, but otherwise he seemed completely unharmed.

"Naya. Good, you're alive. Where are the others?" He caught her, steadying her with a hand. His grip was strong and wonderfully warm against her arm. She wanted to lean into him and close her eyes.

Not yet.

Naya drew in a sharp breath of aether, trying to clear away her exhaustion. "They're outside, back that way. What happened to you? I saw you disappear."

"I stepped through to the fringe," Corten said. "I'll tell you about it later. That man with the red hair—he's connected somehow to what the shadow men warned us about. We have to find him."

Stepped through to the fringe? What in creation did that mean? Still, Corten was right, they didn't have time for explanations right now. "If you mean Ambassador Bargal, then I already know about that," Naya said.

"You do? How——?"

Naya shook her head. "No time. The Endrans are trying to escape. They're the ones behind all the trouble at the Congress. But I think everything they've done here is just a distraction. I have to warn Delence."

Corten seemed to absorb all this with a surprising amount of calm. "When we first got here, a man told Francisco that Delence was meeting with the queen. I'm not sure where. If you're going to look for him, then I'll try to stop Bargal from escaping."

"What?" Naya asked. "Corten, no, those men are dangerous."

Corten met her eyes again and smiled. "I can do this." His smile fell a little. "But maybe you should come with me. You're fading."

Naya pulled her hand from his. Where had this new confidence come from? She hesitated. She didn't want to leave him alone. She didn't want to let him out of her sight ever again. But she had to warn Delence, and doing so would mean risking capture again by the Talmiran soldiers. "Find somewhere safe to hide. I'll come back for you, I promise."

She didn't wait for his answer, instead slipping around him and running down the hall. Her eyes burned with tears of relief she couldn't shed. He was alive.

By the time she got back into the main palace, a group of soldiers stood around the bodies Ambassador Bargal had left on the floor. Three of them leveled their pistols at her as she came stumbling out of the servant's door.

"There's been an attack!" she said before any of them could gather their wits. "The Endrans are attacking!"

Commotion sounded from the hall behind her. Naya felt fear and mistrust darkening the soldiers' aether. "Stay right there!" one of them said.

Naya growled in frustration. They didn't have time for this.

"Send someone to block the gates," she said. She didn't wait to see how they'd react before ducking left and running down the hall. One of the guards made to grab her. He caught her sleeve and Naya heard fabric tear. She stumbled but managed to regain her feet and keep running. A pistol shot cracked behind her and a metal ball tore through her stomach to lodge in the wall in front of her.

It barely tickled.

Naya kept running, trying to remember the route she'd taken when Queen Lial had summoned her for tea. Corten had said Delence was meeting with the queen. If that was true, then perhaps she'd summoned him to the same garden. When Naya reached the lift, she found her hopes, and her fears, confirmed.

Two soldiers slumped at the base of the lift in pools of blood. The aether around them reeked with the fear and confusion of their final moments and the blood soaking their uniforms looked fresh. Naya heard her pursuers coming up fast behind her. She pounded the lift's call button, but nothing happened.

"Don't move!" someone shouted behind her.

Naya spun to see ten soldiers blocking the hall behind her. Some still had rune pistols drawn, but most had abandoned these in favor of wraith eaters. Sergeant Leln stood at their head, staring grimly at the corpses behind Naya.

Naya clenched her fists, trying to ignore the tightness in her throat, the pounding in her bones, and the sudden feeling of being trapped. "Please. Whoever did this is already upstairs!" She gestured to the bodies behind her. "Lord Delence and the queen are in danger. You have to send everyone you can up to the queen's garden before it's too late."

She felt doubt flicker across their aether as they eyed the corpses. Naya met Leln's eyes, searching for that hint of kindness she'd seen once before. "Please," she said. "I'm on your side."

Sergeant Leln met her gaze with a cold stare. "You four, go check the stairs," he said to the man standing next to him. "Marn and Bek should be stationed there. And you, get me a set of salma cuffs."

Five of the men split off down a side hall while the rest kept their weapons trained on Naya.

CHAPTER 48

NAYA

Minutes dragged by in tense silence while Naya stared at the soldiers, waiting. She'd backed up as far as she could toward the rune lift, but still she could feel the constant pull of the wraith eaters adding to the pain of her damaged bond. The aether here was growing thin and the edges of her vision were starting to go black. "You're wasting time," she said to Leln. "Ambassador Bargal still has Mel and Francisco. You should send someone to help them."

"Quiet," Leln said. His voice was stern. After a moment he asked, "Is it true you assaulted a scribe at the academy?"

"No," Naya said, trying to fill the word with as much sincerity as she could muster. "I was there, but I didn't hurt anyone."

"Right, like you didn't hurt poor Ralen?" another soldier asked mockingly.

"That was an accident." Naya kept her gaze fixed on Leln as she spoke. "I'm sorry about what I did. I got scared and I panicked."

Leln watched her for a long moment, then nodded slowly. "Ralen shares part of the blame. He should not have grabbed you, and I should have kept better control over my men."

"Sir!" the other soldier said. "You don't have to apologize to her. She's a—"

"I know what she is," Leln said.

One of the soldiers Leln had sent away came barreling down the stairs. There was blood on his coat and one of his arms hung limp by his side. His eyes were wide with barely contained shock.

"What's going on?" Leln demanded.

"Sir." The soldier snapped a wobbly salute. "Queen Lial wants the wraith brought to her at once."

A thousand questions jumped to Naya's mind. At least the queen was alive. She let the soldiers lead her down the hall, then to a stair that wound all the way up to the queen's private garden. The garden looked the same as it had when Naya had last seen it. Plants spilled from delicate pots and late afternoon sunlight streamed down through the glass ceiling. But a copper tang lurked under the sweeter scents of flowers.

The soldiers led Naya down the winding path to the clearing at the center of the garden. The delicate metal table from earlier had been replaced by a more imposing expanse of polished dark wood. Queen Lial stood next to the table. The front of her dress was slashed open, revealing what looked like a chainmail corset beneath. Delence sat on the ground next to her, clutching at a wound in his leg. The bodies of two servants and five soldiers lay motionless on the floor. Two more soldiers held down a wounded young man wearing the uniform of a palace servant. The servant was bleeding from an injury Naya couldn't see, but his lips were set in a small smile and his expression was almost eerily calm.

"Bring her here!" Queen Lial snapped.

Naya stepped forward, painfully aware of the soldiers behind her and the steady pull of wraith eaters. Her clothes were torn and bloodstained from the fight, and a quick glance down proved that despite her best efforts, her skin was fading in spots to show the pale-blue glow of aether. She could feel rage radiating off Queen Lial like heat from a furnace.

"Well," Queen Lial said. "I have been told you drew my soldiers here. How did you know of this attack?"

Naya lowered her head. "Your Majesty, I didn't know for certain, but I was afraid the Endrans might come after you or Lord Delence."

"The Endrans?" Queen Lial said. "Explain."

Naya stood a little straighter. "Your Majesty, you asked me to tell you everything I knew about Valn's allies. When we last spoke, I truly had no useful information. I now have reason to believe an Endran group calling themselves Resurgence was funding Valn and that Ambassador Bargal was a member of that group. I think he and his allies organized Valn's death as part of a plot to destroy the Congress alliance and cause chaos in preparation for an Endran invasion."

Queen Lial raised one carefully plucked eyebrow. "An invasion? Tell me, Miss Garth, do you have any evidence to support these claims?"

Naya drew in aether, then winced. "That man who your soldiers have pinned is an Endran assassin."

The queen looked down at the wounded man. "It is true that he is not one of my usual servants, and I do intend to find out exactly which incompetent allowed him and his companions up here, but I see no evidence that he is one of Bargal's people."

"If I might make a guess, Your Majesty," Naya said carefully, "when he and the others attacked you, did they seem stronger and faster than ordinary men? If you check under his sleeves, I think you'll find runes tattooed there. Not necromancy, but something else the Endrans are using to enhance their bodies."

Queen Lial's eyes widened slightly at this. She nodded, and one of the soldiers lifted the servant's sleeve, exposing the tattooed runes. Naya breathed a sigh of relief when she saw them. She'd sensed the strange flow of aether around the man's wrists, but it had been so dim as to be barely visible. Just because

Bargal and his companion had those tattoos didn't mean all the Endrans would.

Queen Lial frowned. "I thought they were reapers at first," she said, half to herself. Her fingers drifted to a metal box sitting on the table. It was scribed in runes and seemed a match to the one Hest had used against Naya at the Academy of Magics. If it worked the same way, it might offer an explanation for how Delence and the queen had survived the attack. The runes powering the Endran magic weren't the same as necromancy, but they seemed to rely on aether in the same way. Having that energy torn away from their runes would, she guessed, at the very least have slowed down the Endran assassins.

The queen picked the box up. For a terrifying moment, Naya feared she would activate it. Instead she tucked it into a pocket disguised by the folds of her dress. "Summon Grand Marshal Palrak," she said to one of the soldiers after a moment.

"I told you it wasn't us," Delence growled, struggling to stand.

"You might have hired them," Queen Lial said, though her tone was more thoughtful than accusatory.

Naya glanced at the queen and Delence. "Your Majesty. Last I saw, Ambassador Bargal and his allies were trying to escape near the west stables. They had Francisco Delence and Mel Jeden with them as hostages. If you send men now you might still be able to stop them."

"What?!" Delence said. "Why didn't you say that from the start?"

Word was sent down to the gates and to the soldiers stationed near the stables. Delence tried to limp after them but was stopped by a soldier carrying a medic's satchel, who all but forced him down into a chair to examine his leg. Naya longed to sit and rest herself. She was so tired of the pain in her hand and the weight of worry for Corten and Mel and Francisco. But the queen was still watching her and she could feel the soldiers standing at attention behind her.

"Well, Miss Garth, I must admit, your timing in bringing aid was fortuitous. But you should know that if I find out you've lied about anything, then no amount of diplomatic protections will save you."

"I haven't lied," Naya said.

"And how is it you came to know so much of Ambassador Bargal's plots?" Queen Lial asked.

"My father mentioned Resurgence in one of his logbooks. The rest I learned from Bargal and . . . another source. But it wasn't until today that I put all the pieces together."

"What other source?" the queen demanded.

Naya hesitated. "Another one of Valn's spies. Resurgence placed her in the palace to help with their work here."

"Does this mystery spy have a name?" the queen asked.

Naya looked away. "What will you do to her if you find her?"

"Question her," Queen Lial answered. "Anything else will depend on how she answers."

Naya nodded. "She told me her name was Celia. I never heard her use a last name, but she's an older woman, just a little taller than me and with gray hair and brown eyes. She would have joined the palace staff only recently, though maybe not using that name. If you offer her a pardon for her work with Valn, I think she'll be more than eager to tell you everything she knows about Resurgence."

The queen pressed her lips into a thin line. "I will have someone look for her and see if she can confirm this story you tell." She glanced at Delence. "Did the traitor Valn mention any of this in your interrogations of him? And don't bother lying and saying you didn't question him before the Congress."

Delence cleared his throat. "Not exactly. We had been hunting Celia. We knew she'd fled the city, but my agents lost her trail after that. None of the individuals we questioned mentioned Resurgence, but some of the officials Valn bribed were paid in bars of precious metals rather than minted coins. We thought it odd, but that could make sense if the Endrans were smuggling wealth into the country to fund him."

Queen Lial shook her head. "I don't know if I believe all this about plots and wars, but I will consider what you've said."

"Your Majesty," Delence began.

Queen Lial held up a hand, silencing him. "Still, none of this explains what you were doing outside your cell, Miss Garth. Three good men were found dead in the Barrow halls. Did you kill them?"

"No!" Naya shook her head. "Ambassador Bargal came for me. He killed the guards and let me out of my cell. He told me you'd spoken together and that he didn't approve of my imprisonment. He said his people had decided against an alliance with Talmir. He wanted me to come with him to meet his queen." At that she felt a fresh wash of anger through Queen Lial's aether. "Please, Your Majesty. Whatever he said, I don't think he came for me out of any feeling of justice. He meant to use me for something."

"Hmm." Queen Lial tapped one finger against her dress. "And I suppose you have an explanation for the reports of your assault on the Academy of Magics as well?"

Naya bit her lip. "It wasn't an assault," she said, picking her words carefully. Given that the queen had one of the strange cubes, she had to know about Hest's research. But Hest might not have reported anything about Naya taking Lucia's journals. Doing so would have risked exposing her connections to Valn's treason. And if the queen knew about the journals, then Naya would have expected the soldiers to search the *Gallant* before they'd hauled her off in chains.

What to say? She'd already admitted to Leln that she'd been

at the academy. And Hest or the guards had obviously reported encountering a wraith. The last thing Naya wanted was to send the queen looking for other wraiths while Corten was still in the city. She drew in a breath of aether, then gambled on a lie that was at least marginally less damning than the truth. "I went there looking for a possible connection to Resurgence. I knew Ela Hest was Valn's aunt. I thought she might have helped him, but I was wrong. Partway through our conversation, Hest realized what I was and called for the guards. I ran away, but I swear I didn't hurt anyone."

The queen was silent for a long moment. "Interesting."

Naya glanced away at the sound of someone climbing the stairs. A moment later, Grand Marshal Palrak strode into the garden followed by a young soldier in a sweat-stained uniform. Palrak bowed to the queen, then offered a respectful nod to Delence. "Your Majesty, thank the Creator you are well."

The queen shook her head. "I will be well when I know what is really going on here."

Palrak nodded. "Of course. I was intercepted by a runner on the way here. Apparently there was some sort of conflict at the stables." He gestured for the young soldier to come forward.

Delence tried to stand again, only to be pushed down by the medic. "What about my son? Where is he?"

The soldier flinched, then bowed low and gave Palrak an uncertain glance.

"Speak," Palrak said.

"Yes, sir," the soldier said. "Your Majesty, there was a fight outside the west stables, like the Grand Marshal said. We're still trying to figure out exactly what happened, but a carriage left through the gate before the orders to seal it reached the guards there. We don't know for certain yet, but the men there said they think Ambassador Bargal might have been inside. We've found no other sign of him yet, or of Ambassador Noreth, or anyone else from their party. And it seems their rooms have been cleared out."

"What about Francisco and Mel?" Naya asked.

"They weren't in the yard," the soldier said. "It's possible they fled somewhere else."

"So find them!" Delence snarled.

The chaos and confusion only grew as more soldiers and advisers arrived. The gates were sealed and a search begun, and it wasn't long before a stable boy was found who claimed to have seen Ambassador Bargal forcing Mel and Francisco into a black carriage. The stable boy also mentioned a young man matching Corten's description who'd come out just after the ambassador fled, but he apparently didn't know where the young man had gone after that. Naya's heart plummeted at the news of Mel and Francisco's captivity. This was her fault. She shouldn't have left them alone with Bargal. She was the one he'd wanted. Neither one of them would have been there if not for her.

"You have to send out a search party!" Delence said. He was standing now, his leg bandaged and the irritated medic hovering behind him.

Palrak frowned at Delence. "Sir, I understand your distress, but I shouldn't need to tell you that you are here as a guest to Her Majesty. You will conduct yourself accordingly or you will be asked to retire to your rooms at once."

Delence was nearly sputtering with rage. "My son was a guest here as well and look where that got him. I will hold you people accountable if anything more happens to him."

"Rest assured," Queen Lial interjected, "notice has been sent out to every guard and soldier in the city. The gates are being monitored. We will find them." She turned back to Naya. "Now, I suppose I have to decide what to do with you."

CHAPTER 49

NAYA

Naya paced back and forth across her cabin on the *Gallant*. Two days had passed since Ambassador Bargal and his companions had fled the palace. And for most of that time, she'd been trapped here on the ship, watched. Queen Lial had kept her at the palace long enough to interrogate her about Bargal. After that she'd faced questioning by the heads of the other delegations. Delence had taken her aside and demanded answers about exactly where and when she'd met with Celia. The Banians had expressed skepticism at the idea of an Endran attack, while the Silmaran representatives had mostly seemed frustrated that their northern allies had nearly allowed themselves to be baited into a useless conflict. Arguments, theories, and blame had flowed freely. Round and round they'd gone, with Mel's mother and Delence being the only ones arguing for immediate action.

Eventually Naya had been dismissed. Celia was nowhere to be found, and Delence and others speculated that she might have left with the Endrans. No decisions had been made regarding Naya's fate, but the information she'd given up had apparently convinced the queen to let her stay aboard the *Gallant* rather than in a Barrow cell. With three Talmiran galleons watching the ship, and Talmiran soldiers stationed outside her cabin door, she was nearly as helpless as she would have been in the prison. But the fact that she'd been allowed to remain in relative comfort hopefully meant the queen believed Naya's good intentions.

Corten sat at the desk nearby, sketching runes in a fresh journal and speaking softly with Lucia. They'd been that way for hours now, trying to sort through the strange memories Corten had received from one of the shadow men. By some small miracle, Corten had avoided exposing himself as a wraith during the chaos of Bargal's flight. Naya had spoken to Delence, and he'd grudgingly helped escort Corten out of the palace and back to the *Gallant*.

A knock came at the door and Naya rushed to open it. On the other side, she found Delence standing between two grim-faced Talmiran soldiers. "Is there any news?" Naya asked, her chest tight.

"Inside," Delence said. He brushed past her, then cast a dark look at Lucia and Corten, who'd stowed their work hastily.

"I have some good news," Delence said after a moment. "In light of the information you handed over, and your timely intervention in the assault on her life, Queen Lial has agreed to dismiss the accusations of your trespassing on academy grounds. The official reports will state that claims of a wraith spotted on the grounds could not be confirmed and that, after investigating, the Crown lacked sufficient evidence to prove you were there."

"That's a relief," Lucia muttered.

"Yes," Delence said, lowering his voice. "So far it seems your little experiment has gone undetected."

Naya shifted uneasily. "Do you think the queen knows?" There were at least a few people among her soldiers and staff who would have heard her admit to the break-in. She wondered what they would think of the official report.

"She's smart enough to suspect there's more going on. But at least for now I think she's decided that you aren't a threat and that she has bigger problems to worry about. Even if the

Endrans don't attack, the mere fact that they were so easily able to slip spies and assassins into her palace is a serious issue. I heard there's now a small army guarding the prince and princess, and the queen is making plans to move them in secret to one of her country estates."

"Has there been any word about Bargal?" Naya asked.

"Some. The assassin we captured in the garden isn't talking. But spy reports say a group matching the description of the ambassador's party was spotted boarding a ship on the northern coast. Nobody saw Francisco or Miss Jeden, but for the moment our best guess is that Bargal and his people are retreating back to Endra via the northern passage." Delence's aether was black with a bitter mix of anger and helpless frustration. He paused before continuing.

"Queen Lial is sending a regiment of Talmiran forces toward Tel Ver Pass to demand an explanation from the Endrans, or to hold the pass if they try to march troops that way, but it will be at least a week before they can even reach the base of the mountains."

"Surely it would be faster to send a ship?" Naya asked. She didn't know anything about Talmiran troop deployments, but she guessed it would take weeks to assemble supplies and get through to the nearest Endran city-state on the other side of the mountains.

"The queen doesn't want to risk any ships on the passage, not this late in the year and not to go after an ambassador's daughter and an undead, or so Palrak tells me. I've sent word to King Allence via the longscribers requesting a ship, but most of our fleet is stationed south of the Talmiran border. It would take days for them to get even this far north, and with that much of a lead, Bargal will likely already be inland by the time they make the passage."

"So send us," Corten said smoothly. He was still wearing a

set of Francisco's clothes and looked strangely out of place in the cabin. His dark eyes were intent when they met Naya's. She shivered. The memories the shadow men had given him had left him changed in a way she still hadn't been able to pinpoint.

"You?" Delence asked.

Naya turned back to Delence. "Yes. Starting from here we won't be so far behind Bargal's ship."

"You can't be serious," Delence said.

"Why not?" Naya asked, taking a step toward him. She knew why Corten wanted to go. He'd been obsessed with the shadow men's warning ever since they'd filled him with strange memories. Naya couldn't deny what had happened in the fringe, she just wasn't sure what the shadow men expected them to do about it. Perhaps if they traveled to Endra, they could at least find proof of whatever dark magics this new queen had uncovered. And while they were there, perhaps they could rescue Mel and Francisco.

"You said yourself, there aren't any other ships you can send," Naya said, thinking quickly. "Who knows how long it will take for Queen Lial's troops to make it through the pass or what information the queen will decide to share with you when they return? The Powers have ignored Endra for years while they focused on their own struggles. Right now, more than anything, we need information. Ceramor needs information, and I'm the best person to send. Give me funds for supplies and to pay my crew. Captain Cervacaro has made the crossing to Endra before. We can go after Mel and Francisco while pretending to be a trading vessel."

"This isn't the first time you've considered this," Delence said, crossing his arms.

Naya nodded. It was her fault Mel and Francisco got captured. And while Corten's new intensity frightened her, she knew the shadow men's mission wasn't something they could ignore. "I can do this. Give me a longscriber and I'll send back whatever information I find. I'll get your son back, and I'll help you make sure whatever the Endrans decide to do won't be a surprise to Ceramor."

Delence rubbed his fingers over his mustache. "With the charges against you lifted, it shouldn't be any trouble getting you permission to depart. But I doubt you'd be able to hire any new crew here in Lith Lor, and you won't have time to sail south. You'll have to convince Cervacaro and the rest of his men to stay on. From what I know of them, I doubt they'll be keen to make the journey."

"Give me the funds to pay them, and I'll figure out the rest," Naya said. Her father hadn't taught her to sail, but she knew how to outfit a ship. She'd have to move quickly if she was going to get the holds stocked and still have any chance of catching up to Bargal, but she'd manage it somehow.

"Very well," Delence said after a long moment. "It seems we'll be working together again, Captain Garth. Convince your crew to stay on and we have a deal." He held out his hand and Naya took it.

Delence hesitated after letting go of Naya's hand. "There's one more thing. Ambassador Jeden requested a meeting with you this afternoon. If you're willing, she'll be at a restaurant called the Gentle Crossing in the dockside district."

"Why does she want to talk to me?" Naya asked, more than a little surprised.

"I believe it's about her daughter. Given what you're planning, I'd suggest you accept the invitation."

"You don't think it's a trap?" Naya asked.

"I doubt it," Delence said. "That isn't her style."

Delence left soon after that, and Naya went to speak to Captain Cervacaro. He was standing on the deck, staring out at the shore. He nodded to her as she approached. "Well, Miss

Garth, looks like those warships have finally stopped pointing their cannons at us. I take it Lord Delence came with good news?"

"Yes," Naya said. "And I wanted to talk to you about your offer."

Cervacaro raised his eyebrows. "Oh? Have you finally seen the sense in selling the *Gallant* then?"

Naya shivered. She wanted to tell him no. This ship was her home. Even with the dark memories of her father tainting it, she still didn't want to give it up. Naya drew in a breath of aether. "Yes," she said softly. "Under one condition."

"Oh?"

"You let me hire you for your first voyage," Naya said.

Cervacaro dipped into a low bow. "Of course, Miss Garth. Where would you like to go? Back to Belavine? Or perhaps on a tour of the Islands? They're lovely this time of year."

"We're sailing to Endra," Naya said.

Cervacaro's smile vanished. "No."

"We're sailing to Endra," Naya repeated. "You and your crew will be paid for the voyage. And when we return, I will give you the *Gallant*. You can use whatever savings you have to buy cargo. It's a better deal than you could have ever hoped for and you know it. You'll be able to sail at your own whims, instead of having to follow the orders of a bunch of investors."

"Following orders isn't so bad when the alternative is dying in a northern storm," Cervacaro said seriously.

"Fine," Naya said, feigning casual resignation. "Then we'll sail to the nearest Ceramoran port and you and your crew can leave. Lord Delence will be disappointed that you were too cowardly to help rescue his son, but I'm sure I can find another captain and crew who don't suffer that affliction."

Cervacaro's eyes narrowed and Naya felt the anger build like a storm cloud in his aether. "I am not so sure you will. What you call cowardice, most men would name sanity. Besides, you will have no luck finding a crew better equipped to sail the passage than this one. There are few enough who have done it and lived."

Naya shrugged and turned away. "I'll just have to take my chances." She started walking back across the deck.

"Triple," Cervacaro called out after she'd crossed half the distance.

"What was that?" Naya asked, looking back.

"You'll pay every man on this ship triple what we got sailing out here. And if by some Creator-blessed miracle we make it back to port, you'll pay for any repairs the ship needs. I won't risk my life or my crew for a boat that limps home too crippled for another voyage."

"I'm sure that can be arranged. Are you saying you accept my offer?" She doubted Delence would be happy about the cost, but he would find the money if it meant getting Francisco back.

Cervacaro crossed his arms. "I'll put it to a vote. I won't force any man to sail those waters again unwilling. But if enough agree, then yes, we'll sail with you to Endra."

Something in Naya's chest cracked. Bartering with the *Gallant* as tender felt like a betrayal. But in the end, she was just a ship—wood and sail and rope and pitch. Naya had more important things to care for. She let her smile turn sharp. "Good."

Naya found Corten waiting for her at the stairs leading down into the ship. "That was well done," he said.

"Thanks." Naya let out a small, desperate laugh. "Assuming he convinces the crew, I just have to find supplies, sail the most dangerous route in the entire western ocean, rescue Mel and Francisco, oh, and somehow stop this Endran queen from either invading or destroying the world with dark magic. I'm sure it will be easy."

Corten smiled softly, and for a moment all the strangeness

left his eyes and he was again the boy she'd met in Ceramor. "Well, Matius always told me learning a new skill was just a matter of practice. You've already done the impossible once by bringing me back, and with all this practice coming up, I'm sure you'll soon be an expert at it."

Naya shook her head. "It wasn't just me who brought you back. And it doesn't feel like practice if failing means people might die."

"I guess not," Corten said. He stepped forward, wrapping his arms around her. Naya leaned into his chest and breathed in deep. His borrowed clothes lacked the orange-oil scent she remembered from Ceramor, but the warmth of his body against hers was still real and solid and right in a way she couldn't put into words.

They stayed that way for a long moment before Naya finally stepped away. She smiled up at Corten, then frowned and glanced over his shoulder as she noticed something in the aether. "Who's there?" she asked.

Felicia peeked around the corner of the door to the deck and offered a sheepish grin. "Sorry, couldn't help but overhear your conversation with Captain Cervacaro. I wanted to know if you have any preferences for jackets for the journey north."

"I don't need a jacket," Naya said. "Wraiths don't get cold."

"Well, maybe you won't need one, but I will, and I thought if I was going to try and get something before we depart, then you might want something too, just for appearance's sake."

Naya realized what Felicia was saying and shook her head. "Felicia, you're not coming with us."

"Oh, but I am," Felicia said, smiling brighter. "I've already spoken to Lord Delence about it and he doesn't mind me staying on as your maid."

"No. This trip is going to be dangerous. I can't be always worrying about keeping you safe."

"So teach me to fight. Or let me worry about myself. I'm not asking for your protection, I'm asking to continue working for you."

"I don't need—" Naya began, then sighed. "You're really set on this, aren't you?"

Felicia's expression turned serious. "I am. I've been working in Lord Delence's household near three years now. Francisco was always kind to me there, and if you're going to rescue him, then I want to help however I can. And," she added, "I don't want to go back to Belavine and be a maid for the rest of my life. I want to see something of the world, even if that means facing danger."

Naya met Felicia's eyes, then glanced at Corten. He shrugged. "Seems to me we're going to need all the help we can get."

"See?" Felicia said, smiling. "Even your prince agrees."

Corten groaned. "Only if you promise to never, ever call me that again."

Naya smiled, feeling the weight looming over her lessen just a bit. The tasks before her were no less daunting than they had been, but at least she wouldn't face them alone. "I don't need a maid," Naya said to Felicia. "But I wouldn't say no to a friend."

CHAPTER 50

NAYA

After another brief conversation with Cervacaro, Naya and Felicia arranged to have a few of the crew row them back to shore to begin procuring supplies and meet with Ambassador Jeden. Naya was a little surprised when they found Baz and Tren, Mel's guards, waiting for them on the docks.

Baz's eyes were shadowed and his expression bleak. Tren offered Naya and Felicia a small smile and a bow, but the aether flowing around him was just as dark as his partner's. "Miss Garth, I take it Lord Delence delivered the ambassador's message?" Tren asked.

"He did. He said she's at the Gentle Crossing?"

"Indeed. We'll take you there now," Tren said.

"Thank you." Naya hesitated, feeling their aether settle dark and heavy around her. Mel had obviously been more to them than just another charge. "And I'm sorry. I wish I'd done something more to help Mel."

"It was not your duty to protect her," Baz said grimly.

They rode the lifts, and the two soldiers led Naya and Felicia to an expensive restaurant a few blocks away. The windows were open to the morning breeze and inside men and women lounged over plates of pastries and small delicacies. Naya didn't need Baz and Tren's help to spot Mel's mother.

The ambassador sat alone at a table near the back of the

restaurant. She was dressed in a fine Talmiran gown with a high collar and wore her hair up in a tight bun. The way she held herself was nothing like Mel, but Naya could see the undeniable resemblance in the lines of her jaw and forehead. She looked up as Naya and Felicia approached.

"Miss Garth, thank you for coming." Her voice was cool and calm, but Naya sensed the same heavy weight in her aether that shrouded Baz and Tren. Lurking beneath the darkness was something sharp and desperate that made Naya's shoulders want to hunch all the way up to her ears.

"What did you want to speak to me about?" Naya asked as Baz and Tren took up positions behind the ambassador.

"First, please have a seat," Ambassador Jeden said, gesturing to the empty chairs across from her. As they sat, the ambassador's gaze turned curiously to Felicia, who shrank back a little.

"This is Felicia," Naya said quickly. "She's going to be assisting me in preparing for our journey later."

"A journey? So you'll be leaving Talmir then. I think that's wise. Where will you go?"

"To Endra," Naya said.

Ambassador Jeden went very still, her eyes locking on Naya. "Why?"

"Because I intend to find Mel and Francisco."

Naya saw Baz's gaze focus on her. Ambassador Jeden leaned forward, the sharp note in her aether taking on a hopeful glimmer. "All on your own?" she asked.

"I have my own ship," Naya said. "Delence says the spies reported Bargal sailing toward the northern passage. I intend to follow him." Naya hesitated, looking down at her hands. "I don't know if I'll be able to find them, but I have to try."

"Ambassador—" Baz took a step forward, but Ambassador Jeden silenced him with a raised hand.

"You know, Miss Garth, I brought my daughter to the

Congress because I hoped she might finally find her place at court. She's an impulsive, reckless girl. But she's also smart and an excellent judge of character." Ambassador Jeden folded her hands together, her knuckles standing out pale and harsh against her bronze skin. She opened her mouth to continue, but her voice caught, and she took a moment to steady herself. "She is an excellent judge of character, and she trusted you. You were one of the last people to speak to her before she was taken. I had to see . . . I wanted to meet you myself."

"I didn't mean for Mel to get caught up in all of this," Naya said.

"I believe you." Ambassador Jeden met Naya's eyes. "And I believe you're serious when you say you mean to find her. So, tell me, how I can help?"

"I—thank you," Naya said. A part of her hesitated, remembering everything she'd heard about the ambassador. But the intense emotions in Jeden's aether told her the offer was sincere. "We'll need supplies for the journey. Lord Delence has agreed to fund us, but it's possible not all of the sailors on my current crew will agree to the journey."

Ambassador Jeden nodded. "I'll speak to my contacts in the Banian delegation. I'm sure we can find a few sailors if you need to round out your crew."

"Ambassador." Baz stepped forward. "Please, allow me to go as well. Let me make up for my failure."

Ambassador Jeden turned in her chair and raised an eyebrow. "You're not a sailor, Baz."

"No, Ambassador. But who knows what sort of trouble they'll find in Endra. They may need soldiers as badly as sailors."

"What about you, Tren?" the ambassador asked.

Tren nodded. "I agree with Baz. And frankly, Ambassador, if you refuse him this, I'm worried he'll just turn in his resignation and try to go anyway."

The ambassador shook her head, but Naya saw the way the corner of her mouth twitched and the little thread of warmth that wove through her aether. She turned to face Naya again. "Well, there you have it. Tren and Baz are both good fighters. They've been with our family for well over a decade, so I can testify to their loyalty. Will you take them?"

"Yes," Naya said, her throat feeling suddenly tight. She exchanged a quick look with Felicia and fought back a grin. A few hours ago, this idea had felt almost hopeless. But now, well, maybe they really could pull this off.

They spent a while longer discussing logistics, then left to place orders at a few shops Naya remembered from her time with her father. Some of the shopkeepers recognized her, and not all of them were interested in offering service to a wraith. But not even that could stanch the hope growing in her chest. Maybe Corten had been right. Maybe doing the impossible was only a matter of practice.

When they got back to the *Gallant*, Naya was surprised to find Delence waiting for her on deck. Beside him stood a woman in rough sailing clothes with a wide-brimmed hat covering her eyes.

Delence waved Naya over. "Miss Garth. Good, you're back. I've heard the captain will be calling a vote from his crew tomorrow. Meanwhile, I've got one sailor from the *Lady* who's interested in joining you."

"All right," Naya said. She wasn't sure what good one sailor would be, but she could hardly refuse anyone willing to attempt the dangerous crossing. She stepped closer and peeked under the sailor's hat. Then her jaw dropped. "Celia?" she whispered.

Celia looked even more exhausted than she had when she'd met Naya at Hal Garth's house. Her dry lips cracked into a grim smile. "Hello, Blue. Seems you and I will be working together again."

"How? Why?" Naya turned to Delence. "You said you thought the Endrans took her."

"I may have speculated," Delence said. His tone was evasive, but she could sense the smug satisfaction in his aether. "She knew too much for me to be comfortable with Queen Lial getting her. I assumed she would be smart enough to not have stuck around the palace once the trouble started. So when you said you'd met her at your father's house, I figured that was a good place to search. My men found her hiding in the cellar. And after some . . . discussion, I've agreed to accept her request for asylum—once the two of you return with my son, that is."

"And you agreed?" Naya asked Celia.

Celia shrugged. "I find myself short on alternatives."

"She was working for the Endrans," Naya said, keeping her voice low. "Are you sure we can trust her on this?"

"She knows more about their operations than anyone else I know of in Talmir," Delence said. "Besides, my offer of asylum was for two. Her brother will be staying under our protection until she returns."

Celia's face didn't so much as twitch at the implied threat, but Naya sensed the dark frustration swirling through the older woman's aether. "What do you say, Blue?" Celia asked.

Naya stared at her. Corten, Felicia, Baz and Tren, and now Celia. They'd make a strange crew. But she couldn't deny Celia was talented, and her experience working for the Endrans could prove invaluable in tracking down Bargal.

With an uneasy heart, she extended her hand to Celia. "If you try anything, I'll throw you off my ship."

Celia laughed. "Deal."

ACKNOWLEDGMENTS

Whew. Here we are again.

I've always loved reading (and now writing) acknowledgments because they offer a peek into the back rooms where stories brew and a chance to celebrate all the often unsung heroes who reside there. I would not be able to do what I do without the support of my family and friends both inside and outside the book community.

Thank you to my editor, Monica Perez, who helped transform my rambling early drafts into an actual book. Thank you to my copy editor, Jackie Dever, for finding the things I let slip. Shayne Leighton absolutely killed it with this cover, and Jared Blando took my awkward sketches and transformed them into a truly gorgeous map. As always, thank you to my agent, Lucienne Diver, whose support and critiques continue to help me level up my storytelling skills.

Thank you to my family: Mom, Dad, Zach, Aaron, Aleise. All of you have helped shape this book in little ways. Your love and support remind me why I do this. Special thanks to Caroline for reading so many drafts and sharing my enthusiasm for these characters. Thanks in no particular order to Jeremy, John, Paul, Tim, Jack, David, Alex, Mel, and Nick for all the shared stories and tabletop adventures. Thank you to Beth for listening to me whine about every stage of the writing process, and for all the random conversations about books and dogs and life. Thank you to Matt, for everything.

Finally, thank you to all the readers who've found their way to this story and made it to the end of book two. I hope you're enjoying the journey.

CAITLIN SEAL is a writer and compulsive reader living in Northern California. She says, "Death is maybe the most personal and universal of all human experiences. I love the idea that there could be something so powerful about an unfulfilled purpose, or the pull of a person's relationships with those they love, that it would draw them back to the living world."

When not writing, Caitlin GMs tabletop games, practices aikido, and hunts for portals in old wardrobes.

WWW.CAITLINSEAL.COM

HER DEATH WAS ONLY THE BEGINNING....

TWICE DEAD

CAITLIN SEAL